# CRITICAL PRAISE
## FOR LENORA WORTH:

"Suitable for CBA readers,
this title is also a good pick for romance collections
and those who enjoyed Kristen Heitzmann's *Halos*
or Hannah Alexander's *Hideaway*."
—*Library Journal* on *After the Storm*

"Worth takes readers on a thrilling ride...."
—*Romantic Times* on *After the Storm*

"...an inspirational romance and
mystery thriller rolled into one...
For a sweet, heartwarming story that is full of
suspense, I recommend *After the Storm*."
—*Romance Reviews Today* on *After the Storm*

"Talented new writer Lenora Worth combines
heart-stealing characters and a tragic secret to
make this page turner worth every reader's while."
—*Romantic Times* on *The Wedding Quilt*

"Ms. Worth puts a most unique spin on the
secret baby theme to make this wonderful
love story positively shine."
—*Romantic Times* on *Logan's Child*

"Lenora Worth creates another gem—a great, easy,
entertaining read for everyone, inspirational or not."
—*Romantic Times* on *His Brother's Wife*

# LENORA WORTH

# ECHOES OF DANGER

Steeple Hill®

Published by Steeple Hill Books™

If you purchased this book without a cover you should be aware that this book is stolen property. It was reported as "unsold and destroyed" to the publisher, and neither the author nor the publisher has received any payment for this "stripped book."

STEEPLE HILL BOOKS

**Steeple Hill®**

ISBN 0-373-81124-1

ECHOES OF DANGER

Copyright © 2005 by Lenora H. Nazworth

Special thanks and acknowledgment are given to Lenora Worth for her contribution to the LOVE INSPIRED COLLECTION.

All rights reserved. Except for use in any review, the reproduction or utilization of this work in whole or in part in any form by any electronic, mechanical or other means, now known or hereafter invented, including xerography, photocopying and recording, or in any information storage or retrieval system, is forbidden without the written permission of the editorial office, Steeple Hill Books, 233 Broadway, New York, NY 10279 U.S.A.

All characters in this book have no existence outside the imagination of the author and have no relation whatsoever to anyone bearing the same name or names. They are not even distantly inspired by any individual known or unknown to the author, and all incidents are pure invention.

This edition published by arrangement with Steeple Hill Books.

® and TM are trademarks of Steeple Hill Books, used under license. Trademarks indicated with ® are registered in the United States Patent and Trademark Office, the Canadian Trade Marks Office and in other countries.

www.SteepleHill.com

**Printed in U.S.A.**

The end of the matter; all has been heard.
Fear God, and keep His commandments;
for this is the whole duty of man. For God
will bring every deed into judgment, with every
secret thing, whether good or evil.

*—Ecclesiastes* 12:13–14

To my friend Jean Duncan.
You're not in Kansas anymore and you left Louisiana
for Texas. Jean, I miss you and wish you well.

And to Tom Palczynski—
a great teacher and a good friend.

## Chapter One

"He's dead, Dana. Murdered. He's murdered!"

Dana Barlow looked at her twelve-year-old brother Stephen's tear-streaked face and wondered how life could be so cruel. She'd always been honest with Stephen, while trying to make allowances for his physical problems. She'd have to be honest with him now.

"I know, Stevie," she said, looking down at the bloody carcass of one of their two prize Brangus breeding bulls. Thinking of all the money wasted, of all the time spent in caring for this eleven-hundred-pound animal, she wanted to sit down and cry like a baby. But she couldn't do that. Stevie was watching her; she was the only family he had and she had to stay sane for his sake.

*Why, God?* she asked silently.

"Who'd go and do a thing like that, anyway?" Stephen said in a voice edged with pain and anger. "Don't nobody around here act like that, Dana. Everybody knows Otto was my favorite. He won the Grand Championship! Otto was Stephen's favorite!"

Dana watched as her brother rocked back and forth, holding his hands to his stomach, repeating that same phrase over and over, his mind recoiling into its own little world. A world of autism.

Dana looked around the stark, flat Kansas prairie, her eyes

scanning the rippling waves of bluestem for any signs of intruders, but the wind, dancing and prancing with unabashed boldness, was the only thing moving through the tallgrass. Stephen, highly intelligent and highly perceptive, was right. Prairie Heart, Kansas, was about as mid-America as you could get and none of the five hundred or so residents would be so mean-spirited and uncaring as to deliberately kill a prize bull, especially when the whole town knew how important the animal was to Dana and Stephen's livelihood. Who would commit such a crime?

Dana's green eyes shifted to the west, where thunderclouds darkened the sky with an ominous intensity, to the distant steeple of the Universal Unity Church. The religious complex bordered her hundred acres of land on two sides. And the church's leader, a woman named Caryn Roark, had been badgering Dana for months. Caryn wanted Dana's land.

Only, she wasn't going to get it.

Could this be Caryn's way of trying to nudge Dana into selling? Why would the woman resort to such a thing? When the church had taken up residence a few years back in an old farmhouse on the neighboring Selzer place, Dana hadn't paid much attention to the comings and goings. She was a Christian, and a firm believer in the live and let live theory. As long as the strange cult members left her alone, she'd do the same by them. But lately, Caryn's followers had been harassing several of the local farmers. And now, many of the small struggling landowners living around Prairie Heart had given in to Caryn's tempting offers to buy their land.

"We're the only ones left," she said out loud, her words flying on the rising wind.

Stephen looked away from Otto's bloated, bullet-ridden body. "You'll find them, won't you, Dana? Dana will find the bad guys." He rose, sniffing back tears, smearing his dusty face in the process. Jerking his green-and-white Kansas Co-op cap down over his green eyes, he stalked to his sister. "You already know who done this, don't you?"

Dana kicked at the tallgrass at her feet, scaring a concealed walking stick out of his hiding place. Stephen automatically tried to catch the spindly bug, but the creature sauntered away, so he turned back to his sister.

"Tell me, Dana."

Dana sighed long and hard. The school counselor and his former teachers at Prairie Heart School, where Stephen had attended before she started homeschooling him, might think Stephen was a slow learner, but sometimes Dana thought the boy was smarter than any of them. His autism was mild, a form of what the doctors termed Asperger's syndrome. In spite of his odd social behavior and awkward motor skills, he had a way of seeing through the clutter right to the truth, and he was very clever at picking up signs or figuring out puzzles. Since the night three years ago when their parents had been killed in a car accident along the long stretch of state Highway 56 that had once been the Santa Fe Trail, Dana had never lied to him.

But she didn't have any easy answers for something this awful.

"No, Stevie, I don't know who did it. But I'm sure going to find out. I'm going into town to talk to the sheriff, then I'll send Doc Jeffers around to take Otto away."

Stephen glanced down at the big, dark-skinned animal. "I'll sure miss you, old fella."

Trying to find any excuse to take the boy's mind off his loss, Dana tossed back her chin-length reddish-brown curls and playfully snatched her brother by one ear. "Hey, remember why I was headed to town in the first place?"

Stephen smiled then, his green eyes matching a lone cottonwood tree's rustling leaves. "Yeah, sure. You gonna buy my new Ruby Runners, right? I get to stay with Mrs. Bailey."

"That's right," she said, leading him to the old Chevy truck that had belonged to their daddy. "They're on order and should be here today, and thanks to that pig you sold at the spring fair, we've got the money now."

Stephen gave her a lopsided high five. "Yeah, and I'll run twice as fast, I bet, huh, Dana? I'll be ready for that track meet over in Kansas City, won't I, Dana?"

As usual, Stephen's mind wandered from current pain to future pleasure, so for a brief time, he forgot that big Otto had been brutally murdered. Dana hadn't forgotten, though. She planned to make a stop on the way to town. It was high time she paid the devout folks at Universal Unity Church a little neighborly visit.

An hour later, Dana waited in the whitewashed reception room of the newly built offices of the Universal Unity Complex, which now consisted of a magnificent glass-and-stone chapel, a long white row of three-storied dormitories and Caryn Roark's own private quarters—a modern, stark white mansion setting where old Hiram Selzer's 1885 farmhouse had stood for over a hundred years. The farmhouse was long gone, old Hiram was long dead, and this rambling complex seemed out of place in rural Kansas.

Eyeing her surroundings with distaste, Dana shifted in the white leather chair where a young girl in a flowing blue dress had guided her. Everything in this place was a stark, crisp white. White-on-white carpets and tiled floors, white drapery and heavy silken sheers, white leather and wood furniture. Even the flowers were white—azaleas and gardenias growing in stone pots, petunias and roses cascading out of huge planters—except for one lone, stark amaryllis sitting on the table near Dana's chair. That heavily blooming flower was white with threads of red and pink stripes shooting out over its lush blossoms. The lily looked strangely out of place.

Dana felt out of place herself in her T-shirt, faded jeans and heavy work boots. But, hey, why should she feel disoriented? This was her home, not theirs. She'd been born and raised here—born in the house she now lived in, and raised by two wonderful, loving people who had met their Heavenly Maker on a rain-slick road in the middle of a cold, dark night. No, she didn't have any reason to feel out of place, but she had a whole lot of reason to feel cheated and fighting mad.

When she looked up to see Caryn Roark approaching her down a sweep of wrought-iron spiral stairs, she wondered if she'd somehow stepped into the twilight zone. The woman was downright spooky.

Caryn had platinum-blond hair that was coiled up on top of her head and threaded with brilliant golden braids of rope. She wore all white—of course—a flowing sweater-type material that looked comfortable but would probably be hot if she decided to venture out of the cool confines of her air-conditioned palace. Overall, Dana supposed Caryn was an attractive woman, until you looked into her eyes. They were a clear, cold blue, and coupled with the woman's long, beaked nose, presented a chilling countenance.

*Evil.* Dana didn't know why the word popped into her head, but it did. And it stayed with her the whole time Caryn glided toward her to extend a bejeweled hand complete with silvery painted fingernails.

"Hello, Dana Barlow. So good of you to come by. Now, what can I help you with today? Are you interested in attending some of our enlightening services here at Unity?" Caryn stood back, her hand trailing over the amaryllis while she waited, her gaze expectant.

Dana knew instantly that this was no ordinary church, not at all like the small wooden church she'd attended all her life on the outskirts of Prairie Heart. She got the feeling Sunday school here would take on a whole new meaning.

Clearing her throat, Dana got right to the point. "No, Ms. Roark—"

"Caryn, please."

"Caryn, I'm not here to attend services, but thanks for asking. I came because I'm concerned about something I found on my land today."

Caryn settled herself on a thronelike chair by a ten-foot window, her face serene, her eyes keen, her slightly foreign accent held in check. "Oh, and what might that be?"

"A dead Brangus breeding bull."

Caryn looked appalled. "Oh, how dreadful. We're all vegetarians here, so I do not tolerate hurting God's creatures." She gave an exaggerated shudder. "What does this horrible crime have to do with me, my dear?"

Dana leaned forward in the squeaky leather chair. "I believe it has everything to do with you. I think someone from your complex deliberately shot my animal."

Caryn's eyes lifted slightly, the only sign that Dana's direct accusations had affected her. "Tell me who did this, and I will take swift action!"

Dana gave her a skeptical look, wondering if she practiced that stilted, phony voice in front of the mirror each day. "Will you really? Or did you order this slaughter?"

The other woman didn't move a muscle, but she looked as dangerous as the rolling clouds floating by on the horizon. "Why would I order such a thing?"

Dana tapped the fingers of one hand on the arm of her chair. "Oh, maybe to convince me that I need to sell my land to you after all?"

Caryn rose to stand behind her chair, so she could look down on Dana. "You really should attend one of our services. You seem to be holding a lot of anger inside, young lady."

Dana rose, too. "I'm angry. That's a fact. But I'm not one to hold anything inside. And I'm warning you, if I find one more dead head of cattle on my land, I'll have Sheriff Radford investigate this whole place."

With that she turned to leave, but Caryn's shout halted her.

"Miss Barlow, you've just made a grave error in misjudging me."

Dana turned in time to see the look of pure malice shaping the woman's flawless complexion. "Are you threatening me?"

"I am the law here," the woman said in a rasping voice. "How dare you talk to me that way!"

"I'm not one of your groupies!" Dana shouted back, her own anger and frustration matching that of the other woman. "You don't fool me, and you'll never get my land."

Caryn's cackle echoed over the distant sound of thunder. "Oh, yes, I will. You'll see. Soon, you and that retarded brother of yours will be out on the side of the road."

Dana could take anything anyone dished out, but nobody picked on her brother. Stepping back into the polished foyer, she glared across the marble floor at Caryn. "You stay away from Stephen. He's just a boy. He's never done anything to you or any of your people."

Caryn's smile was triumphant. Dana guessed she'd been looking for a weak spot. The woman's next words proved it.

"If you care about your special little brother, you'll be careful. I don't take to false accusations."

Dana pointed a finger at the stone-faced woman. "And I don't take to people destroying what's mine. If I see any of your people on my property, I'll shoot first and ask questions later." *And forgive me, Lord, for even suggesting that.*

With that, she turned and slammed the glass door, rattling the thick panes against their heavy brass hinges.

A storm was brewing. Dana knew enough about Kansas weather to realize it was going to be an ugly one. She could hear the echo of distant thunder miles away, carrying through the lifting wind. She was a mile from town, though, and if she hurried, she could get those Ruby Runners she'd promised Stephen, and maybe have a quick word with the sheriff.

Actually, storm or not, she wasn't ready to head back to the farm yet. Finding Otto dead, and then the confrontation with that horrible woman, had left her too keyed up to face the mounting problems her little bit of land was causing her. If she didn't do something quick, they'd lose everything and then Caryn would come in and take Dana's property. Dana couldn't let that happen. She'd fought too hard since her parents' deaths to give up now. And she didn't like being bullied.

At first she'd thought about selling and moving to Kansas City. She'd majored in business administration at Kansas State, so she had the credentials to find a decent job in the big city, and her sweetheart from high school, Tony Martin, was already there and earning a good living as a computer analyst. They'd been engaged and had big plans to marry and move to Kansas City, until Dana's parents had died. Tony hadn't wanted the burden of raising a hyper preteen with learning problems and the mannerisms of a kindergartner.

Now Stephen depended on her, and he loved the farm. She hadn't wanted to uproot him, so based on some advice from the local bank president, and after consulting with Stephen's doctors, she'd made a decision to keep the farm. And had instantly gone into debt by borrowing money to raise enough cattle to get a small herd going. She had fifty head of prime Brangus heifers, steers, calves and two bulls—make that one bull now.

Still in shock, she couldn't believe Otto was gone. She didn't need this right now, not when things were just starting to turn around. Pulling the old rickety Chevy into the parking place by the general store, Dana glanced at the erratic sky, then rushed inside out of the wind. She'd get the shoes, then go talk to the sheriff.

Not that that would do much good. Sheriff Radford was getting old and he just didn't care much about random crimes against animals. People didn't fare much better, but then nothing much more exciting than a rowdy cowboy at the pool hall around the corner ever stirred the mundane daily life of this prairie town. But still, a dead prize-breeding bull wasn't exactly something to turn the other cheek about.

"Honey, you look like you got the weight of the world on your pretty shoulders," Emma Prager said from behind the counter and her ample bosom. "What's eating my little Dana?"

"Just about everything," Dana said, afraid if she laid her burdens at kind Emma's matronly feet, she'd burst into tears. "I lost Otto today, Emma. Somebody shot him."

"Goodness-a-mercy!" Emma exclaimed, bringing up the head of the one other paying customer in the cluttered store, and catching the attention of the regulars at the dominoes table in the small café at the back. "What an awful thing to happen, and you trying to hang on to that place with every ounce of gumption you got." Heaving a heavy breath, she came around the counter. "I do declare, what's the world coming to! Did you tell old Radford yet?"

"I'm headed over there now," Dana said, spotting the blazing red Ruby Runner emblem on a nearby shoebox. Emma had promised to hold the athletic shoes for her. "I came by to get our Ruby Runners—I thought maybe it'd cheer Stephen up, since I promised him I'd get them today."

"Got 'em right here," Emma said, turning her bulk to get the pair of shoes she'd saved for Dana. "One size fourteen youth. That child is steady growing, I tell you!"

Emma's straight, scrawny husband, Frederick, came plowing through the curtained door leading to their living quarters in the back of the cluttered store, the German still in his accent coming out strongly. "Get you home, little girl. Tornado's a-coming. Spotted it due west about ten miles from here."

"She don't have time," Emma said, dropping the package she was about to hand Dana. "We gotta get in the cellar!"

Everyone started running toward the back of the old store. Confused, Dana searched for her package on the counter at about the same time the other shopper, a young man in grubby jeans and a blue T-shirt, grabbed a similar package and fled out into the storm before Emma could herd him around. The two old-timers who'd been heavy into their dominoes game sprinted for Frederick's storm cellar.

Dana looked around, then grabbed the only package left on the counter. But Dana didn't follow Emma and Frederick. "Stephen!" she said, her voice rising. "He's at home with Mrs. Bailey. I have to get back!"

"He knows what to do," Frederick shouted over the roar of the approaching storm. "You come in the cellar with us."

"I can't," Dana replied, hoping, praying that Stephen and the frail neighbor woman would be able to get in the cellar and lie down under the blankets they kept down there for just such emergencies.

There was no time for anything else but prayer. The twister was sending its calling card, sucking the old general store into a vortex of rumbling fury. Dana ran to her truck, willing the ancient contraption to crank. The sound of glass shattering and trees snapping left little doubt that this storm was doing some serious damage, but she didn't heed the storm's wrath. She planned to outrun it.

And she almost did. But it seemed as if the storm wanted her and her alone. She watched in her rearview mirror as the twister followed her out of town, hurling and hissing like a giant snake as it chased her down the county road.

"Dear God, help me," she prayed out loud, her heart beating so hard she knew she'd surely die of a heart attack if the storm didn't kill her first. She knew she should stop the truck and dive for the nearest ditch, but she had to get back to Stephen. Mrs. Bailey was great in helping to homeschool the boy, but the aging senior citizen was a nervous wreck in any little storm. She'd go into a tizzy and be useless, especially with a storm as powerful as this twister headed right toward the farm.

Dana rounded the dirt drive to the farmhouse, her foot pushing the gas pedal beyond its endurance, the truck's sturdy tires squealing their displeasure at being forced to turn so quickly.

She didn't make the turn. The truck careened out of control and did a fishhook, spewing mud and rocks toward the tornado like a runt fighting off a bully. Dana screamed and tried to hold on to the swirling steering wheel, but without power-steering the truck got the best of her. The last thing she remembered was the door flying open, then her whole world went black.

She was dreaming, of course. That had to be it. She felt strong arms pulling her down, down into the wet bluestems; she heard a soothing male voice close to her ear, telling her to hold on, hold on. Then a powerful body covered hers, warming her, comforting her, protecting her as the storm swirled around her. Dana kept her eyes tightly shut, afraid to open them and find out if this was really happening.

The storm hit. She could feel the wind sucking at her skin, could feel the debris cutting against her hair and her exposed hands and arms, could taste the dust and rain and power, but somehow she knew she was safe. That strange, lilting voice, that warm, clinging body—who was he and why was he holding her so close she could hear the echo of his heartbeat over the dangerous rush of the storm?

It was all over in a matter of minutes. Nothing seemed real. It was as if Dana *was* dreaming a *bad* dream where she'd woken abruptly only to find that she hadn't been dreaming at all.

She was alive and this was very real. That much Dana knew as she groggily tried to open her eyes. Her head hurt with all the roaring of a tractor-pull. But over the roaring of pain, she heard another more ominous noise. Silence.

Seconds passed, as she listened to the quiet that was even more deadly than the storm's rumbling rage. Dana didn't like silence.

"Stephen?" she called, trying to pry herself out of the stranger's iron grip. "Stephen, where are you?"

She looked up at the brooding, foaming dark sky. This storm wasn't finished yet. "Stephen?" she called again, trying to raise herself up. A bump on the side of her head throbbed in protest, but she tried again until she realized that the grip on her arms was caused by a set of strong hands holding her down. A man's hands.

She was flat on the ground, with a big man holding her there. Then Dana remembered how the man had thrown himself on top of her to shield her from the tornado.

"Stephen?" she asked again, hoping the man would tell her something about her brother.

The man lifted his head and looked straight into her eyes. The first thing Dana noticed was that his eyes were as blue-black and cloudy as the storm's lingering coattails. The second thing she noticed was that he wore all black, from his button-down shirt to his Levi's and boots. His long dark hair was pulled away from his face in a ponytail, but the wind coming through the open field where they lay was doing its best to unleash his thick mane.

"Who...who are you?" she asked, her voice shaking. "Where's my brother? Where's Stephen?"

The big man looked down at Dana. "It's all right, lass. You're safe."

He had a lilting accent that immediately flowed like a fine melody over Dana's shot nerve endings. Scottish? Irish, maybe? What in the world was he doing holding her down in the middle of a field in Prairie Heart, Kansas?

"Who are you?" she asked again, thinking of looters and dangerous criminals and the fully loaded .38 she had in the glove compartment of her truck.

He shifted closer, giving her a black stare that left her both breathless and wondering. With one hand he touched the tender, bruised spot just over her right temple. "You've bumped your head. How does it feel?"

Dana swallowed back the knot of fear forming in her throat. "It's aching, but I can handle it." The knot came back, causing her next words to sound raw and husky. "My brother—he's only twelve and, well, he's a very special boy." She inclined her head toward the farmhouse. "He's all alone with my neighbor. She's eighty and afraid of storms. I have to get to him."

The stranger's inky eyes softened as a look of concern tightened his face. "We'll go find him." At the apparent worry on her face, he added, "You have nothing to fear from me. I was pulled over on the road, watching the storm. I saw you wreck your truck. You were thrown out, and by the time I got to you the storm hit."

So he'd thrown himself over her to protect her. She hadn't been dreaming, after all. And he was still holding her, his big, powerful body still warming hers, from her hurting head down to her shaking toes. Needing to distance herself from the memory of her strange dream, she tried to wiggle away. "I've got to find my brother."

The man rolled to sit up, then helped her to her feet, holding her against the remnants of the wind. "I'll go with you."

Shocked, Dana stepped back. "No, you don't have to do that. I'm fine, really. I just need to find my brother."

The man looked around at the flat countryside, then back to Dana. "We're wasting time. I'll not let you go up to the house alone. You might not like what you find."

Never in her life had anyone said that to Dana. He didn't want her to go there alone. He wanted to be there with her if she found the worst. Well, she'd been through the worst. And in spite of the whole town's support and warm, loving concern, she'd always had to face the nightmares when she was alone at night in her bed…wishing…wishing.

She looked up at the intriguing man standing before her and told herself to run, run as fast as she could. He could be a serial killer; he could be a bank robber on the run; he could be a million horrible things. But she knew instinctively that he wasn't. She didn't know *how* she knew. She just knew.

Dana said a silent prayer. *Lord, I haven't talked to You for a very long time, and You know the reasons. But I'm asking You now to protect my brother. And while You're at it, could You give me a hint as to why this handsome, mysterious stranger is reaching out to help me?*

When she turned to see the house, or what was left of the house, she understood why this man had offered to stay with her. Her home, the only home she'd ever known, was in shambles. Half the roof was gone, exposing her own bedroom to the wind and the rain. Shingles lay across the expanse of the field, and twisted ribbons of tin hung from jagged, split tree limbs all around the house. She saw her pink nightgown flying in the wind, unfurling itself like a pretty spring flag from the tip of what was left of a giant cottonwood tree.

Swallowing, she turned back to the stranger, thankful for the hand he offered her. "I'd appreciate it if you would go with me to the house, mister."

"Call me Bren," he said as he gently guided her up the dirt lane toward the broken house. Giving her an encouraging smile, he said, "Are you all right?"

"Yes," she said, unsettled by someone else taking charge for a change. Then, "I could have faced it by myself, you know."

"I do know," he said, his smile making his harsh features turn handsome. "It's no bother." Looking toward the sky, he added, "Looks like more's coming."

Dana nodded, casting him a quick look. "Yep, these storms like to play tag with us sometimes."

"My first tornado," he admitted, his blue-black eyes scanning the horizon. "But at least I got to spend it with a beautiful woman."

Dana looked down at her muddy boots, embarrassed by the flirtatious compliment. "Thanks for what you did."

He gave her another direct, black stare. "You're quite welcome."

The small talk was almost surreal, set against the ghastly scene before them, but the meaningless chatter kept Dana on an even keel. She couldn't take the silence.

When she did grow quiet, the man spoke softly to her. "Your brother...I wager he's going to be just fine."

As they approached the house, she said a little half prayer, half plea. "Oh, Lord, make it so."

Bren, still holding her hand, helped her around to the back of the house, guiding her through the rubble that minutes before had been her home. A few feet from the white, wooden-framed house, a framed picture of her parents lay shattered and torn in the mud. Dana reached down to pick it up, a small sob catching in her throat.

The man named Bren gently took the damaged picture from her hand. "Careful, you'll cut yourself on the glass."

Dana wanted to laugh. If only he knew. Her cuts went much deeper than any made by a shard of glass. Nodding, she stepped over the pile of kindling that had been their breakfast table, then made her way to the closed cellar door.

"Stephen?" she shouted, afraid of what she'd hear in answer. Afraid of the silence. "Stephen Joshua Barlow, are you in there?"

Pulling away torn shingles and little bits of splintered wood, she banged on the weathered trapdoor. "Stephen Joshua Barlow, are you in there?

"Stephen, you answer me," she called again, her voice cracking in spite of the tight rein she was trying to hold on her fear, on her pain, on her rage. Finally, falling down on her knees, she whispered, "Stephen, please, please."

In the next instance, the door banged back on its hinges and Stephen pushed his bushy golden head up into the wind. Grinning, he didn't even look at her as he said, "Hey, sis, where's my Ruby Runners?"

The man standing there let out a slight gasp of surprise. Probably as glad as Dana to find Stephen alive and in one piece.

Dana grabbed Stephen in a suffocating hug, not caring that his condition sometimes made him shy away from being touched. "Oh, you're all right! You're okay. Is Mrs. Bailey down there with you?"

"Sure she is. I brought her here," Stephen said, obviously surprised that she doubted him. "Stephen knows the rules. Tornado comes, get to the cellar. Tornado comes, get to the cellar." Looking with a matter-of-fact shake of the head over to the stranger's feet, he said, "She was so scared. She was so scared. I got kinda of scared, but I remembered everything you told me, yeah, I remembered everything." His green eyes shone with a light of hope. "I remembered that you said Mom and Dad were always watching over us, from Heaven. Remember, you said even through a storm, they could see us. I should always look past the storm, for them." He bobbed his head, still looking down. "Look for Mama and Daddy."

Dana cried against his tousled hair. "I remember, Stevie."

While Dana held Stephen, tiny Mrs. Bailey emerged up the steps, her watery eyes wide with fear, her stiff gray hair standing on end around her round face. "Land sakes, that near scared me to an early grave."

Dana opened her arms to encircle the shaken woman. "Thank you, Mrs. Bailey. Thank you so much."

Bren stood aside, watching the emotional reunion. Dana watched him over Stephen's head. He looked as if he felt uncomfortable. She supposed this was unexpected for him, being here so far from his home, wherever his home was, being in on this family scene, in the middle of so much destruction.

But then Dana watched as his gaze shifted to the west, to the silvery white spire of the Universal Unity Church, which stood gleaming and intact against the backdrop of a purplish-gray sky.

Dana looked up at him, about to thank him again for helping her, but she was startled by the look in his eyes. It was a heavy blend of hatred mixed with pain. And something else. A determination that bordered on vengeance. Following his gaze, she saw the church complex off in the distance. Had Bren whoever-he-was come to visit the Unity Church?

Dana stared at him, trying to read his strange, still features. Then she looked back at the complex. And up on the top turret of the church, near the tall steeple, she thought she saw a platinum-haired woman standing there with the wings of her white robe flapping in the wind.

## Chapter Two

"Looks like the Universal Unity Church survived," Dana said, squinting toward the beautiful, untouched mansion. Before she could get a better look, the lone figure standing on the tower whirled and vanished into the dark recesses of the upstairs turret room.

Clutching Stephen close to stop his fidgeting, she looked back at the stranger, remembering he had the same accent as Caryn Roark—the woman who called herself the law. "Are you a member of that church?"

"No," he said, the one word speaking more than a lengthy explanation ever could. He stared across the field, the granite-hard expression on his face making him resemble a piece of carved flintrock. Then he turned back to Dana. "I'm not quite sure where I belong."

A shiver dripped down Dana's spine, a slow, trickling warning that set her nerves and her intuition on edge. Giving him a long look, she wondered again who this man was. "Look, mister—"

"Bren," he said, repeating his name to her, his eyes lifting away from the church to pin Dana to the spot. "Call me Bren."

Dana nodded. "Okay, Bren. Call me Dana. Look, thanks for your help. We're okay, so you don't have to stay with us."

Stephen pushed away from Dana's smothering embrace. "We ain't okay, either, Dana. We don't have a house no more."

He stomped his feet and flapped his hands. "House gone. House gone. Room a mess. Room a mess."

Dana knew Stephen would keep repeating these phrases to himself while he tried to absorb this sudden shift in his orderly, structured world. "It'll be okay, Stevie. I promise."

Stephen kept stomping his feet. "Room a mess, Dana."

"I'd better go see about my own house," Mrs. Bailey said, her little legs moving across the damp earth. She took Stephen by both arms, her words loud and precise. "Stephen, listen to your sister." Then she turned to Dana. "I'll call you if I need you, and you do the same."

"Wait and we'll go with you," Dana called.

"No need. I'm sure my son is on his way." The spry little woman was off down the lane. "Y'all can stay at my place if need be. You know you're always welcome."

Dana held a hand to her eyes and glanced toward the west. It looked as if Mrs. Bailey's small white house was in one piece, at least. She'd go check on the Baileys later. And she might have to take her dear friend up on that offer.

"Dana, what are we gonna do?" Stephen asked, bringing Dana's attention back to their immediate problems. His agitation did nothing to calm Dana's own jangled nerves.

Bren's features softened as he turned his attention toward Stephen. "He's right. Where will you go?"

Pushing away the fringe of hysteria that promised to be more intense than the storm that had just passed through, Dana looked around, knowing that they couldn't possibly stay here tonight or any other night for a long time to come. "I don't know. We've got friends in town—Emma and Frederick can take us in for a while. Or maybe Mrs. Bailey. She has a spare room." Thinking of how hyper Stephen could get in small places, she added, "But Emma and Frederick probably would have more space."

Bren looked back toward the church, then back at Dana. "I'll take you to Emma and Frederick, then."

Dana hadn't missed the hesitation in his eyes. Why did he keep looking at that spooky church? He reminded her of a black stallion old Mr. Selzer used to let her ride—wild and proud, and forbidden since her mother was terrified of the animal. Mr. Selzer had called the horse Black Blizzard, because he was always kicking up dust. Oh, she hadn't thought of Blizzard in years. Mr. Selzer had been forced to sell the animal to try and save his property. Why, now, of all times, did she want to sit down and cry for an animal she'd almost forgotten?

She didn't, couldn't sit down, and she wasn't about to go into hysterics—yet. "I— We need to get a few things. And I want to look the place over. I have cattle…I'll need to check on things."

Bren took her arm, gently guiding her around to face him. "I'd like to help, if you'll let me."

She wanted to tell this intriguing man to let her alone, to leave her to wallow in a good dollop of self-pity. She wanted to scream to the heavens and ask, "why?" But Dana knew that she wouldn't get any answers; she'd been that route before and she'd only heard silence, the killing silence of unanswered prayers and a faith that had been tested to the limit.

Oh, well, time enough to argue with God later. Right now, Stephen was looking everywhere but at her, but she knew he was waiting for her to decide what to do about this mess. She was just too shocked to think straight.

As if sensing her shock, Bren placed a hand on each of her slumping shoulders, then leaned his head down close to her face so she was forced to look him straight in the eyes. "Are you sure you're all right?"

Shooting a desperate look toward her brother, she managed to whisper, "I can't let him see how upset I am. He has Asperger's syndrome—it's a very mild form of autism. He doesn't like any sudden changes. He'll get even more upset and scared if I break down. He's so brave, but it's only because he emulates me. Don't let me lose it, okay. Help me, please."

She'd never begged for help before in her life, and the words let a bitter gall in her throat, but this day had gone from bad to worse and it wouldn't take much more to push her over the edge. She certainly wasn't in the habit of begging strangers for help, either. But this man had saved her from that storm and he was here now. The warmth of his hands on her shoulders steadied her, while his blue-black eyes guided her like a dark beacon. She clung to that guiding, dark light, deciding she'd just have to trust him. She didn't have much choice at the moment.

Still holding her shoulders, Bren squeezed his hands against the shivering flesh underneath her damp T-shirt. "Here's what we're going to do," he said, his eyes still locked with hers. "We'll take care of what we can here, then I'll take you into town, to your friend's house. If you get scared, just look at me. I won't leave you until I'm sure you're all right."

Feeling silly for being so weak, Dana lifted his hands away from her arms. "I'm not scared! I'm just so mad!"

Whirling, she blinked away the insane need to fall into his arms and cry like a baby. She wouldn't burden this stranger with her troubles, but she would take advantage of his generosity. For her brother's sake.

Marching to where Stephen sat rocking and digging with precise movements through the remnants of what had once been his prize collection of baseball cards, she patted the boy on the head. "Up, up, Stevie. Let's see what we can salvage before that second line of thunderstorms returns."

Stephen hurled himself up, clutching a stack of soggy

cards, his eyes brimming with tears. "Need to fix these, Dana. Need these straight. They're all wet. I don't like them wet. I want them dry."

"Won't hurt to let them dry," Dana said, silently vowing to replace each and every one of them. Motioning to Bren, she called, "Hey, you ever herded scared cattle before?"

Bren gave her a wry smile. "I've herded sheep. Cattle can't be much different, right? Just show me what to do."

Two hours later, they stood surveying the damage once again. Tired, dirty and muddy, Dana had little hope that they could rebuild. They'd herded cattle in the pouring rain of a renegade thunderstorm, with lightning dancing to the west, just to tease them and remind them who was in charge here. Luckily, most of the cattle were now safe inside their paddocks near the lower field.

The storm had concentrated on the house and surrounding buildings. All the other livestock, some chickens and pigs and the two horses, seemed to be intact, as well, in spite of the nervous squawking and fearful grunting they'd encountered after checking what remained of the barn.

Bren had helped Dana move through the house, half of which was missing, to find enough dry clothes to last them a few days. The combination laundry room/porch on the eastern side of the house was intact, and that's where Dana had found fresh clean jeans and T-shirts. Now Stephen was wet and complaining of being hungry, and Bren, silent and alert, was watching Dana for further instructions.

Then he did something that made her smile in spite of her problems. He turned to Stephen and said, "Did you find all of your baseball cards?"

"Not all of them," Stephen said on a whining voice full of growing anger. "Need to find all of them."

"I think I can help there. I know a man who has a Lou Gehrig in mint condition. Would you like to have it?"

Stephen clapped his hands. "Lou Gehrig—Henry Louis Gehrig—born June 19, 1903. The Iron Horse. First base for New York Yankees. Played 2,130 consecutive games. June 3, 1932, four home runs in one game. Baseball Hall of Fame—1939." Stephen grinned, his eyes lighting up in a moment of clarity. "Can't afford that card!"

"Well, just let me worry about that," Bren said, his own voice soft with joy. Glancing at Dana, he said, "I'm impressed."

"He has a way with remembering statistics," she explained. "Especially baseball stats."

"Then we have something in common," Bren said, his own grin making him look younger and less sinister.

Surprised at how he'd calmed her brother with his elaborate promise, and how he'd silently followed her every command without question, Dana felt a firm bond with the rugged stranger. Or was he still a stranger? Maybe she should look on him as a friend, or an angel, a dark avenging angel who'd saved her from two storms, the one in the sky and the one raging in her overworked mind. Shrugging, she told herself to be practical. So the man had a few connections. No need to go staring off into fantasy land, thinking he'd come to rescue her from all her troubles.

Telling herself to stay clear, she glanced around one last time. "Well, that's about all we can do until tomorrow. I'll have to talk to the insurance adjuster, see where we stand. Of course the livestock will have to be taken care of—that can't stop."

Bren nodded. "You run this place all by yourself?"

Dana pushed back tufts of naturally curly hair. "I try."

His gaze circled the land. "Looks like you've done a good job."

She scoffed. "Yeah, until Mother Nature decided to rearrange things for me."

His gaze touched on her face, then stayed to travel slowly down the rest of her. He took her hand. "You should get into some dry things and try to rest."

"Sure," she said, thinking she'd never be able to rest easy again, not after running from a twister and meeting up with an interesting stranger, all in one afternoon. Just the shock of all this, she supposed. "You don't have to take us into town. We have the truck." She saw the relief pour over his face and asked him, "What about you? Where are you headed?"

She felt his grip on her hand tense, saw his head swing back toward the Universal Unity Church before he looked down at her.

"To Wichita," he said, his expression evasive. "I have business to tend to there."

She let go of his hand, then immediately wished she hadn't. It was a spot of warmth in this chilly, grim setting. "C'mon, Stevie," she called, her heart breaking as he struggled with the few treasures he'd managed to save.

Together, they walked back up the lane to the pickup where Stephen deposited the photo album and baseball glove he'd found, along with some books and video game cartridges.

Dana, on the other hand, had saved very little from the house. They didn't have anything of real value, and besides, what should she save from a pile of shattered dreams? The toaster, the working parts of a computer, the soggy white homemade prom dress she'd worn her senior year of high school, the only remaining place setting of her mother's prized china she'd collected with S & H green stamps?

Did she take part of something to remind her of the home she'd sometimes loved, sometimes hated, or did she just throw away every broken piece and keep the bittersweet memories?

Again she felt Bren's presence. Again she marveled at the man's even being here. He'd saved her, no doubt. Each time she'd wanted to let go of the silent scream pitching through her mind, she'd looked to him. And he'd given her that solid, mysterious look, just as he'd promised. His eyes had calmed her, his unflinching resolve had guided her in such a way that she wondered if he ever got flustered or bent out of shape about anything. She wondered a lot of things about him, come to think of it. Like where he was from, where he was headed and why he was here to begin with. But he was about to be gone, out of her life. What would she do then?

Silly, she told herself, you'll do what you've always done. You'll survive.

"I'll take you back to your van," she said, indicating the sleek black vehicle still parked out on the highway.

Smiling, she hopped into the truck and waited as Bren helped Stephen stash his salvage before they both crawled inside the wide cab with her. "So," she said after cranking the truck, "what do you do for a living?"

Bren must have seen the teasing light in her eyes as she nodded toward his van, but he didn't smile. Instead he looked straight ahead at the gray ribbon of road. "I'm a businessman, and it's a long and complicated story."

And one he obviously didn't want to talk about. "I'm not being nosy," she said. "It's just that you appeared out of nowhere, and well, you don't say much, do you?"

He pushed a hand through his damp hair. "You've got enough on your mind, looks like to me. I won't burden you with my sorry life."

He was right there. She had more than enough to keep her thoughts falling on top of each other without listening to him. Yet she'd like to listen to him. His lilting, flowing dialect sounded like a sweet ballad to her ears. Pulling the truck up beside the long van, she noticed the dark-tinted windows and the gold-etched star-spangled trim work running along the sides of the sleek, mysterious vehicle. Then she saw the ancient Christian symbol of the fish centered on the windshield. That brought her a small measure of reassurance, but he certainly was a man of mystery. And now that he'd helped her settle things into some semblance of order, he seemed intent to be on his way.

She watched as he got out of the truck, wishing he didn't have to hurry away.

Stephen called after him, "Hey, Mr. Bren? Thanks—I get that Lou Gehrig card, right? I get Lou Gehrig, for sure."

Bren's dark eyes fell across Stephen with a gentleness that reminded Dana of a calm midnight sky. "Don't worry, Stephen. I know where to find you. You will get your card. You take care of yourself until we meet again."

Stephen bobbed his head. "Me and Dana, we always take care of each other."

Dana put the truck into neutral and hopped out to meet Bren as he rounded the front. Stopping, he tossed up a hand toward Stephen, then turned to gaze down at her.

"I'd like to thank you, too," she said, not knowing what else to say with him looking at her as if he could read all of her thoughts. And right now, she had a lot of them running through her head.

She wanted him to tell her his sorry story, she wanted to know what kind of business he was involved in, she wanted to understand why he'd been so kind to her, and how he'd managed to make her feel safe in the middle of a raging storm. But she could only look up at him, and keep wondering.

Bren stared down at her, his dark eyes searching her face, seeming to memorize her features, which only made her more aware of him. She knew she was a mess, hair damp and probably frizzing to the high heavens, face more muddy than made-up, lips pale and wind roughened, but she didn't stop him from looking. She studied him just as candidly. He, too, was wind tossed and dampened. She'd never seen a man with such rich, dark, too-long hair, and with eyes to match the finest black-blue velvet. He looked like some dark lord of the manor from another time.

Before she could look away, Bren reached for her and tugged her close, his fingers moving over the tender spot on her head. "If you need anything—"

"I'll be all right," she said into the soft cotton of his black shirt. "I'll never forget what you did."

He reached inside the pocket of his jeans and handed her a soggy card. "There's a number where you can reach me— a private cell phone number. Call me if you need help. All I ask is that you don't give that number to anyone else." Then he let her go.

The warmth from his body left her, to be replaced with a cold, uncaring wind. She stood in the misty rain, watching as he got into the big, black van and drove away. She couldn't see him, but she knew he was watching her. Dana waited until his van was out of sight down the long straight road. Then she looked around over the torn and battered countryside, finally turning her face toward the heavens.

And off in the distance, a satin-sheened watercolored rainbow shot over the clouds, blinding her with its sparkling brilliance.

"You can stay as long as need be," Emma said the next morning as she handed Stephen another chocolate-covered doughnut—his and Emma's version of breakfast. Stephen champed down on the drippy confection, leaving a wide ring of chocolate around his mouth.

The Prager General Store had been spared. Except for a leaky roof where a few shingles dangled, and a strip or two of missing tin, the sturdy old building was still intact. And so it was the natural place for the townspeople to gather and talk about the storm that had swept over the area. Dana wasn't the only victim, although from all the talk, her place had probably sustained the worst damage.

"She's right, Dana," Harvey Mize, one of the old-timers, said from his perch on a tall vinyl-covered barstool. "We'll all do what needs to be done, to help you out."

Dana looked around the cozy store. She should feel safe here, among these good people she'd known all her life. She was thankful and appreciative, but she also knew she'd have to do most of this on her own. "You're all very kind," she said, taking the cup of coffee Emma shoved in her hand. "I just don't know. I don't think we'll be able to salvage the house. And I don't have the money to build from scratch." Thinking of how tired she was, she added, "Maybe I should sell the place."

"What about insurance?" Frederick asked as he rocked back on the heels of his worn work shoes.

Dana looked down at the planked floor. "It'll cover part of the damage, but I've already got a second mortgage on the house...."

The explanation was left hanging, just as the storm had left her hanging, in limbo, unsure and unprepared. Needing to be away from the pitiful looks and shifting eyes of the townspeople, she called to Stephen. "Finish your doughnut, brother. We need to go back out to check on the livestock."

"Need a hand?" Harvey offered.

"No. I'll call if I change my mind though," Dana told him with a wave as she headed out the door. She'd gotten a cell phone a few months before, to keep her in touch with Stephen and Mrs. Bailey at all times. It would come in handy now, too, she reckoned.

A few minutes later, they turned the old truck in to the rocky lane leading to the shattered house. Dana saw the spot where she'd wrecked the day before, her hand automatically going to her bruised head. Thoughts of the man named Bren played through her weary mind, the memory of how he'd protected her in the storm warring with the uncertainty of her future. Stephen's hushed words brought her mind back to the task at hand.

"It's a mess, ain't it, Dana? Don't like a mess."

She stopped the truck near the ripped, gaping remains of an ancient oak tree. In the brilliant, ironic sunlight, the damaged house looked forlorn and still, as broken as Dana's spirit. Funny, for years before her parents' death, she'd wanted so much to get away from this old house, to go out in the world, to find a place of her own. Right now she'd gladly give anything to have the old farmhouse back, for Stevie's sake, if nothing else. The boy loved their home.

"Yep, it's pretty much gone," she said as she slammed the steering-wheel-mounted gears into park. *So this is it?* she asked God. *This is my future?* No plans for a husband and a family, no hope for a normal life like her parents had? Just a mundane existence, here in this sleepy town, waiting and wondering, hoping and praying that she could save this pitiful old farm? Was this how it was meant to be, she had to wonder.

"We still got each other," Stephen said, his soft green eyes watching her face. "You got Stephen. Stephen's got you. Each other, Dana."

Seeing the solid fear in his eyes, Dana chided herself for being so bitter. Taking his hand in hers, she forced a smile. "Yeah, we sure do." Then, looking down in the floor of the truck, she added, "And your prized Ruby Runners!" She'd forgotten all about those shoes.

Stephen's face lit up. "Can I put 'em on?"

"They'll get all muddy."

"Oh, okay." He hopped out of the truck. "But I am, when we get back to town. I am. I am."

Relieved that he hadn't thrown a tantrum, Dana followed. As they neared the house, she realized something was terribly wrong. Carefully making her way up onto the torn porch, she saw it immediately.

The side of the house that the storm hadn't destroyed had been ransacked. It had been hit, but not by a storm.

"What in the world!" she shouted, her frantic words carrying out on the constant, moaning wind.

Startled, Stephen looked up at her. "What's the matter?"

"We've been robbed," she said, each word ground out between a held breath. "Somebody looted what little we had left."

It was true. The kitchen drawers were torn out of their sockets. Silverware had been strewn all over the soggy wooden floor. Dishes were shattered, clothes strewn, closets left open and emptied, books tossed about. Nothing had been left untouched. But even more odd, nothing much had been taken.

Looking up at a fluffy white, overstuffed cloud, Dana shouted to the wind, "I can't take much more, really I can't!"

Stephen started to cry, the tears full-bodied and rushing, but the sound soft and keening. "I'm scared, Dana."

Rushing to where he stood in the middle of a heap of torn books and strewn clothes, Dana pulled him into her arms. "I'm sorry, Stevie. I didn't mean to upset you. It's okay. It's okay."

Stephen buried his tousled head against her chest. "I miss Daddy, Dana. I wish he'd come back. He'd know what to do.

And Mama, too. She'd—" he hiccuped "—she'd have this place fixed, wouldn't she?"

Dana's own tears tasted bitter in her mouth. It was little comfort to know that no matter how fiercely she loved her brother and wanted to protect him, she could never take the place of their parents. "Yes," she said on a raw, torn whisper. "Yes, Stevie, Mama and Daddy would know what to do, and I'm sure they're watching over us. But they can't help us now. We have to take care of things ourselves."

Lifting his head, she wiped a fat tear away from his chubby cheek. "You know I love you, don't you?" At his bobbing nod, she continued, "And you know I'll always, always take care of you, no matter what, right?"

"Yeah, I know," he said, running his T-shirt sleeve over the embarrassing tears, his eyes as bright as a summer stream. "And you do a good job. It's just that—"

Dana finished for him. "It's just that we've had one too many raw deals. This is the last straw. How could anyone rob us when it's obvious we've suffered enough?"

As if by instinct, she looked toward the white brightness of the Universal Unity Church. Why did she get the gut feeling this attack had been deliberate? Maybe it was the creepy feeling in the pit of her stomach, maybe it was the memory of Caryn Roark's unguarded expression when she hadn't seen Dana watching. Maybe she was just going crazy. No, she wasn't crazy. This was very real.

But why?

Was this someone's way of kicking her while she was down? The bank might as well come on out right now and take the land, since Dana didn't see any clear way of keeping it at this point. But this second attack of pure meanness left her more disgusted than the storm ever could. Should she question Caryn Roark again? Could it be someone from her compound, just some kids out for kicks, not willing to accept that consequences came from their random acts of terror?

Telling herself it really didn't matter a whole lot at this point, Dana resigned herself to defeat. She couldn't hold on to this land. Might as well accept that.

Well, whoever was behind these attacks might try to get the land, but they wouldn't get what was left of the inside of her house. Her anger acting as a balm, she stepped back to look down at Stephen. "You okay, sport?"

He nodded. "Sorry I'm like a baby."

"You're not a baby. That little cry did us both good. Now here's the plan. Remember that camping tent out in the barn?"

He nodded, his boy's eyes lighting up. "Yeah, you won't ever let me use the thing. Can't put up the tent."

"Well, today, you not only get to use it. You get to set it up." She looked around. "Let's see…how 'bout over there by that small cottonwood where it looks high and dry."

"Okay, but why? Why do we need a tent, huh, Dana?"

Her eyes held a determined glint. "We're going to sleep there tonight."

"All right!" He danced around in a small circle. "In case they come back?"

"You got it, bud."

Stephen regained his spunk, strutting around with a new purpose. "You gonna use the shotgun, Dana? We ain't supposed to play with guns. No guns for Stephen."

"I just might have to break that rule this once," she said, her tone firm while her heart skipped and swayed like the beaten bluestems nearby. "I'll show them they can't get the best of us."

The prairie at night was a live thing. Like a great rippling snake, the flat fields around the house slipped and curved and moved in a slithering symmetry. The new wheat and bluestems parried and tangled together in the whining wind, the cottonwoods moaned a soft, rustling lullaby, whispering their secrets to the bright stars that looked so close, Dana thought surely she could reach out and grab one for herself.

She'd never wished upon a star before, but tonight as she lay inside the small close confines of the sturdy tent they'd erected and stared out the opening to the night sky, she picked the evening star, and she said a little prayer for guidance, for strength, for control. *Please, God, let my troubles be over. Let me find some peace, let me do the right thing, for Stephen, for myself. Let me do it right, for Mom and Dad.*

She'd been thinking about moving to Kansas City for a long time. Tony called at least once a week, telling her of all the fun he was having, the restaurants, the parties, the entertainment, the wonderful social life. "You're missing out, Dana. This is where the action is."

Yeah, right. She knew Tony Martin. His only social life consisted of his computers and the Internet. The man lived and breathed technology. It had landed him a great, good-paying job, but it didn't leave much room for real relationships. He was like a piece of shining tin, brilliant and gleaming on the outside, but shallow and hollow on the inside.

Which is why Dana had turned down his invitation to marry him and come live with him in the big city. Tony didn't have an ounce of romance in him. Since he'd never taken the hint and even remotely tried to woo Dana back, since he just didn't get that she had to have more than a live-in computer genius, since he had never once thought about anyone but himself, she'd sent him on his way, alone.

Tony was married to his work, plain and simple. He didn't have an inkling of what was involved in hearts and flowers, and he certainly didn't have the patience to deal with a slightly autistic, hyper preteen boy who had the emotional maturity of a seven-year-old. Stephen was one of the main reasons she and Tony weren't together. They'd never discussed it; he'd never come right out and told her, but she knew by his words and actions that Tony didn't want to deal with Stephen. Tony wanted her. He didn't want her little brother.

But he was a good friend in spite of their breakup a couple of years ago, and he did have connections. And Stephen could thrive there with the proper therapy and some new doctors who actually understood his condition. Maybe it was time to cut her losses and head to Kansas City.

She glanced over toward the murky white silhouette of the Universal Unity Church, sitting in the distance like a giant piece of rock candy. The place had suffered little to no damage in the storm. Her neighbor's good luck had held. And the strangest part, Caryn Roark had sent over two young girls with clothes and food for Dana and Stephen. She'd even extended an invitation for Dana and Stephen to stay at the church compound until they were back on their feet. Dana had declined the invitation, her memories of the meeting she'd had with Caryn Roark still fresh in her mind.

"We're the only ones left," Dana said again, wondering where Caryn got all the money to finance her operation. The woman was generous to a fault with the community, and that was part of what worried Dana about her neighbor. Caryn seemed to expect favors in return. "Something just doesn't set right over there."

Oh, well, soon it wouldn't matter to Dana. Soon, she supposed, she and Stephen would be moving on. Once the dust settled and she found out just how much she had left and how much she could sell to make a little moving money, at least. After paying off her debts, she'd take her pittance and start over fresh somewhere else.

Only, in her heart, she wasn't quite ready to give up the

fight, even if she didn't have much fight left. She didn't think she had the courage or the fortitude to face such a formidable task. And she wasn't about to go begging for charity, whatever Caryn Roark's intentions were.

Instinctively she touched a hand to Stephen's head, gently pushing a tuft of thick golden hair off his brow. The boy sighed again and flipped to his side in his Kansas City Royals sleeping bag.

Left alone with the stars and her worries, Dana again thought about the man named Bren. Bren. An unusual name for an unusual man. Definitely not a standard Kansas-type name. But then, she'd known from the start that Bren wasn't from Kansas. Touching the pocket of her jeans, she remembered she had his card tucked inside. She'd kept it there, close, instead of putting it in the bottomless pit of her shoulder bag.

He'd said he'd help her. She'd been taught not to ask for help. It was going to be a long, lonely night. Or so she thought.

A creaking noise off in the distance grass made Dana's head come up. A prickling of fear, like needles hitting the center of her spine, warned her that someone was nearby. She listened, her breath stopping, her eyes trying to penetrate the darkness, one hand on Stephen and the other one on the shotgun lying next to her left thigh.

Then everything shifted and moved. The night came to life as a brilliant light glistened near the farmhouse. A minute later an acrid smell drifted out over the prairie.

Fire. Someone was trying to burn what remained of her house!

Grabbing the shotgun, Dana pulled up out of the tent like a madwoman. "Hey, you—"

Her words were cut off by the shots that rang out into the night. Only, Dana hadn't fired her gun yet.

Rolling back inside the tent, she hushed the now-wide-awake Stephen. "Stay down and stay quiet. Somebody's trying to shoot us!"

Stephen buried himself inside his sleeping bag, his breath coming in great, scared huffs as his body rocked against the ground in a nervous fidget. "Dana?"

"I'm right here, sport. Just do what you're doing. Stay hidden and don't move."

She watched as the fire grew stronger, leaping and dancing like a laughing demon toward the front of the house. Aiming her gun at anything, hoping to scare the intruders away, she pulled the trigger and waited for the old shotgun's kick to bruise her shoulder. The lone shot exploded into the night. Dana sucked in the smell of gunpowder with each deep, frantic breath she took.

Then she took one long breath and shouted, "Get off my land!"

Silence from the intruder, hissing from the hungry fire.

Dana tried to raise up again, and another bullet whizzed by, this one coming from a closer angle. Stephen's muffled cry only added to her own solid fear.

"What do you want?" Dana shouted to the wind.

A harsh laugh echoed through the night, but Dana got no answers to her question. Since Dana already had a sick inkling of who she was dealing with, the silence made her more mad than scared, even though deep down inside she knew she should be afraid.

"Leave us alone," she called. "Can't you just leave us alone!"

Dana heard laughter, then footfalls, as if someone were running away. Then only the hissing of the fire as it snaked up the porch railings.

A sick feeling shot through Dana's stomach, making her

want to retch. All sorts of horrible images ran through her mind. These people were mad! This wasn't just kids out for kicks, and this certainly wasn't a faith-abiding church like the one she'd always known. Caryn had threatened Stephen earlier and now Dana supposed she had sent her thugs to act on that threat. She had to find out if the other woman was doing this, and she had to keep Stephen safe.

"If it's the land, you can have it," she whispered, wishing she hadn't been so direct yesterday with the crazed woman. But she had to wonder if there wasn't something more here. Why would Caryn taunt her with threats against Stephen? She'd purposely pulled him out of school to avoid such teasing and taunts. These people didn't even know Stephen.

*Oh, God. Oh, God. Help us, please.* She clutched Stephen close, soothing his keening cries with a murmured whisper. "It's okay. I won't let anyone hurt you." She thought about calling for help on her cell phone, but realized it would take the volunteer firemen at least fifteen minutes to get here.

When she was sure it was safe, Dana pulled her brother's covers off his head. "I've got to put out the fire, Stevie. Can you stay here?"

"No."

Afraid to leave him alone, but even more afraid to take him out in the open, she wrapped an arm around him. "We're going to crawl through the grass to the house."

"Okay," he said, this new challenge temporarily calming his earlier fears.

"We need to stop that fire from spreading," she explained. She saw his eyes in the moonlight, saw the fear mirrored there inside him. "Stevie, you have to be brave. We're going to get away from here and go to the sheriff."

"Okay," came the feeble reply. "I'll be brave. Stephen can be brave."

"Okay," Dana echoed, the shotgun clutched close. "Stay low and stay right beside me," she said as she inched her way out of the tent, belly-crawl fashion. The going was slow, and the fire was fast. The wind picked up, causing Dana to urge Stephen on beside her. Determined, she struggled to her feet, pulling Stephen up with her to run the last few yards. By the time they made it to the house, the whole remainder of the front porch was on fire. If she could only find the water hose.

They made it to the side of the house where a long spigot ran from the well to underneath the porch steps. Dana always kept a hose connected there to wash mud and dirt from their work boots.

Out of breath, her nerves tingling with fear and worry, she slid up the wall, still clutching her brother, spitting away the grass and dirt they'd gathered on the way. Behind them, the fire hissed and curled, its wrath causing beams to pop and aged frames to cave in like kindling.

"It's all right, sport," she said on a windy breath. "All I have to do is turn the water on and we can wash down most of the porch. Maybe we can save it."

She stood, looking around to make sure the intruders were gone. Then she groped for the long thick noose of the hose, searching in the dark for the fat coil of rubber. Her hands reached out to emptiness. They'd disconnected the hose. It was nowhere in sight.

Above them, the fire rose up, triumphant in its snap-happy victory. The sound of bursting glass shattered the night, and Dana watched as the blue lace curtains of her parents' bedroom curled and crumbled, too dainty, too delicate, to survive the heat of the angry, leaping flames.

## Chapter Three

"So you're telling me that you can't do anything to help me?"

Dana looked at the robust face of Sheriff Horace Radford and wondered why she'd even bothered to drive over the speed limit, straight to his house about five miles up the road, and pull him out of what looked like a sound sleep. The man didn't seem to care one way or the other about all the happenings out on her land.

Remembering how he'd only shrugged and told her how sorry he was about Otto when she'd talked to him yesterday after the tornado, she wished the man hadn't been reelected. She certainly hadn't voted for him. Oh, he'd promised her a full investigation, but having a tornado drop down on his town's doorstep had given him a pretty good excuse to sit on his hands. But having her house deliberately burned to the ground meant Dana didn't have the same luxury.

"It's all gone, Sheriff," she said now, her voice still and resigned. "And I found this note underneath my windshield wipers."

She read aloud the cryptic note. "'You have something that belongs to us. Until we find it, watch out for your brother.'" The note had ended with a Bible verse, Proverbs 18:21. "Death and life are in the power of the tongue."

Reading it again gave Dana the creeps and put a solid fear in her heart. They thought Dana had something of theirs, and they were threatening her brother to get it. The verse was almost like a warning, telling her not to speak. But what did they think she would have to speak about?

"That don't make much sense," the sheriff said after Dana read him the note.

"No, but it's a threat. I don't know what they think I have of theirs. Surely you can send some men out to look around. I saw them set the fire, so I know it wasn't an accident, and I believe these people are a part of the Universal Unity Church. That's the only ones I can think who'd do something such as this."

"Dana, Dana," he said, raising a beefy hand to ward off any further protests, "I'm sure sorry you've had all these troubles, sugar. I hate that you've lost your house, honey. But you can't go around accusing people without some sort of proof."

Dana stepped closer to the sheriff, her footfalls causing his creaky front porch to groan in sleepy protest, her face just inches from the oblong pink wart growing on his crusty nose. "Look at me, Sheriff Radford," she said on a slow, even keel. "I've got dirt all over me. That's from trying to save my house. Stephen and I fought that fire as hard as we could, but we couldn't save anything. That's because they cut off my water supply." Lowering her eyes to the peeling green paint on the floor, she added, "I couldn't even get inside to the phone, not that that would have mattered. My line's been down since the storm. And my cell phone didn't help. It was too late to call the fire department."

The sheriff patted her on the arm, then pulled his dirty plaid flannel robe closer around his puffy white-haired chest. "I'm sorry, honey. Do you have a place to stay?"

Dana gave him another disbelieving stare. "Are you listening to me? They looted and then burned down my house and shot at us!" Her voice rose an octave higher with each word.

Sheriff Radford rubbed the salt-and-pepper beard stubble on his fat jaw. "It don't sound good, do it? But I declare, I ain't never heard of any trouble from that Unity woman and her kids. You sure you saw some of them?"

"Yes, I saw two young men dressed the way they all dress, from what I could tell. I've been thinking maybe it's some sort of revenge against me, maybe because I talked to her the other day about my bull getting killed. But why they've decided to pick on me is beyond reason. Whoever sent them meant business. They tore up what was left of my house and burned the rest. Now everything I had is gone."

"Think you could identify them if you saw them again?" the sheriff asked, his beefy hand still rubbing a hole in his unshaven face as he pondered all the details.

Glad that he was finally comprehending what she was trying to tell him, Dana pushed on. "Maybe. It was dark and I only got a glimpse, but I could tell from their actions, they looked young—two of them, dressed in what looked like baggy clothes and big coats—that much I remember." She let out a long sigh. "I'm pretty sure they shot my breeding bull, and now this. And they looted the house right after the storm. I can't imagine what they're looking for, though."

The old man leaned back against the planked side of the house wall. "I'll go 'round and have a talk with some of your neighbors first thing in the morning. Maybe somebody saw something."

"Talk?" Dana pushed smoke-scented hair out of her eyes. "These people killed an expensive animal and then destroyed what little was left of my home. And that's just this week. Goodness knows what they're planning next. You need to do more than talk. If these kids are from that church, you need to arrest them before somebody else gets hurt."

"I can't arrest anybody until I have proof!" he shouted, his eyes bulging. At Dana's look of surprise, he added, "And you'd better stop accusing Ms. Roark's pack. That woman has become a pillar of this community and she's got lots of money tied up in that place out there. We have to consider all the angles before we go blazing in on a high horse, accusing her of things."

Dana gave him a puzzled look. "I'm not accusing *her*. I just think somebody living there isn't exactly nice. And I think she needs to know about it. When I talked to her yesterday, she practically threatened Stephen herself."

"I can't believe it's anybody from her place," the sheriff responded, shaking his head. "That woman makes them kids behave. Holds them to a tight schedule and has them praying all day and night. They plum don't have time for much outside activity."

It suddenly hit Dana why the sheriff was being so indifferent toward her. The Roark woman had helped the man get reelected. That, plus the fact that the sheriff was lazy and didn't really want to put himself in any danger, made Dana think she could give up ever finding the criminals who'd destroyed her home. No, Sheriff Radford wouldn't make any effort to arrest someone who might put his own life in danger. He only worked enough to keep himself supplied in liquor and cigarettes.

"What are you going to do?" she asked, just to test his thin mettle.

"I'll post guards on your land," he supplied, pleased that he'd done his sworn duty. "Keep any mischief-makers away."

"Mischief?" Dana laughed bitterly. "I'd call arson and slaughter a little more than mischief, Sheriff."

"Crazy kids," he said, shaking his head. "Are you sure you got a good look at them?" he asked again, his words stretching out in a long whine.

"Not a real good one," she admitted. "They stayed hidden like the cowards they are, but I saw them in the light from the fire." She glared pointedly at him. "And you're just as big a coward. You've sold out the people of Prairie Heart, Sheriff. How do you sleep at night?"

Anger puffed his face to a glowing red. From the yellowed glow of the porch light, Dana saw she'd struck her mark. The man sure didn't have a poker face.

"I do what has to be done," he said in a wheedling voice, "to keep the peace around here. And since you ain't got one dab of proof against anybody, I suggest you stop barking up the wrong tree."

Dana lifted a finger to his chest, poking him as she spoke. "Oh, you're right about that. I am barking up the wrong tree. I've lost everything, but you don't care, do you?" Pushing him away with a repulsive jab, she added, "I guess I'll have to deal with this on my own."

"Don't do anything stupid, Dana," he warned. Then his wide face took on a sympathetic demeanor. "How 'bout I give you a little money to tide you over?"

Dana wanted to spit at him. He was telling her not to do anything stupid, when he was the biggest idiot of all! "No, thanks. I don't want your money, Sheriff. I'd prefer some justice, though."

Looking affronted, he said, "You don't know Caryn the way I do. She's a very peace-loving woman. She wouldn't do something like this."

Dana was already heading back to the truck, where Stephen sat watching. Then she turned to glare back up at him. "You know, I never once accused *her* of any wrongdoing. I just happen to believe it's someone living on her property. Seems you're mighty worried about that woman. Sure makes me wonder what you're hiding."

"I ain't hiding nothing," Sheriff Radford called out a little too defensively. "And just to prove it, I'll send them deputies out right now."

"I feel better already," Dana called. She got in the truck and slammed both palms against the steering wheel, a fresh batch of tears brimming down her cheeks. She was going to have to take Stephen to a safe place. And she needed some time to think about what to do next. She was going to have to ask Tony Martin for help sooner than she'd planned.

Dawn greeted them as they entered Kansas City by way of Interstate 35. They'd left Prairie Heart behind. They'd left their little corner of the Flint Hills behind. They'd left their charred and splintered farmhouse behind. They'd left their home, their land, their life, behind.

Dana had made a snap decision, based on a long stretch of determination. She only hoped Tony would welcome them and help them. Maybe, at least, Stephen would be safe in the city until she could figure out what to do next.

After waking Emma and Frederick to ask them to look after her stock, she'd discussed her options with them. She still had her cattle; she could try to save them at least.

"We'll herd them over to Harvey's place," Frederick assured her. He called several burly, dependable, well-armed men to meet him at the crack of dawn. He'd get the animals to a safe pasture. "And I don't mind shooting any trespassers, thieves, or travelers, not one bit."

"Tell the men I'll pay them all back, somehow," Dana promised. "When this mess is settled."

"That Sheriff Radford," Emma hissed, her pink foam curlers contrasting sharply with her bright red-and-yellow-flowered housedress. "We'll vote that lazy old man out come next election!"

"Somebody's got him in their pocket," Dana explained, her instincts telling her that someone was Caryn Roark. "Voting doesn't count out as nicely as cold cash."

"Where you going, child?"

"Kansas City. To see Tony."

Emma smiled knowingly. "'Pride goeth before a fall.'"

"I don't have any pride left, that's for sure," Dana said. "I don't have anything."

"Poor child. We could take care of you two. You know you can stay with us, don't you?"

"I won't put you in danger. I'm going to fight this, Emma, but I have to come up with a plan. I can't fight if I don't have any ammunition, and if I don't know who I'm fighting."

"Bless your heart. You be careful, you hear?"

"I'm afraid for Stevie," Dana replied by way of an explanation.

Emma nodded. Family came first, no matter the cost. "Go to Tony then. Let him help you. He's always wanted you with him, anyway."

Dana looked away. "But he doesn't want Stevie."

"If he loves you, he'll take Stevie, too."

And so Dana and Stephen had taken off into the night, fleeing. Dana had never run from anything, not hard work, not tragedy, not her responsibilities, but now, for Stephen's sake, she was officially on the lam.

She couldn't help but wonder how long it would be before she found her way home again.

"Do people really get up this early?" Tony asked, one eye cocked toward the digital clock over his elaborate computer system. "And did I ask you yet, what in the world are you doing here, and what's that smell?" He held two long, white fingers to his nostrils, pinching them together while making a disgusted face.

Dana pushed Stephen onto a nearby black leather sofa, ignoring the clutter of newspapers and high-tech magazines littering one corner. "Try to go back to sleep, sport." Then she turned to Tony again. "Tony, we need your help. Otto got shot, then half the house got blown away in a tornado, then they burned down the rest. Somebody's trying to either scare us or get something from us. Or just plain murder us."

Tony was wide-awake now. "All of this happened in Prairie Heart? Maybe I'm living in the wrong town."

Dana looked over at the man she'd once thought she loved. Thank goodness she'd figured out it wasn't love that held her to Tony. Convenience, friendship, companionship, loyalty— it was all of these, but not love. She hadn't realized that until this moment, when in the light of harsh morning, she saw him for himself.

He was handsome, in a scrawny Nicholas Cage kind of way. He looked like a Kansas farm boy, but he had the brains of a rocket scientist. His entire head was covered with red tufts of thick, coarse hair that looked like rusty steel wool. Dana had never once seen him comb it. He wore a holey Star Trek T-shirt that featured a faded Mr. Spock and Captain Kirk. Tony was a Trekkie, but he was also a Techie. People teased her brother, calling him a geek, but Tony was the real geek. He was very smart. Too smart.

In their junior year of high school, he'd been one of the best basketball players on the team. But during a play-off game, he'd been fouled and injured. Laid up with a broken ankle, he'd turned to his computer for comfort. Since then, he lived and breathed technology. His ankle still gave him trouble now and then, but he was in pretty good shape considering he rarely moved from his desk except to go down to the nearby park and shoot a few hoops with the inner-city boys.

Tony didn't drive a car; he cruised the Internet. Even now, his e-mail was signaling that he had an incoming message. He ignored it, a rare concession to Dana's paying him a visit, and took another less sleepy look at her. "You've been through a fire."

"Yes," she said, plopping her elbows on her knees so she could bury her smutty face in her hands. "I've been through more than a fire. I've been through the worst kind of destruction."

"I'll make coffee," he said, tugging at his faded red sweatpants. "Then you tell me exactly what's going on."

She did, spilling the entire story out between fits of crying and fits of anger. "This woman wants to either scare us or kill us, for some reason. They said I had something they needed. They torched my house. And I know in my heart these people shot Otto. But the worst of it—they said they'd get Stephen." Glancing over at her sleeping brother, she whispered, "You know how he is. He's friendly to everybody. He's too innocent to know that some strangers are dangerous. I had to get him away from there."

Tony nodded to the same rhythm his fingers drummed on the cracked yellow countertop of the island bar that served as dining table and control station central in his kitchen. "Yeah, I know how he is. That boy's a handful, for sure. What can I do?"

She pushed back a red-brown wave of hair, the hurt of his jab toward Stephen's hyperactive nature making her feel small and doubtful about asking for his help. "Just let me stay here a couple of days. I need a place to hide, while I decide what to do. I went to the sheriff, but there's no help there. He might be in cahoots with Caryn Roark. He thinks I'm just ranting because I'm under so much stress—ha, this is beyond stress."

"Yeah, I'd say you've been through it." Tony took her empty coffee cup and uneaten cornflakes. "Go take a long shower and let me absorb the scarce data you've given me, then we'll talk some more after you've rested." When she glanced at her brother, he added, "Stevie's okay. He can clean up when he wakes up."

Dana nodded, then rose to move down the short hallway to Tony's bedroom, her entire body sore and bruised, her entire system begging for a meltdown. She turned at the bathroom door. "Thanks, Tony."

He winked. "Hey, I've been trying to get you to Kansas City. I'm sorry about things, but I'm glad to have you here." His computer beeped and said something and he absently turned back to the blinking lights of his monitor. Somebody badly wanted him to respond to his e-mail.

Dana came out of the bedroom feeling refreshed if not recharged. She wore her only other set of clothes, a pair of Levi's and a T-shirt with a huge sunflower painted on the front. Now she needed to find something for Stephen to wear when he got up.

Digging through the tote bag she'd brought, she found Stephen's new Ruby Runner shoes. They were clean and smoke-free at least. But Emma had given Stephen the wrong pair of shoes. This wasn't the pair Dana had ordered. These shoes were the latest model, more expensive and much more cushioned than the ones she could afford, but they were the right size at least. They were white with a wide red triangle that resembled a real ruby on either side—the symbol of all Ruby Runner shoes. That same design pattern was molded on the thick soles, too. Stephen would love that continuing pattern.

As Dana turned the shoes over in her hands, the little ruby designs seemed to glow from inside. She was too tired to appreciate it, however. "Fancy," she mumbled, thinking Emma normally didn't order such expensive shoes. Well, she certainly couldn't return them now. She'd settle up with Emma later.

Coming out of the bedroom, Dana saw that Stephen was still asleep, and he still smelled of smoke. She'd have to get him cleaned up and into his new shoes. That would perk him up. She was worried about how all of these changes were going to affect her brother. He didn't take change very well. Kids like Stephen needed routine and structure; in fact, they demanded it.

She looked from her brother to Tony. Still in his T-shirt and sweats, he was engrossed in the many machines that covered one wall of his tiny apartment. Three monitor screens, several powerful system units and a whole lot of multimedia equipment—scanners, fax machines, telephones, modems, printers and cell phones—all sat like dominoes, leaning here and there, arranged in and on each other, just waiting to set things in motion with the touch of a button.

Dana had never understood computers. Her father had bought her one years ago, at Tony's insistence, and she had used it to keep up with the farm's business. Other than that, gadgets didn't impress her much. They did Tony, however. He was almost like an appendage of his many machines. A walking, talking computer, programmed and ready to run as soon as he saw the blinking cursor. He didn't even know anyone else was in the room.

"Tony?" she called.

His long fingers danced across the keyboard in front of him, his thick glasses reflected the bright green lettering on the screen he was studying so intensely. His hair seemed to be glowing, as if the entire process demanded that the energy flow directly through his fingers into his brain, bypassing his heart and soul. "Tony?"

"What? Huh?" Absently he held up one hand.

How many times had Dana seen him do that? How many times had she left him in his room back in Prairie Heart, with his machines and his programs? They'd start out studying for a test, and he'd invariably wind up at the computer, under the pretense of typing up some study sheet. Before long, Dana would be left with her textbooks and Tony would be lost in the vast world of a tiny one-inch microchip.

A girl couldn't compete with that kind of power.

"Tony?" she said again. "Is there any way we could pull up my bank account? I don't know how much cash I can get my hands on."

Now she had his attention. Next to setting up computer systems, Tony loved nothing better than hacking into one.

"Sure," he said, his eyes already back on the screen before him. He was in a chat room on the Internet, and apparently the conversation was lively. "Just give me the name of the bank and your account number."

Dana dug through her purse and handed him her checkbook. She stood over his shoulder, waiting for him to take the information. "Here."

Tony stopped typing, then pushed his glasses up on his nose. "I got the funniest message on e-mail. Wanna read it?"

This was part of the routine. Tony loved sharing his e-mail.

"Okay." Dana took the printout he handed her, not really interested, but needing something to focus on. The words on the page brought her head down. With both hands clasping the sheet of paper, she brought it closer to her face, so she could be sure of what she was reading.

"'What's more precious than rubies and gold?'"

Somewhere in the tired recesses of her mind, Dana connected on the familiar, but it slipped away in a pool of cold fear. She didn't like the tone of this message.

"Who sent this?" she asked Tony, her eyes shifting from the words to the back of his head.

"Don't know," he admitted. "They didn't sign it and I couldn't trace it. Got jammed out on the first try. Whoever it is, they're good. They don't want to be found. But it's pretty obvious they're using a forged e-mail address. Their IP numbers are way off and they used a single cap in the address for the Received heading—Uareit." Still keying in information, he added, "Pretty weird name, though, huh? Almost as if they're saying 'You are it.'"

Dana sank down in an old overstuffed beige plaid armchair. "Yeah, too scary. I think this message was sent to me, Tony. I think I am it"

Tony's head peeled around. "You? How? Who knows you're here?"

"Only Emma and Frederick," she said. "And they don't know a thing about e-mail."

"That's for sure." He went back to his typing. "Hey, maybe you're just tired. Getting a little paranoid?"

"Maybe," she said, her eyes automatically going to Stephen. "And maybe not. Have you ever heard of the Universal Unity Church?"

Tony frowned, squinted, scratched his head. "Rock band?"

"No." Dana smiled in spite of herself. "My threatening neighbor is Caryn Roark. She's the leader of some weird church group—a cult, maybe—and she's been my neighbor for three years now. They have a big compound over there, behind closed gates and tall stone fences, but I've never bothered them and up until this week, they've never bothered me, other than constantly making me offers to buy my land." Shaking her head, she added, "I did sort of threaten her the other day, since I'm sure someone from her compound shot my bull. They claim I have something they need, but I don't have a clue what that might be. And if that's true, why would they go to all that trouble—destroying my house—when they could just as easily have confronted me and asked for whatever they think I have."

"Let's do a little search," Tony said, his fingers already doing the walking across his keyed-up keyboard. "See what we can find. If this church lady is as high and mighty as you make her out to be, there should be plenty of information about her online. Especially if she tries to win over recruits to her way of thinking."

Knowing that would be the only way Tony would be impressed or willing to help, Dana shrugged. "I would like to know more about her. I just don't trust the woman. But I can't understand what she wants from me, other than my land. I guess she decided since I was so angry, she'd run me off, even if it meant nearly killing Stevie and me."

Tony grinned, then rubbed his hands together gleefully. "Well, if this Caryn is on the Net, I'll find out everything we can. I've got sources in places where no source would dare show up."

"What if they find us first?" Dana asked. "I think they know I'm here."

"What can they do, but send a few hits on the e-mail?"

"They might send more than messages," Dana replied in a whisper. "They might come after us." Her eyes centered on her brother. "They might come after Stevie."

The day progressed without any more excitement. Much to Tony's dismay, Stevie ran around in his Ruby Runners, practicing sprinting. Her friend and her brother had always irritated each other.

"Hey, watch the cords, kid. One trip and you'll unhinge part of my system. My clients wouldn't like it if I lost part of their records."

Dana realized they'd already overstayed their welcome. Tony bit his nails and worked—drinking massive amount of black coffee as he tapped into Dana's sparse bank account and informed her that she had about ninety-eight bucks in her checking account and about five hundred dollars in her savings. Not much.

"If someone's tracing you, they'll know the minute you withdraw any money," he explained. "Better just let me loan you some cash. What are you going to do, anyway?"

Dana didn't know. "I haven't thought that far ahead. I only know that I've got to prove they're coming after me. If she wants my land, the bank will practically hand it to her now. I borrowed money against the house to buy the two bulls, but now I can't make the loan payments. Tony, I'm afraid not just for Stephen, but for everyone in Prairie Heart. That woman could take over the whole town."

Tony scratched a hand through his wiry head. "Relax, doll face. I've got my markers out there. We'll see what we come up with."

That gave Dana another idea, something that she'd kept in the back of her thoughts. Now instinct told her to pursue it. "Can you pull up information on someone else for me?"

"Give me a name."

"Bren." She pulled the card out of her pocket. "He told me not to give anybody this number, but I have to know who he is. He helped us out after the tornado hit." Quickly she explained meeting the mysterious man and how he'd been so kind to Stephen and her. "He said he had to go to Wichita on business." She looked down at the card in her hand. "Brendan Donovan. Wichita Industries. That and a phone number are all I have."

Tony snorted a laugh. "Good one, Dana. Yeah, right."

"No, I'm serious," she said, wondering why he thought this was so funny.

"*The* Brendan Donovan?" Tony asked, his face turning a blotchy red. "Are you sure?"

"That's the man's name," she replied.

"Okay, if you say so," Tony said, scratching his head. "But I can't imagine why the wealthy, worldly Mr. Brendan Donovan, better known as the 'Geek from Ireland,' would be out on a county line road in rural Kansas. Maybe it was someone pretending to be him."

Dana studied her friend, suspicious of that bright knowing light in Tony's eyes. To her way of thinking, Brendan Donovan was anything but a geek. The man oozed handsome. "What do you know about him?"

"Enough," Tony replied, already focusing on the task at hand. "Let me pull up a few things and then I'll explain."

A few hours later, Tony emerged from his corner with printouts an inch thick. "Very interesting. When you make someone mad, you go for the big guns, huh?"

Dana dropped the magazine she'd been leafing through. "What'd you find?"

Tony settled down in the plaid chair and adjusted his bifocals. "Universal Unity Church—founded by Caryn Roark. Started in Europe, specifically Ireland, has ties with extremists groups, cultlike following, over a thousand sworn members worldwide, very secretive, very powerful. Members have to swear loyalty to the church and give up all worldly goods. Had some run-in with parents who claim she's brainwashing their teenagers. Moved to rural Kansas about three years ago to start a new arm of church. Still has headquarters in Ireland, but has a growing following in United States. Claims to have channeling powers, uses the occult and spirituality to convey her messages to believers." He stopped, tipping his head so he could see Dana over his bifocals. "And here's the part I especially like—owns stock in various companies, including technology and activewear."

Dana sat listening, surprise and disbelief growing with each word. Now she let out a shocked breath. "I knew she was powerful, but I had no idea. You're telling me I'm in a lot of trouble, right?"

Tony bobbed his head. "Yes, I guess that's what I'm telling you, doll face. Should have kept better tabs on your neighbor, I reckon. And probably shouldn't have picked a fight with her over a dead bull."

Dana dropped her head into her hands. "They moved into the Selzer place a few years back, not long after my parents were killed. They didn't bother me and I tried to stay clear of them, until she tried to buy my land. Ever since I turned her down, she's been rather cool toward me, but no one from over there has ever harassed me before."

"But they may have shot your bull?"

"Yes," Dana said, groaning. "I told you, I went there the other day, after Otto was shot. I told her I thought someone from her complex had done it."

"And you threatened her."

Dana thought back over the conversation. "Yes, I guess I did get a tad mad. But she was so smug, so high and mighty! Okay, I did suggest it might be someone from her group. She didn't take too kindly to that, either."

Tony gave her a worried look. "Dana, this doesn't sound too pretty. No wonder Sheriff Radford didn't get all bothered about the looting and fire."

"No, because she's probably paying for his extra little luxuries," Dana said on a hiss. "He kept trying to protect her, assured me she'd have nothing to do with something like this.

I can't believe this. Why would she get so angry just because I suggested this might be someone from her complex? And why do they think I'm hiding something they need?"

Tony's white teeth played across his bottom lip. "Maybe because she knew you were correct in that suggestion, and it made her look bad? Maybe because she was afraid you had figured some things out? Maybe they're saying they know you have proof and they want that proof?"

"What things, what proof?" Dana shouted, getting up to pace around the room. "I was trying to mind my own business. I never once messed with those people until they messed with me."

"Maybe this Roark woman has something to hide, besides murdering animals and setting fires, and she thinks you know more than you really do."

Dana's head shot up. "That has to be it. Here I was thinking it's just about the land, but they came in and tore up my house, so they were obviously looking for something."

"What could you possibly have that they'd want, though?" Tony wondered. "If this woman is as powerful as this report claims, then she doesn't need anything else."

Dana shook out her wavy mane. "Technology and active-wear? Pretty strange for someone who forces her followers to live in virtual poverty."

"Or virtual reality," Tony added. "If she's into technology, there's no telling what she's got going on. She might be conning them with this spirituality gig. I'll bet she uses technology to conjure up all sorts of dire things."

Dana shivered. "You mean she uses scare tactics?"

He nodded. "Yes, mind control, hypnosis, brainwashing. Dana, you've got yourself into some pretty heavy stuff here."

Dana shot him a wry look. "I went to see her because I was concerned. I must have opened up a whole new can of worms by threatening her, but I never meant for it to go this far."

"Smart move. Are you sure someone from this church could have had Otto done in?"

She shook her head. "No, I'm not completely sure, but that was the only explanation. I'm sitting right in the middle of their complex, so they'd have to cross my land to get back and forth on the property. I just figured one of her wards decided to have target practice on old Otto. We both know there's nothing for miles and miles around. It can get pretty boring out there, especially for those kids from the big city."

Tony squinted at her. "You said your property is surrounded by church property?"

"Yes," Dana replied, nodding. "Everybody else either lost out or had to sell out. The church has bought up just about every bit of land there is to have out there."

Tony leaned back in his swivel chair. "And she's offered to buy your place?"

"She's hinted at it very strongly, but I never offered to sell."

"You thought about it, though. Maybe now would be a good time to do just that. Maybe that's all she's after."

"I am the only holdout," Dana said. "And she does seem to want all the land around there. But I don't want to lose it, not even now. And I certainly don't intend to be bullied out of my daddy's land."

Tony rolled his eyes. "You don't have many choices left, sugar. Time was, you would have gladly sold that land to anyone with a good offer—let alone someone trying to kill you."

"That was before," she said, looking over to where Stevie sat playing a maze-type video game with Tony's state-of-the-art gadgets. "When Mom and Dad died, Stevie didn't take it so well, remember. I couldn't uproot him so soon after all that. He loves the farm, so I stayed. And I'll keep on staying until he's better able to handle a move."

"I've heard this tale before," Tony reminded her. "That's all very noble, but it also means you don't have a life. And we both know that's why you and I aren't together today."

She made a hushing sound. "I don't want to get into that, Tony. Stevie and I are a package deal, take it or leave it. You chose to leave it."

He twisted his lips tightly together and shrugged. "But hey, you're here now, both of you."

"Not for long," she reassured him. "I've been thinking about my options. I can't get the sheriff to help me. I don't have much money. The creditors and the bank are probably closing in right now. If this Roark woman bides her time, she'll have my land anyway."

"So—" Tony raised both hands and let them drop on the worn chair arms "—exactly what are your options?"

She gave him a direct look. "What'd you find out about my friend Bren?"

Tony sat up straight, then eyed her curiously. "Oh, that one. Well, as I said, when you play, you run with the big dogs." He shifted through his download to find what he was looking for. "Bren, from Wichita—if I have the right Bren from Wichita based on the phone number and full name of Brendan Donovan on that card—is one powerful dude, too. And he seems to be the same Brendan Donovan I've heard so much about over the years. I read all about him in my techno magazines. That is what they can find on him. The man is very reclusive and secretive, and very powerful in the technology world."

That caught Dana's attention. She had mixed feelings about the stranger, and she had to know more before she followed through on her plan. "Tell me."

"Wichita Industries is a catch-all name for various businesses and holdings owned by Brendan Donovan. He has so many holdings and companies, it's hard to say what all he does own. In Wichita, he for sure owns a private airplane factory, which he bought out when it was going under a few years back. Donovan Aer—spelled *A-E-R*—builds private airplanes for people who have lots of money to spend, but there is a small chain of computers and software equipment under that name, too. So that's probably why your friend Bren was headed to Wichita. Checking on business, I guess."

Dana took a sip of Coke, the syrupy sweetness hitting her churning stomach at the same time her doubts hit home. "Okay, but what was he doing on a county road in the middle of Kansas?"

Tony grinned. "I'm getting there, sweetheart. It seems Brendan Donovan is the heir to a vast fortune, which he's doubled over the years. The man's into everything, technology—there's that word again—manufacturing, airplanes, land... Oh, and this is a really good one—shoes."

Dana scrunched her brow. "Shoes?"

"Yep." Tony playfully kicked one of her feet with his own bare toes. "He owns Ruby Athletics, doll face. He owns the very shoes your brother is wearing, the hottest active shoes on the market right now, the Ruby Runners."

Dana looked down at her brother's feet, not believing what Tony had just told her. "You're kidding, right?"

"I don't kid when I'm reading a printout," Tony informed her. "And as to why he was on that road the other day, I think I can help you there, too. Did he happen to express any interest in your friend Caryn's church?"

"Not really. He said he didn't have a church home." But she remembered how he'd stared across the prairie at the church. Dana sat up, waiting for Tony to spill the rest of his findings. "What about it?"

Tony's smile was pure enticement. "Just as I suspected

when you mentioned his name, and now that I know we're talking about the same Brendan here, our friend Bren hails from the same hallowed ground as your enemy Caryn. In fact, if my research is correct, why, they're practically neighbors; they both own estates in County Cork."

"Ireland?" Dana asked in a whisper.

"Ireland," Tony repeated dramatically. "Now, how's that for coincidence?"

## Chapter Four

Dana jumped up to pace around the unlit, windowless room. "It might be just that, a coincidence." She refused to believe Bren could be mixed up with the likes of Caryn Roark.

Tony dropped the papers on top of a pile that seemed to be growing from the dark brown carpet next to the chair. "Yeah, but what are the odds of two people from Ireland being in rural Kansas at the same time?"

Dana whirled to face him. "Caryn didn't speak with an Irish accent." Trying to remember how the woman had sounded, she admitted, "She is very cultured. Very formal. Maybe there was a trace, but Bren—he could definitely be Irish."

"Maybe he was visiting the complex," Tony offered as he popped the top on a soda, then took a huge swig. "Hey, I'm hungry. Want Chinese or pizza for dinner?"

Dana continued to pace. "I don't care."

"Pizza," Stephen said from his crossed-legged stance on the floor in front of the television. "Stephen wants pizza."

Dana watched as Tony conjured up the nearest pizza joint on one of his monitors and ordered a large with everything. She had to wonder if he ever left his apartment.

Having provided dinner, Tony turned back to her, his eyes as bright as the simulated picture of fish swimming on the monitor behind him. "Hey, you don't want to believe this man is in with Roark, I know. But it sure looks that way. I've heard things about Brendan Donovan—how he doesn't like to be in the limelight, how he shuns publicity, and maybe this is why. Maybe he's one of her followers."

Dana watched the bubbles floating on the screen behind Tony. "No, he was interested in the church, but when I asked him if he was a member, he…he said no."

Tony's lips tipped up at the corners. "Could he have been lying?"

She shook her head. "It was the way he said no, and the way he looked. I got the feeling he did not approve of the church at all."

"Then why was he there?"

"I don't know." She sank back down on the couch. "All I know is that he protected me during the storm, and he helped us afterward. He even told me if I needed anything to call—"

Tony groaned, lifting his eyes to give her a long stare. "And you're thinking about doing just that?"

She shrugged. "Well, I was. He seemed secure. I believe he'll help me."

"A perfect stranger! Get real, Dana."

Before she could respond, a message came through on the e-mail again. Tony jumped over to the terminal to read it out loud.

"'What is the most important thing in life? To lay down one's life for a brother.'"

Dana looked around as if someone were watching them. "She knows I'm here, Tony." Lowering her voice, she whispered, "She knows and she's threatening Stevie again. She's aware of his problems, and she could easily influence him if she gets her hands on him. I've got to get away from here!"

Tony grabbed her to pull her around. "Hold on. Where will you go?"

"I don't know," she said, a mortal fear pumping through her system. "I don't know."

"What's the matter?" Stephen asked, his attention diverted completely from his video game to Dana's frightened face. "Dana's sad. What's wrong, Dana?"

"Nothing, Stevie. I'm just worried, is all. Your pizza will be here soon."

Stephen watched his sister. "You sure, Dana? You sure you're all right?"

Tony clapped his hands together. "She's just being a drag," he said. "Hey, ready to take on the champ, pal?"

"Yeah," Stephen said, "but I'm warning you. I'm real good at video games."

"Give me that other control," Tony said, his tone mock-deadly. "I'll take you on anytime, anywhere."

Dana, thankful that Tony was at least trying to pacify Stephen, thought back over the message they'd just received. How did Caryn Roark know she was here? Maybe she'd asked around town and found out that Dana and Tony were friends. Maybe she'd had them followed. Or maybe not. That would be too obvious for someone like Caryn Roark. No, whatever method she was using, Dana was sure it was very underhanded and very secretive. And very high-tech, since someone had obviously found a way to get to Tony's computer files. But why was the woman still after her? She'd won, hadn't she? Dana had lost the farm and she'd run away, to protect her brother, to think her way through this, to save her sanity. What more could the woman want?

What if the woman didn't stop until she had Stephen?

"I can't let that happen," Dana said out loud.

Luckily Tony was making such a ruckus with Stephen, neither of them heard. They didn't hear the doorbell, either.

"I'll get it," Dana said. "Probably the pizza man."

"There's a twenty on the counter," Tony said, his eyes never leaving the blur of speeding cars on the television screen.

Dana opened the door and absently took the warm pizza box, her mind preoccupied with other things. Then she handed the delivery boy his money, her eyes touching on his briefly. He looked familiar—

"Thank you," the boy said, a serene smile plastered across his skinny face. He left so quickly, Dana didn't connect on why he looked familiar. Shutting the door, she said, "This is one large pizza, and heavily loaded from the weight of it."

"Set it on the coffee table," Tony said over his shoulder. "We'll be there as soon as I finish winning this race."

"Right." Looking for a fairly level spot on all the magazines and papers on the long, beat-up table, Dana dropped the pizza box on top. That's when the lid popped open just enough for her to see the gadget inside.

"Tony," she said, her heart jumping right along with whatever was in the box. "Tony, come here a minute."

"Hold on."

"Now, Tony."

Something in the panicked tone of her voice got Tony's attention. "Pause it, Stevie," he said as he pushed up off the floor. "What's the matter—no jalapeños?"

Dana pulled him close. "No, something we didn't order. Listen."

He did, his eyes widening as they locked with hers. "Get Stevie," he said, "and go, go as fast as you can. Get out of the building. It might be nothing, just a joke. Just go and I'll come down and get you after I check it out."

"I can't leave you," she said, her hands clutching his arm. "Come with us."

"No way. I can't let anything happen to my equipment."

"Forget the computers. Come on, Tony!"

He leaned toward the box. "Go on. I know a little bit about detonating bombs. I learned it on the Internet. Go! I'll call 911, I promise."

Afraid to leave, but even more afraid to stay, Dana lifted Stephen up. "Listen, sport, I want you to come with me for a few minutes."

Stephen looked confused. "Hey, what about my pizza? I want pizza."

"We'll eat when we get back," she explained. "Right now I want to try out your new runners. We haven't really had a chance to go for a good run since we got them."

"Dana, now?" He rolled his eyes. "I'm hungry and I want to finish this game." He placed his arms over his chest in a defiant stance.

The box ticked away.

"Now, Stephen. Don't ask questions, just come on."

"But I don't want to run. It's getting dark out there and we don't know our way around. You told me, never run in the dark."

"We'll be okay. Now, don't argue with me, Stephen."

Throwing his controller down in a fit of anger, Stephen glared at his sister. "I don't want to go."

"But you are, sport." Eyeing Tony, who stood staring at the ticking pizza box, she heaved Stephen by the collar, praying he wouldn't have a tantrum. "We'll just go around the corner."

She reached the door, grabbed her purse and took one last look at Tony. "Be careful," she said. "Call a bomb squad or something—call somebody, Tony!"

"I'll be fine," he said, his grin fixed and unsure. "Go, and Dana, you be careful, too."

"Okay." She felt the tears pressing at the back of her eyes. "Ready, Stevie?"

"No, no. Don't want to go."

"You don't get to decide," Dana replied. "We have to leave now, Stephen."

They made it to the small lobby, where a security guard nodded indifferently at them.

Dana called to the man, "I think we've got a bomb threat in apartment 201."

The guard snapped to attention, automatically reaching for the nearest phone. "Hey, wait a minute!" he shouted to Dana.

She didn't stop. She pulled Stephen along at a brisk trot, mindless of his complaints. The city was dark and misty. It had been raining. Car lights flashed in her face, but Dana didn't notice. She looked down the nearly deserted street.

She turned back to get a grip on her exact location, taking one last look at the apartment building. Then the earth shook and in a matter of seconds, part of the building blew up and out into the sky. The blast sent glass flying and bricks falling. Somewhere someone screamed and a baby began to cry.

Frozen in horror at first, Dana sprang to life. "Tony!" she cried as she ran back toward the building. "Tony!"

Stephen screamed, too, then began to cry. "Dana? What happened? Where's Tony?" His screams turned into a high-pitched wail that would only get worse if she didn't calm him down.

People began to run out into the streets, pushing and shoving, questioning. Dana held Stephen close, watching as the remainder of the building settled back into itself, hissing and burning. What used to be Tony's apartment was now a hollowed-out hull with charred, tangled computer equipment strewn across its blank face. The air was heavy with smoke and falling cinders, the acrid smell cutting off her frightened breath. Closing her eyes, she bit back the tears wailing inside her. A silent scream roared through her pounding head. This scene was too familiar. This was too soon, too quick, too much.

Tony was dead, and it was her fault. All her fault.

"I have to find him," she said out loud, grabbing Stephen to pull him back toward the building.

Sirens blared all around her; paramedics arrived in ambulances, pushing the sightseers and shocked neighbors aside.

"Tony," she said, trying to tell someone, anyone, where he was. "Tony is in there."

"Step aside, ma'am," a young fireman said. "We'll find your friend, but you can't go in there."

Shocked, Dana could only nod. She gripped Stephen so hard, he cried out again. Easing up a little, she held him close, her eyes searching the crowd. Maybe Tony had gotten out, too.

*Please, God, let him be okay.*

Then she spotted the pizza delivery boy in the crowd. He raked a hand through his bob of a haircut, then leaned back nonchalantly on the fender of her parked truck. He gave her the same serene grin she remembered from—

"From Emma's store," she said in a shaky whisper. The other customer. The one who'd run out when the storm had hit.

One of Caryn Roark's boys.

A chill careened down Dana's back. They not only knew where she was; they had planted a bomb just for her.

"I'm sorry, Tony," she whispered to the horrid scene in front of her. "I'm so sorry."

With that she waited, watching the grinning boy as she talked quietly to Stephen. "Listen, sport. We're going to have to get away from here, because, well, some bad people are after us and we've got to find a safe place."

"Mean people?" He sniffed and looked up at her, his body rocking back and forth in shock.

She nodded, her eyes watching the teenager across the way. She couldn't lie to Stephen, and she couldn't do anything more for Tony. They had to run, to get away, and she needed Stephen to understand the urgency of their situation. "We've got to sneak away, somewhere where they can't find us."

"What about Tony? Don't leave Tony, Dana."

She swallowed hard, her hand tightening on her brother's shoulder. Stephen wasn't supposed to be in such situations. He wasn't supposed to be removed from his daily routines. And without his medication, he'd soon be bouncing off the walls. If she couldn't handle all of this, how in the world would her little brother? "I don't know about Tony," she admitted. "I hope he got out."

"Do we have to leave now?"

"Yeah, I'm afraid so. We can't take the truck, but don't you worry. I'll take care of you, I promise."

She tugged him close, her eyes on the teenager standing in the crowd, watching her every move. Her gun was in the truck. "Here's what we're gonna do, Stevie." She directed him around, away from the bomb scene. "We're going to start running. We're gonna run faster than we ever have. I want you to concentrate, like you do when you're in track, or playing football. I want you to run as fast as you can, but don't leave me. Don't let go of my hand, okay. We have to stay together, no matter what. Okay?"

"Okay. Good thing I've got on my Ruby Runners. Yeah, Ruby Runners are fast."

Thinking of Brendan Donovan, Dana nodded. "Yeah, let's just hope they live up to their name."

And so they ran, following the yellow ribbon of the streetlights, following the dirty gray-black ribbon of the sidewalks. They turned a corner that circled to the back of the apartment complex. She didn't know where they were going, but she had to get away from that pimply-faced teenager with the stringy brown hair and the vacant eyes.

"Did you find her?" Caryn Roark asked into the slim, silver phone at her ear.

"Yes and no," came the shaky reply. "We found her and we tried to scare her."

"That doesn't sound promising," Caryn replied into the phone, the rage inside her simmering in a calm facade of control. "What happened?"

"We followed her from the sheriff's house, all the way into Kansas City. She went to an apartment downtown. We monitored the apartment and we were able to get into the electronics system. We sent your messages via e-mail, hoping she'd leave and we could nab her outside. But she didn't leave. Until a few minutes ago."

"Where is she now?"

"Uh, we don't know. The bomb—"

"You set off a bomb? You idiot, you could have killed them both. I need them alive and shaken, not dead and completely stiff. How else will I find what I need?"

"We were only trying to scare her out of the building, but it went off and…Derrick made it too powerful…and the building blew up. She got away in all the confusion and now we've lost her."

Caryn glanced around the stark white of her office. Everywhere she looked chrome and glass reflected her image back at her. Forcing a serene look back to her face—she didn't need extra wrinkles over this bit of trouble—she said into the phone, "You'd better find Dana Barlow and that stupid brother of hers. Do you understand me? Bring them to me alive. No more shooting or bombs, or you will be sorry you ever failed me."

"Yes, ma'am."

Caryn hung up the phone, then placed her fingers together. Admiring the smooth creamy tone of her perfectly manicured fingernails, she sat down in the white leather chair behind her desk, then glanced at the clock. "Almost time for late prayers. I'd better calm myself down."

After all, it wouldn't do to upset the children unnecessarily. No, that wouldn't do at all.


Dana looked over her shoulder, thinking they'd outsmarted the smirking youth who'd been caught in the sway of the crowd gathering to view the bombing sight. She didn't see anyone behind them.

"Ahhh!"

Stephen's scream and the tug of his body being pulled away from hers brought her head around.

Someone was holding her brother.

"Let him go," she said to the dirty mass of a man standing in front of her. Winded and tired, she squinted at the huffing figure holding her squirming brother. "Tony?"

"It's me, doll face."

Dana threw herself into Tony's arms, tears of relief streaming down her face as she reached around Stephen to hug Tony. "You're all right. Thank goodness! How did you get out of there?"

"Can't breathe," Stephen said, his hands flapping between them.

Tony pushed Stephen back toward Dana, then bent over to take a deep, calming breath. He was covered in dirt and soot from his head to his feet. His left temple was cut and bleeding, his bifocals were bent, but all in all, he seemed to be okay.

"Well," he began, breathing between words, "when I opened the box, I realized the bomb was too complicated for me—not your average-grade pipe bomb, more like an alarm-clock bomb. So I grabbed my cell phone and I hauled myself away. I took the back stairs, screaming and yelling to people as I went. I dialed 911, told them I had a bomb ticking in my apartment, then I got outta there."

Dana sighed long and hard. "And just in time. Oh, Tony, if anything had happened to you…"

"Hey, I'm all right. My computers are gone, but don't look so sad. I've got a back-up system at the main office downtown. And I'm fully insured. They haven't won yet."

"Why are they after us?" Stephen asked, rocking back and forth on his feet. "Why, Dana? Why?"

Dana gave her brother a worried look, then followed it with one to Tony. Too scared to stay out in the open, she pulled them both over to a cluster of trees that formed the beginnings of a huge park. A sign a few feet away announced the fenced area as the Wyandotte County Lake And Park Grounds. "We don't know why they're after us," she tried to explain. "But I think our neighbor is trying to scare me. I made her mad, and apparently, she doesn't forgive and forget."

"But she runs a church," Stephen said, thoroughly confused. "Church people are supposed to follow the ways of the Lord, and forgive everyone. Should forgive, Dana."

"Not this particular church lady, sport. For some reason, she's got it in for us." She didn't dare tell him that Caryn had threatened him.

Slumping down against an ancient oak tree, Stephen asked, "Dana, are we ever gonna get back home? Stephen wants to go home."

Dana brushed his hair out of his face. "Sure we are, sport. Sure we are. But it might be a while, and I can't promise we'll have anything left to go back to. You just hang in there, okay."

Stephen looked around. "This place is spooky. I want my baseball cards."

Hoping to distract him, Dana pointed to his shoes. "Boy, you ran so fast in those Ruby Runners."

Stephen stared down at his feet. "Ruby Runners. Yeah, I have Ruby Runners. I like them. They make pretty noise."

Dana figured her brother was talking about how his new shoes squeaked. "That will stop once you get them broken in."

Tony stood and took in their surroundings. "The park's okay, but sometimes vagrants do hang out in there." He lifted his chin toward a secluded spot behind a service building, then his eyes flashed wide. "Hey, I know someone who might be able to help us. He lives on the edge of the park."

"Are you sure?" Dana asked, afraid to trust too many people. Or cause anyone else to get hurt.

"Yeah." Tony nodded as he stretched and brushed at his clothes. "He's a retired police officer who doesn't always play by the book, if you get my drift. Leo will know what to do." Then he stopped and gave Dana a sharp-angled look. "But I have to warn you, Leo is really weird. I met him when I went to fix a computer at a local church. He was attending an AA meeting there. Helped me move some tables so I could get to the plugs. We kinda clicked, but he's out there, if you know what I mean."

"Great," Dana said, too tired and worried to argue. "That's comforting."

Tony took her by the hand. "But I trust him, Dana. He's helped me out of a lot of tight spots."

Dana decided that was good enough for her. Tony didn't trust that easily.

"Okay, let's go," she said, turning to grab Stephen by the hand.

"C'mon, there's a hole in the fence over there where I climb through to go jogging sometimes. We'll cut through and be inside the park. We'll be safe there, at least. We can call Leo from my cell phone."

"No," Dana said. "What if they trace it?"

"Good point." He put the phone back in his shirt pocket. "If they found you here, and planted a bomb in a pizza I ordered online, then it stands to reason they can find us anywhere." Then he shrugged. "Leo's house is just on the other side of the park."

"Let's head deeper into the park," she said, taking Stephen by the arm. "At least out in the woods they can't link us to any computers."

They hurried along, following a trail that circled the lake. The woods were quiet, except for a few nocturnal animals here and there.

"Sure is dark," Stephen whispered, his hand clutching Dana's arm. "Don't like dark, Dana."

"Lots of shadows," Tony added, sticking close to Stephen's other side. "Nothing to worry about, sport."

"Hope they didn't see us come in here," Dana whispered back.

"Are there any bears in here?" Stephen wanted to know.

"Nah, but we might run into a deer or a fox. Maybe a really mean squirrel or two."

"Hush," Dana said, smiling for the first time in a long time. Then she thought about the bomb again. "That was definitely a strong message back there. I hope no one was hurt or killed because of that bomb."

"Well, we can't get information out here," Tony said, his tone mourning the loss of his lifestyle. "They destroyed my computers!"

Tony guided them through the vast park until they reached the other side of the perimeter. "There," he said, motioning toward a street beyond the fence. "I know another place where we can climb through the fence."

They headed up a hill where a clump of trees formed black shadows on either side. The scent of decayed leaves assaulted Dana as she tried to catch her breath. Giant sycamore trees stood sentinel, their pale gray bark looking ghost-white in the muted moonlight. The night was so still, Dana could hear their breathing growing more rapid, could hear the patter of their shoes on the worn, cushioned path. It was if they were alone in the center of the world.

"Through here," Tony said, guiding them behind a clump of hedges that covered a torn part of the fence.

Soon they were in a small yard that backed up to the park. Dana squinted toward the square, squatty house in front of them.

"Let's just see if Leo's home," Tony said. But he didn't sound very confident.

They were halfway up on the back porch when a huge figure jumped out in their path, growling and snarling at them like a madman. They all three screamed in unison, then clung to each other, Dana holding tight to Stephen while Tony held tight to her.

Dana took in the sight before her, thinking this had to be some kind of macabre dream and that surely she'd wake up in her bed, in her little farmhouse, all safe and sound.

The man was huge. The moon acted as a spotlight as he bent forward. His shirt gaped open to reveal a tattooed chest. That massive chest was heaving up and down as he stared at them, his eyes holding them penned with an unnerving glare. His hair was a mixture of gray and black, and hung around his face in flowing straight locks. He wore twin white feathers on either side of his parted hair. They hung down around his ears, making him look like a giant winged bird. A pair of army fatigues covered his legs, and heavy hiking boots encased his feet. Each time he inched toward them the silver bangles on his massive arms jingled a warning.

For a full minute, the man stared at them and they stared back. In her mind, Dana kept thinking they should run, but her feet wouldn't obey the shouting command.

Finally Stephen spoke. "An Indian. We found an Indian."

The man stepped forward again, and they all retreated another inch. "You're trespassing," he growled.

"Leo, it's me, man," Tony said, his voice shaky at best. "It's Tony. We were in that building back there—the one that blew up. Someone planted a bomb in my apartment—actually, in my pizza."

"This is Leo?" Dana whispered, her arms protecting Stephen as he stared up at the imposing man in front of them.

"Yep," Tony said, indicating the little frame house behind the man. "He lives right here. But he likes to roam the park at night sometimes."

"Uh-huh," Dana replied. "And he's supposed to *help* us?"

The man stared at them, then snarled. "Get out of here, Tony."

"Okay." Tony tugged at Dana's arm. "Let's go."

"But what about—"

"He might be having a flashback," Tony said under his breath. "We don't even want to be here for that, trust me."

"Then let's go," Dana said, frightened all over again.

They were just about to do that when more sirens blasted through the night, startling all of them. Dana, Tony and Stephen took that as their cue, and started to make tracks back toward the woods.

Dana ran right smack into the strange man. He'd also heard the sirens, and now he was trying to block their way. He grabbed Dana to keep them both from toppling over.

"Let me go!" Dana shouted, her eyes widening as she stared up at the man. Even in the darkness, she could see the fear in his eyes. "Please, let me go," she said again, hoping this weirdo wouldn't harm them.

"Do you hear that?" he asked, his eyes brightening like a shard of crystal. "Hear them? They're looking for me."

Tony stepped forward. "Yeah, and they're coming to take you away. Let her go, man."

The man looked at Tony as if he'd just noticed he even existed. "They won't get me if they can't find me."

Tony seized that notion. "Yeah, well, if you don't let us go, they will find us, Leo. And they'll find you, too. And it doesn't look like any of us want to be found just yet. We came to you for help, man. Can you understand that at least?"

The man jerked his head around. "You hiding out?"

Dana didn't dare make a quick move. She'd heard about people like this man. People who lived in their own little worlds; people who went berserk and killed everyone in sight. People who lived in the park, in the dark, people who lived on the fringes of reality. From the way he was dressed, and the way he acted, she'd say this man was on the verge of some sort of rampage, and she didn't want to stick around to find out what it was.

"We're trying to get away," she said in a calm voice, her body protecting Stephen behind her. "So we do need to keep moving." Inching closer, she added in a whisper, "And you're frightening my little brother. Mister, we've had one really bad week, and you're not helping matters."

The man waited for the sirens to die down, then he released her to step back. "I'm sorry. It's just that I used to be a cop, and when I hear that sound, well, it reminds me of things I don't want to think about."

Stephen's eyes lit up. "A cop? Wow! Policemen are our friends." He shook his head back and forth. "Got to get away from bad people. Bad people are after us. Policemen are our friends."

Dana grabbed her brother by the collar. "Hush, Stevie. Let's just get going now."

Leo lifted his head. "What kind of *bad* people?"

Tony sighed, then wiped a hand across his dirty brow. "Look, Leo, we don't want any trouble. We have to keep moving. This woman and her brother are being harassed by some strange cult—the Universal Unity Church—and we need to get out of here."

"Caryn Roark, the woman who speaks with a false face," the man said, nodding his head in slow motion. "I've heard stories about her."

"You know about her church?" Dana asked, curious in spite of her fear.

"I used to be a cop," he repeated. "I heard things down at the station. Parents called in, telling us their kids had run off to join the Universal Unity Church. Sometimes we could get them back, sometimes we had to let them go...." His voice trailed off, and he seemed lost. He sat down on a wooden bench, then froze like a statue, his back straight, his hair flapping in the soft night wind.

"We need help." Stephen paced before the man. "We need help. Right, Dana? Yeah, we need help."

Tony tried to pull Stephen back. "We're wasting time, people. Let's get out of here."

"I used to help children," the man said, his head down. "It's been a while since anyone's asked me to help." He rose up then and smiled down at Stephen. "I'd be honored to help you."

Dana looked over at Tony. Tony lifted his eyes heavenward. "Thanks, buddy, but we've got to get on down the road."

Leo lifted a hand. "Tony, I'm all right, honestly. I didn't mean to scare y'all. You just never know who's going to be passing through this time of night. I have food and drink. Would you like to rest a bit?"

"Food? Where?" Tony asked, his gaze moving toward the

dark, hulking house. "And why are you out here in the dark anyway?"

"Just bored," Leo said, gesturing toward the house. "C'mon in. Nobody'll bother you here, I promise."

Dana leaned toward Tony. "He'll probably lure us in there and kill us."

"I've never killed anyone intentionally," Leo said, a hand still waving in the air as he spoke over his shoulder. "Not in 'Nam, not when I was a cop. I didn't like the killing."

"Weird," Tony whispered to Dana. "I told you he's weird, but he is very smart about bad people."

"You got that right, friend," Leo said, apparently completely lucid now. "Tell me some more about this church. I still have connections down at headquarters, you know."

Tony scowled. "Yeah, that's why I brought Dana to you. Only, we're not sure who we can trust at this point."

"I was a detective," Leo explained as he herded them up onto the porch. "Twenty years on the force. Then one night—"

"Maybe we should just go," Dana said, not wanting to hear why the man was no longer a cop.

"She'll find you, you know," he said, his gaze as steady as a silent pool of water. "She sends her recruiters to the city to find easy prey."

A shiver went down Dana's back. She could well imagine Caryn Roark manipulating runaways and rebels into her cult. She didn't want to think about what the woman did to control them.

"Well, she's not getting my brother," Dana said, wishing that she believed her own vow. "We'll be okay as long as we keep running."

"I can help," Leo repeated. "I need to help."

Tony stomped the hard ground. "Can we trust you, Leo?"

"I'm not as crazy as I seem. You know that, Tony." Then

he turned to Dana. "My name's Leo Ryan. I live near the park because I choose to do so. I like the outdoors. I didn't like Leavenworth."

Tony groaned. "Leavenworth? Dana, he never told me he had a prison record."

Dana looked at the stranger with wide, frightened eyes. "You were in prison?"

"Not the prison," the man stated calmly. "The Veterans' Center. I'm a retired vet. Served two tours in Vietnam. You got a problem with that?"

"No," Dana said, thinking she had a big problem with psychopaths, however.

"Good. Then let's go inside and talk about what's going on. Like I said, I still have connections. And I can turn you in just as fast as I can turn you on the right path. The choice is yours. But either way, you've still got somebody chasing after you."

Tony looked at Dana, then shook his head. Dana looked down at Stephen.

He rocked back and forth, his eyes on the ground. "Policemen are our friends." Then Stephen grinned. "I like him."

"Okay," she said. "We could use some advice."

Stephen smiled, then lifted his face to the huge man leading them inside, his voice singsonging out into the night, "You got courage. Fighting war. Being a policeman. Dana says I need courage."

The man stopped and looked around, his silvery eyes moving across their faces. "Son, I don't have one ounce of courage. I'm nothing but a frightened coward."

## Chapter Five

Leo took them inside the house where a big window showed off the shadows of the surrounding low limestone bluffs. Stopping, he waited at the entranceway for them to walk through, then quickly followed them inside.

He was silent as they gazed around. Then he spoke quietly, like a tour guide. "The rangers run me out of the park every now and then, so I bought this house right next to the hills. I can get back into the park this way. I work in the park during the day as a guide of sorts to the visitors."

"An Indian," Stephen said, his eyes wide with excitement as he looked around the small shadowy building. "I knew it. I knew you were a real Indian."

Dana had to agree with him. The room was bright with the light of a single candle, which burned a strong-smelling incense as its flame danced shadows across the paneled walls. Strange drawings sprawled across the perimeter of the square little room. And all around, different artifacts sat on display— a dream catcher, an old earthen pot, a spear, a bowie knife, books, provisions, hats, small stools; some of the stuff was authentic, some right out of a stereotypical tourist store. The room was a strange blend of reality and dreams.

"Wichita, Wynadot, Huron, Iroquois, Kanza," Leo Ryan said. "I don't care anymore which I descended from. They are all here, the ghosts of my ancestors. They are all here with me. Together we travel in darkness." He looked ahead, his shoulders held at a proud angle.

"Wacko," Tony mumbled, shuffling his feet impatiently.

"I'm not crazy," Leo said, turning to shift his eyes on to Tony. "Or at least you never used to think so."

Tony stopped squirming. "Well, Leo, I've never seen you like this before. I mean, it's bad enough you live near the park like a hermit, but now you're pretending to be a native. I think you need some new medication, my friend."

"I *am* a Native American," Leo corrected. "And I'm not a hermit. I came home to heal."

"Are you sick?" Stephen asked, plopping down on a rag rug laying near the doorway. He immediately started rocking back and forth. "A sick Indian, Dana."

"No, I'm not sick. Not in body," Leo explained. He placed his big, meaty hands on his chest. "But inside here, son. In my heart. I let my fellow officers down, and now I'm too chicken to go back and face them."

"What happened?" Dana asked, fascinated in spite of the numbing shock that wanted to pull her down into a deep sleep.

"I suffer post-traumatic stress syndrome," Leo said without hesitation. "From my Vietnam days."

He went to the refrigerator in the small kitchen, then came back with three sodas. Then he settled down on the blackened floor next to Stephen. He handed the drinks to Dana, Stephen and Tony, then pulled out a bottle of Jack Daniel's. He didn't drink from the bottle, just sat there staring at the amber liquid.

He let out a big sigh, then continued. "I have flashbacks. One night, during a drug raid, I had a particularly vivid flashback. When my partner called me to move in on the suspects, I couldn't do it. I hid in a ball behind a Dumpster, like a coward. My partner had to go in alone. He was killed."

He got up again, rumbled around in the dark kitchen, then came back with a pack of cheese crackers. He opened them, took one and passed the pack to Dana. She took one and passed it to Tony. Even Tony, as cynical as he seemed regarding his friend, was moved by Leo's gripping admission. "You never told me any of this."

"You never asked," Leo said on a calm breath, his eyes still on the whiskey bottle.

"What caused the flashback?" Tony asked, then handed the crackers to Stephen.

Leo finished chewing, then got back up and got a soda for himself, opened it and took a long drink as he sat back on the floor. "I think it was the children. There were three of them inside the house. The mother had been cooking methamphetamine on the stove—an illegal lab right there in the house. We were all set to go in when I heard a baby crying. Suddenly I was back in 'Nam. I could hear the children crying. I could hear my commander telling me to go in, go in."

He stopped talking, stared with black eyes at the bottle on the floor in front of him. "I couldn't do it. My partner went in, and the house blew up. That happens with meth, you know. He died trying to save those children, but he couldn't save them. I stayed behind the trash Dumpster, and the mother ran out the back door right past me and got away."

Dana sucked in her breath, then let out a great heaving sob. She'd held herself so tightly, she'd held herself in check, she'd held back all the frustrations and the fear, and the aching need to scream, but now it all came pouring out. She cried for Leo's pain and the children trapped in that house; she cried for Tony's lost apartment and the people the bomb had hurt; she cried for Stephen in his helpless innocence, and she cried for herself, and the overwhelming burden of being lost in a dark forest with no hope of ever going home again. While she cried, she prayed, hoping that God would turn His face back to her and help her. Then she realized she'd been the one to turn away from Him.

Leo let her cry. Tony sat still, his eyes fixed on the feathered dream catcher that swayed against the silent wind moving through the shadowy room. Stephen took his sister's hand and held it, his gaze staring out into space as he rocked back and forth.

After a long while, Leo finally spoke, "So you see, our paths were destined to meet tonight. I heard the blast. I came out to see what had happened. I thought of those children I didn't help. I can help you now, though. I can help the children that evil woman is holding under her control. I need to help."

Dana sniffed and brushed her hair away from her face. "I don't know what to do. She's destroyed my home, she's threatened my brother and now she's bombed a building, all to get to me. I probably should go to the police, but I'm so afraid. I don't know who I can trust."

Leo lifted his head. "You can trust me. And you can start by telling me who you are."

Dana hung her head, then lifted her chin in the air. "I'm Dana Barlow, from Prairie Heart, Kansas—it's about thirty miles to the west." She motioned to Stephen. "This is my brother—"

"Stephen Calvin Barlow, Jr.," Stephen interjected. "It's just me and Dana. We don't have anybody else. Nope, nobody else."

"Our parents died in a car wreck," Dana said.

"Yeah," Stephen echoed. "Died. They died. Heaven. They live in heaven."

Leo didn't flinch, but his silvery eyes went one shade deeper into gray. He looked over at Tony.

"You know me," Tony said. "And up until tonight I was running a successful computer programming company from my home. Dana and I grew up together, so she came to me for help. After the bomb, I remembered you lived here, so I brought Dana to you."

"And now you all have me," Leo replied, his entire body so still he looked like some sort of monument to a carved wooden Indian.

"What can you do?" Tony asked, his cynicism not quite as sharp now.

"I can find out things. We have to have proof. I can find out if the police have any clues about the bombing."

"It was the pizza delivery boy," Dana said. "Or someone who took his place. Who knows what they did to the real delivery boy?"

"We'll start there," Leo said. "Do you have any more information?"

Tony quickly filled him in on what he'd found out about Caryn Roark and about Brendan Donovan. "I think he's in cahoots with her, but Dana seems to think he might be able to help us."

Leo took in all the information, then sat silently for a few minutes. Finally he put the bottle of whiskey back in the cabinet, then raised a long thick wooden stick into the air.

"What's that?" Stephen asked, still holding his sister's hand, his lone cheese cracker half-bitten in his other hand.

"A prayer stick," Leo explained. "Tonight we will rest. Tomorrow we will be guided by peace, wisdom and the heart of Christ." He held the stick high. "And courage. We will need all these things to complete our journey."

"So we're just going to keep running?" Tony said through a snort. "I can't do that. I have responsibilities. If I let my business get rusty, I'll have to start from scratch."

"I'm sorry," Dana said. "You don't have to help us if you don't want to, Tony."

Leo gave Tony a long, measured look. "They will kill him if he goes back there."

Tony slapped a hand on his knee. "Well, thank you, all-knowing one. Since you're so smart, why don't you tell us what we should do?"

"We're going on a long journey," Leo explained. "And when we come to the end, we will be home. And that will be the beginning, for all of us."

Later as dawn turned to early morning, Dana watched from her spot on the couch where she lay curled up, as Leo got up and took a bundle with him into the bathroom across the narrow hallway. She heard the door opening and shutting. He was gone a few minutes, but when he returned to the small den, he looked so completely different, she almost didn't recognize him.

His gray sprigged hair was wet and brushed back from his craggy face. He was wearing a pair of jeans and a plaid cotton shirt, and a pair of worn brown cowboy boots. In the light from the sunrise, Dana saw that he was just a middle-aged man with a slight paunch and gentle gray eyes that seemed centuries old. There was still something melancholy and mysterious about him, though. Maybe it was in the way he moved, so silently, so carefully.

"Do you have a family, Leo?" she asked later as he handed her a cup of coffee he'd made in an old aluminum pot that perked on the stove. The brew was bitter and black, but it had a bite that ate its way down to her stomach to wake her up completely.

"Once I did," he answered as he sat down on the floor beside her. "A wife, two sons. I see them every now and then, very little. They have given up on me, but I haven't given up on them."

"Family is everything," Dana said, wishing she could turn back the clock.

"You are your brother's protector," Leo stated, nodding toward the sleeping boy beside them.

"Yes, since our parents died."

"You are running from a lot of things."

Dana looked down at the dregs of her coffee. "Yes, I guess I am."

Leo finished his coffee and stood. "I will go to my friends at the station and find out what I can about the bombing."

"How long will you be gone?"

He turned at the doorway. "Until I find some answers." Then he added, "Stay here in the house. Don't go outside. They could be watching. If anyone comes, you can escape up the bluff but you have to hurry."

So Dana was left with her sleeping brother and her pouting friend, and a deep-seated fear that someone was out there watching her.

"I don't like this," Tony said as he crawled from a sleeping bag Leo had offered into a sitting position a few minutes later. "What if he brings the police here? What if I get blamed with planting that bomb?"

"In your own apartment? Besides, I saw the boy who delivered the pizza, and I can identify him as the same one I saw in Emma's store the day of the tornado. That's pretty strong evidence."

Tony nodded in agreement. "If you live long enough to tell it."

Dana didn't respond. Tony didn't need to remind her that someone had tracked her here to Kansas City, or that Caryn probably had thugs out looking for them right now. But why? What did Caryn want from her and Stephen?

She thought back over the days since the tornado, trying

to remember everything that had happened. She didn't believe Caryn would go to all this trouble just because Dana had confronted her about shooting a bull. There had to be something more. Would the woman really go to such extremes to get Stephen?

Dana didn't want to stick around to find out. She paced the small structure, picking up and tidying up the combination workshop and kitchen/living room, taking in the complex decorating scheme of a man who'd lost everything.

Just like her.

Just like Tony.

"Dana, when can we go home?" Stephen asked, coming up out of his blankets to peer around the hazy room. "Tired of this. Stephen is tired of this. Stephen missed baseball practice and track at church league. Coach ain't gonna be happy."

Stephen talked faster with each sentence. Oh, boy, stuck in a small house with a superhyper kid who didn't have his medicine, and a friend who resented being involved in this mess in the first place. In a few minutes, these two would probably clash and things would turn nasty. And where was Leo?

*Call me if you need help....*

Brendan Donovan's words came back to her. She needed help, all right. And fast. But how could she contact Brendan without that Roark woman finding her? And how could she place her trust in a man she didn't even know?

The morning wore on and Stephen's patience wore off. He paced and talked and whined. Dana tried every tactic the counselors had taught her. She touched him often, to calm him down. She answered each of his questions accurately and to the best of her knowledge. She offered him an old beat-up book to read. When he argued, she tried distracting him by changing the subject. It worked for all of five minutes.

Tony sulked, his fingers tapping away on some imaginary keyboard as he sat stony-faced and brooding. Probably calculating how much the insurance company would reimburse him for the damages. If, he'd stated earlier, if he could get out of this mess long enough to stake a claim.

"Wanna go outside," Stephen said for the hundredth time at around noon. "Don't like this place."

"No, you can't go out. It's too dangerous."

"But why? I like parks. Play in the grass, climb a tree, search for rocks. Can I, Dana? Dana, are you listening to me? Why can't Stephen go out?"

"Can you get him to shut up?" Tony asked in a controlled tight-lipped tone.

"I'm trying," she snapped. "Sit down, Stevie. Let's talk about baseball. Let's talk statistics. Or how about some trivia? Where was Willie Mays born?"

"Alabama," Stephen answered with a pouty snarl.

"Where in Alabama?"

"Westfield, and don't want to play trivia. Want to go outside!"

"Stephen, sit down," Tony shouted. "Didn't you hear your sister?"

"Don't boss me around!" Stephen hollered, tears welling in his eyes. "You're not the boss of me."

"How about Lou Gehrig?" Dana said, her voice rising in a slow panic. "What language did he speak before he learned English?"

"German," Stephen hollered, his hurt eyes centering on Tony. "Tony don't like Stephen."

"'Cause *Stephen* can't mind and *Stephen* won't sit down," Tony bellowed, jumping up to do some pacing of his own.

"Will both of you stop it?" Dana said, a long sigh emitting from her entire body. Looking up at Tony, she pleaded, "Be patient with him, please. This has all been really hard on him."

"You always make excuses for him," Tony told her under his breath.

"And you always think the worst of him," she retorted.

"We've had this fight before," he reminded her.

"Yes, but I actually thought you'd matured a little bit," she shot back. "I thought maybe living on your own would make you a little more human."

"I was fine until you two came along."

"I said I was sorry."

Tony stopped pacing; Stephen had grown quiet. They both looked down at Dana as she sat in a defeated position in one corner of the room.

"I'm sorry, too," Tony said at last, his eyes softening as he looked over at Stephen. "Hey, buddy, how about we toss that soccer ball I see over there under that stool."

"What ball?" Stephen pivoted around, squinting hard.

"The one I spotted early this morning," Tony replied, lunging for the battered, dirty ball. "I was saving it for just such an emergency."

"Great!" Stephen had forgiven him already. "Look, Dana, Tony found a ball."

Dana sighed again, then leaned back to watch them pass the ball back and forth. Tony was trying, but he'd never be as patient with Stephen as Dana had learned to be. Would any man?

She thought of Bren. She remembered how he'd distracted Stephen during the awful time after the tornado. She remembered how he'd talked in a soft, calm tone to Stephen, even when Stephen ran his sentences together and made no sense in his excitement. She remembered how Bren had held her, covering her from the surrounding storm.

*If you need anything....*

Leo entered the door, carrying lunch from McDonald's.

"Hello," he said as he tossed each of them a bag. Stephen squealed in delight, and Tony thanked him.

Dana took her hamburger, her throat suddenly dry with doubt and worry. "What did you find out?"

"A lot," Leo said as he sat down to open his own large order of fries and huge hamburger. He took a big bite and chewed quietly.

"Well?" Tony asked, his mouth full of lettuce and tomato.

Leo leaned back, then gave Dana a direct stare. "Sister, I don't know how you managed to do it, but you've got some pretty powerful people looking for you. And they all want answers."

Dana set her food down. "Who's looking for me, besides Lady of the Weird Church?"

"Try the sheriff from Prairie Heart, the state police, the Kansas City police, the ATF people and the FBI, for beginners."

"The FBI?" Tony sat up straight, his crooked glasses slipping down his nose. "Why?"

"The bombing," Leo explained. "The blast hurt two people. They want to question everybody. They think it was a terrorist attack. It was a homemade pipe bomb set with a kitchen timer, nothing sophisticated, probably just meant to scare you."

"Oh, no." Dana lost what little appetite she'd had. "Two people hurt because of me."

Stephen looked scared and confused. "Are they going to arrest us? Are we in big trouble? Big, big trouble?"

"No, son," Leo explained. "But they do want some answers. They need a description of the teenager. They need information on Caryn Roark. They're very serious about bringing her in."

"Then they do believe she's involved?" Dana asked.

"They do indeed believe she's involved. Seems they've been watching her entire operation for some time now. But they work on facts. And the facts indicate that you three know a lot more about things than anyone else." He glanced at Dana. "You said that kid was hanging around your truck. I think maybe he coulda planted some evidence there, to put everyone on the wrong track. That's one more reason you're wanted for questioning."

"Are you going to turn us in?" Tony asked, his eyes bright with fear.

Leo looked over at him, then shook his head. "I haven't decided. I have friends down at headquarters, but I have enemies, too. I have to decide who we can trust."

Tony took a swig of soda, then asked, "Why can't we just go to the police and explain? Maybe they could protect us—you know—witness protection program and all."

"That's what scares me," Leo admitted. "Roark's got some powerful connections. I don't know if they *can* protect you." He gnawed on a long crisp French fry. "Besides, I got some bad vibes down at the station. Something isn't quite right. If this woman is really after you, and everything seems to indicate this is the case, she'll find you."

"But why does she want us?" Dana wondered out loud.

"That's the big question," Leo said, nodding. "That's what the police and the FBI want to know."

Dana shuddered. "Why is Sheriff Radford looking for me?"

"Seems you went off half-cocked and threatened to take the law in your own hands. Someone filed a harassment complaint against you."

"That's ridiculous!" Dana threw her French fries down. "He's just trying to scare me. He knows who's been doing the harassing!"

Tony touched her arm to calm her. "What do we do now?"

"I can take you to a safe house," Leo said. "I have a place out on the river that no one knows about—belongs to my family."

Dana shoved Tony away, her expression grim. "We can't just keep running. Maybe I should turn myself in. But then what would happen to Stevie?"

"They might try to separate you," Leo admitted. "Especially if this sheriff can show you're unstable."

"And especially if I'm involved in terrorist operations."

"You ain't done nothing wrong, Dana," Stephen said, his voice rising. "Don't let them do that. Don't want to separate. No separate."

"I won't. We won't be separated, Stevie. I promise." She looked from his face to Tony's. "Maybe I should call Brendan Donovan. If he's as powerful as everyone claims, he might be able to give me some legal advice, at least."

Tony groaned. "Not him again. Dana, why do you insist on trusting that man?"

She couldn't answer him.

Leo cleared his throat, his eyes touching on Dana. "Speaking of Brendan Donovan, didn't you say he was driving a black van the day you met him on the road?"

She nodded. "Yes. Why?"

"There's a witness who says she saw a sleek black van driving away from Tony's building just before the bomb went off. The police are looking for anyone with information regarding the van. It sounds a lot like the one you described, Dana. The one your friend Mr. Donovan was driving."

## Chapter Six

"I told you we couldn't trust him!" Tony shouted, throwing his hamburger wrapper to the far corner. "I told you, Dana."

Dana's shock pushed deep into her numb nerve endings. "I don't believe Bren is involved. I just can't believe that. If he wanted me or Stevie, he had every opportunity to hurt us. He was alone with us for several hours after the tornado."

"She has a valid point," Leo said calmly.

Tony whirled to face them. "Yeah, but he was there just before all of this started, and you yourself said he was mysterious. Maybe he doesn't want to kill you, maybe that's why he didn't harm you, but he's after something. Why else would he have been snooping around your house in the first place?"

"He wasn't snooping," Dana reminded him. "He was parked up on the road."

Leo lifted a hand. "Did you ask him what business he had there?"

"We talked," Dana admitted, "but he was evasive. He told me not to tell anyone about the phone number he gave me. Of course, I told Tony." She glared over at her friend, wishing he wouldn't be so judgmental.

But Tony was pumped and primed. "And I put the information to good use. Now we know he was in the area the night of the bombing. I think we ought to go to the police right now."

"Why would he give me his number, if he wanted to harm me?"

"Another valid point," Leo stated.

"He could have been setting you up," Tony replied. "It's just a phone number. For all we know, he gave it to you deliberately, thinking you would try to reach him. That way he can keeps tabs on you."

Stephen took the soccer ball and began rolling it up and down the length of his legs. "Bren was nice. Found most all of my baseball cards. Herded cattle with us, helped us clean up the mess. Bren won't hurt us." He lifted his grubby face to Dana. "Remember, Dana, he told us—he'd do anything for us."

"I remember, sport."

She did remember so many things about Brendan Donovan, things that didn't make sense. Such as the way he made her feel, safe in the storm, strong for Stephen's sake. She just couldn't picture that kind, quiet man as someone who would do her harm. "He was very good with Stephen," she said to Tony in a whisper.

"Maybe he was buttering you up," Tony suggested. "Maybe he wanted to gain your trust, so he could do whatever despicable thing he's planning on doing."

"Why do you distrust this man so much?" Leo asked, his eyes centered on Tony.

Tony paced and stammered. "Well…because."

"Because why?" Dana asked.

Tony ran a hand through his brittle hair, then let out a shaky sigh. "Well, because he's the first man you've ever expressed an interest in, I guess."

"Besides you, you mean?"

Tony looked down at her, his eyes a bright translucent blue. "Well, yeah. I've never met the man, but I've read things about him and heard things, and now I'm imagining things. I mean you

seem so smitten with this tall, dark and handsome stranger—
like he's going to rush in and save us all or something."

"I don't need anybody to rush in and save me," she replied,
careful to keep her tone even, "but I do need help and advice.
Someone is trying to either ruin my life or kill me, and I have
to think of Stephen. So, yes, if this man can help me, can help
us, then I think we should consider finding him."

He gave her a curious stare. "Is that the only reason you
want to find this man?"

She had to look away. That gave Tony all the ammunition
he needed. "That's what I thought. You've got a thing for
him—a complete stranger. A stranger who could have planted
a bomb in my apartment!"

"He didn't do it."

"You don't know that."

But somehow she did know that. She didn't have any valid
facts to back up her claim, but her gut instinct told her that
Brendan Donovan wasn't behind all her misfortunes. She just
didn't know what exactly he was behind, though. And now
she had to consider Tony and Leo. She wouldn't want anything else to happen to either of them.

"You're right," she finally said to Tony. "I don't know
what Brendan has to do with any of this, except that he
seemed to know about the Universal Unity Church. Maybe
you're right. Maybe they are somehow connected."

"And maybe Caryn Roark hired him to make a hit on us—
on you, because you have something she wants."

Tony's statement caused a chill to run down Dana's spine.
Could the man who'd held her, who'd protected her, who'd
murmured such sweet endearments in her ear, be the one who
was actually trying to kill her?

"Why would she have me killed? Then I could never give
her what she's after."

"Maybe *that* is what she's after," Tony replied, his eyes going cobalt as he searched her face. "If she gets you and the kid out of the way, she'll finally have your land."

Dana glanced up at Tony, suddenly understanding his fear. It mirrored her own fears. Funny, she'd always accused him of not having a heart. He had one, all right. And right now, he was wearing it on his sleeve. He loved her; he just couldn't accept everything loving her entailed. So he didn't want anybody else to have a shot at her, but he was fearful for her life.

That realization was sweet and endearing, but it didn't solve her immediate problem. She was still on the run, and now she had a whole entourage running with her. *Lord, help me,* she thought. She just wanted to get back home.

"You have a good point, Tony. But if she did hire Brendan Donovan to do the job, he failed miserably." She stood up, then looked down at Leo. "We can't hide out in this little house the rest of our lives. Can you take us to the house on the river?"

"After dark," Leo said. "Until then, we wait and try to reason this thing through."

Dana reached out a hand to touch his massive arm. She noticed his tattoo, a drawing of a star over a lone pine tree. "What does it mean?" she asked.

Leo twisted his face to see the tattoo. "The morning star," he explained, "gives us our power for each day. And the tree—that's me, standing there waiting for my life force to guide me. God will show us the way, Dana."

She smiled softly. "Thank you, Leo, for helping us."

He rose up to take her hand in his. "Thank you, for letting me help."

Leo had a Jeep that he kept parked in a shed out back. They all piled in that and left Leo's house at midnight. They traveled in darkness, skirting the major roads to take the back ways.

"What about your cool stuff?" Stephen asked, a little boy's worry creasing his brow. "I liked your stuff."

"It will be there when I return. It has been there for many years now."

"And we're the only ones who know, huh?"

"Yes. Can you keep it a secret within your heart?"

"Sure I can. Sure I can."

"That is a good thing. Sometimes we need to stay silent."

"My sister says I talk too much. It's part of my problem. I have a hard time being still. My teachers all think I'm stupid or something, but I try. Really, I do. Then I have to take this medicine. It's supposed to help me, but I hate it. I really, really wish I didn't have to take it. The other kids make fun of me. Yeah, they laugh."

"I really, really believe you truly want to be a good boy," Leo replied as he drove the Jeep down the dark road, the yellow marked center lines guiding them along as the vehicle wound around the big lake in the park. "I occasionally take pills myself. Prozac, Zoloft, Elavil. They are supposed to help me feel better, but I believe I could use a good dose of *peyote* instead."

Stephen giggled. "Cactus juice makes you hallucinate. Dana says it's bad stuff. Bad stuff, bad dreams."

"So do pills, if you take too many."

"Your pills don't work right?"

"Sometimes. Sometimes, though, I'm so sad nothing can work."

Stephen stared up at him. "You don't drink that bottle of whiskey? Whiskey is nasty and bad."

"I can't drink it," Leo replied without elaborating.

"Dana says drinking is bad. Bad."

"It is. Very bad. It makes you do things you regret."

"Do you get lonely and scared? I get that way. Stephen is always scared."

"Really?"

"Really. Mighty scared when the tornado came, and when they shot at us. Burned the rest of our house down. But Dana was there. Dana takes care of me. Always around. Only, now we don't need to be so worried. I'm not as scared now, not since we found you."

Leo didn't speak for a full minute. From the small back seat, Dana watched as he brushed at his eye with one hand and held the steering wheel with the other.

She looked from Leo to her brother. They'd built an immediate trust. She could tell that in the clear, concise way Leo talked to Stephen. That in turn helped Stephen to talk slower and not in the third person, as if he were describing another little boy and not himself. Once again, Stephen's power of innocent wisdom amazed her. He had a hidden instinct for saying the right thing to a person who'd been wronged. She knew Leo would guard her brother with his life. Had Stephen been right about Brendan Donovan, then? Could she trust him?

Tony sat beside her, his face turned toward the moving countryside. Dana wanted to love Tony; wanted to pour herself into his arms and find what little security his love could bring, but her thoughts kept returning to another set of arms and to that vivid dream she'd had during the storm, when she'd moved from consciousness to semiconsciousness.

As if reading her mind, Tony shifted to look over at her. "Are you going to contact Donovan?"

"I haven't decided." She watched the road ahead. "I can't keep running and hiding away. If I do contact him, maybe he'll be honest with me. Maybe he can explain what's going on."

"And maybe he'll come after you—one way or another."

She touched Tony's arm. "You don't have to be involved

in this, you know. Leo can get you to a safe place and you can take care of your business. I know you're worried about your computer company."

"I'll start another one. I have some good connections. People know they can count on me to get the job done. And I'm sure the whole city's heard about the bombing by now."

Leo heard them and said, "Oh, yes. It was in the *Star.* They even mentioned your name. You're officially listed as missing. And wanted for questioning."

"Missing," Tony echoed. "Maybe I should stay that way until this thing blows over."

"Then you'll come with us?" Dana asked.

"I can't let you go without me," he said, taking her hand in his. "Besides, I needed to get out and find a little adventure. I was starting to get cabin fever."

A few minutes later, they pulled up to a secluded spot set back on a sloping wood overlooking the Missouri River.

"Speaking of cabins," Leo said over his shoulder, "we'll hike the rest of the way. I'll hide the Jeep here, so they can't spot it near the cabin. You should be safe there until we decide what needs to be done."

They got out of the Jeep, unloading provisions and stumbling up a broad-faced hillside. Dana sat down to wait while Leo pulled the vehicle into a dark, shadowy alcove of green ash trees and overgrown coneflower bushes, then she watched as Steven and Tony helped him top it off with bramble and tree limbs to conceal it further. Then they headed on up the bluff, for what seemed like miles, to come to the almost hidden porch of the small cabin.

Dana turned to look out into the thick clusters of hackberry and sycamore trees, her heart pounding a steady, cautious beat. She felt a tingle of apprehension rushing like a cold breeze up her backbone to lift her hair on end. She felt as if a set of eyes were centered directly on her. She felt as if someone, something, evil and dark, was hiding in those dense woods, watching and waiting.

Watching and waiting…for her.

Leo stood watch the rest of the night while Dana and Stephen curled up in the small bed tucked in one corner of the big, one-room cabin. Tony camped on the long cushioned couch, bundled underneath a patterned quilt with more holes than patterns in its faded blues and minty greens.

The cabin was sparse, but comfortable. Dana slept for the first time in days, one hand instinctively on Stephen's bare arm. He slept heavily, deep in his trust for Leo, far away from the horrors he'd seen on his little piece of earth.

But Dana couldn't run from the horrors, even in her dreams. She tossed about after a couple of hours of hard sleeping, the images in her mind bringing her subconscious into full focus.

They were chasing her through a white mist. She could hear dogs barking; she could feel Caryn's cold blue eyes following her in the white light. Caryn's laughter echoed through her brain, harsh and brittle, like ice hitting a tin roof.

"I'll find you, Dana. I'll destroy everything you hold dear. More precious than rubies. You know the answer."

In her dream, Dana ran faster and faster, looking for Stephen in the heavy fog, calling his name over and over again until she was hoarse and exhausted. But Stephen was gone and Caryn was getting closer and closer.

Dana ran until she saw a great light through the mist. She followed the light, ran headlong into it's warmth.

And ran straight into Brendan Donovan's arms.

Then the dream changed. The mist turned into a storm raging with an angry, snarling wind. Bren pulled her down, down into the wildflowers where everything was warm and soft, so soft. He clutched her close, telling her it would be all right. "If you need anything," he whispered against her throat, his breath fanning away the choking mist, "call me...if you need anything."

"I need you," Dana whispered, her eyes opening in the dream to find him staring down at her. "I need you."

"I'm here." He bent to kiss her and she felt safe, so safe. Only, she had to find Stephen.

She tried to raise up, but he held her down. Panic erupted in great waves. "Stephen?" she called. "Stephen, where are you?"

"He's safe. Stay, Dana. Stay here with me."

"I can't." She tried to rise up again, but she was paralyzed with a great, numbing fear. "I can't leave Stevie."

In the next instant, Brendan was gone and she was alone and cold. The mist came back, choking her, holding her. In the distance, she heard Caryn's laughter.

Dana woke with a start. Sweat poured through her T-shirt, making her shiver in the cool night air. Instinctively she glanced over at Stephen's silhouetted form, thankful that she'd been dreaming.

Leo stepped out of the shadows. "A nightmare?"

"Definitely." She rose up, careful not to wake Stephen. "Not so very far from what's been happening in real life, though."

"You had a powerful dream, then?"

Dana found a bottle of water and twisted off the lid to drink deeply. "Very powerful. Caryn was after me, and I couldn't find Stevie. Then Bren—"

"He draws you to him."

Leo's statement didn't question or judge.

Dana tilted her head to one side. "He intrigues me."

"His *orenda* is very strong."

She squinted toward him in the darkness. "What's that mean?"

Leo sat down on a kitchen chair, then stared up at her. "Our *orenda* determines all things. It is sacred and divine, and it relates all of us to each other."

"Like karma?"

"Much like that. Destiny, fate, karma, belief. They are all the same. It sounds as if this Brendan's *orenda* has summoned your soul to his."

"Because I dreamed about him?"

"Because your destiny has met his. Certain men carry more *orenda* than others. It can be very powerful, very useful, if it is used wisely."

Dana tossed her hair back. "Well, that seems to be the question of the day. What's Brendan Donovan's intent? What's he up to?"

"Did your dream give you any answers?"

"No."

"Think about it. Are you sure?"

She remembered Brendan's whispered words in her ear, on her skin. She remembered his black, tormented eyes. "He told me he'd help me. He asked me not to leave him."

"Then that is your answer."

Dana shifted around the tiny kitchen corner. "That's silly. It was just a dream, and besides, I barely know this man."

"You don't want to ask anyone for help."

"No. I've depended on myself for so long, why should I start begging now?"

"Begging is one thing. Reaching out to someone is another. You reached out to me, when you could have easily turned and run away. Most people do."

She gazed at him, looking down at his craggy, cratered face. "You *needed* to help, remember?"

"Maybe Mr. Donovan does, too."

Suddenly it all made sense. Brendan had wanted to help her, but he'd been hesitant. Why? Because of Caryn? Because he knew something Dana didn't? Because he was afraid? No. He didn't seem afraid, just so sad, so wounded. Just like Leo. Needing to heal. Needing to find some redemption.

"Do you think I should go to him, Leo?"

"I think you have to follow your heart," Leo replied. "I know that's cliché, but it's the best advice I can come up with at four in the morning. And, all this talk means nothing if you don't ask for guidance from the Lord. I believe God puts certain people in our path, good or bad, as part of our destiny. It's up to us to discover that destiny, but it all depends on which path we take."

Dana nodded, then sat down on the chair next to him, thinking Leo seemed lost in another time, but he also seemed as wise and aged as a great oak tree. "You know, the day I met Brendan, I saw a rainbow as he was pulling away in that big black van. Maybe that was a sign or something." She shrugged, then gave him a bittersweet smile. "Leo, you've got me talking like you."

Leo smiled, sending his leathery skin into several scattering wrinkles. "There is a Native American legend about the rainbow. If you shoot the rainbow and cut off a piece to place on a runner's shoulder, he will stay ahead of his opponents. You see, the rainbow is always ahead of us, just out of our grasp."

Dana rose and placed her hands in the pockets of her jeans. "Maybe I am chasing a rainbow." She started back to bed, then turned. "I think tomorrow I'll head to Wichita."

"To find Brendan Donovan?"

"Yes. I need some answers."

His gray splattered head moved slightly. "I think you have

the answers already, but I understand your need to keep searching."

"Running," she reminded him.

"Yes, but remember, when you run away from one thing, you usually run into another."

"Good night, Leo."

"I don't like this, Dana. This isn't like you, to go off half-cocked. At least, think about it some more."

Tony sat at the kitchen table, a half-eaten doughnut in his hand. He looked pale and drawn and tired. He took another bite, his blue eyes still centered on Dana's face.

"I have thought about this. I've thought about nothing else for the past several hours. I think Brendan knows something about Caryn Roark, and I think that's why he was on that road that day."

"Since when did you get so perceptive?"

Dana lowered her gaze to stare into the black depths of the strong cup of coffee Leo had handed her. "It's a gut instinct, Tony. I can't explain it. But I've gone over the way Brendan acted that day. Every time he glanced toward that church complex, he had such an intense look on his face. He was there for a reason, and I believe it had nothing to do with me. I just got in the way  me and that tornado, that is."

"The tornado hit. So now maybe he wants you out of the way."

Dana shoved her coffee cup across the table. "Look, I'm going to Wichita to talk to Brendan. If that doesn't work, I'm going to the police. That's all I can do."

Leo had been standing at the back door, his gaze roaming the surrounding woods. "I can take you to the police right now, if you want. You have nothing to hide, and you have a lot of ammunition to use against Caryn Roark."

Dana leaned into the table, placing her hands underneath her chin. "Yeah, but for all we all know, she's twisted everything to make me look like the culprit. I can't risk that. I can't let the authorities take Stevie away from me, and they might if they listen to her." She cast a pleading look toward Tony. "Then she might be able to get to him. He's safe as long as we stay in hiding."

Tony saw Leo's expression and raised a halting hand. "I know, I know. She has a valid point."

"And this Mr. Donovan might be the only person with enough power to stop the church woman," Leo added.

"Then we all agree?" Dana asked, her gaze moving from Leo to Tony. "We go to Wichita to find Brendan Donovan."

Tony let out a sigh, then threw up both hands. "Sure. But I don't like it."

Leo nodded. "We'll leave tonight. Better to travel in darkness."

Dana glanced over at Stevie, still asleep on the corner bed. "It's going to be all right," she said. "We'll be safe in Wichita."

Moving from the shed to the cabin should have relieved some of the boredom for both Tony and Stephen, but the two seemed to clash at every corner, and by midday the tiny cabin was closing in on both of them. Leo had gone out the back way to scout around and make sure no one had followed them.

"Can't I go outside?" Stephen asked for the hundredth time. "I want to see the river, Dana. Could have gone with Leo."

Dana glanced out the tiny kitchen window. "Leo knows what he's doing, and he doesn't need a noisy little boy tagging along with him."

"I would have been quiet. Leo could have shown me how. He's good at that stuff."

"Exactly. Which is why you had to stay inside."

"I want to see the river!" Stephen repeated in a high-pitched voice.

Tony groaned impatiently, then threw down the sportsman magazine he'd been reading.

"You can see the river from the back window," Dana reminded Stephen as she busied herself tidying up the place. It didn't look as if anyone had thought about doing that in a great while. "Or you can help me dust."

"Yuck!" Stephen said, wringing his nose. "Why won't Tony play checkers with me? Tony should play."

Dana glanced over at Tony's sulking form on the worn green floral velvet couch. "Tony's not in a very good mood, sport. Just leave him alone."

Tony lifted his head then, his eyes bright. "Uh, I think I'll go in that small storage room off the kitchen and see if I can find any other books and games."

"I'll help you," Stephen offered, hopping around in his Ruby Runners.

"I'd rather look by myself," Tony said, a firm set to his lips.

"Stevie, help me move this table," Dana said to distract her brother. Giving Tony a quick look, she motioned for him to go ahead.

He slipped into the tiny room while Stephen pushed and shoved the table aside so Dana could sweep underneath.

"Good, now bring me that trash can over there."

Stephen obeyed his sister, but his gaze kept moving back to the door of the storage room. "Why'd he shut that door? He doesn't want to play a game."

Dana glanced at the shut door, worry creasing her brow. When she thought she heard Tony's voice, she went to the door to see if he needed anything. And found him talking quietly into his cell phone.

"Tony?" she questioned, her eyes bright with fear and concern.

"I gotta go," Tony said, quickly hanging up the phone to spin around and give her a hard, daring stare. "I'm sorry, Dana, but I had to at least check in, let the main office know why I wasn't online."

Dana lifted her chin. "And did you assure them that you're alive and well, and you'll be back online soon?"

"I talked to one of the supervisors," he said, his tone defensive. "Told him I'd be out of commission for a few days." He shrugged. "I was only on for a few minutes."

Dana ran a hand through her hair. "I understand, Tony. I don't want you to lose your clients. Is everything okay, then?"

Averting his eyes, he placed the tiny phone back in his pants pocket. "Uh, not exactly. They know about the bombing. The police and the FBI have been down there to talk to them. They've been through my files."

Dana's hand went to her throat. "Did you tell him what's going on?"

"He didn't give me time. He said I was in a lot of trouble and I'd better just turn myself in. But that's not the worst of it."

"What else?"

"He said I'd gotten some strange messages from an e-mail source in rural Kansas. Something about rubies and gold. 'The price of wisdom is above rubies.'"

"That's a Scripture verse from Job. What in the world is that woman after?" Dana wondered out loud. "I don't have anything except the clothes on my back."

Tony pushed past her to the kitchen. "Well, whatever it is, she's not the only one looking for it. I got another message. Someone called and left a number. Said it was urgent that I get in touch with them."

"Who?"

He glared at her, his eyes full of distrust, his expression full of scorn. "Someone from Wichita Industries, *in Wichita*. The man didn't leave his name, but I think we can figure out who it was on our own."

## Chapter Seven

"Bren." The one word tore out of Dana's throat.

"Yeah, *Bren*." Tony threw himself down in a chair to glare up at her. "I told you he's in cahoots with her. Now do you believe me?"

She shook her head. "This doesn't mean he's in with Caryn Roark. You said he wanted you to call him—that it was urgent."

"Yeah, so he can find us and kill all of us!"

Dana tugged at the pocket of her jeans. "Hand me my tote, Tony."

Tony gave her a shocked look. "You aren't going to call him now, are you?"

"Yes, I am," she said, digging for her cell phone. "I'm tired of running. I'm tired of these threats. I've messed up not only my own life, but yours, and probably Leo's, too. If Brendan Donovan is looking for me, I have to know why."

He tossed his hands in the air. "Well, go ahead then. Sacrifice yourself to them. It won't be long before either the law or Caryn Roark tracks us down anyway."

"You're right. And if Brendan Donovan and Caryn Roark are somehow connected, I can't hide forever. I have to find out what they want with me." She read the number on the bent card she'd been carrying for days. "But I don't intend to sit around waiting anymore, and I can't keep Stevie out on the lam. If this man doesn't give me any answers, I'll go to the police and take my chances."

Stephen came running from the back door, his hands flapping, fingers out. "I see Leo. Leo's running fast. He's hurrying!"

Dana had already dialed the number. It rang once, twice, then she heard the click of the receiver.

"Hello."

It was Brendan Donovan. She'd know that deep, resonant voice anywhere. She'd heard that same voice in her dreams.

She hesitated, her heart hammering loudly all the way to her temple. "Bren?"

"Dana, is that you?"

"Yes. I—I need to know what's going on. I need to know who you are and why you were on the road beside my house. I'm in a lot of trouble, and please tell me if you know what this is all about."

Leo burst through the back door. "They're on to us. I saw several of them moving through the woods."

"Oh, no," Dana said on a breathless whisper. "Caryn Roark's after me. Can you help me?"

She heard the hiss of air leaving his body. "Dana, listen to me. Get out of there. Just go. Wherever you are, leave now."

"Okay, but where can I go?"

"Come to Wichita. There's an airfield south of the city— Wichita Aer. If I can't get you on a plane, I'll get you somewhere safe."

Dana glanced around the room, fear coursing through her body. "Okay, but only if you tell me what's going on."

Leo motioned to her. "Dana, hang up. They could be tracing the call."

Overhead, the sound of a helicopter chopped through the afternoon stillness, its repetitive beat following the flapping of her brother's arms. Stephen didn't like the noise. Dana's heart lurched to a racing beat. "I have to go," she shouted into the phone, her eyes on her brother.

Bren spoke quickly. "There's no time to explain—just get to Wichita. I promise you'll be safe."

The phone went dead. In her shock Dana could only stand there staring at it.

"Dana, I don't like this!" Stephen said, his voice shrill with fear. He put his hands to his ears and started screaming, "Make it stop. Make it stop."

Dana snapped into action, throwing the phone into her tote. Leo gathered a few provisions and motioned them out the back door. "We'll hike to the highway, where we hid the Jeep. Hopefully they didn't spot it."

Dana dragged her screaming, protesting brother down the steps. "Stevie, I'm right here. We have to run fast. Do you hear? Run fast."

"Shouldn't we spread out?" Tony asked, following Leo, Dana and Stephen right on his heels.

"Normally I would advise that," Leo retorted over his shoulder. "But they're already spread through the woods. We need to stick together so nobody gets trapped. If they take one of us, they'll have to take all of us."

Dana silently agreed as she held her brother's jerking body close to calm him down. She wouldn't let them take Stephen without a fight. Slowly, following Leo's lead, they wound their way through the heavy foliage along the river bank. Overhead, aged cottonwood trees and giant, glistening sycamores shaded them from the hot afternoon sun, while river reeds and spindly oak saplings shielded them from sight as they slipped and slid their way through the dense woods.

Through the trees, Dana spotted the helicopter hovering near. "It's not the police," she said on a winded breath.

"Doesn't look like the FBI, either," Leo replied.

"Church woman," Stephen said, his fingers pointing. "That helicopter lands at the big white church. Like a big bird."

"Are you sure?" Dana called over the blasting roar of the machine as it got closer.

Stephen bobbed his head, his eyes going wide. "UUC! UUC!" Then he put his hands over his ears again.

Dana squinted through the trees to the distant shape of the helicopter sweeping low over the secluded cabin. The machine was a gleaming white with gold trim. On the side the letters UUC were emblazoned in an etched gold script, centered in a gold crest that rested in a set of white lace covered hands. An impressive logo, to say the least. One would think Caryn Roark held the fate of the world in her hands.

Dana held to her brother. "She is not a church woman, Stevie. She is evil."

"Evil," Stephen repeated. "Evil woman. UUC."

Dana turned away from the roar of the helicopter to hop up into the Jeep. They had to hurry and make it to the highway before the chopper discovered them.

Leo didn't wait to make sure everybody was securely belted in. He moved the Jeep through the woods, spinning up dust and grass as he careened the sturdy, beat-up vehicle up one slope and down another, taking a path only he knew. After several minutes of bouncing and sliding, he pulled the vehicle off onto a main road, peeling rubber as he straightened the spinning machine into a fast-paced rhythm.

"We made it," he shouted, whooping his satisfaction. "We've lost them for now. I haven't had that much fun since I got kicked off the force!"

Tony, sitting up front with a white-knuckled grip on the dashboard, let out a long-held breath. "Maybe that's one of the reasons you got kicked off."

"Never heard any complaints," Leo said, his aged eyes

watching the rearview mirror as they merged into traffic on the main highway. "I don't see anything behind us." He turned to Dana. "Where to?"

"Wichita," she said, ignoring the groan coming from Tony's vicinity. "Brendan Donovan has promised to get us to safety."

"Oh, sure," Tony countered.

Stephen heard and sat up, his face lighting up. "We're going to find Brendan Donovan? Really, really?"

"Really, really," Dana tossed back, still doubtful that she'd made the right move. "Stevie, don't get too excited about this. We might have to change our plans again if things don't feel right."

Stephen started rocking on the seat. "Feel right. Have to feel right."

"Things already don't feel right to me," Tony insisted as he slumped down in his seat. "Dana, are you sure about this?"

"What other choice do I have?"

"What about the police?"

Leo shook his head. "Not a good idea right now. I recognized one of the men in the woods. He's a rogue cop who's been on the hot seat more than once for his extremist views. I watched him for a while and I got the impression he wasn't here on official police business. I believe he's working for Caryn Roark. If he is, you can bet there are others. For all we know, the FBI agents looking for us might be bogus, too."

"Great. If we can't trust the cops and the FBI, who can we trust?" Tony asked.

"Brendan Donovan," Dana said, turning to face him. "He's our last hope."

"Brendan Donovan," Stephen echoed. "Yeah, he's our last hope."

Tony threw up his hands. "Then, hey, we're off to see the

great Brendan Donovan, lord of the manor, protector of young women in distress, the great man himself!"

Stephen grinned, thinking Tony was pleased. "Tony's happy! Tony's happy!"

Tony made a sarcastic frown. "Yeah, and you're so smart, you figured that out all by yourself!"

"Tony," Dana said, her tone filled with anger, "we can stop right here and let you out."

Tony had the grace to look embarrassed. "I'm sorry. I'll shut up."

Stephen looked hurt for a minute, then continued his rocking, his eyes downcast. "We'll find Brendan Donovan. Yeah, Brendan Donovan. He has my baseball card. Lou Gehrig. He owns a computer company. He's smart."

Tony sat back up. "Yes, Einstein, he does. And he owns a shoe company. Those Ruby Runners you're wearing, to be exact."

Stephen bobbed his head. "He told me when we were cleaning up. He said he'd send me a brand-new computer. He owns a computer company."

Tony looked surprised that Stephen knew that, but nodded. "Okay, hotshot, what's the name of his company?" Dana gave him a disapproving look, but Tony just shrugged. "Hey, we know he's a big shot in the technology world, but we don't have specifics, right? That's information we could use. Bet he didn't tell you that, did he?"

Dana cast a worried glance behind them, then turned back face forward to poke Tony. "Leave him alone, please."

"Just trying to distract him," Tony whispered, his head twisting to make sure they weren't being followed.

Stephen became excited, his fingers twisting and untwisting. "Brendan Donovan owns a computer company. WCC. He owns WCC."

"WCC?" Tony was at full attention now, his blue eyes going wide with surprise and realization. "Stevie, did you say WCC?"

Stephen bobbed his head and rocked back and forth against the seat, straining at his seat belt. "Yeah, WCC. Wichita Communications Company. Yeah, WCC."

"Do you know it?" Dana asked, holding on tightly as Leo took them way beyond the speed limit.

"Oh, yeah. I know it all right," Tony replied, his face pale in the waning afternoon light. "Most of my equipment is supplied by a technology distributor in Kansas City, and I get a lot of work through this distributor. But I was under the impression the company I work for was owned by some other company, you know. Like a subsidiary of a subsidiary, that type thing. Apparently, the people I consider boss are just front men. It never occurred to me to connect on the WCC thing."

"Which is?"

"Exactly what your brother just said, Wichita Communications Company. And that's information I didn't find in my Google search of the famous Mr. Donovan. Secret information, apparently."

"How do you know that he's keeping that a secret?"

Tony gave her an incredulous look. "Because around the home office, we've always called it WicComCo. That's how everything's set up, that's the only name we've ever known. But some of the packaging comes in under WCC. It has to be the same company. Only, no one has ever bothered telling me that I work for WCC, or that it's owned by Brendan Donovan. My checks come in under a corporate name that doesn't even begin to match WCC." He rolled his eyes. "Interesting, huh. This little adventure just gets better and better."

Dana sat back in her seat. "That would make Brendan the head of the company you work for, so to speak."

Tony's breath fluttered out of his lungs as he glared over the seat at her. "So to speak, yes, that would make Brendan Donovan the *silent* owner of the company I work for. In other words, my boss."

"Brendan's your boss?" Stephen asked, another grin cresting his young face even though he wouldn't look at Tony. "Brendan's Tony's boss."

"You catch on quick, don't you?" Tony replied. Then he gave Dana a patently sweet look. "Which means it would be extremely easy for Mr. Donovan to access my files." His voice deepened as his eyebrows lifted. "To send messages to someone, to track someone down, to plant a bomb!"

Dana lowered her head. "This can't be happening."

Leo steered the Jeep from one lane to another, his silvery eyes bright and alert. "That's not all that's happening. They've spotted us. A black Camaro's been tailing me for the last five miles, and—"

Off in the distance, the distinct sound of a helicopter could be heard.

"The chopper," Dana said, her breath stopping to form a lump in her throat. "They're coming for us." Instinctively she grabbed Stephen to hold him close. He protested and pushed at her, but she held on to him anyway.

"Buckle in and hang on," Leo advised. "This could get messy."

It did. They sped down the interstate, headed southwest toward Wichita with the helicopter and the racy black Camaro keeping a steady pace behind them. Leo wove in and out of traffic like an expert race car driver, with both their assailants close on their heels. When a passenger from the Camaro pulled out a semiautomatic weapon and aimed it for the Jeep, Leo managed to swerve toward the median.

"We need to get off the main road," he explained, his eyes

darting to the rearview mirror. "The passenger in the Camaro is packing."

"Great. A shoot-out on the interstate," Tony said, moaning. "This is not my idea of fun."

"Dana, I'm scared," Stephen whined. "I want to go home!"

Tony groaned again, but he did turn around to nudge Stephen playfully. "Hey, you're not gonna let these bullies get the best of you, are you, sport?"

"I'm tired," Stephen said. "And I'm hungry. I don't like that noise!"

"He's always hungry," Tony countered, his generosity quota gone as the helicopter came closer. "I can't take much more of this."

Dana wanted to scream. Did he actually think she was having a blast herself? She glanced at Leo. How could he remain so calm and stoic?

In the next instant, the sound of gunfire boomed out, causing all of them to duck.

"They're aiming for our tires," Leo shouted, both hands holding tightly to the wheel. "I don't think they want to kill us. Maybe they're just playing around to scare us."

"Well, that's because we're so much fun to play around with," Tony said, slumping down. Dana had managed to twist down in the seat with one hand held over Stephen.

"Dana, I can't breathe," he said, squirming.

"Stay down, Stevie," she said, giving his head a firm push. "It's just a game. Just stay hidden."

Stephen stopped pushing and listened, but Dana could feel his body trembling. If she didn't get him somewhere safe, he was going to have a major tantrum. Dana felt tears pricking at her eyes. "Help me, Lord. Help us." Then she thought of her parents. "Help us, Mama," she whispered as she held her brother close.

"We've obviously got something they want very badly," Leo shouted as he swerved on the road. "Here they come again."

The Camaro zoomed up on their rear, almost touching the Jeep's beat-up back fender. Dana lay crossways along the seat over her brother, not daring to look up to see who was chasing them. Her heart boomed with each rut in the road, and her hands, sweaty and shaking, refused to let go of the back of Stephen's shirt.

Leo threw a message out over the tense air. "Hold on. I'm going to take the next exit to try and lose the Camaro."

That sounded simple enough. He'd neglected to tell them that the next exit was three lanes over in the other direction. With a loud, groaning squeal of all four tires, he crossed the path of several lanes of traffic, dodging honking, angry drivers and almost causing a major pileup.

They made the exit by the skin of their teeth, but the Camaro didn't fare as well. Leo watched the car skid and slow down as a semitrailer truck got between it and the Jeep. By the time the Camaro could find an opening, the exit was gone and Leo was headed away from the interstate.

"One down," he stated, slapping the steering wheel in celebration. "Now, where's that fancy chopper?"

As if on command, the helicopter appeared in front of them on the two-lane road, its blades roaring a warning as menacing as any tornado.

Dana screamed, her eyes going wide when she saw the two men in the giant machine. "I—I think I know one of them. He used to own a small farm not far from mine. Rick Calloway—he sold out to Caryn Roark."

"In more ways than one," Leo commented.

"She sent her henchmen. She's not in there," Dana replied, her eyes centered on Rick's hulking form up above. Good grief, he used to drink coffee and eat doughnuts in Emma's place every morning. What kind of spell had Caryn Roark cast over Prairie Heart, anyway?

Dana instinctively knew that Caryn Roark was probably watching from a distance, that she somehow knew every move they were making. Her power went beyond the confines of her stone white church compound. How would they ever escape?

"What now?" she asked Leo as the helicopter dipped closer and closer. A hooded man leaned out, his eyes squinting at them through his rifle scope. "He's going to shoot us!"

Leo didn't answer. Dana watched as he careened the Jeep up the winding road. He seemed so calm, so sure, that she found it hard to picture him cowering in a ball behind a trash Dumpster. Maybe this was one of his more lucid encounters. Or maybe he had just needed to prove himself to someone.

In all the commotion, Tony and Stephen took turns whining and screaming.

"We're going to die," Tony stated through clenched teeth.

"I don't want to die," Stephen cried, the fear in his voice real. "Dana, I don't want to die!"

"I will not let you die," Leo shouted. "Just stay down."

Dana held on to her brother and prayed silently. This whole thing seemed so surreal, like some awful dream that refused to end. What did Caryn Roark want from her anyway?

Then she heard Stephen's shrill shout. "Leo has a gun. Yeah, a gun. Leo can shoot the bad man."

Leo still didn't move a muscle, nor did he respond to Stephen's words.

But Stephen was persistent and scared enough to keep asking for a reassuring answer to what he considered a reasonable question. "Hey, Leo, where's your gun?"

Leo continued to drive the Jeep, his head up, his eyes open

and alert, his whole countenance so still, so taut, Dana could have sworn he was etched in stone. The helicopter hovered closer, swooping down so low, she could feel the whirl of wind brought on by the rotating blades. The whole Jeep shook from the machine's proximity. Her whole body shook from shock and fear and confusion.

She thought about her dreams, all the nightmares she'd had since the tornado. She wanted to wake up with the sun shining and cows to milk and feed. She wanted her home back safe and secure. She wanted to put the disturbing image of Caryn Roark high on top of her stone turret out of her mind for good.

Then Dana thought of Brendan Donovan and wondered at her own sanity. He'd said to come to him. And right now Dana felt as if that was her only option

They were on a deserted stretch of highway now, a back road running along the river, with pastures on one side and on the other, a levee of dense bramble holding back the river's gurgling brown waters. If those men wanted to kill them, this would be an ideal spot. Why had Leo brought them here anyway?

She soon found out.

It all happened so quickly. Leo turned down a bumpy, pebbled stretch of road that seemed to be headed right into the levee. Then he slowly rolled down his window, and motioned for the chopper to come closer.

"Are you crazy?" Dana shouted. "Leo, what are you doing?"

"Where's your gun, Leo?" Stephen said for the tenth time. "Shoot them. Leo can shoot them."

Tony slunk farther down in the seat. "I told you this was crazy!"

Leo acted as if he were taking a leisurely drive in the country. Then in a motion Dana would later remember as only a blur, he stopped the Jeep, and with one hand, reached underneath his seat to produce a .38 Magnum. With the same grace-ful, fluid motion of a hunter stalking his next meal, Leo quickly and swiftly took aim and expertly shot at the helicop-ter's belly, each round sounding off in rapid secession as he emptied his revolver into the roaring, snarling machine perched over their heads. In seconds, he was back behind the wheel, shifting the Jeep into Reverse as the wounded bird danced and fluttered. With the chopper out of control, it could only spin downward, right toward the Jeep.

"Oh, no—" Tony shouted, his expletive covered by Ste-phen's piercing squeal and Dana's own dry-throated groan.

Leo pressed his booted foot to the gas pedal. The Jeep pealed backward about fifty yards, kicking up mud and dirt as he moved it away from the falling chopper. In the next instant, the chopper hit the banks of the levee and exploded in a bril-liant, white-hot boom that rattled the windows and shook the earth beneath the still-purring Jeep. Then everything went still.

For a long while no one said anything. They all just sat star-ing at the leaping flames of the damaged helicopter.

Finally Stephen spoke in a voice quiet with reverence and awe. "Leo got rid of the bad guys. Yeah, Leo took care of the bad guys."

Dana dragged her brother close, tears streaming down her face. "It's okay now, sweetie."

Leo turned around to Stephen, his silvery-gray eyes as gentle as a dove's, his whole demeanor as calm as a summer day. "Don't play with guns, Stephen," he said in a firm tone. "They can kill you."

Stephen looked out toward the carnage of the destroyed helicopter, then brought his gaze back toward Leo, but he didn't make eye contact with the man. He just started rock-ing again. "Yes, sir," he said in a quiet solemn voice. "I think I understand. Don't play with guns."

## Chapter Eight

Wichita appeared shrouded in a dark fog that was only il-luminated by the yellowed lights of early evening. The trip had been tediously long, because Leo had woven the vehicle in and out of county roads and access roads, taking the less obvious, least crowded way to avoid any more confrontations with souped-up cars and armed helicopters.

So far, the trip after the helicopter explosion had been fairly quiet, except for Stephen's nervous questions and con-stant tappings and shufflings. He couldn't be still and Dana couldn't make him stay still, no matter how much Dana and Tony tried to distract him. Dana saw with a certain amount of regret that she'd never be able to have a life with Tony, be-cause he couldn't live with her brother.

This only added to her already-explosive mood. She was on her way to find a man she'd only met briefly, a man with whom she had to trust her life, even though that man had given her no reason as to why she should come to him, and no answers as to why she was being chased by the cult leader of Prairie Heart, Kansas. Dana had prayed with every breath, and with every dark mile they traveled had asked God to show her the way, but she knew that this was about more than someone wanting to get their hands on her little piece of farmland. No, this cult was after something else. And Dana believed it had something to do with her brother.

*I have to protect him, Lord,* she thought now. That was her only mantra. To protect Stephen.

If she weren't so tired, so very tired, she could probably put all of this together. Something in the back of her consciousness kept nagging at her like a missing puzzle piece. From a distance, it looked like she'd find the piece and everything would fall into place. Yet each time she went over the events in her mind, the one missing link eluded her sleep-deprived, aching brain. Caryn Roark wanted more than revenge; she wanted more than control over Stephen. She wanted something very important; something that she needed, had to have. Dana had no idea what that something was; she only knew that she didn't have it. And she really wanted to go home.

She thought about just surrendering to Caryn Roark and telling the woman she didn't know what in the world was going on here, but even in her harried state, Dana didn't think that would be a good idea. The police couldn't be trusted; the authorities would take Stephen from her. Now, even the townsfolk back home, with the exception of Emma and Frederick, couldn't be trusted. Rick Calloway had died for Caryn Roark today. Who else was caught up in this mess?

Brendan Donovan? Somehow he was connected, but he was her only hope; he was the only thing keeping her from crumbling in a heap. She had to believe he could help her, yet she couldn't explain why her gut instinct told her that. She didn't like this dependence, didn't feel comfortable in letting someone else control things, but she was caught up in this now, and she had to find a way out. Brendan was her last hope.

*God is your eternal hope,* she heard a voice say inside her head. Tears pricked at Dana's eyes. Maybe she should start depending on God more and other human beings less. Or maybe she should believe that God was somehow leading her, guiding her to make the right decisions.

Leo shifted in the driver's seat. "Wichita Aer should be out near the other aircraft factories. We'll head southeast."

Tony snarled and stretched. "There's a private airport on every corner in this town. How will we ever find the place?"

"Yellow stars," Stephen said, hitting the back of the seat. "He had yellow stars on the side of his van, remember, Dana? Yeah, I like yellow stars."

Dana nodded. "Yes, he did, didn't he, sport?" She sent up thanks that Stephen's keen awareness to detail had helped them with some of their questions. He'd noticed things about all of this that none of the rest of them had picked up on. "Maybe that's the same logo he uses on his airplanes," she said.

Tony shook his head. "Well, that certainly narrows things down a bit."

"Just help us look, okay?" Dana said over her shoulder.

The night fog had settled in, making it hard to read the road signs. Leo made a loop through the city, heading down Interstate 35. They passed Boeing, then Cessna, and were headed toward Beech Aircrafts when Dana glanced off to the right.

A small tower beckoned toward them in the night. And on the side of the tower was the bright twinkling shape of two yellow stars with a shooting tail of spangled glitter—Wichita Aer. The Irish version.

"There it is," she said, her heart racing with anticipation and fear. "Take this exit, Leo. We should be able to get there from here."

"Just follow the yellow stars," Tony said as he sat up to stare over at the closed factory and adjoining private airstrip. Then he whistled low. "Check out that jet."

Dana squinted toward the airstrip where a sleek gray-and-white private jet sat like a giant bird perched for flight. The same logo of two yellow stars followed by the trailing spangles was highlighted across the plane's exterior. Underneath, the scrolled gilded letters spelling Wichita Aer shimmered brightly.

Dana's heart began to beat erratically again as a cold sweat popped out on her hot, moist skin. *Lord, am I going mad, bringing these people here to face this man?* Was she putting them all in jeopardy? Thinking Tony might be right and this could very well be a trap, she braced herself and tried to say another prayer. *Just don't let anything happen to my brother or my friends.* That was all she asked. Just let them be safe.

"This is it," Leo said solemnly as he pulled the Jeep up to a closed security gate. The gate swung open.

"Don't go in there," Tony warned. "Let him come to us, if he wants to help us so much."

Dana twisted around in her seat to stare out into the fog. "We can't just sit here all night. He's probably been waiting for us."

"And watching," Tony reminded her. "This place gives me the creeps."

Stephen leaned forward to touch Dana's arm. "I'm not scared, Dana. I'll be all right. Don't worry about me anymore, okay. Stephen's a big boy."

Dana bit back the tears blocking her sight. Her brother was growing up. He'd been forced to do so over the past few days. "I know, sport. I know you can handle things. It's just that I love you, you know."

Stephen pulled at her sleeve. "I know. But Leo will take care of me. Leo hurts bad guys."

Leo looked straight ahead into the night. "Don't depend on me, my friend. I just might let you down."

"No, you won't," Stephen insisted, leaning up to rock. "I know you won't, Leo. You'll take care of me."

Leo didn't look at Stephen; he didn't even flinch. "I might

not be able to help you, Stephen. But I appreciate the vote of confidence."

Tony lifted both gangly hands to his hair. "This little gab-fest is touching, but shouldn't we just get out of here? We can go to Mexico or head to Florida. I'm telling you, I've got a very bad feeling about us hitching our wagon to yonder yellow stars."

Dana glanced back at the jet. "He said he'd get us to safety. It's the only plan we have. Go on in, Leo."

Leo pressed the accelerator and aimed the Jeep for the airstrip where the jet was parked. "Whatever you say. I'm just along for the ride."

"No, more like you're just as knee-deep in it as the rest of us," Tony reminded him.

"Shhh!" Dana cautioned. "Just park and we'll wait here."

They sat in the silent, warm night, listening to the sounds of the deserted factory—a pop here, a creak there. Somewhere a piece of loose tin flapped in the wind, banging a steady rhythm that matched the hesitant rhythms coursing through Dana's racing pulse.

Dana shifted nervously, trying to calm herself. She didn't know if she was scared because someone was trying to kill her, or if her worst fear was in seeing Brendan again. The man had had a profound effect on her. That scared her more than anything.

They waited several more minutes, when finally, Tony, impatient and obviously spooked, hissed, "Let's get out of here!"

Dana was just about to do that, when two armed men came out from behind a shadowy building. They both wore black. Craning her neck, Dana tried to see through the shroud of the fog if one of them might be Brendan, but the night and their attire gave little away.

"It's showtime," Leo said on a calm whisper. "Looks like these two are to be our escorts."

"Why armed?" Tony whispered.

Stephen gripped Dana's arm. "Are they going to hurt us? Don't want bad guys to hurt us."

"I don't think so," she answered in a whisper. "Let's just see what they want."

One of the men stopped and scoped his rifle on them, while the other one approached the Jeep and motioned to Dana.

"Dana Barlow?" he asked in a low-throated command.

Dana cracked her window about two inches. "Yes," she said, hating the breathless croak that formed the one word.

"Come with me."

Dana looked shocked, then asked, "Where's Mr. Donovan? He told me to meet him here."

"Come with me," the man commanded again, stepping closer to the Jeep.

"Not without my brother and my friends," Dana replied. "Mr. Donovan promised we'd all be safe."

"Mr. Donovan has requested to speak with you—alone," the man informed her, his eyes glinting in the moonlight.

"Don't go. It's a setup," Tony whispered, his lips barely moving. "Tell him it's all of us, or nothing."

"I won't see Mr. Donovan alone," Dana told the stoic man. "We prefer to stay together."

The man stepped closer, his gun trained on Dana.

Then another man stepped out of the mist, the fog caressing him with a soft-focused intensity that washed him in gray-white shadows.

Dana's head shot up. She gulped in a deep breath of humid air. The lone figure stalked toward them, then stopped a few feet away. His face was still in shadows, his whole body covered in what looked like a black jumpsuit. Dana knew instinctively this man was Brendan Donovan.

She wanted to throw open the door and run to him and demand some answers, but she wasn't that desperate yet. She held back, waiting, wondering, watching.

Then the man spoke. "Dana, come here."

"It's him," Stephen said, clapping his hands together. "It's Brendan."

"He looks dangerous," Tony surmised, his own curiosity causing him to lean forward. "He's playing us like a violin."

Dana scowled at Tony's melodramatic declaration, but she had to agree all of this cat-and-mouse intrigue was starting to wear thin. Frustrated and too tired to be cautious, she called out. "What do you want from me?"

"Come here," he stated again, holding out a hand. "I give you my word, you're in no danger from me."

Tony huffed. "That's not exactly reassuring, is it?"

Brendan shifted, his stance steady and sure. "Dana?"

Dana let out a long-held sigh. That voice. Her name on his lips danced through her consciousness like a waltz, coaxing and enticing and intoxicating. She wanted with all her being to trust him; indeed, she'd started out hours ago on this quest to do just that. But now that she was here, shrouded in darkness, with his presence just a few feet away, she wondered if she were just caught up in some sort of illusion that would be broken once the fantasy of him became the reality. Glancing up at him, she tried to read his expression. Darkness became him, silhouetting him in a mystery that intrigued her as much as it repelled her.

He spoke again. "Dana, we don't have very much time. You're all in danger. And I'll do what I can to protect you, if you'll just trust me."

His words, spoken to reassure her, brought back full force the feel of his sturdy, hard-muscled body covering her, covering her from the storm, protecting her from the cold. She remembered tattered shreds of some tender endearments spoken so close to her ear, some ancient language, so lyrical, so intimate, so moving, that she had instantly understood and accepted that this man would protect her. Always. What had he said to her that day in the bluestems? Why couldn't she remember on a conscious level?

"I'm going to talk to him," she announced, her mind made up. Her instincts were humming to new heights. She was very aware of the man standing in the shadows, waiting, watching, holding out his hand to her. She was very aware that if she took this step, if she chose this way, her whole life would change forever. There would be no going back. But then, she really had nowhere else to go.

And so, she gave her brother a reassuring look, refused to look at Tony and touched Leo on the arm when he tried to reach for his gun. Then she pushed open the squeaking Jeep door to step out into the night wind. It whipped around her, lifting her curls away from her sticky neck, laughing its secrets in her ear, whispering its taunts as she started walking toward the dark form waiting for her on the other side.

He stood, still and unmoving, as if he were waiting for her to come and bring him to life. The only sound was the mournful chant of the wind and her sneakered feet falling against the broken, ripped asphalt. In her ears, her heart sang its own humming tune, a pulse song that radiated through her body and whizzed through her system.

She stopped about three feet from him, her eyes wide, her lips parted, her heart in her hand. "Will you help me?"

"Will you trust me?"

"I want to. I don't have any other choice."

"Then promise me, no matter what happens over the next few days—"

"Promise you what? I need answers."

"Promise me that you'll try to trust me. You'll have to understand that what I'm about to do is what I have to do."

She backed away. "You're scaring me. Just tell me what's going on, please."

"Aye, in time," he said, moving toward her. "Come with me, Dana."

"No." The fear pushed at her. Her instincts told her to run. "No. Something isn't right. You're asking too much."

He grabbed her then, and held her to him, his hand gentle but firm on her wrist. "I'm asking you to trust me with your life."

She saw him motion to the men; she felt him tugging her toward the plane. Then the still night became alive with movement.

The two armed men surrounded the Jeep. "Get out."

Dana twisted in Brendan's arms. "No. What are they doing? You told me—"

"Trust me," he stated, holding her with his hands pressed against her midsection as she fell back against him and tried to twist away.

"Let me go!" she screamed, her gaze locked on the scene before them. The men were taking Stephen, Leo and Tony away. "Don't. Let them go!"

"Dana, don't make this any harder," he said against the back of her head, his words strained and hoarse. "Just turn around and do as I ask."

She fought him then, like a wildcat trying to protect her young. "No," she screamed, kicking and hitting and biting out all the rage and fear she'd held back for so long. Then she heard Stephen's high-pitched protests as he called her name. She tried to answer him. "Stephen!"

"He's going to be all right," Brendan said, his grip on her iron-clad and firm in spite of her struggles. "He's safe now."

Tears streamed down Dana's face. "Where are they taking

him? What is going on! Why won't someone tell me what's going on?"

"I can't explain right now," Brendan said as he pulled her toward the jet. "Not here, not yet."

"You tricked me," she cried, her head twisted toward her brother. "Stephen!"

She could hear her brother's careening wail of fear. "Dana? No, don't take my Dana!"

She called to her brother. "Stephen, I'll find you. You're going to be okay. Please, God, let him be okay."

"Dana? Dana?"

Her brother's voice faded away behind a huge metal warehouse as she heard a heavy door slam shut.

All of the fight gone out of her, she slumped against Brendan and sobbed until she was hoarse and weak, then lifted her head to look at him, all her illusions gone now.

The compassion in his blue-black eyes did nothing to ease the pain ripping her body into jagged pieces.

"I hate you," she said on a steady, calm whisper. "I hate all of you, with your games and your power and your weapons. I'll go on hating you until I find out what's going on and why you and that Roark woman are after me. And I promise you this—if I get the chance, I'm going to make sure you pay."

He didn't respond; he just stood there like some ancient statue, taking her taunts and her threats with the countenance of a man who'd lost all means of understanding and compassion.

"I hate you," she said again, whispering the words at him.

In a soft, controlled voice, he finally spoke. "Aye, you'll hate me even more before this is over. And—" he reached inside the pocket of his lightweight black jacket "—you'll truly hate me for this."

She felt the injection at the same time her gaze locked with his. Within seconds, she saw his face go from stony and cold, to caring and almost…almost tender with regret.

"I'm sorry, *cara*," he whispered.

Dana moaned and collapsed into his arms. She felt herself being lifted, felt as light as air, as fickle as the sad wind surrounding them. She moaned again and snuggled closer to the warmth of the arms holding her. She thought she heard those beautiful, soothing words again, those words he'd spoken to her in the storm. Gaelic love words. Centuries old, but so very pure and untouched, and meant just for her.

In her dream state she cried. And then her world turned to black, and she slept.

## Chapter Nine

In her dreams the tornado came again. The wind carried her away, far away from her home. She could see everything from a large window that looked like one of those big-screen televisions Stephen was always wishing they had.

Everything whirled by—her house, her life, her hopes and dreams. Everything was destroyed. There was nothing left except the mournful wind on the empty, golden prairie.

And Caryn Roark's white, cold hand reaching, reaching for her like the tentacles of a giant spider, grasping and spindly. Then she heard Stephen calling to her, "Dana! Dana! Help me!"

Dana woke with a start, then sat up groggily to adjust her vision. The sound of a humming engine brought her further out of her nightmare. Something was terribly wrong.

"You!" she said, sitting up full force now to stare up at the man seated in the corner beside her. "Where are we? What have you done with my brother?"

She didn't wait for him to answer. She started to rise, then, feeling a cool draft on her skin, sank back down on the cream leather seat to pull the exquisitely soft, patterned blanket back up around her body. Shocked, she looked down at the blanket, then the seat, and slowly realized they were not on board the jet.

Adjusting her eyes, Dana saw that she was in a limousine.

A big black limousine. "Where are you taking me?" It all came tumbling back then, the real nightmare. The man had kidnapped her! "Why are you doing this?" she asked again, gaining strength with each word.

He sat in the shadows, looking over at her with a twist of a smile forming on his wide, full lips. "Which question would you have me answer first?"

His lyrical, lilting voice did nothing to ease her anger or her frustration. Holding the blanket securely around her shivering body, she came up at him with all the force of a mad she-hen, slapping and hissing and pushing and clawing until he was forced to pull her tightly against him for his own protection.

"Dana, will you try to calm down long enough for me to answer you?"

Dana's rage seethed to a slow burn. Taking a long breath, she stopped struggling and looked up at him, her eyes clashing with his. He stared back at her, the rich blue depths of his gaze drinking her in as his eyes slipped over her face. She was shaking, whether from adrenaline or the drugs he'd used on her, she wasn't sure. But she had to get herself in control if she planned to get away from him. And get away she intended. She had to find Stephen.

So she took another breath and tossed her tangled mane back so she could glare up at him. "What do you want from me?"

Brendan Donovan looked down at the woman in his arms and tried to think of a proper response to that particular question. He couldn't tell her that since the day he'd thrown himself over her in that storm, he'd been obsessed with thoughts of her, for more reasons than just simple attraction, although, God help him, that was there right on top of the list. He couldn't tell her that he wanted nothing more than to protect her from an evil she couldn't even begin to imagine. He wouldn't tell her his reasons for doing what he was doing, not just yet, not until he was sure of her motives. And his own. Not until *he* could trust *her*.

And he certainly couldn't, wouldn't tell her that her hair was as fiery and wild as the wind buffing the cliffs surrounding his ancestral home back in County Cork, or that her eyes had instantly reminded him of the green land he held dear. Nor could he tell her that she'd saved him that day during the storm, as they'd lain together in the wildflowers and prairie grasses.

He wasn't ready to tell her anything, so he just sat there staring down at her, hoping she'd see that he only wanted to protect her and her brother. He couldn't allow these possessive feelings to control him. He had to remember why he'd captured her and tricked her in the first place.

"Answer me!" Dana said, shouting the words up at him, a look of hatred and fear on her face. "Why can't you talk like a normal human being! Why all the suspense?"

With practiced control, Brendan pushed her away, closing his eyes to her pretty pink lips and that wind-tossed red-brown hair. Dana plopped down on the puffy seat, silent now, but with a demanding green-tinted bubbling anger still simmering in her wide, beautiful eyes.

He opened a small built-in refrigerator. "Do you want a drink?"

Dana seemed to think about that. "Is this a trick question? Are you going to put me to sleep again?"

Brendan tried to be patient with her. "I'm merely offering you something to drink, nothing more."

"Coffee," she said in a voice tight with a thousand emotions. "I could use a cup of coffee."

"Aye, you Americans love your coffee, don't you?"

"Strong and black," she shot back. "I want to be fully awake when you finally explain all of this to me."

Brendan remained silent. He'd tell her everything soon enough. Right now he only wanted her calm enough to listen. "I don't have coffee. Just water and soda."

"Water, then."

He got out a bottle of water and opened it for her. "How do you feel? Are you comfortable?"

Dana gave him another glare, then sat back to look regal in the cashmere blanket he'd wrapped her in. "How do you expect me to answer that? You've kidnapped me." She looked down at the water bottle, tears forming in her eyes. "Where's my brother and my friends?"

He didn't answer. Instead he sighed, whipped out his silver cell phone and punched at numbers. He spoke into the phone, instructing one of his men. Then he handed the phone to Dana. "Talk to your brother."

She snatched it from him, her eyes full of loathing and distrust. "Stevie? Stevie, are you okay?"

Brendan watched as her face changed from worried to relieved in a matter of seconds. "Okay, baby. Yes, I'll be with you soon. Oh, that's good. I'm so glad Leo is with you and that you like all the games. Where's Tony?" She listened, then shot a frown toward Brendan. "Well, I'm sure Tony is just fine. And I promise we will all be together again very soon."

Brendan motioned for the phone, and reluctantly she shoved it back at him, tears streaming down her cheeks.

"Stephen, your sister is fine. She's with me. I promise I won't let anything happen to her. We'll be there soon and you can see her for yourself."

"Where is he?" Dana asked, sniffing back tears with a stubborn glint in her eyes.

"He's at my estate. I have a large game room there. I put Leo in charge of your brother. He will protect him." At her look of utter confusion, he held up a hand. "My estate is heavily guarded and secure."

"Oh, I feel better now."

Brendan reached for her free hand and took it into his. "I told you to trust me, remember? They are all safe. I give you my word on that."

"How can I believe that? I don't even know who you are, really. I only came here because I'm so tired of running. And I wanted to protect Stevie. He—he can't take this kind of upheaval."

"Your brother is with a trained specialist who knows exactly how to handle children with his condition."

She sat her water down in a holder, then ran a hand through her hair. Her voice went soft. "Am I supposed to believe that, too?"

"It's the truth," he replied. "I would never do anything to hurt you or your brother, Dana. You have to believe that."

"Sure," she said, tossing curls out of her face. "Why wouldn't I believe you considering I've been on the lam for days? I've been shot at, bombed, kidnapped and now I'm stuck in a car with you." Sitting up, she glared across at him. "Tell me what you've done with my brother and my friends!"

He tilted his head, wanting to reassure her. "I can only tell you that they are safe—just as I said—and that no harm will come to them, if everything goes according to plan."

Lifting her chin, she asked, "And what exactly is the plan?"

"To protect you," he said. The words fell like a heavy mist between them. "It's a long story, but I have my reasons for separating you from your brother and the others."

"So that's why you kidnapped me and took them away, to *protect* me?"

"Aye."

"Where are we going, anyway?"

He finished his own mineral water, then set the crystal glass down in a holder before he relaxed back into the seat and stretched his long legs. Staring across at her, he placed his hands behind his head and sighed, but still he gave her no answers. He didn't know where to begin. So he did what he was best at—he remained silent.

Lowering her gaze in defeat, she whispered, "Why can't you tell me what's going on?"

He kept staring at her, captivated by her innocent charm and her brave determination. She looked very frail and sad, curled up on the luxurious seat. Again he was reminded of the effect she'd had on him when first he'd met her. Hair blowing in the wind, fear cresting in her shimmering green eyes, love, deep and abiding, coloring her every word when she spoke about her brother and her land.

Something about her had caught him, captured him that day, and something about her had changed him, saved him from sure destruction. How could he tell her that he had to protect her in order to save himself?

"We're going nowhere right now," he said, watching as she came up off the seat.

"What do you mean, *nowhere?*"

"We're circling the city, just until things settle down and I'm sure everyone involved is safe."

She gave him a look full of disbelief. "This is crazy. Can't you please tell me what's going on? Why is that woman chasing me? And why have you been following me?"

A voice came over an intercom. "Excuse me, sir. We're set to arrive in about twenty minutes."

Brendan motioned toward Dana. "Thank you, Gareth. Please leave us alone until we reach our destination."

Dana lifted her brows. She looked beaten, but he saw a

spark of a question in her eyes. She'd try to escape, that he knew for sure.

"What is our destination?" she asked, her tone casual in spite of the dare in her green eyes.

Brendan gave her a polite smile. "Why don't you just relax?"

Dana looked out one of the darkened window. "I can't relax. You should know that. And if you really want me to trust you, you need to tell me the truth."

She was right, of course. But he needed more time. "For now, all I can say is that you are safe and your brother and your friends are safe." Then he shook his head. "So don't even think of trying to get away when we stop."

He could tell from her next words that was exactly what she'd been thinking. "I can't go anywhere without my brother. And I will find him." Then she glanced away. "You told me you'd help me. I don't call this helping. I should have listened to Tony."

"Tony is very intelligent, but he is in way over his head."

"Then you do know what's going on?"

"Yes, I know some of it. And together we're going to figure out the rest of it." He held his clasped hands up to his mouth, his index fingers folded together as he tapped them against the padding of his bottom lip. "Which is precisely why I had to separate you. I need your full cooperation, you see. This drastic measure was the only way I could be sure I'd have it."

Dana's heart sank with a sickening, plunging thud. How could she have ever trusted this man? "So, you're holding Stephen as a pawn in this little game, to make me behave and be a good little captive?"

"I see you're beginning to listen to reason, but I wouldn't exactly call any of you captives, and your brother is certainly not a pawn."

"There is no reason to any of this," she retorted, trying with all the might she possessed not to lunge for him again. And she wouldn't cry for him anymore, either. No matter how much her heart was breaking, no matter how much fear she felt for Stephen's safety. "So he's with Leo?" she asked, her voice cracking in spite of her resolve. "Just tell me you don't have him locked away somewhere all alone. He's different, you know. And he needs his medication. He gets uncontrollable and hyper when he's upset."

"I've taken all of that into consideration," Brendan said, his eyes going a murky shade of blue-black. He leaned forward then to reach a hand out to her again. When she refused to take it, he dropped it to his side. "I won't let anything happen to your brother, Dana. I know how to handle him."

She didn't trust him past the scant space between them. "And Leo and Tony?"

"Perfectly safe, and yes, Leo is with your brother, as I've said. I thought it best to get Tony out of the picture for a while. If those two don't wind up killing each other, it'll be a miracle."

She couldn't help the smile. It shot out before she could capture it. "How do you know so much about my friends and me?"

"I'm a quick study. I learn a lot by watching and listening. You should try it yourself, lass."

"You're not making any sense," she told him, her chin back up. "You tapped into Tony's computer system, didn't you? You sent those threatening messages just before the bomb."

The look he gave her told her he had no idea what she was talking about. Alert now, he asked, "What did the messages say?"

When she could only sit staring at him with an open mouth,

he leaned over to her to shake her gently. "Dana, what did the messages say?"

Lifting her arms away from the too-warm feel of his big hands on her skin, she recoiled. "Why should I tell you? Don't you already know since you seem to know everything else?"

For the first time since she'd met him, Dana witnessed an impatient exasperation in Brendan. He heaved a frustrated sigh and ran a hand through the dark hair at the nape of his neck. "Tell me, so I can help you!"

"Why should I tell you anything?"

"Because I am your only chance of getting out of this."

"Or so you said. I'm beginning to doubt that."

"Dana, you came to me for help. So let me help you. Now tell me about the threatening e-mails."

Tossing up both hands, she said, "They were references to Scripture. Something about 'What's more precious than rubies and gold' and 'The price of wisdom is above rubies.' To me, that means that my brother is the most precious thing to me. But I don't know why anyone would threaten us." Leaning back with a sigh, she asked, "Can you just answer me this? Is Caryn Roark behind all of this."

"Yes," he said, the mention of that name causing his eyes to go black. "Yes, she is."

Dana again felt that instinctive tug. Somehow he was connected to Caryn Roark. She was sure of it now. "How do you know that?"

The blank look on his face gave nothing away, but Dana wouldn't be silenced. "Okay, then, what on earth would Caryn Roark want with me?" She stared at Brendan, not really seeing his face as she went back over the day of the tornado. "I've rarely had contact with the woman, but the other day I went to see her because I thought some of her kids had killed my bull."

"How did she respond to that?"

"She didn't like it. She got very angry. But I can't see how that would cause her to trash and then burn down my house and chase us all over Kansas."

"She has her reasons," he said. "And that's why we have to work together to find out what she's after."

"If that's true, why all this secrecy, Brendan? Why did you take my brother away?"

"To throw them off," he said, his eyes hooded and full of shadows. "I have a plan, Dana. I aim to get you out of this mess."

"Why were you on the road that day?"

"I was watching the Universal Unity Church compound."

"So you do have connections with this cult?"

He nodded, that look of dark danger moving through his eyes. "I can't explain right now, but I am no friend of UUC, trust me. I'm on your side in this."

Just knowing that helped calm Dana even while it scared her. At last, she had a clue as to what was going on, even if she was still angry at him for his actions. And she wouldn't stop until he told her everything. If Brendan Donovan thought he could spirit her away and use threats and manipulation to sidetrack her, he was wrong. She could play games, too.

She would get her brother back. She would get her land back.

If he didn't truly help her, Brendan Donovan would regret the day he'd laid eyes on Dana Barlow. She watched him now and gave herself a secret pat on the back. From the look on his tormented face, she was already starting to wear thin on his patience. If he only knew. By the time she got through pestering the truth out of him, he'd be more than glad to let her go.

She rose up again and dropped the blanket, using every bit of courage she possessed to question him further. Forcing herself to stay calm, forcing a controlled, calculating expression on to her flushed face, she said, "I'd like to know where you're taking me."

He stared up at her, his eyes moving over her face. "We're going to stay on my estate. It's about thirty miles from Wichita. It has the best state-of-the-art security money can buy—I should know, I designed it—so I can assure you, you'll be safe there. The others have already been taken there."

"So we've just been driving around in circles to throw off Caryn's people?"

"Something like that, aye." With a low growl he shifted against the seat. Then he turned, closed his eyes tightly shut, took a deep breath. "Don't ask anything more right now, Dana." Then he tossed her a shopping bag. "Clean clothes."

Taking it, Dana looked down at the feminine clothes inside. "Thanks."

"You can change now or wait until we arrive."

"I think I should wait," she said, wondering if he actually expected her to change clothes in the car with him sitting two feet away. She'd accept his kindness, but she had one more question. "Why did you put me to sleep?"

"For your own protection," he said, his knuckles white against the seat. "I didn't want you to worry about your brother." Then he motioned. "You'll feel better soon. Once you're in a warm bed and can get a good's night sleep."

Dana went silent, her thoughts shifting from trusting to accusing with each new revelation. The man had offered her help, yet he'd tricked her and drugged her. Now he was telling her that together they had to find a way to stop Caryn Roark. Did she dare believe his motives? How could she, when she didn't even *know* his motives for doing this? Could she trust in her heart that Brendan hadn't intentionally harmed her? She badly wanted to believe that.

With the muted streetlights passing by, she tore open the

package and pulled out a gathered floral cotton skirt and a soft white cotton scooped-neck top. "At least you know how to dress a woman," she whispered as she stared at the pretty outfit. Too bad she didn't plan on sticking around to find out more about him.

Brendan watched as she came out of the powder room on the first floor of his estate, her rustling movements going still as she waited for him to turn around. Seeing her in the dainty outfit, he instantly wished Gareth didn't have such instincts about what women liked. The feminine attire only added to her natural country-girl appeal, and only added to his already-acute awareness of her. He swallowed back a snarl and shot his eyes down the length of her without saying a word.

"Glad you approve," Dana said. "I appreciate the clean clothes. Now take me to Stephen—and later you can tell me everything you know about the Universal Unity Church."

He leaned into the ancient desk of his huge downstairs study, bracing his tired body against it. "I do not wish to discuss Caryn Roark."

"But you know why she wants me, don't you?"

He turned away to stare out a window, into the open, black sky, wondering who was out there watching them. While he had the best security his technology and his money could buy, he still worried. And so he stood stoic and silent, fighting a raging battle within himself. How could he tell her everything that had brought him to the county line road the day of the tornado? How could he tell her that by helping Dana and her brother he'd somehow redeemed himself?

She lashed out at him then, stalking the small space between them to tug him around, her eyes flashing, her nostrils flaring. "I had a home. I had a life. Sure, it wasn't the best life, and maybe I resented it at times, but I was willing to make the most of it. And I was willing to put up with Caryn Roark as a neighbor, even though people whispered strange rumors about her, about how she manipulated her followers, about how she lured teenagers into her cult, about how radical her views really were. I ignored them, tried to shut myself off from the world, because I had to keep things going. I had to take care of my brother and the farm. Something always got in the way of my having time to worry about some strange woman next door. Then she started pestering me, trying to take my land. I ignored her. The townspeople warned me. They said she had ways of controlling people."

She stopped to take a breath, her eyes widening, pleading, for him to help her understand. "But I refused to listen. I tried to mind my own business and now I've lost everything, including my brother."

She jabbed at his chest, her fingers hitting a rock-hard wall of flesh and resistance. "Now, here I am, miles away from my home, with a man who kidnapped me and drugged me and who knows what else you've got planned!" The jabs turned into fists, tiny, ineffective fists hitting against his chest. "All I'm asking is the truth, Brendan. You tell me where my brother is, you tell me what's so important that people would try to kill me, you tell me the truth. I deserve the truth." Tears streamed down her face now. Her voice cracked and softened into an almost whisper. "Tell me, Bren, what's your connection to Caryn Roark?"

Brendan took her fisted hands, easily lifting her wrists away from his body. For a minute, he just stood there, looking down at her, the hurt in her eyes a reflection of the torment raging through his system.

Dana used that obvious torment to break his resistance. "Bren, please?"

She was right, of course. She deserved the truth, or what

little bit of the truth he could give her. He saw the need in her eyes, saw the tears falling like broken crystal shards down her face. Maybe it was the look in her luminous eyes, maybe it was the way she said his name, but something in him softened and he decided to trust her just a small bit, just enough to ease some of his own pain.

Then he took a harsh, forced breath and said, "Caryn Roark is my sister. That's my connection to her."

## Chapter Ten

Dana's mouth went dry. She started to shake as her knees began to cave in; her legs seemed to turn to rubber. She wobbled, then reached for the sofa behind her.

Brendan caught her, guided her down. "Are you all right?"

The concern in his voice didn't soften the fear and pain merging in Dana's soul. "Your sister?" she repeated, her words barely above a whisper. "Oh my goodness, what have I gotten myself into?"

"More than you can deal with alone," he said, his hands still on her arms. Her skin was cool; he felt the grain of chill bumps on her slender wrists. Gently he leaned her back on the sofa cushions, then grabbed a chenille blanket from a nearby armchair and draped it around her shaking body. "That's why you have to trust me."

Dana laughed harshly. "Trust you? Trust you! You just told me that madwoman is your sister, and you still want me to trust you? Surely you don't think I'm that stupid!"

He closed his eyes to gain control. He had to be very careful in how he handled this situation. "I don't think you're at all stupid. But I do know that you can't fight Caryn alone."

Something in his words and actions must have penetrated Dana's shock and revulsion. She nodded her head in a slow, steady acceptance. "You're right. I can't fight this alone. But why should I depend on you of all people?"

Brendan felt the darkness shadowing through his mind. The old familiar darkness of despair. "Because I know her better than anyone. I know exactly what she's capable of."

He hated the fear clouding Dana's eyes, but he wanted her to understand what they were up against.

"So you're going to help me. You're going to fight your own sister?" she asked, disbelief warring with hope in her expression.

He leaned forward to gather her close in his arms. She tried to protest, but the drugs and this last bit of news had obviously made her too tired, too lethargic to do anything but slump against him. She suddenly seemed so dainty and vulnerable, like a little girl afraid of monsters. And his sister was a monster.

"I've been fighting my sister all my life," he said against her hair, his tone hushed and grim. "And that's all I can say right now."

"How can I believe you, after what you've done, after everything's that's happened?"

"Believe this," he said, then unable to tell her everything he wanted to say, he made a silent vow, promising her that she would not become another victim of his sister's evil. "Believe that I only brought you here to help you, to keep you and your brother safe, until I can decide what's to be done."

Dana felt safe in his arms, in spite of her doubts. He said something, something so beautiful, in the language she recognized from her dreams.

"What does it mean?" she asked, drowsy again. Had he put something in her water or was she just that tired?

"It means 'Sleep the night, my love. I'll keep your dreams safe until morning.'"

She didn't want to sleep; she didn't want to feel this good in his arms. He had tricked her and he'd taken her away from her brother. How could she expect him to keep her safe. "How can you do that?"

"Just go to sleep, Dana," he said, his mouth dangerously close to her own. "I promise you, the time will come when I'll explain everything, but for now it's best you don't know too much of this."

"For my own safety?"

"Yes, and for your brother's sake."

She had to trust him on that, she conceded. For Stephen. "I miss him," she said, her voice edged with tears.

"I know." He trailed strong fingers through her hair. "I know you're worried, but Stephen is safe, I promise. He's asleep now with guards watching over him. And Leo is nearby. He refuses to leave the boy. You'll see them tomorrow."

That something in his voice, that gentleness, that tenderness she'd first noticed about Brendan, caught at Dana, making her forget her worries for a brief time. So she snuggled closer in his arms and felt the weight of fear and worry lift from her shoulders. For just a little while, she decided, already seeking those safe dreams he'd promised her. For just a brief time she'd trust him. But she wouldn't let it continue. No. She planned to get away from him to find Stephen.

But first she needed to find her way out of this big, dark house.

As if he could sense her need to escape, Brendan scooped her up into his arms. "I'm taking you to your room now, love. You need to rest. Just rest."

She fell against his chest, her eyes closed. A kaleidoscope of colors played through her head, like a brilliant rainbow covering the blue sky. Vaguely she remembered Leo's story, the legend of the rainbow.

Was Brendan carrying a piece of the rainbow on his shoulder to protect her?

She thought she felt the brush of his lips on her own, but

it could have just been her own sigh whispering past her heart, longing for all the brilliant colors she couldn't touch.

Dawn was floating by when she woke again. At first she didn't recognize her surroundings. She'd been dreaming such a sweet dream. Her parents were still alive and Stephen was just a toddler. They were running through the pasture beside the old farmhouse. Her mother's sunflowers were blooming all yellow and brown in a carpet of deep green. The flowers nodded their elegant heads at Dana, smiling and preening for her as she rushed by. Stephen giggled and fell into the prairie grass. Her mother called them to supper.

Just a dream. A sweet, simple dream.

But the dark dawn was reality. As was the man sitting in a chair by her bed, watching her with those midnight-black eyes.

Being here with Brendan, being caught up in this mysterious chase with Caryn, that was reality. The sense of being lost and in limbo, that was reality.

"Where am I?" she asked him, her throat raw, her voice low and hoarse.

"In my home," he replied, his dark, brooding gaze dancing off her to stare out the window. "In your bedroom."

"And how long do you plan to keep me here?"

He looked at her, long and hard and considering. "That depends on so many things, Dana. Your safety. Caryn's determination."

"And *why* are you keeping me at your home, Brendan?"

He smiled, a tired, tension-filled smile, but a devastating one at that. "You ask too many questions."

"That's because I need so many answers." She sat up, pushing a hand through her wild, tangled locks. "I don't know what's waiting for me back home. Caryn's probably bulldozed what was left of my house. And my cattle, well, I can only hope the Fredericks were able to load 'em up and get 'em to safety."

"Your livestock has been taken care of," he said quietly with a flick of his wrist.

"How do you know that?"

"Try not to worry," he replied by way of an answer. "You shall get your land back, I promise."

"You sure do promise a lot."

He lowered his head to stare across at her, his dark eyes reminding her of stars at first dawn, brilliant and taking her breath away. "I've promised you protection and that includes your land."

She adjusted her bedcovers, not missing the way his eyes moved slowly over her while she did so. "So, you're in some kind of war with your sister?"

"Something like that."

She saw that brooding darkness she'd first witnessed after the tornado when he'd glared across the way at the big white Universal Unity Church compound. "How sad. Stephen and I argue all the time, but I can't imagine something like this happening with us."

Brendan looked at her, captivated by her sleepy-eyed beauty, and remembered how touched he'd been the day of the tornado, touched by her loving concern for her younger brother, by her fierce need to save what was her own. Maybe that was what had saved him from sure destruction that day. He'd been headed on a path more deadly than the tornado they'd faced down. Except for Dana, he might be dead right now. And his sister along with him.

His eyes held hers now and he wished for carefree childhood memories, wished for a sister's love, wished the dark agony that came just before dawn would ease away. "Then consider yourself very lucky," he said, his tone soft with regret.

"I do," she said, worry coloring her words. "That's why I want to see my brother again—today."

"You will," he returned, all his defenses softening. "Just as soon as morning comes and we make sure things are okay."

"This is a very big house," she said. "I remember the drive last night up a winding road, and this big, hulking mansion up on a hill. It reminds me of a castle."

Brendan nodded, glad that she was willing to talk about something besides her brother. "It is, in a way. We call it Castle Donovan, mainly because it was built from a real castle in Ireland, along with limestone from Kansas."

"You actually live in a castle?"

"It's more a rather large estate, but parts of it were brought over from Ireland, piece by piece. My great-grandfather built it after making a fortune in railroads and cattle at the turn of the century. Then when my parents came to America, they worked to restore it. I inherited it from them."

"Your parents are...dead?"

He nodded. No point in going into detail there.

"Mine, too."

"We have that in common."

Dana sat up, eyeing him with a new interest. "How can you be so nonchalant about living in a castle? Stephen will love this place." Then she asked, "Why did you separate us?"

"To confuse Caryn. To check each of you out. To make sure you didn't compare notes."

"This is too weird. You make it sound like some sort of espionage."

"It's very complicated."

She sat propped up against the ancient rococo-style rosewood headboard, her green eyes vivid with doubt and distrust. "You certainly cover all the bases."

"I have to. I deal in a highly competitive, cutthroat business."

"Do you think I'm that way—cutthroat?"

"Not at all."

"So why did you take me?"

Ah, a fair question, asked so directly. He couldn't explain that just yet, so he just lifted a brow. "To offer you my help, and for my own reasons. I wanted to get to know you better, Dana."

That silenced her for a full minute. She clamped her lips tightly together and looked around the room. Then she glared across at him again. "You could have just taken me to a movie."

He had to smile at her practical nature. "There was no time for that, but we might try that later downstairs in the media room. My only concern last night was getting you away from Caryn." Then he leaned forward. "And making sure you weren't one of her underlings."

That caused her to sit up. "What? You thought I was working for Caryn Roark?"

"I didn't want to think you were, but I had to be sure."

"So that's the real reason for all this intrigue and mystery," she said, the words full of a soft fury. "You had to debrief me, sort of? Make sure I wasn't hiding something?"

"I had to be sure. And now I am. Very sure."

He could tell by the way she crossed her arms and held them tightly against her midsection that he'd destroyed that little bit of trust he'd tried so hard to gain. Well, better that she knew that much of the truth at least. Because he had a feeling things were going to get much worse before they were all out of this mess.

But he couldn't tell her that yet, either.

As the sun came up over the lake, Brendan rose and extended a hand to her. "Welcome to Wichita, Dana Barlow."

"But we *left* Wichita hours ago."

"And now, we're back—about thirty miles south of the city."

"It would really help if you'd explain all of this," Dana said. "Was this really necessary?"

"Very necessary. If I hadn't rescued you and sent all of you in different directions, you'd probably be either held against your will or...dead by now."

"I hate this," she replied, closing her eyes tightly. "And I'm still leaning toward hating you."

"Aye, I think you are," he agreed, pushing memories of her snuggled close in his arms out of his frazzled mind. "I can live with your hatred, Dana, as long as you can manage to stay alive."

"Thanks to you?" She snorted, reopened her eyes and looked toward where the heavy drapery opened across a huge, arched window. "Don't do me any more favors, okay?"

Brendan decided he was caught between two very dominant forces. His sister and this innocent, intriguing woman.

And he vowed that only one of them would win his complete loyalty.

He was sitting close, too close for comfort, in the opulent room. The sun had risen a while ago, but Brendan refused to leave. And he still hadn't offered to take her to see her brother.

"I can take care of myself without you," Dana whispered as she huddled in the big bed. "So just let me go."

"Yes, I've seen how very good you are at taking care of yourself," he retorted dryly, his fingers drumming away on a fancy laptop computer he'd apparently brought with him. "Just how far did you plan on running, anyway?"

She tossed her head. "As far as I needed to get to protect my brother. Caryn is playing some sort of sick game. She threatened Stephen, but for the life of me, I don't know why. I can't let her get to him." She slumped back against the elaborate headboard. "Bren," she said, her voice going soft as valor turned to fear, "Bren, just tell me that you won't let her hurt him. If you can just promise me that, I'll make you a promise." She rubbed her cold forearm with one hand. "I promise I won't make any trouble. We can work together on this. Whatever I need to do to end this nightmare, I'll do it. Just keep my brother safe."

Brendan sat in the chair, watching the proud, frightened woman he'd rescued. He'd faced down corporate giants, he'd walked right over hostile takeover attempts, he'd fought and scraped his way to the top with a ruthless, calculated determination, and now he was sitting here about to turn into a puddle of putty simply because this tiny woman had just begged him to keep her brother safe.

Fighting for control, he retreated further into his own dark secrets and asked God to show him the way. Then, unable to stop the simple gesture, he got up and reached a hand down to her face, his fingers barely touching on the single tear that trailed its way down her cheek from a spot just below the soft flutter of her lashes.

"You have a deal," he said, his finger tracing her tear. "I'm telling you, Dana, I will not let any harm come to Stephen or you. And I only ask that you trust me and do as I ask, without question."

Dana sniffed back tears, then reached up a hand to grasp his fingers. "Why are you doing this, Brendan? Why are you going to such lengths to protect us?"

Brendan closed his eyes to the bitter memories swirling like haunted dreams deep in the recesses of his brain. He wasn't ready to talk about his motives—not here, not yet.

For now, he had her with him. For now, she was safe. and her brother was protected. This time, Caryn wouldn't win. "I said no more questions," he reminded her in a gruff voice.

Dana turned her head away, but he didn't miss the flash of wrath in her green eyes. Good. He could take her anger a lot more than he could stand her pain. Let her think the worst as long as he could keep her safe.

Wrapping his hand around hers, he leaned close, a dark humor cutting off the brooding fear deep inside him. "Maybe," he said, his breath flowing out over her jawline, "maybe in spite of how much you despise me, you will listen to me and follow my instructions—for your brother's sake."

Dana's whole body went on alert, the chill bumps popping out on her skin now surfacing from anticipation and apprehension instead of the chilly elegance of this big room. The man holding her, the man who'd kidnapped her and brought her all the way around by Laura's house, as her mother used to say, remained a mystery to her. A fascinating, intriguing, frightening mystery. Was he being sincere with her? Or was he playing his own dangerous game?

Did she dare trust him? She'd promised she wouldn't cause any trouble. And to protect Stephen she'd honor that promise. She hadn't promised anything else beyond that, though, because she couldn't be sure if his requests were veiled threats. Yet his touch, her name on his lips, his breath on her skin, spoke of untold promises. Promises of safety and hope, promises of protection and security—things she'd missed out on since her parents had died. Things she'd asked for from God, but it had seemed even He had turned his face away. Brendan promised all of these things and more, as he sat there so close, yet so unreadable. Had God sent Brendan just in time? Or had God forgotten her altogether?

Trying to lighten the dark trepidation curling in the pit of her being, Dana asked, "Do you always have to kidnap women to get them to cooperate with you?"

He laughed then, a strong, deep rumbling that stirred his body and shook Dana's soul. "Only when I want to have them completely to myself," he said, his smile lifting the tense angles of his face.

Wanting to gain information, Dana lowered her head and decided to test his mettle. If she had to flirt with the man to find a way out of this, then she'd do it. "And will you...have me completely to yourself at this castle?"

"Aye." He leaned close, his eyes holding hers. "Of course, we're never really alone here. Castle Donovan sits on a slope above a large private lake. It's survived every sort of weather and every sort of suburban encroachment for close to a century. My home is a virtual fortress, but I have guards everywhere."

"A prison," she said, willing herself to stay calm. "But we have chaperones."

"Depends on how you want to look at this situation," he offered, his eyes locking with hers. "Aye, people watching over us."

Dana backed away, the temptation of his touch too much to comprehend just now. She'd never been good at flirting anyway. And she suspected flirting with this man would only lead to more trouble. "Well, since I can't find out much from you, I haven't decided if this is a date, or a trip to the loony farm."

Dana watched, and too late, saw the dare in his expression just before he hauled her close, his hard eyes softening as he gazed down at her. "That also depends," he whispered on a low growl. "I can keep you safe, and we can get to know each other better during our forced time together. But you have to play by my rules."

Right now, right this very minute, Dana opted for that challenge. But she intended to make some rules of her own. He was holding her against her will. Well, almost.

She wanted to get away. Badly. Well, almost.

She couldn't deny that she felt safe in his arms. But she'd make him miserable until he told her the truth and brought her brother back to her, even if she had just promised to cooperate.

Lifting away from him, she caught her breath, alert to how this man made her feel. "You're right, Bren," she said on a breathless voice filled with awe and understanding. "I guess it does depend on you, on me, on what we can accomplish while we're working together. My main goal is to get my brother to a safe place. And then I intend to find a way to bring your sister to justice, one way or another."

"I don't like that stubborn tone in your voice," he said, concern shadowing his eyes. "You can't do this on your own, Dana. She's too powerful."

"And you think you can do it on your own?"

Her words hit too close to home. "I have to do this. I have to stop Caryn before more innocent people are hurt. You asked what I was doing on the road that day? Well, I was trying to help another young woman."

Her hiss of breath only caused him more agony, but she had to know some of the truth, at least. "Her family hired me to get her away from the cult." He closed his eyes, blinked away the weariness seeping through his bones. "I failed—because of—"

Dana lifted off the bed. "Because you stopped to help Stephen and me."

He could only nod. "I don't regret that decision, because now you're in this, too." He shrugged. "Maybe God wanted me to find you that day."

She let out a breath. "And what about the other girl?"

"She's still inside the compound back in Prairie Heart. I haven't been able to pinpoint exactly what Caryn has done with her."

"Are you saying that girl might be punished or worse?"

"I don't know. But I intend to find her, for her parents' sake. They need closure, good or bad."

"But how can you help that girl if you're trying to protect Stephen and me?"

"You're in a lot of danger, and I've vowed to protect you."

"Yes, so I've heard. But why me, Brendan? I'd really like to know the answer to this whole puzzle."

"I can't tell you anything more right now."

"Then I intend to keep pushing."

He watched her face, knew she meant it. Dana Barlow had that prairie spirit that came from generations of hardworking people; people who worked the land and made a living off all the good life had to offer. People who were loyal to God and family. He had no doubt that she would fight his sister—and him—with every fiber of her being.

And that fight could be the end of her.

Well, not if he could help it. He'd lost one woman to his sister's evil ways. And since that day, he'd tried to save so many children from Caryn's charismatic trickery. Sometimes he'd succeeded, other times he'd failed.

But not this time, he told himself. He wouldn't lose this one. He'd keep Dana and Stephen safe if it was the last thing he ever did.

## Chapter Eleven

He'd left long after the dawn came and went. The morning sun brought the room into a vivid focus, highlighting the gilded mirrors and brocade tapestries, while his leaving left Dana with abstract thoughts of a man she didn't understand at all.

And he had not yet taken her to see her brother. In spite of her pleas to see Stephen, Brendan had assured Dana that Stephen was safe and that she'd talk to him soon. Then he told her to get some more rest.

How could she rest when he'd locked her in with a click that had sounded with electronic precision around the entire room? After giving up any hope of sneaking out of the room, Dana had forced herself to relax and think things through.

First thought—she was a prisoner here. But, oh, what a luxurious prison. It had been so dark last night, and she'd been so tired and groggy that she hadn't paid much attention to her surroundings. But she could see everything now in the light of day.

Crimson. Crimson satin stretched over the elaborate headboard of the big intricately carved bed, where a golden crest complete with the image of a savage black falcon bearing his claws, the Donovan coat of arms, no doubt, rose up out of its center. Heavy crimson velvet curtains covered the tall, floor-to-ceiling windows that formed an oriel at the end of the huge, carpeted room. Two fat, crimson-covered armchairs with matching ottomans, all styled in the same ornate dark wood, sat by the massive black marble fireplace where even now, on a crisp spring morning, a fire crackled. Everywhere she looked, Dana was faced with something in the color crimson. And since there was a large gilded mirror on every wall, the reflections of her surroundings shot back at her a hundred times over, along with her own wide-eyed, dazed image, making her dizzy and disoriented.

The walls, a mixture of heavy marbled stone and dark, polished paneling, also boasted several large, gold-encrusted portraits of elegantly clad, stern-looking men and women whom Dana could only imagine must be some of Brendan Donovan's ancestors.

Stalking around the room, Dana talked out loud to the image of a dark lord who bore a remarkable resemblance to Brendan. "He has no right to treat me this way, you know. I won't let him bully me. I won't. I'm being held against my will, and I'll find a way out of here—and with my brother." Somehow.

She had to remind herself that Brendan was trying to protect her. Maybe there was a method to his madness, but Dana had yet to understand it. Why all the secrecy and drama?

Because he's protecting you from a very dangerous woman, she reminded herself. "Be grateful, Dana," she said to the portrait. Then she decided she'd be grateful when she found Stephen safe and whole.

If she concentrated on her brother, she could put all the rest out of her mind. All the danger and the fear. And the way she seemed drawn toward Brendan, the way she felt all mushy and disoriented whenever he said her name in that beautiful Irish brogue. She had to put that out of her mind, too. Those particular revelations conflicted sharply to her claims of being here against her will.

Stalking the spacious confines of her elegant prison, she remembered how last night he'd carried her through the so-called castle, taking her on twists and turns that she couldn't see, his voice pushing ahead of her grogginess as he made low comments in her ear.

"Watch yourself. Hold on."

"We're turning right here."

"Sorry I bumped into that stone wall."

All sweet terms of endearment as he shifted her weight in his arms to keep her out of harm's way. All protective and caring, so she wouldn't get hurt by even a splinter or a rough wall.

"I don't get him!" Dana said, the harsh tone of her words echoing in the high-ceilinged room, even as Brendan's gentleness sounded inside her mind in sharp contrast to the echoes of danger she felt all around her. "He's still living in another century, thinking he's some lord of the manor who can push innocent women around."

But even as she said that, Dana knew Brendan had been kind to her from the beginning. And he'd put everything else aside to find her and help her. Including the rescue of a young girl caught up in Caryn's schemes and lies.

Stopping in the middle of the carpeted floor, Dana said a prayer for the unnamed girl. "Lord, let her be okay. Let her be alive."

And then a light seemed to glow white-hot inside Dana's brain. She suddenly realized that instead of fighting against Brendan's help, she *should* be trying to work *with* him. She had told him she'd cooperate, but what had she done but whine and ask pesky questions? Together they could bring Caryn Roark to justice, just as she'd suggested to him earlier. She'd been grasping at straws then, but now she knew she had to give in to his rules after all. It was the only way.

But how? She had to stop plotting escape, because right now Brendan was her only means of protection. She couldn't leave without Stephen and Tony and Leo, anyway. Better to be cooperative and get to the bottom of ending this horror.

"I hear you, Lord," she said, wondering when she'd turned back to God for help. Well, getting shot at and threatened with a bomb and chased by dangerous people sure could bring a lost soul back to the fold rather quickly. But it was more than all those things. It was the look in Brendan's eyes when he'd finally told her that Caryn Roark was his sister. It was the agony on his face when he'd confessed he was trying to rescue a young girl.

There was in this world, after all, the kind of organized but false religion that people such as Caryn Roark thrived on, using others to gain power and means. And then there was the kind of honest intensity of a man like Brendan Donovan. He was trying to save one young girl, trying to bring her home to her parents.

"That did me in, Lord," Dana said, tears pricking her eyes as she thought about Stephen. What if he had been enticed by the cult members? She'd certainly want someone to help her rescue him, if that were the case. And Dana certainly knew the one true way, the only way, to get her brother into heaven. And that had nothing to do with following Caryn Roark. No, that only had to do with faith, keeping faith in God, no matter what.

She lifted back a flap of velvet drapery, felt the warmth of the morning sun hitting her face, and said a prayer. *I will do my best, Lord, to honor You, always.*

A knock sounded at the door, causing her to jump. Wrapping her arms across her chest in an ineffective protective stance, she called, "Come in." Which was really redundant, since she was locked in.

After the click of the lock moving, a young maid entered, carrying a silver tray full with bread, cheese, fruit, fancy little cakes and coffee. She smiled as she lowered the tray onto a marble-topped table by the covered windows. "Mr. Donovan sent you some breakfast, ma'am, with plenty of strong coffee just the way you like it, and a pot of hot tea, too, just in case," the girl explained. "And I am to draw your bath while you eat."

"Th-thank you," Dana stammered, embarrassed to be waited on by someone who appeared years younger than her, someone who used very proper, old-fashioned language. When the girl started to pour steaming coffee into a rose-patterned cup, Dana held up a hand. "I can do that. And I can run my own bath. Just show me where everything is."

"Oh, no," the girl insisted. "Mr. Donovan gave me specific instructions. He told me to make sure you were fed and comfortable. You eat, ma'am, and I'll do my job."

Not wanting to get the girl in trouble, Dana nodded, then sank down to stare at the bounty set before her. Well, she was hungry, and as far as she could tell, it was nearly noon anyway.

When she'd finally found a window behind all that heavy drapery, she'd lifted the curtains to get a glimpse of her surroundings. The window, as well as the paned doors to the terrace, had been locked, of course. And Brendan had explained in detail earlier how this vast estate, set along the plains and hills of Donovan Lake—could it be named anything else?—was equipped with the latest security measures. No one could get in or out, without him knowing it immediately.

Frustrated, but wanting to keep up her strength, Dana tore into the crusty bread, then dipped a hearty dollop of fresh butter from a stone crock to smear across the moist, warm chunk. It was delicious, so she decided to try the cheese and fruit, too. Wonderful. The delicate tea cakes were just as good, and the coffee was strong and soothing. She had a cup of that, then decided to test the tea.

Her mother used to drink hot tea in the afternoons after all the chores had been done. When Dana was small, they had elaborate tea parties and dressed up in fancy church hats and Easter gloves. That bittersweet memory only brought the threat of more tears, but Dana pushed them away, determined to get herself together.

By the time the maid emerged from a nearby room, Dana was full and drowsy, almost complacent. "Please tell whoever cooked this, I thoroughly enjoyed my meal."

"Oh, I will," the girl said, beaming with pride. "Miss Gilda made the bread. You'll get to meet her soon, I imagine."

Thinking Miss Gilda was the main cook, Dana made a note to get her bread recipe. "What's your name?" she asked the dark-headed maid in an attempt to get her bearings.

"Lara," the girl said. "And you're Miss Barlow, right?"

"Call me Dana," Dana replied, liking the girl's dimpled smile and warm attitude. "And thank you so much for everything."

"If you need anything else," Lara said as she made to leave, "just pick up the phone."

"How about a map?" Dana asked sweetly, knowing it probably wouldn't get her very far anyway. "Or a clue as to where I can find my brother."

Looking confused and flustered, Lara said, "I'd have to clear that with Mr. Donovan."

"Of course." Dana looked down at her plate, her appetite suddenly gone. "I was only joking."

Lara looked relieved. "Is there anything else I can get you?"

"I need more clothes," Dana said, looking down at her frazzled outfit. "I changed into this last night, but I slept in it all night and it's wrinkled."

Lara pointed to a large wardrobe dominating a far corner of the shadowy room. "I think you'll find everything you need in there, ma'am." Then she pointed to the skirt and blouse. "I'll have this cleaned and back to you soon."

"Wait," Dana said, causing the girl to halt at the door. "How long have you worked here?"

The girl looked evasive, but finally said, "Almost a year now."

"What made you want a job here?"

Lara's smile was tentative, like a shy ray of sunshine. "Mr. Donovan rescued me."

"Rescued you?" Then a shard of bright light seemed to pass through Dana's tired, numb brain. "From...from the Universal Unity Church?"

Lara nodded. "But please, don't tell anyone you found me here. I have no family left. And *she'd* want me to come back." Lara twisted her hands together. "I can't go back to that place, ever. This is my home now."

Dana's stomach lurched and churned as the hair on the back of her neck stood up. "She? You mean Caryn Roark?"

Lara nodded, held her head down. "I'm afraid to even go outside, I'm afraid of the dark. Sometimes she would lock me in the isolation room, so I could mend my ways and ask for proper guidance. Mr. Donovan—he's brought in doctors to counsel me, though. I'm much better now."

Too stunned to say much else, Dana watched as the slender maid left, shutting the door quietly behind her. Dana didn't miss the click of the lock, though.

"So you really are a rescuer," Dana whispered, wondering what would have happened to her, and especially to Stephen, if Brendan hadn't stepped in. Whatever Lara had been through, Dana didn't want to experience. She didn't want to be afraid like that poor girl. And she didn't want Stephen to be left alone or taken from her.

*This is too much for me, Lord,* she thought. *I need to get dressed and get on with finding out how to get out of this. Oh, and I could really use Your help, if You can see fit to watch over us.*

"But right now, I have to be practical about this, and find something to wear."

Curious, she marched to the wardrobe to throw open the doors. With a gasp, she stared at the rows and rows of feminine clothes floating on satin covered hangers, in every shade of the rainbow. Reaching out a hand, she touched on the sleeve of a plum-colored robe and matching lacy gown. Soft and silky. Then she found a more practical hooded velour jacket and matching sweatpants in a mint-green.

"This will do me," she said, sensibility overtaking the feminine urge to wear something fancy.

After searching for underclothes, she headed to the big, airy bathroom, wondering how Brendan had managed to get all these clothes so fast. "Maybe he keeps them here for his girlfriends," she mused out loud as she sank with a gasp of joy into the hot, soothing, scented water.

She sat there enjoying the bubble bath since she hadn't had time for one in years. Her gaze landed on the beautiful flower centered on the pale gray marble vanity across the room.

An amaryllis lily. This one was a brilliant red, its petals so thick and lush, they looked like pure velvet.

Dana laughed, almost to the point of hysteria. This was getting too weird. She'd thought she could trust Bren, would have bet the bank on it, yet really, she knew nothing, nothing about the man, except that he was rich and powerful and as handsome as…well, as handsome as the Irish lord in that big picture in the other room.

And he and his sister both grew amaryllis lilies.

Feeling a sudden chill, Dana sank down deeper in the

warm water, closing her eyes to the panic that moved like a prairie wind through her body.

This chase, this game, had grated on her nerves to the point that she couldn't think straight anymore. Bone weary, Dana prayed for the strength to keep ahead of the game, whatever the game might be. And she prayed for Stephen's safety. Brendan had told her that her brother and her friends were safe. She intended to make him prove that.

Just as soon as she could get out of this tub and get dressed.

From his vantage point in front of a panel of television screens, all trained on various entrances and doorways inside the estate, and with one particular camera trained on the door to Dana's room, Brendan wondered for the hundredth time if he'd done the right thing by forcing her to come here.

*I only want to protect her, Lord,* he thought as a silent prayer ran through his tired brain; the pitter-patter of a gentle rain hitting the stone terrace outside singing a refrain to his mantra. Then he felt a sharp pang of guilt cutting through his conscience. He hadn't just brought Dana and her brother here to protect them, although that was top priority. But he wasn't ready to tell Dana all his reasons for forcing her to be a guest in his home. Not yet.

He wouldn't let it happen again. He wouldn't let Caryn win this time. He'd saved many children from Caryn's religious cult, had made it his mission to do so years ago. But this time he had to stop her for good. This time she'd gone too far in coming after Dana Barlow and her brother. The stakes were much higher now.

And his sources told him that Caryn wouldn't stop until she had what she was after. But what was she after? Brendan thought he already knew the answer to that question and it sickened him.

He had to watch out for Dana and her brother until he had the answer, the proof he needed. Caryn could have killed all of them with the first try. Instead, she was harassing Dana. That made him think Dana had something Caryn needed very badly. And that was why he had to make sure Dana was protected at all times. But since he hardly knew whom to trust at this point, he'd personally see to that. And, as much as he hated doing it, he'd have to use Dana and her brother to draw Caryn out.

He couldn't quite admit that he liked being around Dana, liked her vitality and her practical nature. He wasn't ready to delve into those feelings yet. He accepted that since the day he'd found her there in the storm, he'd been captivated by her. And afraid for her. Because Dana was so practical, and yes, stubborn, he realized that she'd try to get away and do this on her own.

That would be a mistake.

He couldn't let her out of his sight for too long. He wouldn't let his sister win again. He wouldn't let Caryn destroy this young woman. Bitter memories of a porcelain-skinned, dark-haired woman swirled up like laughing water, momentarily blurring his vision.

Shaking his head to refocus, Brendan rubbed his tired eyes. "I'm sorry, Dana. But it's the only way. The only way." For so many reasons, he wanted to keep her near. For so many reasons, he knew he shouldn't have her here. But she *was* here. And for now she was safe. And so was her brother.

Until his sister figured out that Brendan had tricked her, that he'd sent her on a false trail. Then Caryn would come looking and he'd have her at last.

Then, only then, could he end the nightmare that his sister had caused, and maybe find his own peace of mind.

* * *

Trying to ignore the beautiful, imposing lily that only re-minded her of Caryn Roark, Dana glanced around the opu-lent bathroom as she hurriedly dressed, her gaze taking in the gold plumbing fixtures on the black-and-white marble tub. Ac-tually, it looked more like a small swimming pool. The thing could easily hold six people with plenty of leg room. So much vanity, so much luxury, was beyond Dana's comprehension.

"Don't get used to it," she warned herself. But she couldn't help gaping at her surroundings.

The matching marble vanity, complete with a large sea-shell-shaped sink, boasted the same elegant fixtures, while an ornate brass vanity stool shouted with the same crimson vel-vet she'd seen everywhere else.

"Hmm. Not quite Elvis, but not exactly country charming, either," she quipped as she watched bubbles going down the drain in the tub. "If this is the guest room, I can't wait to see the rest of this little homestead."

If she ever got the chance. Oh, she ached to her very bones, ached with worry and wonder and confusion and fear. In spite of her enforced stay here, she couldn't help the relaxing ef-fect the bath had had on her. The water felt like silk, and held the scent of wisteria and honeysuckle. Nothing like the anti-bacterial soap she used back on the farm.

"But, hey, if it gets me clean…" She had to stop talking to herself. Where was Bren? She wondered if she'd see him again anytime soon. And what about her brother? "I'll just use that fancy phone and call around until someone listens to me," she said.

What if he were lying about everything? What if Stephen wasn't even here? A horrible thought centered itself in Dana's mind, making her blood run cold. What if Brendan had tricked Dana and turned her brother over to Caryn?

* * *

In another part of the mansion, Stephen sat playing a video game courtesy of Wichita Communications' latest virtual reality computer game.

"This is so cool," Stephen shouted to Leo, who sat nearby reading a detective novel their absent host had sent down specifically for his enjoyment.

"Glad you like it, son," Leo replied, his eyes on the book, but his mind clicking with the experience of years of police work. Not used to being held captive, he got up from the comfortable leather armchair to pace the confines of the long gameroom where they were being held. "I wonder how our friend Tony is faring?"

"Tony is gone," Stephen replied, then giggled with a mock-menacing laugh as his hero zapped another thug, using his brains and brawn to move through the maze of the game. "Tony is mean to me. Yeah, Tony is mean. I'm glad we got rid of him."

Leo didn't reprimand the boy. He was right. Tony was as impatient as a caged field mouse. Yet, Leo had vowed to protect him, for Dana's sake. Only, he couldn't very well do that locked up in this romper-room dungeon somewhere far away from his own little domain.

"I'm sure Tony is just fine," he said, more to reassure himself than the boy. "Mr. Donovan's men said they wouldn't hurt him."

Only, Leo reminded himself with a grim smile, Tony could drive anyone to breaking a promise with his stubborn resistance and his whining attitude. That would be a shame. The man was a genius with a computer. And Leo had a sneaking suspicion Brendan Donovan knew that, and planned to use Tony for his own means. He just hoped Tony had the good sense to do as he was told.

\* \* \*

"I won't do it," Tony told the stocky man standing over him with a gun. "I will not do it, and you can shoot me on the spot if you want."

"Okay," the man said, raising the gun to Tony's trembling temple, his dark eyes showing not one speck of sympathy or emotion.

"Hey, wait," Tony said, moving his head away from the cold butt of the gun. "Maybe I'm being too hasty here."

"Maybe so," the burly bodyguard said, his tone filled with sarcasm. "Look, kid, all Mr. Donovan wants you to do is—"

"I know what that man you call boss wants me to do," Tony said, the whine in his tone grating but clear. "He wants me to hack into someone's system, mainly Caryn Roark's, and I'm telling you, until I know what's going on, and why exactly I'm hacking, I won't do it. What if she's got ties to the government or something, man? Do you know how many years a man can get for breaking into the Pentagon's files?"

"It's not the Pentagon," the man named Spear told him, rolling his dark eyes heavenward. "You don't need to worry about the hit. You just need to do your job."

"My job?" Tony scooted his swivel chair around, his own eyes flashing back from the reflection on the screen in the muted darkness of the computer room. "Man, I had a job, a good job, until someone decided to blow my equipment to the far corners of Kansas City. Now I'm a free agent, on the run from the FBI and probably the CIA, too. And I'm not doing Brendan Donovan's dirty work. That can get me five to ten in a house much bigger and darker than this one."

"Not even to help Dana?" a deep Irish voice said from the darkened doorway.

Tony pivoted his chair around, his eyes darting up to find

the man himself standing there staring at him with that brooding look he remembered from the airport in Wichita.

"Well, well," Tony said, coming up off the chair like a bantam rooster. "You finally decided to pay me a visit. You know, Mr. Donovan, kidnapping is a federal offense, and I don't even want to get into what holding us here against our will and forcing me to do illegal hacking implies."

"That will all be explained, in time," Brendan said as he strolled into the dark, equipment-stuffed room, his penetrating gaze centered on Tony. "I hear you're not cooperating, Mr. Martin. Why is that?"

Tony swallowed, then tried to find the courage to face down his dark, formidable opponent and...boss. "Mr. Donovan, I refuse to be used in whatever games you and that demented Caryn woman are playing. And I demand to know what you've done with Dana and the others."

"How very noble of you," Brendan said, his expression carved in stone. "Didn't Spear tell you that they are perfectly safe?"

"I don't believe that thug," Tony said, then wished he hadn't. Spear was at least six feet tall, and built like a linebacker. "I mean, I want *you* to explain all of this to me."

Brendan looked over Tony's shoulder at the various computer screens and printers set up in this nocturnal basement office. He didn't want to tarry here too long. Knowing that Dana had finally relaxed a little, he'd left one of his most trusted guards, a woman named Serena, to watch outside her room.

However, he wanted to see Dana again soon and let her visit with her brother—just to reassure her. Which meant, he didn't have time to persuade the reluctant Tony Martin to do the work he'd brought him here for.

"Mr. Martin, do you realize that you work for me? That you have always worked for me?"

"I figured that out, yeah," Tony said, his tone scratchy in spite of the stubborn glint in his eyes. "So what are you gonna do, fire me?"

He grinned, but Brendan didn't find his suggestion at all humorous. "I just might have to," he said, "except that I need your expertise so very much, you understand?"

The compliment won him points. "Why do you need me so much?" Tony asked, intrigued and eager from the glint in his eyes, but still cautious. "I mean, hey, man, we all know you wrote the book on the latest computer software. You can hack into files with one hand behind your back, can't you?"

"I could," Brendan said, treading very carefully. "But this particular time, I need someone who hasn't been tainted or bribed. I need someone I can trust completely. And as foolish as you seem at times, I've checked your background and you're clean. Perfectly trustworthy, except that I happen to have found a, shall we say, secret file on you. You've done some illegal work on the side, and I have proof of that work. Which is why you will now do as I ask, or risk getting into some very serious trouble."

Tony bobbed his head, his scrawny neck lifting as red, blotchy streaks moved down his face. "You've got a spy somewhere, don't you?" He jumped up, hopped around. "That's the only reason you'd want to bring in someone like me. You're *blackmailing* me into doing this."

Brendan stared at him long enough to make Tony stop dancing. "I think this system might have been compromised, yes," Brendan said. "And because I happen to know from thoroughly checking up on you the minute you became involved with Dana, I decided you'd be perfect to help find out exactly who's been toying with my software, and because no one knows you are here, and no one knows what I'm asking you to do, you're fairly safe for now in doing what I'm asking. Right now, it's a win-win situation, Mr. Martin. See to it that it remains that way, do you understand?"

"Oh, yeah," Tony said, slinking back down in his chair. "How convenient for you that Dana Barlow's ex-boyfriend happens to be a computer genius. Almost as if you planned the whole thing." He shrugged, gave a jittery laugh. "So, what's the gig, Mr. D? Find a hole in your latest software? Snare a potential hacker? Do a little encryption work? That's almost too easy."

"How about, stop Caryn Roark?" Brendan asked in a non-chalant fashion that belied the urgency coursing through his blood. "To save Dana."

That got Tony's attention, and caused Brendan to wince inside. Mainly because it wasn't just what he'd said, but the way he'd said it, his voice going obviously soft. He couldn't afford to be soft on any of them right now.

Tony looked doubtful. "We thought you were going to help us, but instead you've kidnapped us. Is this your way of saving Dana?"

"Dana is safe. And so are her brother and Leo. And you, too, for now." He dragged a hand down his face. "And I'm getting extremely tired of having to repeat that to everyone."

Tony lifted his shoulders like an ostrich about to charge. "Well, good. You'd have me to answer to if *Dana* wasn't okay, man."

"I'm sure I would, at that," Brendan said, smiling slightly. "Now, what I need you to do is find out everything you can about Caryn's system. You know from what Spear has told you, that she has a vast knowledge of computer technology, and that she's hired some of the best computer people in the business to help her build on that technology—some of them past employees of mine."

"Yeah, Spear mentioned all of that, but like I told him, I'm not so sure I want to break into *her* files. I mean, not only is that highly illegal, but that woman is evil and very smart."

"And you're out of a job, last I heard," Brendan reminded him.

"Thanks to you bombing my place."

"I did not bomb your apartment," Brendan replied calmly. "You know Caryn was behind that. Don't you want to stop her?"

"What's in it for me?" Tony asked, greed seeming to cloud his better judgment.

Brendan knew what ticked this man's clock. Tony Martin was as predictable as rain in western Ireland. "A new job, a better position within my company and all past indiscretions forgotten."

"You can guarantee me that?"

Brendan nodded. "I do own the company."

"What sort of position?"

Brendan stepped close, moving in for the final offer. "One that will make you a very rich and powerful man, Mr. Martin. How about head of development for new technology?"

Tony looked around the long room filled with the latest gadgets of technology. This place looked like something out of a spy movie, with all its monitors and screens. It was like sitting in the middle of Toys "R" Us, with every play thing he'd ever wanted at his beck and call. He'd been in awe since the minute they'd thrown him in here, and he was itching to click those keys, to rewrite programs, to take this big baby for a spin. Threats and demands didn't do the trick for him though, and right now, he wasn't very afraid of blackmail, either. He needed a proper guarantee.

But money and power, well, hey, they could win him over every time. And he certainly wanted to help Dana, of course, he told himself with a belated self-righteous adjustment of his flushed neck.

"Deal me in," he said. "But I want it in writing, and I want you to personally sign the contract. Oh, and I expect a huge salary increase." With a smug, daring satisfaction, he named his price.

"Done," Brendan said, his expression never giving away the distaste he felt for this heartless creature. Tony Martin would probably sell his own mother down the river for a piece of action involving the latest technology. But Brendan needed his help, and he would make good on his word. Tony Martin could be shaped into a good, loyal employee, heartless or not, as long as he had a keeper to watch over him day and night. "I'll have my assistant work up the terms," he said. "In the meantime, I expect you to get started."

"No, in the meantime, I'll wait on that contract," Tony countered, a slight hint of rebellion in his tone. "That, and I want to see Dana and the others. I have to know they're okay."

Brendan hid his surprise behind a cold stare, but he didn't have time to argue. Dana's life could be at stake. He inclined his head in agreement. "I'll send the contract back with my signature in fifteen minutes. And I'll have someone escort you to see the others."

"I'll be waiting," Tony said, his grin full of tooth and victory.

Brendan headed to the door, then turned. "Thank you, Mr. Martin. Your sacrifice won't go unnoticed. I'll be sure to tell Dana how very concerned you were."

That calculated remark wiped the smug grin right off Tony's face. "You'd better be careful with Dana. She's...she's special to me."

Brendan didn't respond to that. He'd seen that from the very beginning. Spear, however, had to hide his own grin behind his big beefy hand.

"What are you laughing about?" Tony whined. He swallowed the hard, thick lump clogging his throat, and wondered belatedly if he'd just sold his soul.

## Chapter Twelve

Dana jumped at the pounding on her door.

"Come in," she called, thinking she'd never get used to being locked in this room.

Brendan entered, gave her a half smile. "Good, you're dressed. I'll take you to see your brother now. And Tony...is very anxious to see you, too."

Pushing waves of hair out of her eyes, Dana sprinted toward the door. "It's about time. I'll go mad if you insist on keeping me locked up, Brendan. If we're going to fight your sister together, then I think it's high time *you* start trusting *me*."

"I agree," he said as he led her out of the room. "This way."

Dana immediately became suspicious. He was being way too tolerant. "You mean it?"

He glanced down at her as they walked through a long, carpeted passageway, its walls covered with priceless art. "We're here together. Your brother is safe here. Your friends are willing to cooperate—"

"What do you mean, willing to cooperate? You make it sound as if they had to be persuaded."

"They did, at first. But they came around to seeing things my way."

"You threatened them, didn't you?"

He gave her that simple smile again. "I made them an offer they couldn't refuse."

"We're all here at your mercy, aren't we?"

"You're all here to help me, yes. But it's a mutual thing. I will help you in return."

"Okay, all right," she said, letting out a long sigh. "Just let's get on with it. I used to have a life. I'd like to get it back."

"Me, too," he said, the word a low growl.

Dana once again saw the darkness surrounding him. She wasn't sure she wanted to know all the real reasons he was so obsessed with getting to his warped sister, but she knew she had her reasons for the same. "What's the plan?" she asked as he took her down a set of winding stairs.

"Right now, we all get together and I explain things. After you visit with Stephen, of course. He's doing great, by the way. I had my personal physician check him out. He's back on his medication, so he should be fine."

Dana swiped at the tears brimming in her eyes. "He's okay, really?"

"Really. He's been playing video games. I've got some prototypes here and I asked him to test them for me. They're learning games, nonviolent, where the hero solves all the problems without guns or weapons. Mostly these games require a good brain. It helps teach kids to think on their feet."

She relaxed a little. "Stephen would love that kind of game. And it helps him with his motor skills as well as improving his mind."

"Exactly. He's a very smart boy. He played several games, then we coaxed him to bed."

Alarm coursed through Dana. "Who's *we?*"

He guided her across a landing that offered a view of the lake. "Myself and Leo. Your brother has been with Leo the whole time, just as I told you."

"Leo takes good care of him," she said, her heart bursting with relief. "Where's Tony?"

"Tony is ensconced in the computer room, helping me to hack into Caryn's files. I don't believe that man ever sleeps."

Some of her fears evaporating, Dana grinned. "If anyone can get into files, it's Tony. But then, you probably knew that already."

"Yes, I did. I'm using his abilities and I'm paying him a hefty sum."

"You know the way to get to him, too, obviously," she said, smiling in spite of the surreal nature of this conversation. Something about this whole setup worried her. All of this calm and relaxation after being chased and harassed just didn't seem natural. She couldn't settle down and accept that they were truly safe. She'd only believe that when Caryn Roark was behind bars and Dana and Stephen were back home. If they had a home to go to.

"So you have Tony right where you need him," she said. "That's either very convenient or an amazing coincidence."

"It's a little of both, and it works for my purposes. That and the fact that he's in love with you. He's more than willing to help you."

"We were over a long time ago," she replied, a funny feeling sliding down her spine. "Tony can't accept Stephen's condition."

"*I* can," Brendan said, the intimacy of that simple statement sending her into a heightened awareness of him that only left her more dazed and confused. No man had ever said that to her. Why would he say it now, as if it was important for her to understand that about him?

"I appreciate that," she managed to whisper, her emotions churning like the silver waters of the lake below.

She watched as he punched numbers into a keypad next to a massive wooden door. He was so near, and yet he looked like he'd been carved from granite, so hard to read, so hard to comprehend.

"What's in here?" she asked, wondering how anyone could find their way around this huge place.

"Your brother," he answered.

"You've had him locked up, too?"

"For his—"

"I know," she said, holding up a hand. "For his own protection."

He ignored the sarcasm in her words. "We have a lot to talk about, Dana," he said, the weariness of his words seeming to weigh him down. He stood silent, still. "It's a long, complicated story."

"And on a-need-to-know basis?"

"Something like that. The less you know, the safer you'll be."

"I do feel safe, but I'd feel better if you'd quit locking all the doors."

"I can't do that. I can't have you going off on your own. It's too dangerous."

"So I'm like in your own personal witness protection program?"

"Something like that," he replied as the door swung open.

"Dana!"

She put all thoughts of being hidden and locked away out of her mind as her brother raced into her arms. "Stevie." Tears of joy pricked at her eyes as she held her brother close. "You're okay. You're really okay."

"I'm great, Dana." Stephen said, pushing away from her physical touch to rock back and forth, his hands flapping in excitement. "Games—we have lots of games. Puzzles. I like the puzzles best. Brendan lets me do tests and puzzles. He says I'm smart." Then he shifted on his Ruby Runners. "Where you been, Dana?"

"I've been right here, sport. I got a good night's sleep and now I'm good to go."

"I don't want to go," Stephen protested, taking her words literally. "Leo says we have to stay here for a while. I have games. And baseball cards. I have lots of baseball cards—even Lou Gehrig. Yeah, I've got Lou Gehrig."

She shot Brendan a thankful look, then glanced around the sunny room. The brief rain shower had passed and the sun was out again. Even though they were on the bottom level of the house, the high, narrow windows allowed sunshine and light to stream in between their paned slits.

As if reading her mind, Brendan said, "The windows are protected by an infrared detection system that's hooked to the main computer. Your brother is being watched 24/7 by highly skilled bodyguards."

She could only nod, relief flooding through her. Stephen *was* safe. And he looked good. He was clean and well rested. She looked around at the long room. It was filled with television monitors and computers, authentic video arcade machines and lots of books and toys of all kinds. "This looks like a big romper room."

"That's exactly what it is," Brendan explained. "I still have a bit of little boy left in me."

She tried to picture him as a little boy, without all the darkness of a brooding frown clouding his handsome face. "You'll have to tell me about that sometime."

"Sometime," he said. "Perhaps when this is all over."

"Yes, when it's over."

Leo came up to them then, his dark, solemn eyes never blinking. "Dana, you look rested."

"I did get some sleep," she said. "And it's good to have on clean clothes." She didn't miss the appreciate look Brendan gave her. "Thanks for the sweat suit and the other clothes," she said.

"You're welcome."

He motioned for her to join her brother, so Dana went over to the table where Stephen was playing some sort of buzzer game. She sat with him, chatting and laughing for a long time, while in the far corner, Brendan and Leo talked in low, controlled voices.

Finally, acutely aware of Leo's speculative look, she turned her gaze away from her brother. "What now, Brendan?" she asked across the room. "Now that I know Stevie is okay, I'm ready to get on with this."

Leo nodded. "Me, too. Sitting around makes me antsy." He gave Brendan a look that spoke of things better left unspoken. And left Dana wondering what was really going on here.

"Let's go talk to Tony," Brendan said. He stood and pressed a buzzer on the wall. "Serena, would you send in the nurse to sit with Stephen."

Dana lifted a brow, a paradox feeling of relief and disquiet rushing through her. "You think of everything, don't you?"

"I try." He gave her a look of open honesty, an intense look that asked her to believe him.

Dana looked away, toward her brother. "Stevie, I'm going with Brendan to a meeting. Will you be okay here?"

"I'm great, Dana. I'm just great," Stephen said, not even looking up from the wooden puzzle he was now busy putting together. "Leo, too?"

Leo answered, "Me, too, buddy. But I'll be nearby."

Stephen didn't respond. He rocked back and forth, his fingers working some sort of pattern that matched whatever was flashing through his head. "Okay. I'll do more puzzles. Yeah, more puzzles. We like results. We'll record results."

Dana watched as a young woman in a crisp pair of colorful scrubs came into the room from yet another hidden door. The woman smiled and waved.

"That's Stacey," Brendan said. "She's trained in dealing

with special needs children. Stephen will be safe with her." Then he inclined his head toward a discreet monitor in the far corner of the long room. "And we can watch him at all times, if you'd feel better."

"I would," Dana said.

They left after that, moving back across the landing to another set of stairs on the other side of this wing.

"My computer controls rooms," Brendan explained, using a remote control to open doors as they walked through the halls. "I have several prototypes being developed at any given time. Thus the secrecy and security."

Leo nodded. "Technical espionage. You can't have others stealing your inventions."

"That's right," Brendan said. Then he turned at a big door. "And I think that's exactly what my sister is trying to do."

An hour later, Dana sat staring at all the computers and other machines in Brendan's control center, her mind reeling with the significance of what she'd stumbled into.

"It's like the Batcave," Tony whispered while they waited for Brendan to finish a call on his cell phone. "And he's richer than Bruce Wayne ever imagined being. See that phone he's using? It's a prototype that's going to blow the competition out of the water once it hits the market. Downloading, e-mail, multimedia wireless, pictures, GPS—that's just the beginning with that little baby. It's called wearable computing. It's like having a desktop in your pocket. Access to any type information, right in the palm of your hand, or even in your eyeglasses—a computer right there in front of your eyes—with a microchip the size of a grain of rice. It's all about MEMS—microelectromechanical systems. It's amazing. I can't even begin to tell you—"

"You don't need to tell anybody anything," Brendan said

as he flipped the phone shut. "If you want to keep the lucrative job I've offered you, you'd be wise to shut up now, Mr. Martin."

"Sorry, boss," Tony said, his freckled face flushing. "I just can't get over all the cool things we're doing here."

"I like enthusiasm," Brendan replied, his black gaze sweeping over Tony with a hint of disdain and respect. "But right now we have to deal with the matter at hand. Now where were we?"

Tony cleared his throat as he sat up straight, his eyes moving over the thick stack of papers in front of him. "I believe Caryn Roark is after something that she thinks Dana has. I also think, based on the careful research I've done and the tons of information you required me to read, that she is somehow moving illegal goods through her many connections both here and in Ireland. And that those illegal goods—drugs maybe—are the main source of her vast income. The questions we have to answer are what does Dana have that Caryn needs, and how is she moving the illegal stuff without being detected?"

"We have to find out those two things," Leo said, the statement dry and controlled. "Okay, so how do we do that? Illegal hacking won't stand up in court."

Brendan tapped his fingers on the polished table. They were in a long conference room just off the control center. Dana couldn't help but notice the crested gold ring on his left hand. The falcon again. In black onyx and diamonds.

Powerful. That word sprang to her mind. She was sitting here with a very powerful man. But a good man.

She hoped. She prayed. But she had to ask. "Did you bring us here hoping to lure your sister out?"

"Yes," Brendan replied, his gaze meeting hers without flinching. "Yes, I did. I've been working with the authorities for months now, ever since I began suspecting that Caryn was up to her old tricks, and that she might be using technology I'd developed to do so. When she started chasing you, I knew this was about more than just winning converts to her church. Thus the need to branch out on my own without the FBI's input. So far, we've heard nothing from her, however."

"Did you leave her a trail?" Tony asked, a nervous tic causing him to blink in a flashing-light fashion. "I mean, for all we know, she's watching us right now."

"She is indeed, or she soon will be," Brendan said, his calm cool making Dana nervous. She just couldn't second-guess this man. And that scared her.

"So, we just sit here and wait?" she asked, wishing she could change the course of time.

"Yes and no," Brendan replied. "She won't dare try to strike me here. She knows this estate too well, which means she knows it's heavily secured. I just wanted her to know you were with me. *Safe* with me."

"And now she does?" Leo asked.

"She knows she's reached a dead end, concerning trying to scare Dana. Now it's time for us to make our move."

"Which is?" Dana asked.

"I think I'll have to send someone into the cult," Brendan said, the dark torment in his eyes telling Dana he really didn't like this idea. "I need to find that missing girl. Her parents are depending on me for that. And I also need to find out what Caryn is after." He leaned forward, his gaze so intense and focused, it was if he didn't even see the others in the room. "I think she's using some of my own employees to get to me. She's sent cult members into some of my factories, to work and to send information back to her. First, I have to prove that. Then I have to figure out how they are communicating and passing information."

"You need a spy," Leo reasoned, nodding.

"Yes. But first I need to find out where her cult members hang out, in which factories and businesses they work. We know she demands they work outside the cult and give her a tithing of sorts. And she has them placed all over the state, maybe even all over the world, but she monitors them on a daily basis.

"I asked Tony to help me with this because, frankly, I don't think I can trust even some of my own people right now. We can't send anyone to the church compound back in Prairie Heart. That would be too obvious. But we can plant someone in one of the factories."

"I have names of most of the members," Tony said, his hands fluttering through the printouts in front of him. "It wasn't easy to do, but I hacked into her mainframe and got into the membership files. Maybe if we connect on some of them—"

"We could find out where they're located," Brendan finished. "I'll have Serena go in to one of the plants and dig for information."

"Who's Serena?" Dana asked.

"Serena Carson, one of my best bodyguards," Brendan told them. "She's been with me about two years now. She just got back from a business trip last night."

"You have a bodyguard named Serena?" Tony asked, grinning. "Can she guard me?"

"She could easily kill you," Brendan shot back. "So don't even mess with her."

"Why does this Serena have to be the one?" Dana asked, something akin to jealousy warring with reason in her system.

"She's trained," Brendan said, lifting up in his leather chair to stare over at her. "She knows what to do."

"What if I were the one?" Dana asked, her eyes meeting

his in a challenge. "The one to go in to some of the factories and ask questions, maybe find that girl and…maybe find out what else is going on?"

"Out of the question," Brendan replied. "They know you, Dana."

"They don't all know me, at least not outside of Prairie Heart. And I didn't socialize with any of them there, either. Only Caryn knows me for sure. I could change my hair, wear heavy makeup. I could easily become someone else."

"Not a good idea, doll face," Tony said, the look of fear in his eyes matching the twitch of his hands on the papers.

"I think it is," Dana replied. "Find me a spot somewhere obscure, somewhere that one of the cult members is located, but Caryn wouldn't dare visit, and I'll go in, get information and we can end this once and for all."

"Dana, the woman is after you," Leo reminded her.

"All the more reason for me to be the one," Dana said. "I need to find out what she wants, and if there is just one person out there willing to talk, we need to find that person."

"And we will," Brendan replied. "But not this way. It's too dangerous for you to even consider, Dana. I won't allow it."

"You can't tell me what to do."

"I am telling you, and if I have to lock you up again, I will do it. You are to remain here with me until we decide our next plan of action, and no matter what we do, you won't be involved in any way."

"Then how am I ever supposed to find out why she's after me?"

"I will find that out," Brendan said. "I have people working on that right now, and with Tony's expertise we'll soon find the holes in her system."

"While I sit here like a target," Dana replied.

"You're safe here."

"Are you sure about that? You just admitted you brought me here to entice your sister."

Leo held up a hand. "The security here is tighter than Fort Knox, Dana."

Dana shot him a skeptical look, then turned to Tony. "Find out more, Tony. Find out how I can best get to her. There has to be a cult member out there, someone who's not so sure about the University Unity Church."

"I don't like this," Tony said, glancing over to Brendan for instructions.

"Find out what you can," Brendan said, getting up. "And I'll send in Serena, just as we planned."

Dana jumped up. "I told you, we have to do this together. Let me help."

Brendan stood, easily towering over her. "The best way you can help me is to remain here. Can't you see? As long as she knows you're here with me we have a chance of drawing her out, of distracting her while we do our work."

"We'd have a better chance if she thinks I'm gone from here," Dana shot back at him. "That girl is still out there somewhere, Brendan. I'm a normal-looking woman who can blend in with a crowded workforce. Let me help you find her."

He gave her a look that told her she couldn't win this argument. "I won't risk that."

In spite of the way his words washed over her like a soft plea, Dana refused to back down. "And I won't sit here forever."

Leo tapped a meaty hand on the table. "We're not accomplishing much by arguing about this."

"*I* won't discuss this any further," Brendan said. Then he turned to Tony. "Keep digging. We'll find something soon."

Dana gave Tony an imploring look. "Let us know what you find."

"Let *me* know," Brendan said, the tone in his voice firm and full of dismissal. "Remember you work for me, Tony."

Tony swallowed, rolled his eyes. "Sorry, Dana, but the man has a point."

Dana didn't respond. She'd just have to find a way to do this without Brendan's consent if it came to that. Somehow. She reminded herself she was here under his protection, but she wasn't under his control.

She also reminded herself that she was used to doing things on her own. Why stop now?

## Chapter Thirteen

"*Conas ta' tu'?*"

The woman sitting at the long mahogany breakfast table looked up and smiled as Brendan stalked across the in-laid Dutch floor tiles lining the sunny room.

"I'm not too good," he replied, his eyes downcast. His hand grabbed for the silver coffee urn set on a two-hundred-year-old hand-carved rosewood buffet centered underneath a Gobelin tapestry of cheerful cherubs. "I'm tired and irritable. I did not sleep well."

"The woman from the prairie, she is quite a handful," his companion said, her warm green eyes full of charm and mirth. "Do you think it was wise to bring her here?"

"No, I think I'm probably going to regret bringing her here." Brendan slumped down onto a Queen Anne chair and spread his long, jeans-clad legs out in front of him. Staring at the tip of one of his black handmade boots, he added, "She's determined, driven by her love for her brother. And it's beginning to soften me."

The woman gave him a gentle gaze. "You did it for the child, remember? So don't tell me you're not soft on the inside."

Brendan took a long, shuddering breath, then took an even longer drink of the blistering hot coffee he demanded each morning. Closing his eyes, he let the warmth of the brew hit his belly before he lifted his head to face his sister across the table.

Gilda Donovan looked exactly like Caryn, her twin. They both shared the same white hair, once dark like his own, now grayed to almost platinum, and the same smooth, fair skin and slender, tall builds. The only difference was in the eyes.

Gilda's were a clear, clean green, as fresh and open as an Irish field, while Caryn's eyes were a cold, calculating blue, as icy and as fathomless as the Atlantic. One was his conscience while the other was his nemesis.

"Aye, I did it for the child," he said at last, some of the fight, the tension, easing out of him. He wouldn't tell his sister that he had also brought Dana here because he wanted to be near her, too. "How is Stephen?"

Gilda's mouth curved into a warm smile. "The boy will be all right. He is occupied with the games and tests you set up for him, and of course, he has his friend, the *leon*."

"Leo will watch over him. He's a good man, in spite of his troubled background. I just hope he won't cave under pressure."

Gilda's eyes lifted at that comment. "He is a gentle man who has seen too much pain, too much suffering. I think he will live up to his name."

Fascinated, Brendan sat up to grab a fat raisin scone, his gaze focused on his sister. "You've talked to him?"

"At length," Gilda said, her eyes going blank. "I had to make sure he could help with the child. You were right about him. He wouldn't hurt Stephen. He's the best one to guard the boy."

Brendan smiled for the first time that morning. "You are impressed with Leo, then?"

Gilda dropped her gaze to her plate. "I didn't say I was impressed. Just curious." She shrugged. "And naturally, concerned that he was qualified to guard Stephen."

Brendan's smile widened. "Gilda, have you been flirting with Leo Ryan?"

Gilda slapped her linen napkin down, then lifted her head to glare at her brother. "I'm too old to flirt, as you well know."

"But you're not too old to look," Brendan shot back, glad to be distracted from the dark deeds of his sleepless night. "Leo is a fine-looking fellow, and he does have a spiritual presence, much like you."

"Don't be a dolt! I'm an old maid in my fifties, with little presence and even less patience."

"With a heart, and a head and feelings," her younger brother said gently. "It's no surprise you get lonely, living here in isolation."

"I might remind you of the same."

That stopped him cold. "I don't need to be reminded of my monklike status, sister. Ms. Barlow has found my weak spot, and she uses it against me with all the zest of a caged lioness."

"Then let the lioness out of the cage, before she opens a wound you might not be able to heal."

Brendan lowered his gaze, staring down at the worn table. "There are some wounds that will never heal."

Gilda inclined her head, her eyes intent on her brother. "Just what is your weak spot?"

Brendan tapped his fingers against the wood. "The child, Gilda. The boy is my weak spot."

"Perhaps that is the place where you'll find your greatest strength."

Brendan stood, restless now. "Don't give me any of your riddles this morning, Gilda. I know how to handle the situation."

"Do you now?"

"Yes, I do. I'm doing this because I have no choice. But she has to remember who is in charge here."

"And who, exactly, is in charge?"

Brendan had to wonder that himself. "Am I making a mistake, Gilda? Should I just turn everything over to the authorities and let justice prevail?"

Gilda rose to stand by her brother as he looked out over the sweep of the colorful gardens on the side of the house that faced away from the lake. A maze of running roses mixed with fiery Japanese elm trees and towering magnolias. A hedge of pink azaleas burst forth like chiffon on a ball gown.

"She is still our sister, Bren. My twin, my mirror, my soul. I can't be a part of it, but I understand why you must do this thing."

"Sometimes I don't understand myself," he said on a soft whisper. "Sometimes I dream that I find her and hold her close and tell her that all is forgiven. And then I wake up in a cold sweat, and I hear the voices calling to me, and I think I see—"

"Don't speak of it," Gilda warned. "Just do what you must to ease this torment. You need to heal, Brendan."

He looked over at her, seeing the goodness and the beauty in her face. "I don't know if I ever can. How can I heal when our sister is so lost?"

"*Dia dhuit,* my brother," Gilda said, her arm on Brendan's. "God be with you, both of you, I pray, throughout this ordeal."

Brendan looked across at her, wondering how she could be so good, so pure, when her twin was so horribly mean and twisted. They both kept children around them, but Gilda was a teacher, a nurturer who ran her own day school, taking care of the local tykes while their parents worked.

Caryn collected frightened children and disillusioned youths as if they were specimens, to be used in her experiments and wildly insane plots. Caryn wanted power and control; while Gilda longed for the children she would never have.

"Sometimes," he said as he stared up at the stone steps carved into a rising hill that lead to a rotunda behind the formal gardens, "sometimes I wonder if this ordeal *will* ever end. I thought it would be over by now. My trip to Prairie Heart was supposed to be my last. I almost…"

"The woman you're helping now stopped you from doing something tragic, Brendan," Gilda reminded him, her eyes bright with concern. "You were being much too reckless. You weren't thinking straight. I'm glad you found Dana Barlow. I'm glad you brought her and her brother here. At least, we can save them and you're safe now, too." Reaching a hand up to his face, she said, "I couldn't bear to lose you."

"You won't," he replied, kissing her hand and giving her a reassuring smile. "I'm too stubborn to die."

She didn't like his false smile. "So you'll sit here and wait. And what about the woman? What will you do with her in the meantime?"

That was a very good question. Especially since Dana had this crazy notion of going undercover inside the cult. He couldn't let her do that, of course. "I'll try to protect her."

"She won't want to stay hidden here forever. And you can't keep secrets from her forever. If she finds out—"

"Maybe I should introduce you to her, for some company. As long as you don't reveal too much to her."

"Bring her out to the school. She's probably good with children, since she's used to dealing with her brother's special needs."

Bren shook his head. "It's too risky."

Gilda looked shocked. "Surely you don't think our sister would dare harm any of my children?"

Brendan turned away from the window, his eyes going black. "I wouldn't put it past her. She's getting desperate now. She'll do whatever it takes."

"Is all of this really that important to her?"

He placed his hands on his sister's shoulders. "You have no idea how important."

"And you won't tell me."

"No, I can't tell you what I don't understand myself."

She chuckled. "You make it sound like a spy novel. What is that line, 'I could tell you, but then I'd have to kill you'?"

"This is no joke, Gilda," he replied sharply. "Caryn just might kill you. She'd kill both of us if she could. As you well know, she's killed before."

A deep sadness colored Gilda's green eyes. "My own sister. What went wrong with her, Bren?"

"God only knows. Our father loved both of our mothers, Gilda. You have to know that. But Caryn never could accept my mother or me. I can only tell you that she hates me. She always has. She's inflicted pain on me before. And now, I suppose, she's seeking her ultimate revenge."

"When do you think she will come?"

He gave his sister a direct stare. "She's watching and waiting right now. As soon as she realizes I have what she's after, she will find a way."

He didn't tell Gilda, but he could feel it in his bones. Caryn was coming; soon she would be near, very near. It wouldn't be long now. All of this would end soon, one way or another.

"I want them captured and brought to me, one way or another," Caryn shouted at the two young men standing in front of her. "Two of my most trusted men dead, and my helicopter destroyed! I can't understand this. Now tell me once again, Ricardo, how exactly did we lose contact with the woman and the boy?"

Ricardo Amodeo, a slender, attractive killer with dark eyes and jet-black hair, stared at his boss and swallowed back the contempt and fear he felt for her. His silent sidekick looked down at an imaginary spot in the white carpet. "The transmitter we planted in the truck went on the blink," he tried to explain again. "Someone must have found it or it got damaged in Kansas City. Then she abandoned the truck and went on the run on foot. We were getting faint signals from another source, but we haven't been able to pinpoint where they're coming from. For now we've lost contact."

Caryn's cold eyes moved over him like a laser, cutting him with each lift of her dark brows. "How long before the computer can begin tracking her again?"

"My contacts are working on it right now," Ricardo said, hoping he could stall her long enough to get some answers. "But you have to understand, the sensor is very temperamental. Conditions have to be just right—body temperature plays a big part in how strong the transmission will become. Sometimes the sensors go into sleep mode—"

Caryn swept around the desk, her whole countenance stern and stony, her white robes impeccably clean and stark with starch. "I want them found! All of them. I do not understand how four people could just disappear. You told me this equipment was state-of-the-art, the latest from WicComCo. You were the one who also told me about this amazing autistic boy, a boy who seems to have disappeared off the face of the earth. I want to know where you failed me."

Ricardo shifted on his black boots. "If we had the missing sensors—and the codes, of course."

"Ah, we all know we need what is rightfully ours, now don't we?" Caryn replied hotly, her jewel-encrusted fingers rising in the air with a dismissive whirl. "And we all know that your one mistake has led to an even bigger mistake."

"The bomb wasn't my idea," Ricardo reminded her, his voice firm in spite of the squeak he felt in his throat muscles. "Someone else ordered that."

Caryn didn't like a subordinate telling her she'd messed up, or that anyone serving her had messed up. She rarely made mistakes. Grabbing Ricardo by the collar of his white cotton shirt, she hissed, "I told you to scare the girl, not blow up a whole building. You sent Derrick, and his inexperience could have very seriously damaged the sensors. He messed up at the general store, and that's why we're in this fix right now. Are all of you incompetent? Perhaps that's why you can't locate the woman or the boy."

"Someone was wearing the chip when they left the apartment," Ricardo told her, his eyes wide and pleading. "The smart sensor was in place and working, along with our other devices. We tracked them to the river and lost them on the back roads. The sensors fade in and out—right now we think they're somewhere near Wichita."

"But without the sensors working properly, we have no way of knowing that," Caryn reminded him. "We have to have all the pieces in place in order for this to work exactly as it should. And from what you've reported to me, that boy is the key. We've failed in our mission."

"We will get the goods back," Ricardo promised her, his eyes centering on her hand still clutched to his collar. "It's just a matter of time."

With a groan of disgust, Caryn pushed him away. "See to it that time doesn't run out, Ricardo. For the woman, or for yourself."

He knew what that meant. He'd seen what Caryn did to those who failed her. "I'll report back within the hour," he assured her. Then he growled at the other man, and they both beat a path to the door.

"Good. I'll be through with evening vespers by then." With a pat of her immaculate platinum-blond hair, Caryn turned to face one of the many mirrors centered around her spacious office. Composing herself, she closed her eyes and willed her frowning expression into one of peace and utter contentment, before she went out to give a pep talk to her flock. "I have to go and bless the children now. You go and do what I pay you to do."

"Yes, Caryn," Ricardo replied, silently thinking the children Caryn held here were anything but blessed. But, hey, she paid good money and he had no other place to go, but back to the streets. He'd stick it out until she gave him everything she'd promised him.

But if he didn't find Dana Barlow, he'd get much more than he'd bargained for. That thought put an urgency in his step as he headed through the maze of offices and secret rooms centered in Caryn's Kansas compound, to the heart of the building where a laboratory of computers and transmitters harbored every possible means of intelligence information.

If Dana Barlow was still on the planet Earth, he and his computer experts would find her. And that brother of hers.

There really was no place to hide from Caryn. Therefore, there was no point in running. He knew that firsthand.

"I have no place to run," Dana told herself and the captive audience of Brendan's ancestors. "I'm stuck here with all of you until I can find a way to get away. Only I can't really get away, because supposedly we're all in this together, whatever this is."

The faces in the portraits stared back at her with mocking, cold eyes. What did they care, anyway? They'd done their time here on Earth. They were free now, gone and dead.

Remembering the restless night she'd had after all the long discussions about Caryn Roark, Dana once again headed to the locked doors of the terrace. She'd already pushed the drapes back to let in some light, but that didn't give her any freedom. Determined to stay calm until she could find a way to do what she had to do, she stared at the trees on the sloping bluff and the glimmering slit of lake below. Even if she could get past Brendan's security system, she was surrounded by rocks and woods. It would be very hard to just walk away from this place.

So she sat, wondering if she'd get to be with Stephen again today, the open curtains and the light from her bedside lamp keeping her from screaming out in frustration. She sat and watched as the sky changed with the dawn from a deep violet-purple to a soft robin-egg blue. A fog shrouded the woods and water like a sheer cloak, but the sun cut through it with delicate but determined rays. Somewhere a hawk cried out, the lonely, piercing sound mirroring Dana's own melancholy feelings.

If she didn't get out of here soon she'd go stark raving mad. Because right now, the only scenes she had to play out in her mind were the ones she'd shared with Brendan Donovan. And she did not like the pictures she saw. She didn't want to remember the softness of his sweet Irish words whispered in her ear, the warmth that enveloped her each time he touched her. She didn't want to remember how he'd taken her through the house to allow her some light and fresh air in the conservatory, where he grew rows and rows of those imposing amaryllis lilies.

"Your sister Caryn has one of these flowers in her office," Dana had told him as she watched him pruning the giant stalks and blossoms.

"I gave it to her," he'd said, his long fingers moving with a lithe dance over the shooting bulbs and voluptuous blossoms. "Once a few years back when things were better between us. That particular one is called *Bordao de Sao Jose*—St. Joseph's Staff. At the time I thought my sister was like a shepherdess. That's what the word *amaryllis* means in Latin."

"I didn't realize amaryllises could grow all year round."

He'd looked up then and straight into her eyes. "They can if you force them."

She didn't want to remember Brendan, except to remind herself that he'd captured her and separated her from her brother, and now he was using her to get to Caryn. Using her like a sitting duck, while he worked on his own agenda. An agenda that left Dana restless and edgy. She thought about her earlier suggestion that he use her undercover on the outside. That was a whole different matter, after all. That was taking action, not sitting twiddling her thumbs.

"Remember how he's treated you," she told her reflection as she got up to look into a mirror across the room. The figure staring back at her in the full-length mirror looked nothing like the Kansas farm girl she'd been a few days ago. No, now she was different.

Her hair, air-dried by the fire, hung wild and riotous around her face and shoulders. Her eyes stared sleep-rimmed and suspicious, wide and questioning, back at her image. She'd lost weight from being on the run.

It was time to stop running. Time to convince Brendan that she wouldn't just sit still and wait. If he'd just let her out of this room for more than a few minutes at a time, she'd be better off.

She still couldn't be sure if he was truly protecting her, or just holding her here to get at Caryn. Maybe it was a little of both. And she'd really like to know why he wanted to confront his own sister so badly.

What could a sister do to a brother to cause so much pain and distrust?

She'd thought of a dozen reasons to distrust Brendan herself. But each time she decided she couldn't trust him, she'd remember his tenderness, his time spent with Stephen. Surely it wasn't all an act. If he wanted to use her, he could easily agree to put her out there as a lure for Caryn. And he refused to even consider that. No, instead he'd just held her trapped here.

Dana didn't like it, but she had to cling to the hope that Brendan really was protecting her and her brother. Even if she didn't agree with or understand his methods, at least she had to give him credit for getting her away from Caryn's thugs. But now it was time to move on, time to get this over with so her life—so Stephen's life—could go back to normal.

"I have to convince him to let me do this."

Anxious and needing to stay busy, she straightened the big bed she'd lost so much sleep in, an image of Bren standing there at the foot of the bed in the dark making her hurry about her work. Then she tidied up the bathroom, not daring to touch that big, blooming belladonna, and the sitting area. Pulling a chair up to the parted curtains, she planned to sit and think, maybe pray hard, until he came again. She hadn't had that luxury for some time now—just to sit and think. She didn't want to read, even though the room was well stocked with an array of works, from Samuel Beckett to Thomas Wolfe. Someone was sure the serious literature type.

Not Brendan, surely. When did that man have time to read? No, he was too busy chasing around the world, kidnapping farm women and trying to get back at his crazy sister.

And there was that burning question again. Why would a brother and sister hate each other so much?

The click of the door caused Dana to spin around, her eyes out of focus from staring at the bright outside. Through the muted light of the room, she saw a figure coming toward her. A figure with clipped white hair, a slender woman wearing a long flowing dress, carrying a tray.

Dana's heart plunged to the floor. Bringing a hand up to her mouth, she tried to speak, to call out, but the words wouldn't come. It couldn't be. This simply couldn't be happening.

But it was. Caryn was coming toward her, a serene smile tipping her lips, a calm look centered in her eyes. She looked different without her white robes, but she was the same.

And Dana had nowhere to run. There was only one thing left to do. She found her voice and screamed with all her might, as loud as she possibly could.

Then she headed right for Caryn, intent on knocking the woman down so she could escape.

## Chapter Fourteen

Before Dana could reach her, the woman stepped aside to block the doorway, a frightened look on her face. Dana kept coming and screaming, intent on getting past Caryn. As she pushed past the woman, the tray slipped and clattered to the floor, the sound of breaking china chasing Dana's scream down the corridors of the rambling house.

"Brendan?" Dana called out, panicky and panting. Then she turned to face the woman. "You won't get away with this, neither of you. I promise you somehow I'll find a way to get back at both of you."

The woman actually reached out a hand to Dana. "Please, stay calm, dear. I'm so sorry—"

"Sorry!" Dana rolled her eyes and regained some of her courage and composure. "Is that what you came to tell me? That you're sorry for what you've done. A little late now, don't you think? Where's my brother?"

"Please, let me explain," the woman began, her eyes wide with concern. Her very green eyes.

Dana noticed the change, but decided Caryn was so full of tricks, she wouldn't put it past her to change her eye color every day of the week. "Yes, why don't you explain? I'd really appreciate that." Then, another scream. "Brendan, where are you?"

She heard footsteps coming up the long hallway, and anxious to get past the woman, waited at the partially opened door. Brendan ran right into her arms, his eyes so dark and deadly, she was halted by the sheer force of his gaze. A stunning, black-haired woman followed him, a sleek, slim-nosed gun raised between her long-nailed fingers.

"What is going on?" Brendan said as he pulled Dana back into the room, his eyes moving over her face with that dark, intense look. He checked her over, a sigh of relief leaving his body when he saw she wasn't physically hurt.

"She's here," Dana said, pointing to the woman, her finger shaking, her head bobbing. "Are you happy now? You got her to come after me."

Brendan looked around to see Gilda standing there, embarrassed and almost as scared as Dana looked.

"Sister!" he said, his eyes burning fire. "Gilda, what were you thinking?"

"I wasn't," his sister replied evenly. "I wasn't thinking. I thought she knew. I thought you'd explained. I'm so sorry. I—I just wanted to talk to her, comfort her."

Brendan flicked his wrist at the attractive woman holding the gun. "It's all right, Serena. Go back to your post."

The woman, dressed in black, nodded and stalked away like a lady warrior on the prowl.

"Gilda?" Dana huffed a breath, took another look at the woman standing by her. "Another alias, Caryn? You really are in cahoots with each other, aren't you?"

Brendan placed both of his hands on Dana's arms. In spite of her attempts at bravado, he could feel the trembling that rumbled through her body. "Dana, listen to me. This is my sister, Gilda. My *other* sister. This is not Caryn."

Dana glared up at him as if he'd gone daft. "You people are sick, really sick. Do you actually expect me to believe you?"

"He's telling the truth, *cara*," Gilda said, her head slightly bowed, her hands wrapped together in a demure fashion. "I am his sister. I'm Caryn's twin, and I mean you no harm. I simply came to bring you some breakfast and to keep you company. I didn't realize that you didn't know we were twins."

Dana threw back her head and howled with near-hysterical laughter. "Oh, that's a good one. So you're the good twin, right? When will this end?" Turning on Brendan, she shouted, "And when will you tell me the truth!"

"Gilda wouldn't hurt you," Brendan tried to explain, his hands on her shoulders keeping her steady. "My sister is the kindest, most gentle woman in all of Kansas."

Dana stopped laughing to frown up at him. "So, Caryn's the classic evil twin, huh?"

"Yes." Brendan let her go then, his dark eyes whirling with torment. "She is very troubled and conniving. But Gilda is the opposite. She is—"

"A saint, no doubt," Dana interrupted, her eyes moving over his face with disgust. "I'm really tired of your games. You deliberately sent her to scare me, didn't you, Brendan? Is this my punishment for daring to question you?"

Brendan debated whether to shake her or simply take her into his arms. "I did not send her to scare you, and I am not punishing you. We thought you might need some company, but I had planned on introducing you two later."

"What I need," Dana said, spitting each word at him, "is to get out here. I want my brother away from all of you!"

"Stephen is safe," Gilda told her, the compassion in her voice catching Dana's attention along with the mention of her brother. "He's taking his medication right on schedule and we're making sure he has structure and routine in his life."

Shocked, Dana could only stare at the woman. "How do you know about his medicine and his routine?"

Brendan nodded to his sister to speak. Gilda touched Dana on the arm. "My brother made sure he had all the proper information on all of you, before he brought you here. He will do nothing to harm your brother. Indeed, it is because of the child that Brendan is involved in this, and I'm afraid he was forced to bring you here for your own protection."

"Yeah, I've heard that line," Dana said, noticing the dark look of warning that passed through Brendan's eyes. Then her voice cracking, she asked, "Stephen is all right, isn't he?"

"He's in the gameroom again," Brendan said, the compassion in his words melting some of Dana's anger. "And Leo is with him, just as yesterday. They were playing chess last time I checked on them."

Dana breathed a sigh of relief. "And what about Tony? I haven't talked to him today."

Brendan didn't seem to want to answer, but he did. "He's doing research so we can find a way into the cult. He seems to be enjoying himself, in spite of the serious nature of his duties."

"Enjoying himself?" Dana decided Brendan was telling the truth about that at least. "Well, that makes sense. Tony's happy when he's creating new technology or hacking away at someone else's." She relaxed a bit, her eyes on the woman who looked so much like Caryn. "And what has Tony found?"

"It's complicated," Brendan finally told her. "And that's why it's better to keep all of you separated for a little while longer."

"And ignorant, so you can call the shots, no doubt."

"No, so you won't have information that could hurt you. You don't understand the implications involved here, Dana."

She frowned at him, confusion causing her to doubt her own sanity. "You're right there, and since you don't trust me enough to explain the whole story to me, I can't very well put the puzzle together—except that Caryn is after me." She looked back at Gilda. "Can *you* tell me what Caryn's done? Why is your brother so intent on getting to her?"

"I can't talk about that," Gilda said, shaking her head. "I can only tell you that Brendan has your best interest at heart."

"You scared me," Dana admitted, leaning against the wall to take a long breath. "I can't believe this—you really are her twin?"

"Yes. Brendan is our half brother."

At yet another warning look in Brendan's eyes, Dana stood straight again. "Really? So you had different mothers?"

"I have to get back to my work," Gilda said, averting her eyes. "I'm so sorry I startled you, Dana."

"Nothing around here surprises me anymore," Dana said, watching as the woman hurried down the long corridor. "Want to explain, Bren, about the half-brother thing?"

"Not yet."

Dana stepped close, her finger jabbing his chest. "How can I help you if you won't tell me *everything?*"

He swiped a hand down his face, then leaned close. "The less I say, the better. We're still not sure how Caryn tracked you as far as she did. She might have spies here on my staff. There might be bugs—"

"I thought you said this place was a fortress."

"It is, for everyone who has access to it. But if one person inside is on her payroll—"

Dana shook her head, the action causing chestnut curls to spill around her face. "This is too weird. Bugs? Spies? I must have gotten lost somewhere in a really bad spy movie."

Anger flared in Brendan's eyes. "Would you have rather I left you running around Kansas so the FBI could bring terrorist charges against you?"

"Terrorist charges? Now you are kidding, right?"

Brendan touched a hand to her hair. "They think you planted the bomb, Dana. They found evidence in your truck. And you ran. That automatically makes you look like a suspect. Given that and Caryn's tendency to put a spin on things so that she's in the clear, you'd be up against more than just her wrath if you leave here."

Dana found the nearest chair and sat down, defeated. Leo had told her as much, but she didn't want to believe it. "That's insane."

"My sister *is* insane," Brendan said, the growl in his words bringing her head up. "And she has to be stopped, before it's too late."

"When will it be too late?" She had to know.

"Enough!" Brendan said, turning to stare down at the broken dishes inside her room. "I'll call Lara to bring another tray of food."

"Don't bother. I'm not hungry." Maybe a hunger strike would get her somewhere, Dana decided.

Brendan ignored her protests as he punched in codes on an intercom system on the wall and ordered another tray brought up.

"Don't do this," he said as he urged her into a chair with one strong hand on her wrist. "I've seen your appetite. I know you can eat."

It didn't help that her stomach chose that particular moment to growl greedily. Maybe a hunger strike wasn't the answer, after all. "Okay, I could use some coffee," she admitted. "And maybe some more of that wonderful bread. Lara told me that Gilda makes it. It's very good."

"Every day she bakes," Brendan said, his smile relaxing his face, his hand still on her arm. "I am truly sorry we frightened you. But Gilda is nothing like Caryn. She's lived here with me for a few years now. After Caryn became so erratic and volatile, I didn't want Gilda in Ireland by herself, so I brought her here. Gilda never married. I'm all she has left."

Dana stared up at him, then said, "The eyes are different. Caryn's are so cold, so blank." When she saw the pain passing through Brendan's eyes, she quickly added, "It must be hard to see something like this happening to someone you once cared about."

Brendan nodded. "Yes, Caryn is still our sister. But she drifted away from us, got involved in radical groups back in Ireland. Then when our father died...well, Caryn never quite got over his death. This has been a great source of turmoil for many years now. Especially for Gilda."

"Tell me about Gilda," Dana said on a casual note, hoping he'd open up to her at last. She didn't dare ask what had happened to their mothers. Apparently they were out of the picture, either dead or estranged.

"She runs a day school located on the estate grounds."

"She works with children?" It struck Dana as ironic that both of Brendan's sisters were involved with children. She shuddered, then saw him watching her.

He'd obviously read her mind. He stood, away from Dana, his captivating eyes holding her own. "This will be over soon, I promise."

"And then what?" she asked, the very real fear in her voice echoing across the room. "Do I go back to being a Kansas farm girl? Does Stephen go back to track and football and Little League with Special Olympics? Or do I go to prison for something I didn't do?"

"I'll find the proof to show the FBI that you weren't involved in the bombing."

"Oh, really? And how, Brendan? Will you pull a few strings, throw your weight around?"

"Don't," he said as he sank down on his knees in front of

her chair, his hand coming up of its own accord to stroke her hair again. "You have to take this seriously, Dana."

"Oh, I'm being serious. I'm in serious trouble here, and you're the only one I can turn to. But then, you know that already, don't you?"

He dropped his hand, looked away. "And you find that highly distasteful, no doubt."

"No," she admitted. "I think you are a kind man. A tormented, obsessed man, obviously, but you've been mostly kind to me. And to Stephen. Right now, I need you as much as you need me. I want to do my part in all of this. So please, don't keep me locked up here."

He turned and for a minute she thought she saw real need there in his blue-black eyes, but whatever she'd seen was fleeting. Gone, to be replaced by that sinister, blank stare. "You're quite right there, love. We do need each other. And you're doing exactly what you need to do right now. You're under my protection so that means we're stuck with each other. And that means you have to stay locked safely inside these walls—with me."

"You'll regret that decision."

Wanting to test her regarding that theory, Brendan stayed on his knees and leaned close again, so she was forced to look at him. What he saw there in those pure green eyes made him want to protect her even more. Her eyes held a mixture of fear and trust, a confusion between hope and war. She didn't understand him at all. She didn't trust him at all. And she really didn't need him. Or at least she didn't think she did.

Instead of getting caught in an emotional tangle, he decided to persuade her to follow his instructions. "Pity, we can't agree on how to spend our forced time together. There are so many better ways to spend time than bickering and fighting." He lifted her chin with one finger. "Don't you agree, Dana?"

Dana's lips parted as she gripped the brocade arms of her chair. He could tell she was wary of being tricked, even more wary of being vulnerable.

"I don't want to bicker and fight, Brendan. I only want to help. We need to work together. I can help you if you'll just let me go out there and find one cult member, someone who's willing to talk. You said yourself that some of them work in your factories."

"I told you no," he said, wondering when she'd turned the tables on him. "What good is keeping you locked up safely here if you insist on exposing yourself to that kind of danger?"

"My brother *would* be safe here," she said, the determination in her expression endearing her to Brendan even more, and causing him no small amount of guilt. "And that's all I need from you. If you can continue to protect Stephen, I can go out there and help you with the rest."

"I don't like this idea."

"But you'll think about it?"

"I don't know."

He didn't know what to do with her, honestly. Except right now that emotional tug was back. And because he did feel so low about what he was doing, he wanted to test her reaction to that, too.

She waited, her eyes questioning as he leaned in to kiss her. It was a gentle, tentative kiss, since he wasn't so sure about doing this. He wanted his touch to be warm and reassuring to her, even if she couldn't give in to him completely.

But Dana surprised him yet again by returning his kiss. She fell against him, and Brendan couldn't resist the need to pull her close and hold her in his arms. She tasted of morning and tears. And he tasted the fear of emotion again.

"Dana," he said, lip against lip. "Dana."

Somewhere a click sounded. Brendan brought his head up at about the same time the door swung open. Lara entered from the hallway, her eyes centered on the tray she carried. By the time she looked up with expectant eyes, Brendan was standing by the fireplace, one hand tightly gripping the marble mantel, and Dana was sitting up in the chair with such a prim air, she looked as innocent as a schoolgirl, blush and all.

"Good morning, Mr. Donovan, Miss Barlow," Lara said on a cheerful note, so intent on her mission she noticed nothing unusual. "It's sure dark in here. Should I open the curtains a little more?"

"Yes," from Dana.

"No," from Brendan.

"Why not?" Dana asked, her mind still humming from his kiss, his touch. "I'll turn into a mole cooped up in here."

"It's too risky," he said underneath his breath. Then to Lara, "Miss Barlow is still tired. She needs to rest a bit more. And be careful there, Lara. We had an accident."

Lara bobbed her head and put the tray down, then waited, a hesitant smile forming on her pink lips. "Shall I clean up this broken china?"

"That's all for now, Lara," Brendan said with a flick of his wrist, every bit the lord of the manor. "You can send someone from the kitchen to clear that away."

"Thank you," Dana called as the girl hurried out of the room. Then she jumped up to face Brendan. "You can't expect me to stay locked up here again all day. I'll go crazy. Please, Bren, don't do this to me. Put me to work, or let me sit with Stephen, at least."

She watched as he hardened himself to her plea by turning his back, while *she* remembered his lips kissing her. She wasn't going to make this easy. "You aren't a cruel man, Bren. I believe that with all my heart. Your kiss didn't feel cruel. It felt...right."

He stomped to the door, looking intent on going about his work. But he stopped, one hand on the knob, his head down. "Eat your breakfast. I'll send up some magazines and some more books, and maybe some music to entertain you until— until I can break away and come back for you. What would you like to read?"

"Houdini!" Dana shouted, mad at herself as well as him. He's just kissed her as if he meant it. Now he was back to being the boss.

Ignoring her fit of tantrum, he threw a look of steel over his shoulder. "Take a nice long bath, do aerobics, do needlepoint for all I care, but you will not leave this room until I say so."

"Or until you can trust me," she added, the realization that he didn't cutting off her breath and leaving her at odds. What did it matter whether he trusted her or not? She certainly didn't trust him. "You actually think I can get past all your gadgets and guards, Brendan?"

Brendan inclined his head ever so slightly. "You're a very smart woman. I'm sorry, Dana, but I have to cover all the angles. I can't risk the distraction of you going off on your own."

"You *don't* have a heart," she said, her eyes sparkling with a clear green anger. "If you did, you'd let me out of this prison."

He stood with a hand braced on the heavy door, hesitancy evident in his expression. Finally he nodded. "I'll come back for you in an hour," he replied as he opened the door. "I've got pressing business to attend to first, I told you."

"Such as?"

"Nothing for you to be concerned about."

"I'll scream," she threatened, feeling childish but decidedly better.

"I doubt anyone would notice. Besides, others have tried to get through my system. They never succeed."

"So you've held others here?"

He had to grin at that. "Not I. I've had Serena test the system on numerous occasions. But some of my ancestors have…. A colorful history. I think they probably did hold people here against their will."

"Stay and tell me about them, at least. Maybe that's where Caryn gets her domineering ways."

"I can't discuss that with you. I can't be distracted, Dana. One slip, and Caryn will win. *Again.*"

Dana saw the grim expression masking his features as he let that last word slip out in a whisper. So Caryn had wronged him once before. This was about much more than just rescuing teens from a dangerous cult.

"What did she do to you, Bren?"

"I can't talk about it—any of it," he said, a flash of anger making his eyes turn to blue-gray. "Just be ready in an hour. Then we'll see where we stand."

Dana watched as he left, the click of the door echoing after him. Then she sank back down on the chair, hoping that maybe she was finally making some progress with him. But he'd kissed her. Touching her lips, she thought of how soft and gentle he'd been, how that one sweetly intense moment had bonded them in such an intimate way. Had that been deliberate, to throw her into turmoil?

He'd said they would see where they stood. Did he mean with his sister? Or did he mean with that kiss?

Caryn stared across at the sobbing, dark-haired young girl centered in the chair on the other side of her desk. "Samantha, did you call your mother last night?"

The girl refused to look at her, a sure sign that she was hiding something.

"I can't help you, dear, if you don't tell me the truth. Remember, we don't allow personal phone calls here. It interferes with your spiritual awakening. We want our wards to be studious and devoted. Outside forces can confuse the issue. Do you understand?"

The girl started crying all over again. "I miss my mother. I want to go home."

Caryn looked at the picture of her own parents sitting on the edge of her marble-topped desk. Studying the aged photo, she felt the annoying pick of tears forming in her eyes. But she took a breath and willed the tears away. She would not cry for them ever again. Especially her beloved father. He'd betrayed her in the worst sort of way. He'd fathered an illegitimate son.

She'd feel no sympathy for her dead father.

Nor would she feel any sympathy for this pathetic young girl who'd turned to her for help. How dare the child question her.

"But you chose to run away," Caryn reminded the girl. Coming around the desk, she took Samantha's trembling hand in hers. "You're scared. I know how that feels. But we will take care of you here, as long as you obey me and follow the rules. And the rules clearly state there is to be no contact with the outside world, unless it is approved by me."

"Can't I just call her once a week?"

Caryn tamped down the urge to slap the whimpering girl. "Why? So she will worry about you? So she will scream at you? Didn't she do that enough when you were living at home?"

"We had a really bad fight, but now I want to go back," the girl said, lifting her tear-filled eyes. "She said I could come home. She even said my father wants me home. Please?"

Caryn shook her head, her hand still on the girl's arm. "You can't believe their lies, Samantha. They only want you back there so they can control you. Don't you remember the sense of freedom and peace you felt when you came here?"

"I think they're willing to listen to my side of things now," Samantha said, tears streaming down her face. "Can't we just talk to them? Maybe see if they'd like to attend services here sometime?"

"No," Caryn said, taking Samantha up from the chair with a yank of her arm. "Now stop this crying and go and do your work. And I expect you to be at evening vespers. I think you might need to do some extra chores, to clear your head."

"I'm tired," the girl replied through a whisper. "I missed lunch today."

"That's because I had to schedule this session, to discipline you. If you can't get in the right frame of mind by supper time, you'll miss that meal, too."

The girl stood up, cowering, her shoulders drooping. "Stand up straight," Caryn said, the anger slipping out in spite of her need to stay serene and in control. "I can't stand to see a person slouching."

"I'm sorry," Samantha said, her eyes downcast. "Can— may I go now?"

Caryn waved a hand in dismissal. "Yes, go and pout about missing your mommy. Honestly, I feel so unappreciated here. I've given you food and shelter, and all I ask in return is a little loyalty."

"I've been loyal," Samantha said, moving toward the door. "I've done everything you asked, but I'll try to do better."

"Well, that's more like it." Caryn patted her hair, then smiled. "I think I'll let you lead us in prayer tonight, starting with yourself. You need lots of prayers. You are a very troubled girl. We might have to put you in seclusion and counseling if this continues."

"I'll be fine now," Samantha said, her eyes going wide with a fear that sent a thrill of power through Caryn's system. No one wanted to be put into seclusion. It messed with the mind, but it worked so well as a means of discipline and decorum, Caryn had to use it at times. Only when she was absolutely forced to do so.

"I thought so," Caryn said as she watched the girl hurry out of her office, the door closing softly behind her.

A few minutes later, a knock at the door had Caryn gritting her teeth. "What now?"

Ricardo came in. "I have news regarding Dana Barlow."

"Well?"

"You won't like it."

Caryn stalked the cool confines of her inner chamber, her white linen robes billowing out behind her like the petals of a lily following the shift of the wind. "Are you sure, very sure, of this information, Ricardo? Because I don't want to hear it if it isn't accurate. I don't have time to waste on rumors."

"We have witnesses. We have statements from several different people," Ricardo replied, his whole body standing at attention, his expression smug as he became the bearer of news, any news, to please the woman he served. Only he feared this bit of news would make her formidable temper spark even higher. Which was why he was hedging, saving the best, or in this case the worst, for last. "I have every reason to believe someone had taken Dana Barlow."

"Who, then?" Caryn asked, her sharp gaze cutting into his face like a paper shredder. "Do you have a name for me, Ricardo? Was it the FBI, or the ATF people maybe?"

"They could be in on it," he said, knowing she'd want to have the complete report, with graphic pictures.

"'Could be'?" Her hard eyes flashed like ice cubes. "I don't want 'could be.' I want to know details, exact, specific details. I want something concrete. You do understand me, now don't you, Ricardo?"

"I do." He shifted, the smug expression he mustered belying the shaking in his pulse. "We're still working on things, but I have every reason to believe—"

Caryn gave an impatient lift of her shoulders, then moved behind her desk again, folding her jeweled hands and arms across her body. "Tell me what you know. Now!"

Ricardo hunkered down for the inevitable onslaught of foul language that was sure to follow the information he was about to give his boss. "We believe she's with your brother."

Caryn dropped her hands to her sides, fists clenching so tightly, Ricardo could see the white in her knuckles and the blue in the veins lining her slender hands. He watched as her cold gaze flickered across the lone picture on her desk, then back to him. "What did you say?"

"We believe Brendan Donovan has Dana Barlow with him—at that big estate near Wichita." He didn't tell her that he had a source who'd verified this without a doubt. Ricardo had to tread very lightly here, to make sure his volatile boss didn't do anything too rash, too soon.

"Castle Donovan," Caryn said on a soft whisper. The anger came swift and hot, flashing like lightning across the immaculate enclosure of Caryn's shimmering chamber as she reached out a hand to the nearest object, which happened to be a five-hundred-dollar porcelain vase, and sent it flying across the white carpet to land against the gray stone of a massive fireplace. The vase, once stark and domineering in its expressive beauty, now lay shattered in a million sharp-edged pieces.

Ricardo swallowed, thinking that could easily be him lying there, broken. He remembered the boy from California who'd botched getting the shoes from that crazy old woman at the store. Mixed-up, confused, terrified of the storm, the boy had gotten the wrong shoes. A fatal mistake for that young boy, especially since Caryn had, as a second chance, also sent him to Kansas City to find Dana. What was his name—Derrick? Yeah, Derrick had gotten carried away. In an attempt to make up for his mistake with the shoes, in an attempt to impress Caryn, Derrick had decided to scare them with a homemade bomb. But he'd made the bomb too powerful. Blew it. Literally.

Derrick was gone now, vanished, his parts scattered to the wind. Yeah, when Caryn wanted to get rid of something, or someone, she didn't just destroy the object of her wrath. She made sure the parts could never be put back together again. Ever.

She would do that even with her own brother. She'd tried once before, and she'd come close to succeeding. Only, Brendan Donovan was made of tougher stuff. And he'd been a relentless pursuer ever since. Now he was coming back for more. And Ricardo didn't want to be around when these two finally came face-to-face again.

"Why has my brother become involved in this?" Caryn asked, her pacing lifting her body in long, angry strides as she moved like a mad bird around the office. "I'm done with him. I'm done with Ireland. And I want to know why he's suddenly interfering with everything I've worked so hard to build! He shouldn't have a clue as to what we're about here, should he? Why does *he* have Dana Barlow, Ricardo? And why didn't *someone* let me know sooner?"

Ricardo gave what he hoped was a nonchalant shrug, and decided to answer only the first question. "Well, your brother always did have an eye for a pretty lady."

That earned him a piercing slap that sent him reeling back about two feet. Bringing his hand to his bloody lip, Ricardo glared at Caryn, then looked away when her smoldering gaze centered on him with such malice, he wanted to turn and run away from here for good.

"Dana Barlow may be pretty, but she's also very stupid. She should not have gotten herself in the middle of this. And she'd better not be involved with my brother. She should have just handed over her land like a good little farm girl. If she'd done that, just granted me that one simple request, her little brother wouldn't be in so much danger right now."

Backing up to a safe distance, Ricardo reminded her, "Well, at least you've got her on the run."

Caryn nodded at that, then went to the cushiony white leather chair behind her ornate desk. "Yes, and in a matter of days, I should not only have the information we need, but I will also own the deed to her land."

Uh-oh. Ricardo swallowed again. "Uh, Caryn, there's something you need to know about that land."

Caryn's head shot up. "Oh, and what's that?"

"Someone beat you to that. Our records from the bank show that someone made a substantial payment on Dana's mortgage a few days after the fire. Enough to pay the whole thing off. The land's still in her name, and she owns it free and clear."

Caryn didn't move a muscle, but Ricardo could see the slight twitching in her jawline as she held her teeth clenched tightly together, her bright eyes working like a monitor as she did some fast headwork.

"Brendan," she said at last on a whisper filled with enough hate and anger to walk across the room. "He must have paid off the debt on the land." She drummed her fingers on the desk, her cold eyes staring at the picture of her parents. "He sure has gone to a lot of trouble for this woman. That means he suspects something. Someone has leaked information to my brother." Slapping a hand against the back of a leather chair, she gave Ricardo a sly look. "Don't tell me we have a double agent working at the castle."

"Our source there is secure," Ricardo replied. "And gathering more information as we speak."

"What is my brother up to. That's what I want to know."

"He could just be becoming more bold," Ricardo pointed out. "He might not know anything for sure."

"He wants to sabotage me," Caryn replied, her words low. "He doesn't understand the way of things here. He thinks I'm out to hurt people. But I only want what's best for all my children."

Ricardo saw the flash of wrath in her eyes, just before she patted her platinum-haired head, her chin held at a regal angle. "Get the jet fueled and ready, Ricardo. In a couple of days we're going on a little trip."

"Okay. Where should I tell the pilot we're headed?"

Caryn shot him a direct look, her glance pinning him to the carpet threads. "To Wichita, of course. I do believe it's time for a tender reunion with my long-lost brother and saintly sister. It's high time I visit the Castle Donovan."

"What are we going to do?"

"Do? What should *you* do? That's the question you should be asking right now." She advanced toward him, her breath heaving, the harsh lines of her face slashing through the heavy foundation she wore. "You should say your prayers, for starters. Because I think you will soon be out of a job. And then, you should try to figure out a way to get Dana Barlow away from my dear half brother."

"What are you going to do when you get there?" Ricardo, for self-serving purposes, had to ask.

"I'm going to kill him," she replied calmly. Then she turned to leave the room.

"Where are you going right now?" Ricardo asked, afraid of what she might do next, and very afraid that it might involve him.

Caryn turned to face him, a serene smile on her pale face. "Why, I'm going into the sanctuary for evening vespers. After all, it's so important that the children don't miss the message, not even for one day. I want to send them off to bed thinking only of how much I love them."

"Right," Ricardo said, the one word not very convincing. Then he leaned forward. "About Brendan Donovan, you might remember he is a very powerful man."

Caryn turned and pushed him until he was at the door. "Get out. Get out!" Shoving him into the hallway, she shouted after him. "Brendan will never, ever be powerful enough to stop me. Never." Then she slammed the door shut.

Somehow her brother had done it again, Caryn thought as she leaned against the door to control herself. He'd outwitted her. She'd been so very careful, and until that Barlow woman had caught her brother's eye, things had been going very smoothly. And how *had* that happened? How did Brendan even know Dana Barlow?

Caryn pushed off the door, a low groan of rage lifting up from her stomach. Brendan couldn't get to the boy before she did. But even now, her brother might have things figured out. Brendan would know exactly what to do to test the boy, to make sure the child truly was as smart as everyone said.

Brendan would have to pay for this, of course. He'd interfered with her operation here for too, too long. Him and his self-righteous, patronizing ways. She wouldn't let him ruin this for her, too.

"Maybe it is time for Samantha to go home," she said out loud, her heart beat calming to a soft flutter like a tired butterfly as she thought of a surefire way to get back at her brother. "Maybe it's time she went home to her overbearing, overworked mother and cowardly father. In a body bag. That would surely teach my baby brother a lesson. Someone has to pay. It's only fair."

Deciding that was the perfect plan, she picked up the phone and gave the order. Then she sat down, closed her eyes and said a prayer for all involved.

They would all need prayer now, more than ever.

## Chapter Fifteen

Dana stared at the big bed, thinking she did not want to go to sleep tonight, not with all these thoughts of Brendan whirling around in her mind. True to his word, he'd let her spend some time with Stephen today. And true to his word, Brendan had been right about her brother. Stephen was doing great here, better than ever. He was being entertained, stimulated, controlled and constantly watched by experienced, expert people who seemed intent only on what was best for Stephen. Her brother loved Leo and he loved Gilda, too. He couldn't stop talking about all the new people in his life. Seeing him so happy had brought a lump to Dana's throat. What would happen when she had to take him away from this safe haven?

Pushing those thoughts out of her mind, Dana knew she had Brendan and his millions to thank for Stephen's improved life-style, at least. But right now she didn't feel so thankful because while he'd been extremely accommodating toward her brother, Brendan had excluded *her* from the endless meetings in that dungeon room he called a control center. Since Brendan didn't want her in on his plans, she'd come up with a few of her own. She just wasn't sure which one she was going to use.

Right now, however, she had some research to study and mull over, thanks to Tony. Somehow her friend had known she needed to stay focused and busy. So he'd finagled that sweet and gullible Lara into bringing Dana a stack of magazines. But not just any magazines. Tony had hidden some very interesting trade magazines and Internet articles underneath the stack of home decor and fashion publications.

"Read these," he'd scrawled in Sharpie ink on the front of one of the magazines. "All of them." Then, "We're all okay, so don't worry. Tony."

Dana rarely had time to read back home. But she'd caught up on that tonight. Fascinating, since the magazine articles were from techno trade journals, written and produced by insider experts and public relations and technology publishers. Fascinating, since several of the articles within the pages of the magazines were about none other than the man himself: Brendan Donovan.

A scrapper. Rising throughout the ranks of the business world to become an entrepreneur who rivaled the likes of Bill Gates and Ted Turner. The Irish Whiz Kid who'd taken an old family name, with a lineage dating back to the High Kings of Tara, and made it into a modern icon, complete with the respect of his peers and the envy of those lesser mortals trying to rally behind him. Brendan had taken old money and made it into new, with a little Irish luck and a whole lot of what the Irish called *de'anamh*, doing and making.

Educated in America, at Harvard and MIT, no less, and having a head for business, he had begun buying up small, struggling companies straight out of college. With the help of some computer buddies from MIT, he first developed Donovan Industries, starting out with technology in Ireland, then eventually settling in Kansas—apparently because his mother been born and raised there—and adding the aircraft factory and the sporting goods company, all under the new name of Wichita Communications Company.

Listed as one of the hundred richest men in the world, Brendan Donovan held a distinct power within the international business arena and seemed to enjoy the battle to stay on top. Lately, however, his only battles concerned developing new technology before anyone else beat him to it, and fighting off those who would be spies within his organization. It was all very top secret, of course. Which was why it was hard to find out the real story on Brendan Donovan. Of course, there was no mention of his clandestine work in saving people from his sister's dangerous cult.

He had homes in America and Ireland, and several other exotic locations around the globe. And he had once been somewhat of a playboy, from what the older editions of the magazine's social section showed. In his early days as a rising star, he was usually pictured with a beautiful woman on his arm. A different flavor for each month, it would seem. Dana had been through several early editions of the magazine, and each time Brendan was featured, he had a different calendar girl, standing tall and glittery by his side. Now, remembering the lovely woman who'd burst into the room earlier with him, the woman he'd called Serena, the woman who obviously served as a bodyguard and more perhaps, Dana frowned.

"Yes, I'm learning so much about you, Bren."

Well, the way he rescued and bossed and kissed, she could understand women being attracted to him. Needing to know more, she picked up the next magazine to read tidbits about her captor. His womanizing days had apparently changed in the past few years, though. The boss had become reclusive and mysterious over time, and now preferred to stay out of the limelight. So much so, that the majority of his own employees didn't even know they worked for him. *Just like Tony.*

She skimmed through several more magazines, then found other, more recent pictures of Brendan. After reading the caption of one, she began to understand part of why he'd changed. One picture in particular, from a magazine dated a few years back, held her attention. The dark-haired woman standing by his side was stunning, beautiful, her eyes glowing as she stared up at Brendan. They were dressed in black-tie elegance, surrounded by celebrities and the elite at a fund-raiser party for some noble cause, held in New York.

And the woman was listed as his wife. Mrs. Brendan Donovan. The caption read, "Brendan Donovan with his lovely new bride, Shannon."

Shannon. Brendan had—still had maybe—a wife named Shannon.

Which was only one of the reasons Dana felt as if she'd been struck with a physical blow. Where was the beautiful Shannon, anyway, while her wayward husband played his little espionage games? While her husband kissed another woman and made that woman feel as if she were the only woman alive?

Dana stood and looked at herself in the mirror, disgust evident in her frown. Actually she was more angry at herself than Brendan. She'd flirted with him, partly in an effort to save herself and Stephen, partly because it had felt so good, so right.

But he was a married man. Forbidden. Out of reach. Devious. Lying. Tricking. A handsome dark-haired Irishman with startling blue-black eyes and lips that were much softer than a woman could ever imagine. A gentle soul who'd held her through a storm, speaking poetic words in her ear. A kidnapper who'd risked everything to bring her across the state of Kansas to safety. A protector? Or a tormentor?

Plan One was to ask her good-looking host where his beautiful wife was, and just when, exactly, did he plan on telling his wife he had another female locked away in the "castle"?

Plan Two was to ignore the way he made her feel. That meant no more flirtations, no more mind games. That would be too risky. As much as she dreamed about him, Dana wasn't about to get involved with a married man. It was just plain wrong.

Plan Three was to trick, bribe or fight her way out of her elegant prison and get help for her and her brother. But she might have to sneak that plan around Brendan. Maybe start with the innocent, sweet Lara and work her way up to good-hearted Gilda. She'd get Tony to help her, too.

As she sat here, reading and calculating, Dana made notes, sort of a chronological time line of all the events leading up to her being here.

And all of her notes led back to one thing—the kid from the Universal Unity Church who'd been in the store the day of the tornado—the same kid who'd planted a bomb in the pizza box in Kansas City. That scrawny, pimple-faced teen-ager had been in the store for the very same reason Dana had.

"To get a pair of new Ruby Runners," Dana said out loud. "And I picked up the wrong pair."

Shoes that were manufactured by a company owned by Brendan Donovan. "Okay, I have to ask Tony where the nearest Ruby Runner factory is located," Dana said, jotting notes as her mind rushed ahead of the realization forming in her brain.

Up until the storm, Caryn had merely been harassing her for her land. After the storm, came the unintentional shoe switch at the store, then the fire and the threats and the weird e-mail messages, followed by a bomb. Then life on the run, and all for what? A pair of shoes?

"That's ridiculous."

Dana wished she could run this by Tony and Leo right now. "They'd help me figure this out."

"Have you got any of this figured out, Leo?" Tony asked, his voice subdued and quiet since he'd warned Leo he was pretty sure this room was heavily bugged.

Leo stared across at his young friend, taking in the fuzz of beard growth on Tony's gaunt face and the dark circles underneath his eyes. The computer genius had been hard at work for two days now, and still, Tony hadn't been able to crack all the way into Caryn's heavily guarded computer system. He was close, so close. And it was just about to kill him.

Leo, on the other hand, had been given an enforced break from his duty of watching over Stephen. He'd protested, but around here, protests only got a locked door in your face. That Serena woman was one tough cookie. She was buff and a bully, too. Not a good combination in a woman, to Leo's way of thinking. Her beauty impressed him, while her attitude troubled him. Leo had a bad feeling about that one.

"Leo, man, are you meditating again?" Tony asked, snapping Leo out of his thoughts. "I repeat, how do you figure all of this?"

"The only thing I've got figured out," Leo responded in his steady, calm voice, "is that you'll be a dead man by morning if you don't stop and stretch and eat something."

Tony snorted. "No, I'll be a dead man if I don't break into those secret files. Brendan Donovan will personally see to that." Whacking his fingers against the hot keys, he hissed and spewed. "I'm so close, I can taste it."

"But not close enough," said a deep voice from just inside the doorway.

"Man, you need to stop sneaking up on us like that," Tony said, a shudder going down his bony spine. How in the world Donovan managed to walk through closed, locked doors was beyond him. Then he heard the familiar click of the remote Brendan carried in his pocket and relaxed a little. Just technology, plain and simple. Maybe the man was human after all.

"Still no luck?" Brendan asked, his dark eyes roving over

the many screens and modems centered in front of Tony like the control panel of a spaceship.

"I'm afraid not," Tony had to admit, although it pained him to no end. "I'm not used to defeat, Mr. Donovan. I'm circling, getting deeper. But she's got the whole system jammed pretty tight with fire walls and back alleys. Maybe she was expecting us to pay her a visit."

"Aye, you can be sure of that," Brendan said, nodding. "Caryn has some of the best and brightest technology people working for her. I should know. Most of them used to work for me."

Leo didn't move a muscle. "Cyberspace is a very powerful spirit. And a very destructive one, no doubt."

"No doubt at all," Brendan replied. "Especially if the wrong information gets into the wrong hands."

"Is that the case here, man?" Tony asked.

They'd tried to get Brendan to level with them each time he graced them with one of his little nocturnal visits, but the man was worse than any fire wall blocking a computer system, impenetrable.

Brendan sighed, a long tired letting of air, then wiped his fingers over his burning eyes. "Aye, that is the case here. Let's just say that I have something my sister wants very badly. And let's just say that if she gets her hands on it, it could cause worldwide problems, problems neither of you can begin to imagine. Caryn wants power, and with this bit of technology, she would possess all the power she'd ever need."

Tony leaned back in his swivel chair. "Okay, let's just say that. Then why are you trying to crack her files? I mean, if you've got what she wants, what else do *you* need?"

"Proof," Brendan said calmly. "I need the final proof to stop her, once and for all. And the proof is in those files. Unfortunately, I can't count on the FBI to help me with this.

They've dragged their feet for months now. I need information." He lifted his shoulders. "Plus, I need to know her next move."

"A chess match," Leo said.

"Exactly." Brendan glanced around the dark room. "And time is running out. I can't protect you much longer."

Tony's scowl echoed that remark. "Especially since what you're asking us to do is highly illegal and inadmissible in court. I'm wondering how you'll protect me when I get busted."

"You won't get busted," Brendan said. "You're too good for that, right?"

Tony puffed up. "Right."

"Where is Stephen?" Leo asked, his gaze casual, his eyes anything but. "I didn't appreciate the way that Serena woman waltzed into the gameroom and took him."

"He's with Gilda. She requested some time with the boy, and I sent Serena to personally escort him to my sister." Brendan replied. "Leo, don't you trust me?"

"No, we don't," Tony answered for Leo. "Oh, I mean, no, we don't, *sir*."

Brendan actually chuckled at that. "I don't blame you. I'm not so sure I can trust myself right now."

"The question is," Leo said, his dark eyes holding Brendan, "do you trust *us*?"

Brendan didn't say anything. He didn't have to. Leo knew the man was fighting against his feelings, against wanting to trust his little band of reluctant followers. But Leo also knew Brendan Donovan needed to trust someone, something, in order to get that haunted look out of his eyes. Brendan Donovan was seeking some sort of redemption. Leo recognized a kindred soul when he saw one.

"How is Dana?" Leo asked, this time his voice and his eyes going soft. He knew the Irishman had a thing for Dana, so he didn't have to worry about her safety. But he did worry about her frame of mind.

"Dana? Dana." Brendan said the name as if it were a sip of silk moving down his throat. "Ah, there's a different matter. I'm afraid she's not having as much fun as Stephen. She does not like her necessary isolation."

"You'd better be taking care of her," Tony warned, a slender finger flying in Brendan's face. "Dana isn't used to being cooped up, man. She's a farm girl. She likes the great outdoors, fresh air, all that hokey stuff. She'll turn on you if you're not careful."

"The way she did you?" Brendan questioned, curious.

Tony looked mad for a minute, then shrugged. "What can I say? I love her, but we never could work through all our problems. Kinda of a *Green Acres* dilemma. I like the city life. She prefers the country. Not to mention, she has that problem child for a brother. She wouldn't budge an inch without him."

"She is his protector," Leo reminded him in a stiff voice. "I admire her for standing by her brother."

"I do, too, my friend," Brendan said, "and I'm truly sorry that I've had to separate them."

"Then show her," Leo suggested. "Do something nice for her, so she won't be so worried."

Brendan inclined his head slightly. "Good advice, Leo." Then he turned back to Tony. "Keep trying. I have it on good authority that you're one of the best info warriors of this decade. I don't want to be disappointed."

Tony didn't miss the hidden threat, but he liked being called an info warrior. His vanity far outweighed any threats, veiled or otherwise. He'd crack those files, if it killed him. "You won't be disappointed," he said, coming very near to saluting Brendan. "Just get me a glass of milk and a peanut-butter-and-jelly sandwich and I'll be back on the case."

Brendan agreed, then turned to leave.

"Hey, boss, wait," Tony shouted, holding up a hand. "I did find a few names to match to some of your employees. If these are correct, then you do have some cult members working in a couple of your factories. But then, we kinda already knew that."

Brendan hurried over to Tony. "Show me the list."

Tony handed him a rumpled sheet of paper. "It's odd, really. It seems that the highest concentration of matching names is centered in your Ruby Runner factory, right here in Wichita."

"Ruby Runners?" Brendan stared down at the paper, his expression changing from focused to frustrated as he lifted his head. "I think I just figured out what Caryn is doing. And I think it's time I go in to investigate." Then he threw the paper back down. "Tony, I need you to go in and find out about the workforce at that particular plant. Find out who's applied for a job recently, or who's given notice." He turned back toward the door. "And in the meantime, I'll do some research of my own. I think we're finally getting somewhere."

"Yes, sir," Tony said, already heading out, taking the first left on the Internet, heading back through the thin wires of a telecommunications cable and broadband. To his way of thinking, it was the only way to travel.

Leo sat down on the floor, closed his eyes and meditated his fate. To his way of thinking, it was the only way to stay centered in the midst of all this turmoil.

His mind in turmoil, Brendan headed down the tapestried corridors to the far side of the castle, to the rooms he'd occupied for most of his adult life. Private rooms that usually brought him a sense of peace and quiet, away from all the machines and technology.

That is, until a certain farm woman with a fiery temper had taken over the suites down the hall. His prisoner. Dana. Maybe Leo was right. Maybe he should at least let her out for some air, let her roam around the house so she'd feel secure and at home. Dana had enjoyed seeing the conservatory yesterday, but Brendan had not liked the reminder of the gift he'd given to Caryn years ago. But then, a flower couldn't fix what was wrong between his sister and him.

Would having Dana here be any better?

He should have never brought her here. Yet he wanted her near. Wanted her walking around that large, opulent room, hidden safely behind his security, just so he could have the pleasure of getting to know her and the peace of knowing she was safe for now. It was wrong to hold her here, but it was the only way he knew of protecting her, of keeping her safe and near while he figured out what was going on with his sister Caryn and Dana's brother, Stephen.

He'd turned his back once. He'd looked away from someone he'd professed to care about. And Caryn had taken full advantage of it.

It wouldn't happen again. Not now. Not with Dana. She was too innocent in all of this. Too precious to be destroyed by someone as evil as his older sister.

Too precious to keep locked away like some beautiful, breakable doll. She might bend, but Dana Barlow would not break. She wasn't like Shannon. This he knew for certain.

Maybe it was time *he* started trusting again, just as Leo had wisely suggested. Maybe it was time he told Dana the truth. The whole truth.

Brendan had turned to God in his darkest hours, had asked God to guide his soul back after he'd lost Shannon. And God had given him the strength to rescue scared, confused children from his sister's cult, as a means of some sort of redemption. He'd saved a lot of them, but it was the few that he'd lost that still tortured Brendan.

"I won't lose Dana and Stephen, Lord," he said now as he asked God to guide and protect them.

But, he wondered as he rounded the secluded wing where he had Dana hidden away, if he did tell her the truth, would she still look at him with that delicious longing rising like a morning mist in her green eyes? Or would she look away in disgust?

Still tormented, still hurting, he pulled out his cellular phone and called Serena. "Turn off the monitors on Dana Barlow's room and take a break. I will be with her for a while, and I don't want to be disturbed." Then he snapped the phone shut. His mind was made up, his purpose set. He had to trust her, or he *would* most definitely lose her.

Brendan keyed in the remote code to Dana's door, prepared to spend some time showing her that he was having a change of heart, all the way around.

He was greeted with the blunt end of a sharp instrument coming across the top of his head. An intense, red-hot pain centered in his brain, and then, thankfully, blessedly, his whole world went dark.

## *Chapter Sixteen*

Brendan woke with a jerk of his head, followed by a painful moan and a curse. Dana breathed a sigh of relief. She'd practically knocked the daylights out of him, but at least he was still breathing.

"I'm sorry," she said, meaning it. "I thought I could just run out of here, but then I realized I can't do that—I mean I'm not the type to leave someone hurt. I thought I'd killed you."

"You might have at that," Brendan responded, one hand going to the lump on his head. On a winded whisper, he added, "Remind me to remove all the heavy objects from this room."

She stood over him in a pair of black knit pants and a white cotton long-sleeved T-shirt she'd found in the armoire—her escape outfit. "I'm sorry," she said again, her voice calm in spite of the quickening of her heart. "You wouldn't play fair, so I decided to try my hand at being nasty. Turn the tables, so to speak. But I guess I'm not good at being nasty, and I did tell you that we'd work together on this."

He lay there for a minute, analyzing her with a pained, frowning gaze that moved up her body to center on her face. "Well, I'm thankful for that at least, or I might be dead right now. And that won't accomplish anything."

"Oh, I think you're right there," she said, her legs planted firmly apart, her hands on her hips. "So relax, I'm not going to finish the job. I can get things done just fine with you slightly injured. You see, you're down there on the floor, probably with a concussion, and I'm up here." She held up his fancy wallet-thin silver phone and his precious multibuttoned remote that seemed wired to the glowing keypad by the door. "And I have these. I was just on my way out the door, when I heard you moan."

He winced. "So, you'd *just as soon* leave me for dead!"

She couldn't tell him that she'd prayed he wouldn't die. She only wanted to injure him so she could get to Tony and find a way out of here. "No. I mean, I was concerned that I'd hit you too hard. I'm glad you're okay, but now I've got to get going." She pranced toward the door, her fingers trying various buttons on the remote.

Brendan shifted, groaning as he managed to pull himself up with a hand on a chair. "Dana, don't be foolish. If you take off through this house, you'll only get yourself lost, and risk putting yourself in danger. The sensors can spot anything moving in any room in the house."

"I intend to find my way out of here, so I can do what needs to be done."

Brendan didn't miss the determination or the desperation in her voice. He'd pushed her too far. And he had the aching head to prove it. "Listen, *colleen*," he said in a sweet voice, "if you help me up, we'll talk, about everything. I was on my way here to do just that."

Dana turned back to stare at him, then came over to squat in front of him, her green eyes blazing. "Do you really expect me to believe that?"

"I give you my word."

"Oh, that makes it a done deal, I suppose. I'm telling you, Brendan, I'm tired of this 'need-to-know' way of finding out things." She let out a long sigh. "I'm just tired and I want some answers."

Brendan let out a frustrated grunt. "I came here to tell you our plans, but you waylaid me at the blasted door!"

She fell back on her bottom to stare at him, her auburn hair floating like crinkled silk around her face. "I want to believe you, Brendan. And I'm sorry about your head, honestly. I didn't mean to hit you so hard. I broke this little statue." She pointed to a shattered pile of Waterford crystal. "I hope it wasn't valuable."

"Think nothing of it," he said, wondering how he was going to get himself out of this mess. Nothing in this room could be as priceless as her fiery innocence. Her determination, however, was another matter entirely, and could prove to be costly. What was he to do with her?

He tried again, sending up a prayer for patience and strength. "Dana, you need to stop this craziness right now. You won't get far anyway, because Serena will come looking for *me*—since you probably triggered one of the alarms with all your button-pushing."

Her head came up. "Oh, yes, the beautiful, capable Serena. Tell me something, Bren. Do you ever hire men to work for you?"

He smiled in spite of his pain. "Jealous, are you, love?"

Dana hopped up to glare at him. "No, I am not. I just think it's mighty curious, you being surrounded by beautiful women all the time."

"Where'd you get a notion like that? If you'll recall, I had two very capable *men* with me at the aircraft factory. You've met Spear. He doesn't have a feminine bone in his body, and he's been with me for years. And I hired your robotic friend, Tony, didn't I? And Leo, too, even though I find it tiresome— him giving me sage advice all the time."

Ignoring his pointed reminders with a dismissing tilt of her chin, she picked up a pile of magazines from a nearby table and dropped them in a ruffling heap at his feet. "I've been doing my homework, Mr. Donovan."

"Sweet," he said, the word rushing through a hiss of pain as he saw his face glaring back at him in crumbled glory. "Where did you find those?"

"Never mind that," she replied. "They were sent to me. I guess the maid forgot to get rid of them."

Gilda, Brendan thought, his demeanor going neutral in spite of the fury raging through him. His sister was like a little sprite, always trying to stir up mischief. She knew he'd never tell Dana a thing about himself, and Gilda would certainly never betray him by talking about him behind his back, so she'd deliberately planted those magazines here. Now he could only sit here, wondering how much Dana had read.

Apparently enough, from the fuming look on her face.

"Did my sister give you those?" he had to ask as he managed to sit up.

"No, so don't go blaming her," Dana responded as she plopped down beside him and pushed at his arm. "And I'm the one asking the questions right now, so just listen."

"Okay." He gave up and squinted at her. Maybe if he kept her talking, she'd settle down and be reasonable. "What do you want to know?"

"Where is your wife, Brendan?" she asked, scooting away to lean against a two-hundred-year-old armchair. "Does Shannon know you're keeping me here? Are these extra clothes hers?"

Brendan lowered his pounding head and let the memories swirl through the fog of pain. Shannon. He could see her, her long, dark hair flowing, her white skin shining, her black eyes so trusting. Much like Dana's eyes had been that day when the storm had raged around them.

Shannon's trusting look had led them down a tragic path. Dana's trusting look had stopped him from taking a path of no return. He owed Dana the truth, at least.

For a full minute, he just watched her, hoping she'd see that truth in his eyes. "Shannon is dead, Dana," he said on a voice so low she had to strain close to hear. "And, no, you're not wearing her clothes." *And I pray you don't take the same path she did.*

"Oh, no." Dana pushed away from the chair to reach for him, her actions as natural and pure as her honest eyes, her hands on his arms strong and tender all at the same time. "I'm so sorry. I'm such an idiot!"

"No, love. I should have told you. I'll tell you now. If you're willing to listen."

"I am," she said. Then she reached up to touch the purplish lump on his head. "I hurt you. Oh, Bren, I'm sorry. It's just that I'm so confused, so mixed-up. And I'm used to doing, don't you see? I have to do *something.*"

"So am I, *cara,* used to doing. So *do* I—need to do something. I have to end this thing. I've been trying for so long to end my sister's misguided reign. And I'm growing very tired myself."

"Here, let me help you sit up," she said, her tone gentle and caring now. Then her chin jutted out to a defiant level. "But I think I'll just hold on to the remote and the phone until we have an understanding."

He chuckled in spite of the darkness of Shannon's memory. Dana was the first woman who could make him push those memories away completely. He wanted to pull her into his arms, but guilt and sensibility told him to hold back. "Still don't *quite* trust me?"

"Well, it's obvious you don't trust me, either. I'd say we're even. We're both locking things inside."

"Aye. In more ways than one." Then he motioned to the keypad on the wall. "You'd better hit that first grid or Serena and Spear will be in here with guns blazing. You might have triggered an alarm."

Dana jumped up and did as he asked, then gave him a questioning look. "It just lets them know that we want privacy, love. A digital Do Not Disturb sign."

He waited as she struggled with the information he'd just given her, his eyes touching on hers, asking for understanding. Then the minute he saw the resolve on her face, he pulled her down beside him.

"Bren, don't start anything," she said, her breathlessness belying the firm tone of her words. "I want the truth. All of it. And then, I mean it, I want to end this, too."

He settled her next to him, nestling her by his body as he leaned back against the sturdy leg of the table. "Then listen. And decide if you're with me, or against me."

Dana knew in her heart she was with him. In spite of all her doubts, she'd been with him since the day she'd met him in the midst of a storm. But she should be running out of here, searching for answers. "If I listen, will you please include me in on the plans?"

"Yes, yes. I promise, somehow we will figure this out together."

"Then talk fast."

Brendan held her close for a minute, then kissed the top of her burnished curls. A dainty grandmother clock sitting on a nightstand chimed twelve times. It was midnight.

"Shannon and I grew up together," he began. "Her father was our estate overseer back in Ireland, so Shannon and I saw a lot of each other. But we both went our separate ways in adult life. Me, off to school here in America—at my mother's insistence—while Shannon stayed in Ireland and attended university in Dublin. While I was at Harvard and MIT, she finished school and opened an art gallery in County Cork, in the village near our estates there. She was always very close to my two older sisters, so naturally she was like a part of the family.

"When I came back from America, we started seeing a lot of each other again, and we fell in love."

Dana shifted in his arms, the thought of him loving another woman more disturbing than she cared to admit right now. "You got married."

"Aye." He didn't speak for a while. "About a year after our wedding, Shannon started to change. She was lonely, living in our estate house, with nothing much to do. Her gallery no longer interested her, so she took to spending time with Caryn. My father's first wife died when the twins were in their early twenties. Caryn drifted away from the church after her mother died. My sisters had just lost their mother, and then when my father brought home my mother and me, well, Caryn didn't like my mother. My mother was just a few years older than them, you see, and well, a new baby, especially a son, just made the situation even more strained. Caryn never liked me, either. After my mother died of cancer when I was a teenager, I thought maybe Caryn would change, that we'd all become close. But then things got worse when my father died a few years later. Caryn was very bitter because, even though he left the twins substantial accounts and holdings, he left most of his assets to me.

"Caryn didn't even try to hide her displeasure or her hatred for me. She had changed so much, and she got involved in this kind of charismatic religion, branding herself as a minister. She married Sean Roark, the man who'd started the movement, and for a while, Caryn seemed happy. In the meantime, Shannon was fascinated by all of it. She followed

Caryn, listening to her every word. When either Gilda or I would warn her that she was becoming obsessed, she'd lash out at us."

He shook his head. "Then she'd come to me, all petulant and begging forgiveness. And I'd always forgive her. I loved her, you see."

Dana felt him stiffen, felt the tension coiling through his body, but she didn't speak. Somehow she knew in her soul that when Brendan Donovan loved, he loved deeply and with commitment…and passion.

He continued. "I was away on business a lot, setting up new factories and offices here in Kansas while I worked on renovating this house. Caryn hated this house—mainly because my mother had urged my father to move back here and help her oversee the renovations. Caryn used that resentment to bait Shannon, to convince Shannon that I didn't really love her. Shannon complained about my time away, but she didn't want to come to America with me. Caryn used that loneliness to fuel her own desires."

"Which were?"

"She wanted power and control. Unlike Gilda, she didn't approve of my being in charge of the family fortune, so she was out for revenge. You know, in Ireland women have been the heads of clans for centuries. Caryn wanted to run things, and I did put her in control of the estate—the castle and the grounds in County Cork—for a while. But she was using her power for her own agenda. She wanted to turn the castle into a religious retreat. Gilda and I were against this, so we relieved her of her duties, so to speak.

"After Sean was killed in a car accident, Caryn was very distraught, and in spite of our attempts to help her, she became even more distant. She came to America. I thought I could help her more if she came here so I gave her some land not far from here. There was an old abandoned abbey on the land and Caryn fell in love with it. She'd stay here in the house on her visits, but she spent a lot of time at that abbey. She traveled back and forth between Kansas and Ireland, and at the time, she and I became close again. Or at least Caryn pretended to want to end the feud, the battles. But I can see now that she just did that to ingratiate her way back into our lives, so she could control my wife. Even though I felt uncomfortable with it, Shannon would visit Caryn in Ireland and always welcome her here."

He wrapped his arms tighter around Dana. "In an effort to keep Shannon from being so withdrawn and depressed, I started taking her on trips with me. And I thought she'd be content here where my parents had been so happy. For a while, she took an interest in the house and the business, and she soon learned everything there was to know about my various holdings. We were truly happy during that time, but as soon as she went back to Ireland, and went to see Caryn, she began to take a turn for the worst. She became paranoid and unreasonable. I took her to doctors, but no one could get through to her."

"Depression still?" Dana asked, her heart going out to him.

"That's what they called it. Of course, later, much later, I would find out differently."

Dana lifted her head. "Why? What happened?"

He turned her in his arms then, his hands clutching to her shoulders, his eyes dark with the turmoil she'd first seen the day she met him, the turmoil she'd seen when he'd looked toward Caryn's compound. "The same thing that could happen to you, Dana, if I can't protect you."

"What do you mean?"

"Caryn killed Shannon. Even though Shannon's death was

ruled a suicide, Caryn killed her with her lies and her decep-
tion, with her trickery and her technology. And once she used
Shannon all up, she left Ireland for good and headed back to
America. But she didn't come back here. Instead she went to
another part of Kansas, on a spot of land one of her devoted
followers suggested she should buy—land in Prairie Heart.
She's been manipulating people and destroying lives ever
since, all in the name of her fanatical religion. I got involved
in trying to stop her when some friends came to me and asked
me to get their son out of the cult."

He leaned his chin on the top of Dana's head. "At first, I
didn't want to believe the things they were telling me, but I
started investigating and found out it was true. The way she
holds those children hostage with threats and intimidation, the
way she controls their minds and every aspect of their lives,
well, I had to do something. It was just like what she'd done
to Shannon.

"So I've been secretly getting kids out of there for years
now. I can't make you understand how dangerous my sister
is, but you have to believe me. If I hadn't brought you and
Stephen here, you would probably be held against your will
at that church compound right now."

Dana swallowed back the fear rising in her throat. "Brendan, you're scaring me."

"You should be scared."

"This has something to do with the shoes, right?"

His brows shot up. "What makes you think that?"

Dana explained about the day of the tornado, about how
she'd picked up the wrong Ruby Runners. "I think that kid
was supposed to get the pair Stephen is wearing."

Brendan looked evasive and surprised, but finally he nodded, realization cresting in his eyes. "Aye. The Ruby Runners.
Fastest-selling athletic shoes in history. Fully padded, com-

fortable, cushioned. The perfect hiding place for smuggling transmitters or sensors across the country, and across international lines."

"What kind of sensors?" Dana shook her head. "Now you've lost me. Are you telling me the shoes I got by mistake held hidden computer chips?"

"That's what I'm telling you. But it's more than microchips. It's a highly technical GPS—Global Positioning System—that can track anything or anyone. I've been working on a prototype. It's no bigger than a grain of rice, but it could revolutionize the world of computers. These sensors have the capability to go undetected on clothes or shoes, on equipment, to keep track of whatever needs to be tracked. We've been test-marketing them by embedding them in the gel pods of the Ruby Runners. And that might be why Caryn's after you. She must think you have one of those prototypes."

Dana put her head in her hands. "This is unbelievable."

"Then listen, and listen good," he said, his hands digging into her shoulders. "Shannon was a very smart woman. She learned things about my computer business. She learned secrets that weren't supposed to be revealed. And she took that information back to Caryn."

Dana looked shocked. "Are you saying your wife was a spy?"

"Yes. But more like an innocent pawn. Caryn brainwashed her, had her believing I was evil and insensitive to Shannon's needs. And she was right to some extent. I failed Shannon. I was too busy building my companies, my empire, to see that my own sister was poisoning my wife, both physically and mentally. And when Shannon would come to me, all loving and soft, yielding and forgiving, I was too blind to see she was only fishing for more information."

"Oh, Brendan." No wonder he didn't think he could trust anyone.

"Caryn got Shannon hooked on drugs, then she manipulated her into retrieving information about my various business dealings. Soon Caryn knew my every move, and all she had to do to find out more was threaten to withhold the drugs. Shannon was too weak, too far gone, to put up a fight. But in the end, she found her own way out of the horror to which my sister subjected her. You see, I figured out who the spy was and I confronted Shannon."

Dana watched his face, saw his expression harden, saw the clenching of his jaw. His eyes grew dark with a misty blackness. "In the end, in order to save me, in order to keep Caryn from becoming even more destructive, Shannon took matters into her own hands." He stopped, closed his eyes, his breathing coming hard. "One cold winter night, she climbed to the tower of the old abbey on the other side of the lake and threw herself down onto the terrace rocks below." His eyes held Dana's. "Shannon committed suicide. And she carried my unborn child with her."

Dana stared up at him, tears filling her eyes. Then she put her arms around him and rocked him gently to her. "Don't say anything else now," she whispered. "Just let me hold you."

Brendan fell into her embrace, some of the tension leaving his body on a rush of relief. Dana held him for a long time, her hands stroking his back, her lips touching on the wetness slipping silently down his face to mix with her own tears.

Brendan. A tough, hard man, with a soft, gentle, faithful soul. A man who'd immediately accepted her brother; a man who'd risked everything in order to save Stephen and her.

A man who'd lost so much.

A man who was afraid to let *her* take matters into her own hands.

She knew at that moment that she was madly in love with him. But she had to think about that and what it meant.

Finally she looked up at him and said, "Let's go see Stephen, Brendan. I think it would be good for both of us."

"I think you might be right," he said, his hand touching on her face. "I have to examine his Ruby Runners, too. And since he practically refuses to take them off, I'll need your help there." Then he glanced at his watch. "But it's almost one in the morning. He's asleep. And he sleeps with those shoes on most nights."

"He gets attached to things," she said, her voice low and trembling. "Let's just look in on him."

He leaned close then. "We've got time before we rush back into all this ugliness. I'd like to spend that time with you. Just you. I won't be able to sleep, so I want to show you my home, Dana." He shrugged. "I just want to forget for a while."

Dana helped him up, kissed the lump on his head, then turned to take his hand. "No more secrets. No more regrets. God brought us together for a reason. We need to do this together, no matter the cost."

"Yes, I think you might be right there, too."

He leaned down and kissed her, his touch unlocking all her doubts. As Dana kissed him back, she could feel the tension leaving his body, could feel him giving in to her, too. "We'll see Stephen again first thing in the morning," he told her, "but until then, you'll finally get to see my world."

Brendan had taken her out of her prison, had opened her eyes to a new, mysterious way of life. And in doing so, he had also released himself from that same prison.

The house—and yes, it was like a real castle—was magnificent, a splendid, opulent slice of America that rivaled the great Biltmore Estate in North Carolina. The mansion was a mixture of turn-of-the-century America and the rich history of an Ireland that had survived everything from Cromwell's attempts at eviction to the potato famine of the 1800s.

"There are over sixty rooms and various secret hallways," Brendan explained in a controlled voice as they moved through what he called the Outer Hall where more portraits of ancestors lined the gallery, and the arched, whitewashed ceiling held a carved Donovan coat of arms. "One of the reasons I was afraid to let you out on your own."

Dana stopped at an oval floor-to-ceiling window much like the one in the bedroom where she'd stayed locked away. Down below, the illuminated lake greeted her, its white-blue waters licking at black rocks and small bluffs that sat like hunched shoulders over golden, rolling prairies. "Did you create this lake?"

"I didn't," he said with a slight smile. "One of my grandfathers did that. Had the valley blasted with dynamite back in the thirties. And Donovan Lake was formed."

He looked over at her, then back to the lake. "One day, I'll take you to Ireland and show you the Caha Mountains."

Dana sensed a hesitancy in him, as if he wasn't sure he should extend the invitation. "You'd do that for me, Bren?"

"Yes," he said, his dark eyes full of a new hope. "I'd love to show you my other home."

She reached up a hand to touch his face, her eyes holding his. "I wish we could have met under different circumstances." She groaned. "That sounded really lame, but it's the truth."

"It didn't sound lame to me," he replied, taking her hand to his lips. "How we met isn't important right now. But keeping you and Stephen safe is." He looked back out toward the water below. "We've found a connection to the cult, Dana. A woman in Wichita, in one of my shoe factories. I think she might be willing to talk, based on her recent activities. She recently indicated to a co-worker that she wanted to leave the cult, but was afraid to do so. Serena has been watching out for her. She reported this latest development to me earlier. I'm going in first thing tomorrow."

"Let me go with you," Dana said, putting a hand over his. "You'd just intimidate your worker, especially if she's waffling about turning on Caryn. I could get friendly with this woman, try to persuade her to talk. Let me do this, Brendan."

He wouldn't look at her. "Dana, we've talked about this. That would defeat the whole purpose of keeping you here. I can't risk that. What if Caryn captures you? Drugs you the way she did Shannon."

Then he turned to her, and Dana saw the fear in his eyes. Along with something else, something that made her heart turn as flowing and liquid as the waters of the lake.

"I can't risk that again, ever, Dana."

"I'm in this now," she said, trying to reason with him. "You brought me here to lure her out. And I've learned a lot since I started running. My first mistake was in ignoring her. I should have been more careful about keeping tabs on my neighbor."

"You had no way of knowing."

"No, but I still have questions. We know it has something to do with the shoes now. Set me up in the factory and let me ask some questions."

Brendan glanced around the long, wide marble hallway leading to a formal dining room and a matching drawing room, both situated on the side of the house facing the lake. He'd shown Dana both rooms. Enough for her to see the gilded, gold trimmed mirrors and the Aubusson tapestries decorating the high walls that surrounded shimmering Waterford chandeliers. Enough for her to see that all of the walls could have ears and eyes.

"Let's go outside and talk this over," he said now, taking her by the arm.

"Outside?" She reached up to kiss him on the cheek. "Oh, Brendan, fresh air!"

Her innocent action took Brendan completely by surprise. And made him want to do something not so innocent. He wanted to hold her here forever, but he had to be careful that he didn't stifle her. Right now he was too raw, too open, too vulnerable, to show her how he felt. He couldn't yet expose himself that way, not even to her, especially when he hadn't been completely honest with her.

Instead, he opened one of the stained-glass doors and urged her in front of him, his eyes taking in the surrounding well-lit countryside with a practiced, experienced scope. "My men are posted everywhere and the electronic security is top-notch. No one should bother us here."

That statement seemed to remind Dana that she might be out of prison, but she wasn't completely free or out of danger. She sighed, shuddered. "So much for forgetting about all of this for a little while. When will this end?"

"Soon, I hope," he said, taking her hand to lead her to the stone balustrade that overlooked the curve in the lake. "Okay, we know Caryn has someone in place at the Ruby Runner factory in Wichita. We've matched a name to this woman. Her name is Sharon Harper. She's been inside the cult for five years. And she's been working at the factory for three years. We're watching her now, tracking her activities, and she's made some noise about not being happy with the going-ons back in Prairie Heart. I'll go in under the guise of visiting one of my holdings, and find out more information for us."

"You should let me go in first, as a new hire."

"Why are you insisting on this?"

"Because I have to pay you back for all you've done for Stephen and me."

"I don't expect that."

"I know you don't, but I have to do something."

"I'll have to think about this, Dana. It doesn't make any sense to set you up like that, after Caryn's chased you all over Kansas."

"It makes perfect sense to me. I can snoop around while you do your 'boss' thing."

"You'd have to be briefed on what to look for and you'd have to learn all about the new technology my company is constantly updating."

Dana could read the hesitancy in his eyes. "I'm not Shannon, Brendan. I won't do anything foolish."

He pulled Dana into a tight embrace, whispering, "I'm going to hold you close, so only you can hear. Just pretend you're enamored of my every word, darling."

"That won't be so hard," Dana admitted, allowing him to wrap his arms around her in a protective gesture. "All of this secrecy, though. Is it really necessary?"

"Extremely. I told you Caryn planted spies within my company."

"And your own wife was one." Again, Dana could understand why he'd been so distrustful. "I'm not a spy, Brendan."

Brendan looked down at her. "No, you aren't a spy. But you *are* a lot like Shannon. You are a beautiful woman who got caught up in something too powerful to understand."

"Are you talking about Caryn now," Dana asked, her lips parting, her heart beating heavily, "or about us?"

He answered her with a kiss, a real kiss not meant to impress prying eyes. A kiss that she wanted and needed.

Dana fell against him, her hands going around his neck to pull through his dark hair.

The spring air whipped around them in a gust of sycamore leaves and azalea blossoms. Below, the choppy waves of the lake splashed against the shore, taking and giving in a timeless rhythm that lured them into a false sense of security.

"Dana," he said at last, his breath winded, his eyes burning her, "I don't know how much longer I can stand this."

Dana pulled her hand through his hair. "I think I'm falling for you, Bren." Her unabashed honesty caused him to close his eyes and groan. Dana closed her own eyes, too. "I want to be with you, but I still need answers."

He opened his eyes and looked at her again, a resolved frustration marring his features. "And you want to do this for your brother?"

"Yes. More than anything."

He understood her meaning, he understood her motivation. She saw the admiration, and the acceptance, in his eyes.

"I'll let you go on one condition. I'm going to be nearby."

"Okay."

"Okay. Now listen to what I'm about to tell you. It might make you change your mind."

"I won't change my mind."

"There is a lot in Kansas that Caryn can destroy," he said at last. "Fort Leavenworth happens to be one of the high-tech divisions of the United States Army. And Wichita Communications Company is one of their main suppliers, especially with the new smart sensors. We've developed several different types of transmitters and sensors that can be used for all sorts of intelligence. I fought hard to win that government contract. Now Caryn could destroy that as well as so much more."

His meaning became crystal clear. "Are you telling me that Caryn is out to overthrow the American government?"

"She'll do whatever she can to destroy those with whom she disagrees," Bren admitted. "She's very militant, and she hires people who live on the fringes of society—secret militia groups, extreme radicals who think the government is out to get them. If she can get one of these particular smart sensors in place, or hack into the computer system at Leavenworth, through one of her hit men, things could begin to go terribly wrong. She could set off a computer virus that would spread all over the world."

"You're serious."

"Dana, I'm telling you the whole story, everything. I've created programs developed exclusively for the American government as a means of launching a technical warfare in the event of a takeover. In the wrong hands, it can wipe out entire computer systems in a matter of seconds."

Dana stopped to think about how terrorism had already changed the world over the past few years, and realized Brendan was very serious. "Even Congress or the Pentagon?"

"The Pentagon especially. This has to do with booby-trapped computer systems that simply destroy vital information at the click of a button. This has to do with logic bombs, set off within banking systems, or transit systems to snarl people's accounts and travel across the world. These things eat data in the same way the good guys win in some of the kid's games I've been letting Stephen test for me."

She'd seen that while watching Stephen play. "Okay, but what's that got to do with shoes?" Then she gasped. "You said one of those things might be hidden inside my brother's Ruby Runners?"

"That's only part of the problem." He looked out over the water, than back at her. "My company created a prototype—a smart sensor placed in the gel sole of children's shoes to track them in case of kidnapping. It could help with missing children all over the world."

"Unless it gets in the wrong hands."

He nodded. "Yes. We've been testing it in certain shoes,

asking interested consumers to be our guinea pigs, so to speak."

"The boy in the general store? You think he was a tester of sorts?"

"He had to be, although I'm not sure how he got clearance. But Caryn wants to use the shoes to track her cult members and to track her illegal activities, too, I think. Only, she doesn't have all the technology to make it work. If she gets her hands on all the codes and designs, she would be able to control her followers even more. They'd never be able to get away from her. If there is a sensor in Stephen's shoes, we probably jammed it when we brought all of you here, which means Caryn lost track of you after you left Kansas City and hooked up with me. Of course, I'm sure her experts have figured things out by now. I expect to hear something from her anytime now."

"So that's why she's after us. We might have the last part she needed to finish her dirty work—if my brother's been running around, wearing these shoes?"

"I don't know that yet, but it makes perfect sense. We have to coax him to let us have a look at them. I can't be sure we have the right ones. You see, there were several prototypes— some in cell phones, on clothing and purses, and on different styles of shoes. We're working with analog and MEMS and what we call piezo materials. They can manipulate any type of electronic device. We were heavily into the testing stages when we realized there'd been a leak."

"All this technical talk," Dana said, shaking her head. "No wonder you hired Tony."

"Yes, Tony understands the language and the significance of what's going on here. And he's *not* a spy. I made sure of that before I told him what's going on. I've got him working on cracking Caryn's system right now. We've tested this particular sensor at the plant in Wichita and secured its program, but we believe she's managed to smuggle more information out. There are several passwords to activate each sensor, but I don't know which ones she has. We have to get to this contact, this Sharon Harper, before she sends another sensor code to Caryn. If I can persuade her to cooperate, this might be over very soon."

Dana believed him completely. This was too farfetched to be believable, but that in itself made her believe him. How could he make up something like this?

"That explains why you took us, at least." Then she put a hand to her mouth. "Caryn tracked us to Kansas City, didn't she? That's how that kid found us and planted the bomb."

Again he nodded. "Either that or they put a transmitter on your truck the night of the fire. Then he made a simple bomb and rigged it in that pizza box, but it was a very powerful blast. And now he's missing, of course."

Dana could see the face of that kid. "He was so young."

Brendan's frown deepened. "He's just one of many she's trained to do her bidding. Caryn probably had her people sneak into your house and spray your clothes with sensory chemicals, too."

Now she had to laugh. "Bren, please!"

"It's the truth! Did she bring you extra clothes after the storm?"

Dana nodded, her hand over her mouth. "She sent some over, but we never put them on. Is that why you had me change clothes when you brought me here?"

He nodded. "I had to be sure. She could watch your every move, each night, right from the roof of her compound, simply by using a special night device and following the infrared rays coming from your clothes. But apparently she couldn't be sure you had the shoes since Stephen wasn't wearing them then."

"No, they were in the truck in the storage boot. He didn't put them on till later." She gasped. "That's what they were looking for the night they set the fire—and the day they ransacked my house!"

"Aye. Since they didn't find anything after the tornado, that would have made her angry. So she probably sent her boys to set fire to your house, knowing you'd fight back, or hoping you'd turn to her for help. But you got away before her plan worked."

Dana felt weak, cheated, violated. "How long has she been doing that? Spying on me, I mean?"

"Months, maybe. She needed your land to finish out her compound. You were like a thorn in her side already. And I'm afraid you taking off with the Ruby Runners didn't help matters."

"Well, she has my land by now, I'm sure."

"Your land is secure," he said.

"How do you know that?" Then she held up a hand. "Right. I'm supposed to trust you. I keep forgetting that you are much more powerful than even Caryn Roark."

Brendan brushed a hand in the air as if to dismiss her statement. "Don't worry about the land, because she won't stop at that. She thinks you know too much. You have to be eradicated."

She looked up at him, shock numbing her. "I can't believe this is happening. It's just too bizarre."

"Aye. Caryn deals in the bizarre. She'll kill Stephen in a heartbeat to get what she needs, or worse, she'll kill you and *take* him. The only reason she hasn't done it yet is because she probably wants to question both of you to find out how much you know and who you might have told. She lives for such confrontations."

"But why?" Dana tried to pull away, but he held her steady. "Why, Brendan?"

"Caryn thinks she is superior to the mere human race. With this much power, she can pick an army of highly trained, devoted followers who will do her bidding like a pack of robots. She's insane, Dana."

"An understatement." Dana looked up at the man holding her, and knew he held her life in his hands. For the first time, she saw what Brendan had sacrificed in order to follow her and help her. "Thank you, Brendan, for telling me the truth, for helping us." Then she pulled away again. "Now, I only have one question left."

"I'll try to answer it."

"I can understand why you're helping me, but I need to know how you found me when you did. What were you *really* doing on that road back in Kansas?"

## Chapter Seventeen

Before he could answer, Serena rushed out onto the terrace, flanked by the two men who'd been with Brendan at the airplane factory.

"Your beeper wasn't responding," the buff woman told Brendan, her dark eyes flashing. "and when I checked the monitor and didn't see either of you anywhere, we began a search—"

"I told you not to disturb us," Brendan replied, holding up a hand to show Serena he was all right. "We were having a private conversation."

"Sorry, boss," Serena said, putting away the revolver she held, her cool gaze moving over them. "You need to let us know where you are next time." Then she watched as Dana handed Brendan his cell phone and remote control. "Letting her test the equipment?"

Brendan gave his employee a hard stare of a warning. "Serena, I'm okay. That's all you need to know."

"Right," Serena replied, tossing back her gleaming black hair. "We thought the perimeter had been compromised. Guess it was a false alarm after all."

Then Brendan's remote *did* go haywire. At about the same time his cell phone rang. Dana turned to stare up at him, watching his face as he listened into the phone.

"What are you saying, Tony? What body in the lake?"

Dana pivoted as she heard the words, a sick feeling hitting her in her stomach. Her eyes scanned the gleaming dark blue waters. A heavy dread seeped through her system as her eyes landed on something floating under the spotlights in the water on the far shore.

A body.

Dana gasped, her eyes clashing with Brendan's at about the same time he discovered the body, too. "Thanks, Tony. We see it. Save the message. I'm on my way down."

Serena cursed underneath her breath. "Someone did get in. How did that get there?"

"That," Brendan said, his gaze locking with Dana's, "is the body of Samantha Bennett."

"How—how do you know that?" Dana asked, the answer shouting at her with a solid pounding inside her temples as the white-clad body bobbled on the dark water like a dead dove. But she had to hear it from Brendan.

"According to Tony, we got a message on the main Web site," he said, taking her by the arm as he signaled with the other hand to Spear and Serena. They both took off in different directions, cell phones plastered to their ears.

After they were alone again, Brendan turned back to Dana. "My sister has sent us her calling card. She killed Samantha and dumped her body here so we'd see it. And she left us a threatening message: 'He that goeth about as a talebearer revealth secrets.'"

"Proverbs." Dana fell back against the doors leading inside. She felt sick to her stomach. "Oh, Brendan. Oh, how could she?"

Brendan held her by the arms, his gaze bearing down on her. "Because you asked what I was doing that day on your road? Remember, I told you I was headed to the Universal Unity Church—"

Dana moaned low in her throat. "To save a young girl? Oh, no. That girl was Samantha? Was it?"

He nodded, his expression solemn and stern, his eyes black with grief. "Now do you understand why I don't want you going undercover?"

Dana lifted her head, each breath she took giving her new strength. "*Now,* Brendan, can you understand that *you* need *my* help? She knows I'm with you. That's what the verse is saying. She thinks I've told you some sort of secret about the Ruby Runners. She'll probably know the minute I leave here, so what does it matter where I go or what I do? We have to find a way to stop this woman!"

"Dana." Her name on his lips was controlled, low. The look in his eyes held a clear warning, but it also held something else. A wariness, as if there was so much more he wanted to say. "This is not a game. She killed a young girl just to prove a point."

"I can see that," she replied, watching as a vehicle moved slowly around the lake toward the floating body. "All the more reason to get this over with and get her put away for life."

Brendan looked down at her, thinking he could take her anger, but he couldn't bear her hurt. Somehow he had to allow her some sort of closure, but he also had to protect her in the process. The only way to do both was to keep her near and keep her busy, just until he could level with her about everything, including the real reason they'd been thrown together. Finally he let out a tired breath of resolve, then nodded. "We'll work out a plan, a thorough no-mistakes plan. And we'll go in together."

Dana tried to speak, but he held a hand over her mouth, his eyes flashing an intense blue. "I'm not finished. At first, I followed you to watch out for you. Then I tracked you to

Kansas City, hoping to get to Caryn somehow. Then I wanted you near me, to protect you and Stephen and to lure Caryn out. Well, I've done such a good job, Samantha is dead now. And you're asking me to risk you in the same way? Can't you see I don't want to do this, Dana?"

Dana let out a gasp, much like a sob. He lowered his forehead to hers, his emotions at the breaking point. "I promise you this. When this is all past, when Caryn is at last brought to justice, I won't ever use you or lie to you again. I want only honesty between us, Dana. I want a second chance, with you."

He watched as she swallowed, then closed her eyes. "Will I always have to look over my shoulder, Brendan?"

"Not if I can help it. I'll never, ever let you go. I'll always be there with you." To prove his point, he kissed her, his hand still gripping her chin. "This is an impossible situation. But maybe you're right. If I send you in, maybe the FBI will at least drop all the charges they've built against you."

"A plea bargain of sorts? But I'm not guilty."

"We know that, but right now we can't prove it. If we cooperate and get through this, then we might be able to find the proof—that Caryn set you up as the bomber in Kansas City."

"Whatever it takes," Dana replied, glad that he was beginning to see things her way. But she saw that solid concern in his eyes, saw the pain he'd suffered for so long. "Bren, you have to go after your own sister. I understand the danger— that's pretty obvious—but it *will* be easier on you, to let *me* do some of the snooping. Isn't it time you turned some of this burden over to someone else?"

He nodded, his dark eyes filling with a kind of reluctant gratitude, and Dana's heart burned with the loneliness he must have felt all these years. "You're not alone anymore, Bren," she said. "You have me now. And God will show us the way."

"He brought me to you that day, Dana. You asked me why I was really on that road. I *was* there to get Samantha, but that's not the only reason. I was going to confront my sister, once and for all—to the bitter end." And there was another reason, too, but he couldn't tell her that now. "You saved me from doing something that would have destroyed me."

"God saved you," Dana replied. "And now we have to finish this, the right way. We have to be careful," she said as she held to him. "We can't make any mistakes. You've done everything in your power to help me and I've fought you tooth and nail. But I'm willing to cooperate, do whatever I can, to get us through this."

He looked down at her, his eyes full of regret. "No distractions. Until this is over." And when it was over, he'd explain his reasons to her. All his reasons.

Dana lifted a hand to his face, her words echoing his thoughts. "And when it's over, then we'll see what happens."

Brendan lifted away from her and turned toward the downstairs offices, his hand pulling her forward. "Right now we need to gather all our forces and come up with a plan." Then he dropped his head. "And I have to identify the body and call Samantha's parents."

"We're in deep," Tony told her later as they sat around the control room, waiting for Brendan to brief them on what to do next. "I mean, we're talking megatechnology that changes on a daily basis, technology that can control millions of people, and we're caught between two people who both want to control that technology—one for good and one for evil." He rolled his eyes. "Now we find out about the dead wife, who was connected to both of them. And I thought old episodes of *Star Trek* were exciting."

"Yes, I know," Dana replied. "I can't believe she killed that young girl and caused Shannon's death. And Brendan thinks she probably killed the kid who set off the bomb—just because he didn't finish the job."

"And she made sure we knew she did it," Tony said, shuddering as he stared over at Dana. "I haven't had a good night's sleep since we came here, and now I won't sleep for sure. We're dealing with a madwoman, Dana."

Dana wanted her friend to know how much she appreciated his bravery. "Tony, thank you. You could have run away that night in Kansas City. But you stayed with us and helped us find Leo. And you came here, reluctantly and under pressure, but you've stayed the course in spite of everything. I don't know what I would have done without you."

Tony actually blushed. "Hey, don't make me out to be a hero, doll face. Donovan didn't give me much of a choice, between blackmail and a hefty salary coupled with a cushy job—if I come out of this alive. But I've aged a lot in the past couple of weeks. I mean I've matured."

"Yes, I think you have," Dana told him. "Which is why you'll understand when I say I need your help once again."

"How so?"

"I need you to help Brendan when we go to Wichita and talk to this Sharon Harper."

Tony's fingers stopped tapping on the computer keys. "Dana, I'm helping, can't you see?"

"I can see. But I mean, he needs us, Tony. He needs to know that we won't let him down."

"Oh, like, if I mess up? I think you're fairly safe, but Donovan would have *me* tarred and feathered."

"*Donovan* will know you did your best. But that's my whole point. He's a very powerful man, but he's also a very troubled man. We can help him to heal."

"Yeah, right. That man has everything the world has to

offer, and the money to buy all of it. So I don't get how we can help him in any way."

Dana gave him a bittersweet smile. "We can give Brendan Donovan the one thing he's never truly had, Tony. We can restore his faith in God and in mankind. He needs to see that we believe in what he's doing. He needs to see that we will stand by him."

Tony ran a hand down his face. "I get it. Support, teamwork, all that stuff. Except you're in love with the man, and I'm not."

Dana lowered her head. "I'm still working through my feelings for Brendan. You know, I've thought about busting out of here and going out on my own—"

"I don't like that idea," Tony said, shaking his head. "I don't like this one bit, doll face."

"It's okay," Dana said, holding up a hand. "I've made a deal with Brendan. We're going to the factory together. And you'll probably be needed there, too. And Stephen will be here, protected the whole time, thanks to Leo. I'll find Sharon Harper, get to her, appeal to her for help. I'm only asking you to go the extra mile, if push comes to shove, Tony."

Tony stared at the screen before him, his head down. "You want to know you can count on me, even though I've let you down before, so many times."

Dana smiled. "Yes."

He didn't answer her at first. Just sat there, his gaze fixed on the computer in front of him. Then he said, "What if the Harper woman doesn't cooperate or tell any tales? What if she goes straight to the Evil Twin Sister? Who are *we* gonna count on then, Dana?"

"That's a chance we have to take. But we have to do this, Tony. That could have been Stephen," Dana said, her whisper for his ears only. "That could have been my brother floating in the lake."

Tony didn't move a muscle. "I'll see what I can do. I'll try to rise to the occasion."

"Thank you," Dana replied. "Now I'm going to visit with Stephen, to tell him goodbye."

Tony watched her go. Then he turned back to the computer screen. "Doll face, that's one request I can easily grant. And not because I'm scared of Brendan Donovan, or because I want to save the great man's sorry soul. But because I love *you*."

Early the next morning, they found Stephen playing basketball with Leo in the massive basement gameroom. Brendan guided her inside the room, his expression grim. Dana didn't know how she was going to do it, but she had to go to Wichita without her brother. Leaving him here would be so hard and so scary. Steeling herself, she put on a blank face so Brendan wouldn't suspect her fears and make her stay behind.

Stephen was happy; laughing and joking with his new hero, Leo. At the sound of the heavy metal door clashing open, he turned, his whole face lighting up at the sight of his sister. "Dana!" He started talking very fast, repeating the same phrases over and over until Dana acknowledged him.

Dana rushed to meet him, tears welling in her eyes. Brendan stood behind, watching, waiting. Dana could see his heart shattering through the intensity of his blue-black eyes at the sight of them together. He'd never had that chance with his child. Maybe that was why he had such a soft spot for Stephen.

"Oh, Stevie. You're okay. I'm so glad you're doing okay."

"Okay, Dana. I'm okay. I'm okay." Stephen scoffed at her mushy tears of endearment, pushing her away so he could rock and flap his hands. "Bren's been taking good care of me. Yeah, Bren likes me." He lifted a foot. "Bren makes Ruby Runners. Brendan did. Bren makes Ruby Runners, Dana."

"About your shoes," Dana said, leaning down to stare at

her brother's feet. "We might need to borrow them for a while, sport."

"No," Stephen said, running away, waving his arms. "My Ruby Runners. Mine, Dana."

Dana gave Brendan a pleading look. "Do we have to do this—take his shoes, I mean?"

"We need to take them apart, analyze them," he said on a low voice. Then he smiled over at Stephen. "Hey, Stephen, what if I managed to get you a new pair of shoes. A pair that works even better than those you have on."

Stephen shifted from foot to foot. "New shoes. Yeah, new shoes might be nice. Where are they? Where are my new shoes?"

Brendan walked to Stephen and touched him on the arm. "I'll bring them to you very soon, and we'll make an even trade, okay."

Stephen looked toward Dana for guidance. After she nodded, he shifted on his feet again, his eyes darting here and there. "I like the code. Yeah, I like the patterns in the shoes. It's a code, all right. Yeah, that's what it is."

Brendan's eyebrows shot up. "What kind of code, Stephen?"

Stephen sank down on the floor, then rubbed the raised red shapes on his shoes. "Ruby code. Makes noise. Flashes at me. Yeah, it's a code, all right."

"Can I look at one of your shoes?" Brendan asked, careful to remain still and calm.

"No," Stephen replied, his hands moving against his chest. "Need new shoes. Need another code."

"Okay, I'll get you the new shoes," Brendan said. "But right now I'd like you to show me these codes. I know how good you are with codes."

Stephen rocked back and forth, his hands holding on to the

toes of his scuffed shoes. "Number sequence," he said, grinning. "I can write down the numbers. I can write down the codes."

Brendan snapped his fingers to Leo. "Get us some paper and pen."

Leo found the necessary items and brought them to Stephen. "Write down the shoe codes for us, sport."

Stephen did so, drawing out an elaborate mathematical sequence that looked like a scientific formula. "It's in the colors. The beeping colors. And the patterns. I like the patterns."

Brendan stared down at the numbers and patterns on the paper. "He's right. They're sending the sensor codes through the shoes using the computerized GPS. They're trying to pick up on his location. It's in the pattern of the rubies. That's how she's finding out our passwords and encryptions. The employees she's set up are putting them right here in the pattern of the shoe soles. All they'd have to do is reprogram the sensors to send out some sort of messaging system but only in certain shoes. And that's why she's after this particular pair of shoes. This pair holds the last of the sequence she'd need to start mass producing bootleg Ruby Runners with built-in sensors. She'd be able to keep tabs on anyone wearing these shoes."

Dana couldn't make heads nor tails of all the patterns and numbers. "So if that kid in the store had gotten the right pair of shoes—"

"My sister would have the last sequence code to create the smart sensors probably in underground knock-off factories, with her hand-picked workers making sure things went accordingly and that the shoes got shipped to Caryn instead of out to stores. She could not only track people, but goods and probably a money trail and filing system, too." He shook his head. "Amazing. All this time I thought she was just trying to track Stephen to get the shoes, but she needs this code, too. And it's been right under my own nose the whole time."

Tapping Stephen on the arm, he said, "You are brilliant, Stephen. You've helped us solve a big problem."

Stephen grinned, flapped his hands and took that as a sign of dismissal. He trotted off to find the basketball, shouting, "It's all in the codes. Yeah, I like codes. I'm brilliant about codes."

Brendan turned to Leo. "Stay with him. Watch what he does with the shoes. He sees things we can't see. And that is the one thing Caryn shouldn't know. Which means you can't let that boy out of your sight while we're in Wichita, Leo."

Leo nodded. "The boy rarely takes the shoes off. But he does sit and stare down at them whenever he's tired. Sometimes he just rocks and stare, like he's in his own little world."

Dana looked at Brendan. "He has a kind of sixth sense about puzzles and codes." Then she brought a hand to her throat. "What if you sister knows that *about* him? She'd not only be after the shoes, but Stephen, too, just as we feared."

"Did anyone back home know that?"

"Our neighbor, Mrs. Bailey, did. And a few other people. Some of the kids he went to school with, before I started homeschooling him."

Brendan said something under his breath, then started punching numbers in his ever-present cell phone. He walked to a window, issuing orders as he moved.

Leo stepped forward, his sneakers squeaking on the polished court floor. "You look very beautiful, Dana Barlow. More rested now. But I see sadness in your eyes, still. You are worried for your brother."

Leo was much too wise, she decided as she hugged him close. "Thank you for watching Stephen for me."

"I like the boy," Leo said with an eloquent shrug. "And besides, I had nothing else much to do. But, I wanted you to know, that Serena woman makes me take breaks whether I want to or not." Then he whispered, "Now that I've been briefed on the latest developments, I won't leave Stephen's side again, whether that she-cat suggests it or not." He scowled at Brendan when he joined them again. "Will you tell your assistant to stop pestering me? I don't need any more breaks. Especially now."

Brendan nodded, a silent stillness moving around him, as if he hadn't really heard a word Leo had said. Then he gave Dana a questioning look. "We need to talk to Tony." He stalked toward the heavy doors, waiting as they automatically swung open for him.

Dana patted Leo on the arm. "Thank you." Then she said in a low voice, "Now we know why Brendan has been so secretive and stubborn, but I do believe his heart is in the right place. We have a hard task ahead of us, but we have to stop this before anyone else gets hurt or worse."

Brendan's heart seemed to be in his eyes at the moment. Dana could see that he truly cared about her brother and her friends. It brought her a measure of relief in the midst of all this tragedy and gave her the strength to finish this job.

"Sometimes the falcon takes the form of a man," Leo said by way of agreement and understanding.

Remembering the falcon centered on the Donovan crest, Dana was amazed at how Leo had picked up on Brendan's essence. "This has all been so strange."

Leo's expression didn't change. "It will become even more strange before it's over, I'm afraid."

Dana smiled back at her brother, to reassure and distract him. "Stevie, I have to go. Tomorrow I'll leave for a few days. Will you remember to eat right?"

Stephen bobbed his head. "And take my medicine. I like Miss Gilda. She's cool. Yeah, Miss Gilda is real cool. Where's my new shoes? Where's my new shoes?"

After reassuring Stephen he'd get his shoes, Dana turned to where Brendan stood waiting by the door, fear in her heart. "Where is Gilda?"

"At the day school." Then he added under his breath, "With guards."

"Can we see her at dinner?" Stephen asked, rushing forward to rock back on his heels. "Yeah, we can all have hot dogs. I like hot dogs."

Brendan looked up at the expectant faces watching him. He didn't know how to answer that. He didn't have time to eat or sleep now that he'd figured things out. "We'll have to see, Stephen. Right now we've got some business to take care of. But Leo will stay here with you."

As if on cue, Tony burst into the room from yet another hidden door, his eyes blazing like an overworked computer monitor. "I did it, man! I broke all the doors—fire walls, jams, virus protectors and all. I finally found a big hole in their back door." Then, realizing Stephen was in the room, he stopped, his wired eyes lifting in surprise, one hand automatically reaching up to scratch through his steel-wool hair. "Uh, hey, buddy. Just playing one of Mr. Donovan's games."

Brendan stepped forward to take the printout from Tony's jittery hands. Motioning to Leo to take Stephen, he pulled Dana toward the door.

"I'll be back soon," Dana called to her brother, but Leo had Stephen distracted with another round of basketball. She wanted to run back to him and tell him how much she loved him. She didn't want to lose sight of her brother, but Leo gave her a reassuring look. And she heard the click of the automatic doors as they left. Stephen would be safe. And she wouldn't cry. It would be all right once she cleared things up.

"What did you find?" Brendan asked Tony as they hurried toward the other rooms.

"Oh, all sorts of interesting stuff. Like a detailed listing of other Ruby Runner plants she's hitting on, including which workers she's paying off and which shipments include the test sensors from WCC."

"She had to keep it organized to know exactly what was going where," Brendan said as he skimmed the pages in front of him. "Just as I suspected, she's got people planted at both the computer and software plants and the shoe factory." Recognizing some of the names, he hit a hand on the papers. "Some of my highest-paid, best workers are on this list!"

"She's paying more," Tony said blankly. "And get this, she has a stockpile of weapons, both legal and illegal. I've downloaded all kinds of inventory sheets showing deals and transactions with some very shady people. She's controlling a radical army of followers, with all her dough and her pretty talk. And if she gets her hands on all your technology—"

"She'll be controlling much more than their minds and their money." Brendan's expression went from anger to grim acceptance. "At least, with allegations of this information and what Stephen just showed us, we can present enough for the FBI to possibly raid the compound and take some of the members in for questioning, while I go in to talk to this Harper woman. Of course, that might take some maneuvering, since the FBI won't accept our 'unofficial' findings. They'll need to do some digging of their own." He glanced at Dana. "If everything goes as planned, you might not have to be involved after all."

"Is this almost over then?" Dana asked. "Once we talk to Sharon Harper?" She had to make sure she'd be doing the right thing, leaving Stephen alone here.

He gave her a calculated look, as if he already knew her thoughts. "Possibly. I've got to make a few phone calls, see what my people can come up with, give the FBI this new information. This will help nail her, but we still need someone from her cult to step forward to corroborate this information."

As they entered the computer room, he said, "Tony, I need to speak with you about your findings." He turned to Dana. "You could visit with Stephen while I make the necessary arrangements."

"I'm there," Tony said, his shoulders squared with victory while his gaze sent Dana a silent plea to stay put.

Brendan glanced at Tony, then back to Dana. "Tony informed me that you had actually considered going off to Wichita by yourself."

At Dana's surprised look, Tony shrugged. "Hey, I just didn't want the boss to have any last-minute surprises."

Dana gave Tony a furious look, then shook her head as her gaze hit on Brendan again. "I thought I could make a difference. I only wanted to help, to get this over with, but I didn't follow through with it as you can clearly see. I thought after last night you'd finally started trusting me."

"And I thought we'd gone beyond secret agendas," Brendan said, the look of hurt in his eyes causing her to flinch. "Dana, there is no way I'd ever let you strike out and do this on your own." He leaned forward, a finger in her face. "And I will lock you back up if you even suggest that to Tony or anyone else around here again."

Hurt, she lashed out at him. "You think I'll turn on you the way Shannon did, but I've done nothing, Brendan. I've done nothing but watch and wait."

"Just watch and pray, Dana," Brendan said. "I need you to do both right now."

Later that night, Dana sat to the left of Brendan, watching his brooding face through the warm glow of candlelight at the huge dinner table. Watching for signs or clues as to what the man might be thinking. He'd been quiet all night, his whole expression dark and stony, his body coiled and tense. This was their last night together here before they set off tomorrow for the factory in Wichita.

They had a plan now. And she was still included in that plan, thankfully. They were going to set her up in the factory in Wichita, have her work there for a week as a new hire right next to Sharon Harper. And while she was there, Dana would try to get to know the other woman and try to find some answers.

She had to admit, working with Brendan was much better than trying to do this on her own. If only he could see it that way. Instead, he thought just because she'd even considered it, she'd tried to betray him, just as Sharinon had. So much for that fragile trust they'd developed. So much for kisses and promises.

Which was why Brendan Donovan wasn't saying much. He didn't want her to do anything to jeopardize her safety. That was noble, but she refused to stay hidden away here like some helpless princess in a castle. So between the two of them, she and Tony had finally hatched out a convincing cover, with Tony setting up her paperwork in the human resources files, so that things were in place for Dana to act as a liaison and try to get to the Harper woman.

Brendan had managed to get the FBI to agree, too, once his sources at the Wichita plant has assured him that Sharon Harper was ready to get out of the Universal Unity Church once and for all. Even though the FBI couldn't use the information Brendan had obtained, they'd received the news from the FBI that they thought they had enough to go on now, based on the evidence they'd already been gathering, Samantha's death and the threatening e-mails Dana and Brendan had received.

They would be invading the church compound sometime

within the next few days, while Dana was in Wichita talking to Sharon Harper. Brendan and Tony would be nearby. Brendan could rest easy. At about the time they'd be getting an eyewitness account of all Caryn's shady dealings, the woman herself would be placed under arrest for various crimes.

So why wasn't anyone at this table eating, drinking or smiling? Dana wondered as she tried to swallow another bite of the hot dogs and potato salad Gilda had ordered for Stephen.

Gilda sat on Brendan's other side, near Leo. Dana noticed those two hit it off right away. Leo had never grinned that big. Gilda looked regal in a mint-green flowing dress, her smile bright and cheery. Dana had finally gotten over the shock of how much Gilda looked like Caryn, and now she could see that they might resemble each other physically, but they were nothing alike.

"Bren, isn't it lovely to have the house full of people again?" Gilda said, her cheeriness strained.

Brendan looked up from studying the gold-etched Celtic knotwork design of his centuries-old dinner plate. "What? Oh, yes. It is nice, in spite of the circumstances."

Gilda gave her brother a concerned look, then said, "We've been so preoccupied with all of this, I'm afraid we've forgotten how to relax and enjoy ourselves."

"Aye." Bren moved a hand, the only sign that he was actually halfway listening to the conversation. His gaze lifted to Dana's face. He didn't smile, but the look he gave her told her that he was very much aware of her sitting there.

As she was of him. He'd changed into a white cotton shirt and dark jeans. He looked better than the chocolate ice cream, and twice as dangerous. Like a pirate returning from the seas, here he sat, the dark lord at his too-long dining table in his too-large castle-house.

He looked lonely and sad and preoccupied.

Dana wanted so much to reassure him that they were doing the right thing. Dana wanted to confront him, comfort him, conform him. Yet she knew she might not be able to do any of those things. He might have given in to her, but he still didn't trust her. Oh, not because of Caryn. But because of his own bruised heart.

Leo's gravelly voice pulled her out of her musings. "Dana, did you know Bren's great-grandmother back in Ireland used to buy up all the food she could find and give it to her tenants?"

"She was a very kind woman, and she saved many a starving child during the horror of the potato famine," Gilda said, her smile serene in spite of her nervous chuckle.

"You musta took after her," Stephen said just before he slurped his milk down. Then in typical Stephen fashion, he added, "You got a crazy sister. Dana said so. Crazy sister. She scares me."

"Stevie!" Dana said, her gaze flying from her brother's face to Brendan's. "I'm sorry."

Brendan lifted his head, his eyes touching on her before moving to Stephen. The sadness within their depths tore at her heart.

"Stevie, you really shouldn't say things like that," she gently admonished.

Stephen rocked on his high-backed chair. "Tony says she's crazy. She's chased us all around. It's like a game. With codes and puzzles."

Brendan's mouth was set in a grim line. "My sister is ill, I'm afraid, Stephen. She has done some terrible things and she has mental problems. I hope to end all of that soon one way or another."

"You gonna zap her? Tony said we should zap her."

Dana slumped down in the brocade-covered seat of her chair. "Stephen, finish your dessert. It's getting late."

"But I wanna know! I wanna play the game. Brendan says I'm good at the codes and games. We practice. Lots of practice."

Thankfully Gilda took over. "We're trying to stop our sister from making a huge mistake, Stephen. We mean her no harm. We just want to get her some help, and make sure she doesn't do anything destructive."

Stephen rocked and smiled. "I see two of you. I see Gilda and I see the wacky woman. Yeah, there's two of you, for sure."

Brendan rose then, his actions causing dishes to rattle and sway. "I'm going to check on Tony."

"What about the codes?" Stephen asked, rocking back and forth in his chair.

Brendan's head shot up. "Stephen, it's very important that you don't talk about the codes, to anyone."

"The ones in my shoes?" Stephen asked. "The lights come on and they make noise. Like Morse code. Yeah, it's a code all right. And the patterns match up, too."

Brendan gave Dana a worried look. "Hopefully Caryn doesn't yet have all the technology she needs to figure out the sensors, but if your brother mentions the wrong thing to the wrong person—"

"So you *do* think she knows Stephen has figured this out?"

"I think there is a very strong possibility that she's guessed this. Which means, she's after both of you. She wants Stephen, just as we suspected. That's the only reason you're both still alive."

"That and your protection," Dana reminded him.

"I have to go and talk to Tony," Brendan said, his eyes downcast. "Try to convince your brother to forget about the codes, Dana."

"No," Stephen said, rocking harder. "I like the codes. Not gonna take my shoes. No."

"I'll see what I can do," Dana said, her hand on Stephen's arm to calm him. "It's okay, buddy. We're not going to take away your favorite shoes, but we need to find you a new game to play, okay?"

Dana watched as Brendan stalked out of the room, then looked over at Gilda. "He's worried, isn't he? But then, so am I. I won't let that woman near my brother."

Gilda nodded, her eyes on her brother's retreating back. "He doesn't have the heart for this, really. He pretends to be so strong, so tough, but…"

Dana understood what Gilda meant. Brendan knew he had to do this to end his sister's reign of terror, yet he hated doing it. She was, after all, still his sister, and he was, after all, a gentle and caring man.

Dana loved him all the more for his courage and his remorse. Dana loved him, period. End of discussion.


"End of discussion," Caryn screamed at the five or so people hovering around her like pigeons waiting for crumbs in the inner sanctum of her private suite. "I'm going to confront my brother and that little pea-brained prairie girl who's caused me so much trouble!"

Ricardo tried again, his voice sounding weak and scratchy in his own tired ears. "But, Caryn, it's just too dangerous. I'm telling you, the FBI and probably the CIA are working on nailing us. And I'm pretty sure, based on our source inside the Donovan house, your brother is cooperating with them. That means they have *evidence,* Caryn." He held his hands out, palms up. "And if the boy—"

Caryn's crystal eyes flashed icy cold fire. "Forget the boy. I'll take care of him myself. Let them try to get to me. They've got nothing on me. Nothing." But Ricardo didn't miss the frown of worry forming between her eyes. It flashed by as she waved her jewel-clad hand in the air. "We did cover our tracks, right, Ricardo?"

"Umm, of course. I've shredded every piece of evidence I could find and I've encrypted the computers so they can't retrieve any information." He didn't bother to tell her that he'd been a tad too late. If they'd gotten in, as he suspected, then Brendan Donovan was probably calling out his troops right now. Ricardo wasn't going to be the one to tell his boss that, though. "No more delays. If you're really sure about this—"

Caryn rammed her hand down on the marble slab of a desk in front of her. "Of course I'm sure. I've wasted enough time, listening to all your warnings and your paranoid insistence that the FBI is moving in on us."

"Just stating the facts," he replied underneath his breath. "This could be getting out of hand."

Caryn gave him a look that fairly fried him in his pants. "If you've done your job, Ricardo, we're safe. If you haven't, you will pay the consequences."

Ricardo swallowed the bile rising to his throat. Maybe he should just quietly sneak out into the night and disappear. Brazil was sounding better and better.

"What about the sensors? What about the remaining codes?" Caryn asked, her keen eyes noting the sickly yellow pallor of his olive skin.

"We're missing the one," he said quietly, meekly, with his eyes downcast. "The shoes—the boys still has the shoes."

"Which means my dear brother probably has things figured out. He'll know that the boy is the key to all of this." Caryn hissed, her eyes lighting up like a vulture's. "Why did I send that idiot Derrick to do the job?"

"He was your favorite at the time, I believe."

"He was a nice boy, that's so true. Such a shame."

"A child, really," Ricardo said, nodding in agreement. Thank goodness he'd served his time as teacher's pet. He squirmed, remembering her weird twisted idea of what maternal love represented.

Caryn slammed her fist against the desk again. "Now, when can we get on with this and get back to Wichita? I've waited long enough. And don't tell me I have to wait for *this* to be solved, or *that* to be fixed, again."

He opened his mouth to protest, to tell her that they had to wait for the right moment, but she cut him off—

"I'm tired of waiting until we have a way in. We've got a very good contact working for us, so I don't see why I have to wait any longer. I'm going to Wichita. I'm going back to the abbey, and I want that boy brought to me, so I can get the information myself. We're going to find a way to get my brother to cooperate or he just might find another body floating in that lake."

## Chapter Eighteen

"Are you sure you're up to this?"

Dana turned from the hotel window to find Brendan staring at her with that black gaze, his expression etched in angles and planes from fatigue and lack of sleep.

"I'm okay," Dana replied, comfortable in her disguise now, since she'd been acting as Diana Porterfield for the past week. "That FBI man who just left wired me like an electric fence."

Brendan gave a rare grin as he touched his hands to her arms. "I think half the agents are in love with you."

Dana couldn't help her blush. "I doubt that. I'm just glad they're beginning to believe me."

"Well, they've certainly interrogated you enough," Brendan said, his grin vanishing. "And you bring them new information on a daily basis."

"I think I'm good at this," Dana teased, the tension between them as sharp and static as the buzzing light in the bathroom. "I might just have a new career."

"Oh, no," Brendan replied, his hands still holding her by her shirtsleeves, his grin gone. "Remember, when this is over—"

"We get a second chance," Dana finished.

That was something they hadn't mentioned much over the past week. Mostly Dana had gone to work, training to bind shoe soles with the help of fancy machines and smart computer models and scales, beside the timid, frightened Sharon Harper. And mostly she'd reported back to Brendan and a team of hand-picked FBI agents. Now they were all waiting for the final all-clear, the part where they would know for sure that Caryn Roark had been taken into custody.

"So many stories," Dana said now, remembering the bits of information she'd managed to get out of Sharon.

The woman was brilliant as far as being a computer geek, but terrified of going against the cult she'd come to regard as her only place to turn for help. Sharon lived with several other cult members in a house that Caryn had set up in the city. And unfortunately, the same overt control and intimidation went on there, the same as it did at the big church compound back in Prairie Heart.

"Torturing children, brainwashing them into believing their families have abandoned them, withholding food and companionship as a means of mind control. Even the adults who live here in Wichita are watched over like they're prisoners. They have to report to her each week." She shook her head. "I'm sorry, Brendan, but I don't see how that woman could possibly be Gilda's twin. Gilda is so kind and gentle, so loving."

"And Caryn is hostile and full of hate." He let go of Dana, his hands falling to his side. "She started changing the day my father brought me home."

"But why?"

He looked down, a white-hot shame seeming to color his bronzed face to gray. "I was born out of wedlock, Dana. My father married my mother when I was two years old."

"Oh, my," Dana said, one more piece of the puzzle falling into place. "So Caryn resents you for that?"

"Yes. She thinks I'm a disgrace to the Donovan name. And it was only made worse when my father seemed to favor me over the twins. You see, he had an affair with my mother while his wife was still alive."

Dana didn't mean to gasp, but this was just one more shock. Putting a hand to her mouth, she asked, "And he married your mother after his first wife died?"

"Yes. Gerald Donovan married Valerie Caldwell six months after Merline Donovan passed away. Caryn never could forgive my father or me for that."

"That's the first time you've ever mentioned their names," Dana said, reaching out to him. "It's not your fault what your parents did, Brendan." She hugged him close, the beat of his heart a steady reminder to her that he was so very human, after all. "You've been trying to make up for this all your life, haven't you?"

She felt his nod against her hair. "I've tried so hard to bring Caryn back, to show her that we can be a true family, that we can worship the one true God. But she's too far gone now. Too far deep inside her hatred and her paranoia. She's so obsessed with power and control, she's forgotten the real Christ. Somewhere inside her soul is my sister. But I can't reach her."

Dana held his chin with her hand. "Not much longer now. Sharon is going to talk today, I just know it." She looked up at him, seeing the slanted lines of fatigue that cratered his face. "You'll find some peace soon, Brendan."

He pulled her into his arms, kissing her with a fierce tenderness that told her he hoped for that peace. "I'll ask again— are you sure you're up to this?"

"I'm fine," Dana told him as he backed away, worried that he'd pull her out of this if she whined even a little bit. "So far, so good."

"Remember to stay calm," Brendan told her. "Sharon Harper might know you want to talk to her, but she has to be very careful. She's very scared and now we've added our stipulations to her growing list of worries. We've given her an ultimatum, based on the information you've already gathered, but she's seen what my sister does to people who leave the cult. She might not cooperate."

"I've seen that, too, remember?" Dana asked, the memory of Samantha Bennett's floating body still fresh in her mind. "Did you finally get in touch with Samantha's parents?"

"I went to their house last night," Brendan replied, his head down. "After all the FBI red tape, I'd wondered if I'd ever get a chance to talk with them."

"Is that why you made Tony stay here with me? You told us you needed to be briefed by the FBI."

"I did that, then went to visit with the Bennetts. They live on the other side of the city."

She had wondered where he'd gone last night. Not that it mattered. He was gone most nights. He was in a room across from her, while Tony had the room next door. They all had bodyguards. Dana had the tall, cool Serena shadowing her. And she had decided the young woman was downright strange. Serena took her job very seriously. Right now, Serena was just outside the door, watching.

"How did they take it?" Dana raised a hand. "Stupid question. Of course they would mourn their only daughter."

"They are devastated," Brendan replied as he pushed off the wall and came to stare out the window with her. From this vantage point high up in the hotel, they could just see the steel-and-chrome facade of the Ruby Runner factory from here. "They told me they'd testify in court, do whatever it takes to help bring my sister to justice."

Dana shifted her gaze away from the bright red neon of the distant factory's ruby-shaped marquee and touched a hand to his arm. "I know how hard that must have been, Bren, having to talk to them about Samantha."

"I should have saved her," he replied. "I was so close."

"Don't remind me," Dana said, turning away. "So many lives changed the day of that tornado."

"I have to do this, Dana," he said, tugging her close again. "For Samantha. For you and Stephen. For Shannon."

"You'll save others, too," Dana told him as she held him close, careful not to topple the short blond wig she was wearing as an extra precaution. "And then it will all be over at last."

Brendan looked down at her and she saw something there in his tragic eyes that scared her. It would never be over for this man. He would carry his scars and his guilt to his death.

"Brendan, have you ever talked to anyone, I mean, about things with Caryn?"

His features turned as harsh and unreadable as the gray clouds shutting out the sun. "Gilda is my rock. She's the one who's held strong to our faith and pulled me along with her. Gilda has saved me from myself by showing me that God is in control."

"But you want to be in control, right?"

His smile was bittersweet. "I control my empire, but in the end that doesn't really matter, does it? It didn't save Shannon or Samantha." Then he touched a hand to Dana's face. "I don't want anything to happen to you, Dana. But somehow, this time, I think I don't have a choice. I feel as if I'm completely out of control letting you act as a liaison like this. Serena has been trying to get me to send her instead. It's not too late to do that."

Dana shook her head. "I know now how your sister operates. I know what to say to this woman. We always have a choice, Bren. And you and I are here today, making a choice to change things. As Christians, we learn that we have to speak out against wrongs, no matter how much we suffer. We're doing this because it has to be done, and so we can protect innocent people—the people we love. We have to hope that God will guide us."

Brendan moved his hand down her jawline, his eyes touching on hers as he pulled her close. "Dana—"

There was a discreet knock at the door, then Serena leaned in, her steely gaze taking in their embrace with a dismissing look. "They're ready to go, sir."

Brendan let go of Dana and nodded. "We're ready, too, Serena."

Serena quietly closed the door, but not before Dana saw the censure on her face. Maybe the beautiful, exotic Serena had a thing for her boss.

"Okay, I'll be near the room where you and Sharon are to meet for lunch," Brendan told Dana. "And the FBI will be monitoring everything you say, too. Tony will be centered in the main computer room with the management team there, searching for any other clues that might help us." He adjusted her wig, gave her a once-over look. "Serena will be stationed right down the hall from you and Sharon, too."

"Okay." Dana buttoned the denim jacket she wore to hide the wire. "I'll be okay, Bren, honestly. Caryn is on the other side of the state, and hopefully she'll be arrested before the week is over. We're going to be all right."

"I'm praying for that," he said. Then he bent down and kissed her, the dark pain in his eyes momentarily turning to a brilliant hope. "Remember, when this is over—"

"We can begin again," Dana answered.

"Yes, a new beginning for all of us," Brendan replied.

"Start at the beginning, please," Caryn Roark shouted to the man standing before her with a look of sheer terror on his face. "And please, don't tell me the FBI is riding in on their high horse to take me away."

Ricardo didn't tell her that, since he'd been trying to warn her for a week now and she had refused to listen. But the frantic young girl she'd plucked right off Bourbon Street in New Orleans about two months ago did.

The girl burst into the room unannounced, a definite no-no, her long blond hair flying out behind her linen robe, her crystal-blue eyes wide with the same terror Ricardo's held.

Caryn roared her displeasure, "Marcy, you'd better have a very good reason—"

"My boyfriend called me," Marcy said. "He was waiting for me just outside the gates. They're surrounding the compound—an FBI SWAT team. Caryn, they're going to arrest you and probably kill all of us. Jack said we'd better hightail it out of here."

Angry that the girl had been sneaking around and calling some boy behind her back—she'd deal with this ungrateful little troublemaker later—and even more angry that the FBI had the nerve to invade her private domain, Caryn rose up like a tall-necked crane. Her gaze darted here and there, not yet in a panic, but not as sure as she'd always been. "Ricardo, how do you explain this?"

Ricardo saw his life flashing before him and wished too late that he'd stayed in Brownsville, Texas. "I've been trying to tell you for days now that something was up. I have sources—"

Marcy interrupted with a shrill warning. "I don't want to be here when they start shooting. I'm leaving with Jack, whether you like it or not!"

"Enough!" Caryn dismissed the girl with a wave of her hand. "Go, you little ingrate. Get out!" Then while Marcy made a quick path to the door, she reached into a drawer and pulled out a mean-looking .45, aiming it right for Ricardo's forehead. "I ought to blow your sorry brains out."

Ricardo closed his eyes and said a prayer, thinking of his family back home as he waited for the end. Seconds ticked by, and the silence was white with nothing except regret.

"Come on," Caryn said, taking him by the arm to lead him to a secret passage. "I need you to destroy evidence—use the paper shredder, burn something over the disks and CDs, make sure everything is encrypted and help get me out of here. After that, we'll have to reassess your position here, Ricardo. You have failed me miserably."

"But I tried to tell you—"

"You only hinted," Caryn shot back, her eyes blazing. "I don't like hints. I wanted to go to Wichita days ago, but I listened to you instead. If I didn't need your skills, I'd kill you now. But I don't have time to do the job sufficiently. I have to go."

Thankful that she'd spared his life for now—maybe she still had feelings for him after all—Ricardo nipped at her sandaled heels like a cocker spaniel. "But where will you go?"

Caryn did a spin, her eyes piercing his with a white-hot blue. "To Castle Donovan, you stupid idiot! If I hadn't listened to you and our so-called source, I would have already been there three days ago, and this would all be over by now. I'm going to get those shoes off that boy and find out what's trapped inside his head, if I have to kidnap him myself. And I'm going to make Dana Barlow and my brother pay."

"You're taking me with you?" Ricardo asked, half hopeful, half filled with dread.

"No," she explained as she hurried into the bowels of the compound. "You will make sure I get away, then you will stay here and stall the FBI."

"A decoy?"

"Exactly. And I expect you to do whatever it takes to keep them out of here. Or at least make it look like I'm dead. Set the place on fire if you must."

Ricardo understood. She wasn't going to shoot him on the spot. Instead, she was setting him up to die a slow death, to take the fall for all her misdeeds. How many others would die in order to save her aging skin?

He didn't dare ask her that question. And he had no choice, but to do her bidding. Even as they hurried to the planned escape route, he could hear the buzzer indicating someone was knocking at the gate.

"You know what has to be done," Caryn told him, her words hurried and hushed. "Call ahead and tell our contact that things have changed. We go to plan B."

"Yes." Ricardo watched as she slid through a door hidden in a paneled wall.

He knew exactly what needed to be done.

Sharon Harper was a slender, shy woman with thin, stringy light brown hair and big brown eyes. And she was a basket case. Her hands shook and she kept looking around the small break room, her eyes darting here and there. Dana's heart went out to her. She'd had a hard life on the streets and Caryn had taken her in, then trained her in the ways of the cult. After Caryn put the woman through school and helped her get a job in technology, Sharon felt trapped in her gratitude. Trapped and used, since she was now paying for Caryn's generosity. Sharon wanted out of that trap.

"I don't like this," Sharon said, pushing at the loose strands of hair trailing from a beige plastic clip she'd wedged at the nape of her neck. "I wasn't sure about this to begin with, but when Mr. Donovan threatened to fire me and turn me in to the FBI—I don't like being railroaded this way, especially by someone I trusted."

"That's why I'm here," Dana replied, remembering all the instructions the FBI and Brendan had given her. "I'm sorry I had to trick you, but I'm no threat to you, Sharon, and neither is Mr. Donovan. He just wants to end this dangerous, illegal activity, so he can clear his company's involvement and help others."

"He sounds like a regular saint."

"He is a good man," Dana said, keeping the emotion from her voice. "He could have turned you in already."

"But he wants me to rat out everyone else," Sharon retorted. "I'm being blackmailed here, and if she finds out—"

"She won't," Dana said, hoping it was true. "Caryn Roark is going to be arrested today, at her compound in Prairie Heart. So the best thing you can do for yourself is tell us everything you know."

Sharon shot up out of the red vinyl chair, her work-rough hands shaking. "No. Oh, no. Do you actually think that woman will let them take her? She has more exit routes then that magician David Copperfield. I can't do this. I can't talk to you anymore. She'll send someone to kill me, for sure."

Dana took the other woman's arm, trying to guide her back into her chair. But Sharon Harper was in full panic mode now. She pushed Dana so hard, Dana hit her knee on the steel table leg, then fell back against the glass tabletop.

"I'm sorry, but I just can't." Sharon Harper gave Dana an apologetic look, then bolted out the door.

Dana hopped up, wincing as her knee throbbed with pain, then hobbled out onto the factory floor. "Wait, Sharon. Wait!"

But Sharon Harper was running for her life.

In spite of her bruised knee, Dana took off after her.

"What's going on?" Brendan asked as the FBI agents centered in a room down the hall started shifting and pointing. One was speaking into his headphone, shaking his head at Brendan, while another spoke into the tiny microphone at his wrist.

"Miss Barlow? Miss Barlow, can you hear me?"

"What's wrong?" Brendan asked, jamming his hand against one of the agent's dark-suited sleeves.

"The subject just bolted out the door," the man said, his eyes reflecting agitation through his wire-rimmed glasses. "And your friend Dana Barlow has taken off after her."

Brendan felt his heart drop to his feet. "What? We have to go after them."

"Tell me about it," the preppy agent replied, snapping his fingers to his men. "If they make it out of the building, we can't guarantee their safety."

Brendan didn't stick around to hear the rest of that scenario. He had to find Dana now. Before one of Caryn's devout followers did.

Dana followed Sharon Harper down a flight of dark stairs, calling after the frightened woman. "Please, stop. You're our only hope."

The woman kept running, her long hair flying out behind her. Dana could hear the woman's shoes flapping against the steel of the stairwell.

Shoes. This was all about shoes.

Dana ran as fast as she could after the woman, then screamed down the stairwell. "Sharon, my brother has the Ruby Runners. The ones with the code and the sensor. We have them. And if Caryn gets to him, she'll kill him. Just like she killed Samantha Bennett."

She heard a shuffling sound echoing back up at her, then she heard a muffled moan. "Sharon, are you down there?"

Seconds ticked off, each one bringing a new prayer through Dana's mind. *Help me, Lord. Help me, Lord.*

Finally she heard footsteps coming slowly back up the dingy stairwell. Then she saw Sharon leaning her upper body around the stairwell down one flight below. Sharon looked up at her, tears streaming down her face. "She killed Sammie?"

Dana nodded, her heart breaking for the woman. What kind of person put this much fear into another human being's heart, and all in the name of some controlled type of religion? "I'm sorry. But that's why we came to you. You're our only hope of ending Caryn's control over all her followers. We have some information gathered, but we need you to tell us what you know."

Sharon glanced around as if looking for someone, then sniffed, lowering her head to stare down at the dusty floor. "I knew Samantha Bennett. She came to the cult about a year ago. But she wanted to go home. She only wanted to get back to her family. Caryn kept talking her out of it."

"I know," Dana replied as she slowly made her way down the stairs. She was almost to where Sharon stood trembling, but she didn't want to rush in and startle the girl. Standing a few steps above, she said, "That's why we need your help. As I said, we've got evidence against Caryn, but we need eye-witness accounts to back up that evidence."

Sharon looked at her, her eyes brimming with tears, the fear in her expression twisting her features. Her eyes widened as she held back, her expression set in a taut grimace. "I'm so scared."

"We'll protect you, I promise," Dana said, thinking that was exactly what Bren had promised her. If she'd listened to him sooner, Samantha might be alive still. "Mr. Donovan will hide you until it's safe again."

"And will it ever be safe again?" Sharon asked, holding on to the steel staircase with an white-knuckled grip. She kept glancing back down toward the next stairwell.

"I hope so. I hope it will be safe very soon," Dana told her as she took another step and reached for Sharon's hand so they could sit down.

But Sharon didn't reach out to Dana. Instead, she pulled even farther toward the next set of steps. Dana stepped around and saw why Sharon was still being so hesitant. Serena Carson was standing there holding a gun on Sharon Harper.

Brendan burst down the stairwell, two FBI agents with weapons drawn right on his heels. Several workers out on the floor had seen Dana chasing the other woman through an exit door to the stairs, so he'd sent Serena back down the elevator to waylay Sharon's escape. He prayed Serena had made it down in time.

"Dana?" he called, a solid fear holding his breath inside his lungs. This had been a bad idea from the start, and now it had gone from bad to worse. Serena was probably fit to be tied, since she'd tried to warn him about using Dana as an informant.

"Dana?" Brendan called out again, too intent on finding her to worry about Serena's reprimands.

"I'm here," came the answer. "We're down here, Brendan."

"Thank God," Brendan said as he took the first real breath he'd had since they'd bolted out of the conference room.

Then he looked down and saw them. Saw Serena standing there with a gun leveled at Dana's head.

"You shouldn't have sent an amateur," Serena said as she pushed the gleaming gun closer, jamming the butt against Dana's temple while she yanked away Dana's wig then ripped at the wire under Dana's jacket. "She has no idea what she's gotten herself into."

"Stop it," Brendan said, his heart rate accelerating as he watched Dana's brilliant hair tumbling down around her face. He looked into her eyes and felt the cold sweat of a jagged fear rushing down his spine, his glance bouncing from Serena's cool expression to Dana's terrified one. "I take full responsibility for this decision, so don't blame Dana. Don't do this, Serena. Put down the gun, please."

"No, sir," Serena replied in a curt tone. "I can't do that. But you'd better tell the FBI to back off." She pressed the gun tighter against Dana's face, jerking Dana closer as she did it. "I do not have a problem with killing her right here, right now. In fact, I should have done it the night you brought her home."

The sick feeling inside his stomach reaching a pressure point, Brendan motioned to the men behind them and breathed a gulp of air as he heard them lower their weapons. "Why are you doing this, Serena? Haven't you heard the news—my sister Caryn is being arrested even as we stand here. Her complex has been raided by the FBI. She might even be dead for all we know."

Serena's smile was devoid of any loyalty or emotion. "I don't believe you. And I can't let you get to Caryn. Can't you see, I've come further than anyone ever has. I made it into your inner circle, but I had to wait for the right moment." She indicated her head toward Sharon Harper. "I knew she'd cave and bolt. All I had to do was wait down here. Now comes the easy part—your little farm girl here just inadvertently gave me the rest of the information I needed. You trusted me—"

"Yes," Brendan shouted, the disgust in the one word tearing out of his throat. "I trusted you, depended on you to protect me and this woman."

"*This woman* has caused more trouble than you ever did," Serena shouted back, the rise of anger in her voice enough to tell Brendan that she wouldn't hesitate to shoot Dana. "She should have kept running." Her laughter echoed up and down the narrow, hot stairwell like dancing fire. "I bet she doesn't even know the real reason you brought her to our little château, does she, Brendan?"

Brendan swept a hand through his hair. "Serena, I'm asking you to let her go."

Serena jabbed the gun tighter against Dana's head, her face inches from Dana's as she glared up at Brendan. "He knew about your brother from the very beginning. Knew how smart he was. That's why he's been testing him, making him play all those games. He's figured out your brother is brilliant underneath all that autism, but he had to bide his time on exactly when that brilliance would surface. The boy figured out the whole coding system inside the shoes before any of us saw it. Just think what a technology guru like Brendan Donovan can do with a mind like that. And you thought Caryn was the one after him."

Brendan watched, a shock wave of despair shooting over him, as Dana's eyes went wide with horror and realization.

"I don't believe you," Dana said to Serena, but Brendan could see the wheels turning inside her head. "That can't be right." She glanced back to him. "Bren, please tell me she's lying."

"Dana—"

Dana's face went white, then she looked down, tears forming in her eyes. "I can't trust any of you, can I?"

When she looked up, Brendan saw the wrath of his own betrayal reflected there in her vivid green eyes. It was a look he'd never forget.

"Dana, it wasn't like that. I knew about Stephen, but I was trying to protect him, not use him. I only wanted—"

"You wanted exactly what Caryn wanted," Serena interrupted. "To control him. Why can't you at least admit that, Brendan?"

Dana looked up at him, the pain of that question shining in her accusing eyes. She didn't speak, just stood there, watching him, as if she'd given up on him completely. Brendan couldn't explain right now. But somehow, once she was safe in his arms again, he'd have to make Dana see that Serena was wrong.

Sharon Harper stood off to the side, her head down, tears streaming down her face. She glanced up at Brendan. "I'm sorry."

"Shut up," Serena screamed. "I'll gladly kill you, too, you coward."

Sharon started sobbing again, her fear palpable in her darting eyes and shaking hands as she hovered next to Dana. Dana tried to reach out to Sharon, but Serena slapped her hand down. "Please, save me your sanctimonious attempts at helping this woman. None of you care about her the way Caryn does."

Dana stood silent, her eyes on Brendan, her stark, shocked gaze telling him that she thought he didn't care at all.

"Yes," Brendan said. "Caryn cares about both of you, enough to use you, to trick you, to make you do her bidding. Tell me, Serena, did she promise you a prime spot in her ministry? Did she promise you luxuries, riches, anything you ever wanted?"

Serena's laugh sounded like brittle glass, sharp and shimmering. "She can give me something you'll never be able to, Brendan. She can give me spiritual freedom."

"This is freedom?" Brendan asked, his eyes flickering from her to Dana, pleading with Dana to listen and understand. "To have to hold an innocent person at gunpoint? To threaten everyone around you? To spy on me and my organization, just so you can win brownie points with Caryn? She wants to use the technology I created to serve her own selfish purposes, Serena. That's not the kind of spiritual freedom most people crave. Does Caryn even mention how Christ died for you, Serena?"

"Shut up," Serena said, pushing back down the stairs. "I'm taking these two out of here. Don't try to stop me, Brendan. And don't come after me. I'm going to deliver the goods to

Caryn. I know what I need to know now, and I know how to get what Caryn wants. You should have warned your little girlfriend here. You should have told her the whole story."

Brendan watched Dana's face, saw the dead, emotionless expression there in her green eyes. They looked like a silent, dark pool. What was she thinking? Of course, she was thinking that he'd lied to her all along. She was thinking that everything he'd said to her had been a betrayal.

"Dana?" he called, his throat constricting as he watched Serena backing them down the stairs. "Dana, I won't let them hurt you. I promise. Remember, I promised to protect you?"

"Yes," she said, her voice as soft as a dove's call. "I remember. I remember everything you told me, Brendan."

"Hush up," Serena said. "Your little lovefest is over now."

Watching, and unable to make a move, Brendan saw what he should have seen since the day he'd found Dana on that road in Prairie Heart. He was in love with Dana Barlow. No, make that, he *loved* Dana Barlow. He loved her spirit, he loved her faith, he loved her determination, but mostly, he loved her courage. She'd put herself on the line, for him, for Sharon, for all those who'd suffered at the hands of his demented, misguided sister. And now she was paying for that. Because he'd betrayed her. By trying to protect her, he'd done the one thing a woman such as Dana could never forgive. He hadn't told her the whole truth. No matter that he only wanted to take care of her and Stephen. No matter.

He loved her. Which meant he had to stop Serena from hurting her. No matter the cost. That realization made his voice hitch as he called to Dana again. "Are you all right?"

"We're fine," Dana said, looking up at him with watery eyes. "I'll be okay, Brendan. Just do what needs to be done— to protect Stephen. You can at least do that for me, can't you?"

He heard the rage in that simple request. And wished with all his heart he could go to her and prove that he would do anything to honor that request.

Serena yanked Dana's arm, causing Dana to wince. Causing Brendan to take a step toward them.

"Don't," Serena shouted. "You'd better make sure I have a vehicle out of here. You'd better think twice about sending anybody after us. I mean it, Brendan. I'll kill both of them. You keep the FBI and the SWAT teams and the sharpshooters and anybody else who tries to get to us, you keep them away. And I mean *far away*."

Brendan didn't move a muscle. He knew Serena. And she knew all about how things would go down. He had to let her go for now. But he'd make sure he found Dana somehow.

"It will be over soon," he called out as he watched Serena pushing Dana and Sharon down the stairs. "You hear me, Dana? This will be over soon."

He was answered with the slamming of a steel door.

"This has to end soon, you understand," Caryn Roark said into the cell phone, her gaze scanning the flat prairie land before her. From this location atop the crippled stones of the century-old abbey, she could see the entire estate of the Castle Donovan. The estate that should rightly be hers. "Do you understand? I'm tired of listening to your advice on this. We should have moved days ago." She let that settle then added, "Of course, your work today has made up for lost time, no doubt. But I hope you understand what has to be done now."

"I do," came the reply. "I will take care of everything on this end, Caryn. You won't be bothered by any law enforcement officers. You have my assurances on that."

"They took over my church," Caryn said, a hiss of malice in the words, even though she tried to sound distraught.

"There was a fire. Tragic, just tragic. Many of my followers probably died. They think I'm dead. I have to retaliate."

"I understand," came the reply. "I serve here at your discretion. But you know that."

"Yes, I do. You have been very loyal to me. And you have acted very wisely. Your cover was solid and you waited until you had a chance to make a move. Your actions today have impressed me, Serena. Now just do as I've said and soon we won't have to worry about any of this again."

"I'll take care of it. You can count on me."

"Then do it, and quickly," Caryn replied. "In the meantime, I have to pay a visit to my dear sister, Gilda."

She closed the flip-phone, her gaze resting on the house across the lake. It really did pay to keep up old acquaintances. Brendan thought his house was solid, thought his employees were loyal. He was wrong, so very wrong.

Caryn laughed out loud, then bent her head in solace and prayer. They all needed prayers now, lots of prayers. Her poor, misguided brother thought he had won, at last. But he hadn't won. It was his fault—all of this. His and that farm girl's. Her meddling had brought on death and destruction, has caused the peace and tranquillity of the Universal Unity Church to be shattered. And that demanded revenge and regret. But it had to be done.

Caryn couldn't let those within her control be sent out into the world again, not alone and on their own. That would be fatal for all concerned. No, she had to have a way to keep tabs on all of her flock. The world was just too cruel for her precious flock. Just too, too cruel.

She'd seen that when her father had taken up with that other woman. And when he'd fathered a son out of wedlock, only to dote on that son to the point of casting her and her sister aside. The illegitimate baby had become the heir to the

Donovan fortune, only because Brendan's mother had forced their father to marry her. And he'd taken everything that should have been Caryn's. Everything. Then after she'd lost Sean, well, life was just too cruel. Unless one learned to control life.

Now she would have the means to always be the one in control. She'd go into hiding for a while, just until things settled down. Then she'd take the empire that Brendan has stolen and rebuild it again, maybe somewhere across the world. And then life wouldn't be so cruel anymore.

Caryn patted her immaculate silver-white hair and stared across the water at her brother's home. "It will all be mine very soon."

Maybe then she could find some peace at last.

## Chapter Nineteen

"**H**ere's what you're going to do," Serena told Dana as she turned the car down an alley of warehouses on the outskirts of Wichita. "I'm going to let you go back to Castle Donovan, Miss Barlow."

At Dana's shuddering sigh, she held up a hand. "But with stipulations, of course."

"Of course," Dana said, glancing over her shoulder at the back seat where Sharon Harper sat hunched over. Since she'd just learned she could only depend on herself, Dana was no longer scared. Just angry and determined. "What are the stipulations?"

"We have your brother," Serena said, a smirk moving over her full lips. "He's probably with Caryn right now." At Dana's gasp, she shrugged, tossed her thick hair over her shoulder. "They thought Caryn was dead, killed in the raid at the church complex. But she got away. And she's coming to Wichita to claim what is rightfully hers. She has your brother—and the final piece of the puzzle."

Dana's heart threatened to burst out of her chest as she struggled against her seat belt to look at the other woman. "Don't hurt Stevie. He doesn't understand any of this."

"That's not quite true," Serena said, giving Sharon a look in the rearview mirror. "We've been watching your brother for some time now. I've been especially attentive to him since he's been at the mansion. He's very smart. He has it all figured out, but you and Donovan were too preoccupied with each other to even listen to the boy. Brendan lost interest in pursuing Stephen's abilities, but I kept working on him."

Dana caught the hint of resentment in Serena's words and stored that bit of information—that and Brendan's backing off from her brother. But right now, she only wanted to know about Stephen. "What do you mean? He's good with puzzles and codes, but that doesn't give *any* of you the right to harm him. Just let him go."

"We had to put it all together," Serena replied, her tone so conversational, Dana could almost believe they were just sitting here chatting it up. "Brendan knew it even before he brought you to the mansion. But I had to wait before I could make a move. I didn't even let Caryn know we had you at first, because I was so afraid she'd kill all of us in one of her fits of rage. But Caryn didn't want either of you dead—not yet anyway—so I held her off from doing anything too rash. I told her I'd bring you and the boy to her alive."

That acknowledgment caused Sharon Harper to let out a moan. "She's going to kill us *now,* don't you see? This woman heard everything we talked about. She heard us talking about the codes in the shoes. Now that they know that, they won't let us live."

"Hush," Serena said over her shoulder. "No one is going to hurt you, Sharon. You're my hostage. You and that strange brother of *hers* get to live." With that, she tossed a harsh gaze back to Dana. "So here's the plan. You will go back to that so-called castle and if anyone questions you, you will pretend that you got away from me. I'm going to make sure the security cameras and monitors malfunction just long enough for you to go to Caryn. You go on foot to the old abbey. There's a trail that follows the perimeters of the property. Then you will meet Caryn there this afternoon at five o'clock. If you don't show up, your brother will be dead by morning. And our little friend here—" she pointed toward Sharon Harper "—she's our insurance policy. She knows too much."

"Why don't you let Sharon go?" Dana asked, the disgust and worry coursing through her body a roaring noise inside her ears. "And my brother, too. You know about the shoes—"

"Yes, we know everything now. Except the codes for the final sensors. Your brother knows them, though. He's so attached to his shoes, he's managed to see the coding right there in the design pattern—that silly blinking and vibration. That's so like Brendan to come up with something so simple for something so complicated. But your little brother, he thrives on simple but complicated. So he might be spared. Caryn might be able to train him, use him in the future. After we're done with you, of course."

Dana felt the horror of that declaration pouring over her like a hot rain. "What do you mean? If Caryn has Stephen now, why can't she find out what she wants, then let him go? She can take me, do whatever she wants with me. But you need to let my brother go."

Serena cranked the gray sedan she'd taken from one of the helpless workers back at the factory. "Caryn likes to tie up all the loose ends. She wants to make sure you're dead before she takes Stephen away. She'll take him underground until things cool off. And if you don't show up, if you spill your guts to Donovan or anyone else, your brother and this sniveling stool pigeon will both die. But just to make sure you understand, they will suffer before they die. Do I make myself clear?"

Dana could see very clearly what Serena was telling her. She didn't have a choice. She had to go to Caryn somehow, without Brendan knowing. Of course, it was pretty obvious where Serena would take her. Then it hit her.

"Caryn wants to make *her* brother suffer, too, doesn't she? Is that why she's insisting on me going to her? She knows Brendan will come searching for Stephen and me."

"You're smarter than you look," Serena replied, her cool assessment of Dana taking on a new respect. "Just don't get too smart. That could be fatal." Then she laughed, the sound like fingernails hitting glass. "Caryn hates Brendan. But I've filled her in on how very close the two of you have become. He has such a soft spot for women, don't you see? That particular weakness will bring him to her on his knees. She wants to hear him beg."

Dana sat there, her gaze moving over the deserted warehouses where they'd stopped. She couldn't run this time, and she couldn't depend on Brendan or any of her friends anymore. She had to face this head-on and alone. If she tried to leave this car, she'd be dead and so would Sharon Harper. And worse, Stephen would be at the mercy of these insane, disillusioned people. The thought of her innocent brother being a pawn between Caryn and Brendan made Dana sick. It also made her dangerous.

She turned to face Serena, her course set. "I'll go to Caryn, because I don't want anything to happen to my brother." Then she leaned close and lowered her voice to a whisper. "But one day very soon, I will find some justice in knowing that *all* of you will have to answer to someone besides me." She pointed upward. "Caryn is worshipping the wrong god, Serena."

"I'm so scared," Serena said, laughing again.

"You should be," Dana replied. She was rewarded with the brief spark of the unknown fear she saw in Serena's dark eyes.

After saying a silent prayer, Dana remembered her mother's words to her long ago. *He will not leave you comfortless, Dana. Trust in the Lord. Remember, don't seek your own understanding, but trust in Him in all you do.*

Dana didn't have anything left to give. She'd tried depending on Brendan and he'd tricked her just as badly as his sister. She knew to turn to a higher source, to give her the courage to get through the next few hours until she could see Stephen again. God would show her the strength He'd always given to her.

"I'll do what needs to be done," she said to Serena again, a new peace settling over her soul.

Serena nodded, satisfied that she's put a solid fear in Dana. But what Serena didn't know was that Dana was no longer in fear of her or Caryn Roark.

Dana Barlow had a new mission. She was going to get to her brother and save him, if it was the last thing she ever did.

"Which way?" Brendan asked into the phone at his ear.

"They headed south of town. We're trying to follow them, sir, but we've lost contact. The suspect managed to take a side road into the warehouse district."

"You lost them?" Brendan shouted into the phone. "Why didn't you move in immediately and capture Serena Carson?"

"It's a dangerous situation," the agent replied. "I've got agents looking for them right now. We don't want any harm to come to the hostages."

"Neither do I," Brendan said, the thought of Dana being held by a woman he'd considered one of his most trusted aides making him feel physically ill. "Serena is smart," he told the agent. "She'll know we're watching her. But she'll also know that we won't move in on them unless we absolutely have to do so."

"Are you saying she might force the issue?"

"She could. Or she could do something completely unexpected."

"Hold on," the agent shouted into the phone.

Brendan held his breath, expecting the worst, hoping against hope that Dana wouldn't try anything foolish. But knowing Dana, he figured she'd try to get away however she could.

"What is it?" he shouted, the tension inside his body coiling and hissing like a giant snake.

"Good news," the agent said. "We picked up the trail again, out on the interstate."

"Are they still headed south?"

"Yes, sir."

Brendan waited over the next few minutes, waited and wondered how he could ever forgive himself if something happened to Dana.

Finally the agent shouted into the phone. "That something unexpected. She just did it, sir. We just got a call from our operatives. Serena Carson let one of the hostages go."

Brendan closed his eyes, his one prayer asking God to spare both women trapped inside that car, but his one hope that Dana was the one being set free. "Which one?" he said, the words barely audible. "Where?"

"She let Dana Barlow out, sir. She still has the Harper woman."

"Where's Dana?" Brendan shouted into the phone. But the agent had already hung up.


"Where could she have gone?" Brendan asked Spear a few minutes later. They knew Serena had dropped Dana off on the main road near the gates, but Dana hadn't come back to the house.

They were in Brendan's office on the first floor, with agents and authorities swarming around, but Dana was nowhere to be found. They'd searched the grounds, they'd checked the monitors and security systems, and no sight of her. He'd even checked on Stephen at the day care to warn Gilda and Leo to be on the lookout for Serena. No sign of Dana there, either.

Now it was growing dark. And Brendan was slowly losing what little grip he had on reality. He could feel it happening again, that solid, sick fear that something wasn't right. He'd felt it the night Shannon had died, and he was feeling it right now.

"We're searching the grounds, sir," Spear said, a look of empathy in his black eyes as he lowered his voice. "We know from the gate monitors that Serena dropped her off just inside the estate walls, right by the main gate. But Dana set out on foot from there."

"And she didn't come back here to the house," Brendan finished, going over it in his mind for the hundredth time. Not wanting the FBI to hear this conversation, he whispered. "Why would Dana run away now? Where could she be hiding?"

He didn't say it out loud, but even if Dana hated *him* with all her being now, she would have come back to the house for her brother. Dana wouldn't just take off without Stephen.

So why wasn't she here? That was the question that kept forming in his mind. Serena Carson was on the lam with Sharon Harper, but all of his sources told him they'd soon be taken into custody. Serena couldn't get very far with the FBI and the state police after her. So why would Dana be hiding out?

And his sister Caryn—reports from the fiery scene of the church complex indicated that she was probably dead. But they hadn't found anything to substantiate that yet.

Then he remembered Dana's parting words to him—to take care of Stephen for her. What if Dana knew where his sister was and she'd gone after her on her own? "I need proof."

Spear's dark eyebrows brushed up his face at that statement. "Proof of what, sir?"

Brendan's mind started coiling and curling around a

thought so horrible that he knew his gut instincts had been right. Leaning close, he said, "What if my sister didn't die in the fire, Spear? What if she's on the loose and headed here?" He ran a hand down his face. "She could already be here, somewhere on the estate."

His gaze smashed into Spear's just as the other man realized what he was saying.

"She could have Miss Barlow," Spear said, his ruddy face going pale.

Brendan hit his hand on the desk. "And Serena would know how to change all the security codes so we'd have a hard time tracking anyone within the perimeters."

Spears groaned. "Which is why we can't seem to locate Miss Barlow."

Brendan's heart did a hard thump against his rib cage. "We're completely vulnerable to anyone getting inside."

Already, Spears was keying in codes on his handheld remote. "It's not responding, sir."

Brendan went into action. "Have the stableman saddled my horse. I'm going to sneak out from under these incompetent agents and go to the old abbey to search it out, and getting there on horseback will be quieter and easier. Dana must have had a reason for running instead of returning here to the house. I have to find her before Caryn does. And we have to get there before the authorities figure this out and set up camp all over the estate."

Spear was headed out the door to follow orders when Tony pushed him back in, his expression bordering on sheer terror. "We need—"

Brendan nodded, held up a hand. "Let's take this outside, Tony."

Understanding, Tony turned back out into the hallway. "Mr. Donovan, we've got major problems."

"I know. Our security system has been compromised."

Tony bobbed his head. "It's more than that, sir. Leo isn't answering his page and your sister Gilda, she's been injured."

Brendan sank back against a wall, waiting to hear the worst. "What happened, Tony?"

"They took Stephen, Mr. Donovan. Somehow, they got in here—I mean, they took over the day care, right after it had closed for the day. They rigged the alarms and cameras to make things look normal, and they took that boy. Miss Gilda fought them, but they knocked her over the head. Leo was hurt, too, according to Miss Gilda, but he's out tracking them right now, we think, since we can't get a response from him." He stopped to take a breath, his hands shaking their way over his stiff hair. "Dana's gonna have a fit for sure. I...I don't know—"

Brendan stood up to steady Tony. "It's not your fault. Serena Carson was—is—working for Caryn. Serena set the whole thing up, I'm sure." And he hadn't taken the time to send extra security to Gilda and Leo, because he'd been so worried about Dana. He stopped, gripped Tony's bony arms. "Listen, Tony, Dana is missing, too."

Tony's face went red with fear. "Well, that explains why that woman flirted with me so much. She was fishing for information." He stuttered, "Oh, d-dear God, help us. It's—it's worse than we could ever imagine."

"Much worse," Brendan said. "Much, much worse." Then he grabbed Tony and pushed him to the door. "We have to find them, all of them." He hurried toward the lower level. "I think I know where they might be, and I'm not going to wait on procedure and protocol to get them back."

The darkness was alive with shadows and sounds. It moved around Dana in swishing, hissing fingers that seemed to claw close to her ears. Through a jagged hole in the crushed roof of the old abbey, she could see a crescent moon and a few stars scattered like broken glass across the silky night sky.

"Are you comfortable, dear?" Caryn asked from the rotten desk where she sat in the corner, a single candle burning just enough to make her face look ethereal and yellowed with age. "Are you cold?"

"I'm fine," Dana replied, the ropes at her hand cutting through her skin each time she tried to move. "Why don't you let my brother go now, please?"

"I like your brother," Caryn replied, the sound of her fingernails hitting the cracked oak of the desk a constant reminder, like a clock ticking away to nowhere. "I think, yes, I think even after I toss you over the side of this building, I will take your sweet brother out of that basement downstairs and bring him under my wing. He'll be under my constant care. He'll be such an asset to our cause."

Dana closed her eyes to the terror of that scenario. "You can't do that. Stephen is just a boy. He has special needs—"

"He has a special mind," Caryn interrupted, rising to come and stand in front of Dana, her white tunic fluttering out around her like wisps of mist in the moonlight. "A very special mind. Why, just think what one could do with all that locked-up brilliance. With the proper training, he could show me the way to a whole new future. And that would be so good for my followers. They need someone to care for them, to watch over them and control them. They are so lost, don't you see?"

"I see," Dana said, spitting the words at her, "that you are a very sick, delusional woman. I see that you don't understand that you won't get away with this." She tossed hair out of her face. "No matter what you do to me, it's over for you, Caryn. The FBI has raided your building, and I'm sure they have Serena Carson in custody by now. Brendan knows all about how you've been stealing his technology, and he knows what you're trying to do with it. You can't run forever, Caryn."

"Shut up, please," Caryn said, her voice as calm as a schoolmarm's. "I have never had to run. I've always had people around me at my beck and call. People believe in me, Miss Barlow, and they follow my word. Too bad you didn't give it a chance."

"I won't worship at your feet," Dana replied. "I only worship the one true God. And He's a God who is forgiving and loving, not manipulative and cunning."

"'A sound heart is the life of the flesh; but envy the rottenness of the bones,'" Caryn quoted. "I think you are jealous of what you can't understand, young lady."

Dana laughed out loud. "And I think you quote way too many Bible verses that you don't even begin to understand or follow."

"Spare me," Caryn replied. "I would think you'd be tolerant of alternatives forms of religion."

"I'm not tolerant of someone as evil as you," Dana replied, all the while her hands trying to work the tight ropes at her back. She had to hold the fear and hysteria at bay, for Stephen's sake. Because somewhere down in the dark, her brother was locked away.

While she worked on the ropes, she prayed. And while she prayed, she kept her eyes on a stone cross centered on the ivy-covered wall in front of her. The cross was broken and crooked, but it was still there, a constant in this nightmare. "Tell me, Caryn, do you actually believe that your followers have a better life with you?"

"I've had enough of this conversation," Caryn replied. "Serena should be bringing your brother to us very soon. I still can't believe the look on dear Gilda's face when I walked into that adorable nursery school and took Stephen right out from under her nose. And that strange man with her—Leo she called him. Serena had to wound him, I'm afraid. He was fighting like a wild man. He had to be restrained."

Dana listened, images of her brother being taken passing through her mind. "Is Stephen…is he okay? He doesn't like the dark, Caryn."

"He's fine," Caryn replied, sweeping a hand in the air. "I have a way with children." Then she shrugged. "It's all going to work out just perfect. Stephen will be here with us soon. And once Brendan gets here, we will celebrate. He gets to watch you die, much in the same way his poor, weak Shannon had to die. Then, after I kill Brendan, I will take your brother far away from here. Maybe back to Ireland."

Dana saw the condescending dare in the other woman's eyes. It shimmered like a warning glare through the moonlight that filtered into the crippled walls of this old, silent building. "I will not let that happen," she said, her words a firm promise that echoed out into the wind as she finally felt the ropes at her back give way.

Down below the jagged terrace where the abbey stood, Leo Ryan lay gasping for breath. He'd been shot in the right shoulder, and wouldn't you know it, he was bleeding all over the bluestems. But not to worry, Leo thought as he glanced up at the moon and said a prayer for physical courage. He'd suffered much worse in his lifetime.

"Not to worry," he said on a rushed whisper. "I will find you, Stephen. I will protect you. I am not so scared now. I know God will watch over you and me. I feel the spirit of hope inside my wound."

All of that was well and good, Leo thought with a chuckle. "But first I have to figure out what she's done with you."

With a grunt, Leo got to his feet and began tracking again.

Serena had brought the boy this way, he was sure. He'd found footprints in the grass and dirt.

*Serena.* Leo knew something hadn't been right with that woman. She was too bossy, too inquisitive. But she left good footprints. It was her one downfall. She'd forgotten to cover her tracks.

Because one set of those footprints held the distinctive design of a pattern of ruby-cut imprints.

Stephen's shoes. The Ruby Runners.

"You are leaving me a trail, my young friend."

Leo intended to follow that trial, to the bitter end.

Brendan and Tony also intended to follow that trail. It hadn't been easy, slipping away from the watchful eyes of the FBI to come down to the underground control room. And it would only be a matter of time before the agents set up their own perimeter around the property. Brendan had to find Dana and Stephen before that happened. Because he knew his sister would resist authority, just as she'd always done. And she'd do whatever she had to do to get away, with Stephen.

"We might not be able to pick up a strong signal," Brendan said as he punched in codes and adjusted frequencies on the main terminal, "but it's worth a shot to see if the Ruby Runners can lead us to them." Nodding to Tony, he said, "Here, let's try this."

Tony's fingers danced a fast jig over the keyboard. "I sure hope this works, boss. I can't stand the thought of Dana with that crazy woman."

"Me, either," Brendan said, closing his eyes to the dark dread pitted inside his stomach.

It had been two hours. It was full dark outside, but they'd heard nothing from either his sister or Serena. And no one had a clue as to what had happened to Sharon Harper. He'd had a horse ready to go when Tony had pointed out the obvious.

"What about using the shoes to track them?"

Torn between rushing off to find Dana, or trying to think rationally, Brendan had taken a step back to try Tony's suggestion. But he'd never been a very patient man. He was going insane with worry and a kind of dark grief that wanted to pull him under, one last time.

Brendan fought against that dark grief. He wouldn't give up this time. He'd find Dana and make her see that he loved her and Stephen.

"Leo is out there, we know," he said now. "And the FBI will soon be combing the woods for them. But the FBI doesn't know about the abbey, and hopefully we can get there before they figure things out. Caryn has to be there, but she might have Stephen and Dana hidden someplace else."

"I think we're ready to give it a try," Tony stated with a fist in the air.

Brendan stood over Tony, his eyes watching the computer screen in front of them. It showed a grid of the surrounding land and woods, including all the structures located on the property. If Stephen was out there and if he was wearing the Ruby Runners, they should see a signal any second now. Brendan had shown Tony how to reset the codes so the sensors would be in place and accurate once again. If the sensors were still working.

They waited, the silence stretching like a cable cord between them. The seconds ticked off, lost on the echoes of the night like a frequency gone over the air.

"Maybe it was a bad idea," Tony said, swiveling around in his chair. "Maybe we should just go—"

Then Brendan saw it. A faint blinking on the screen.

"There," he said as he leaned close. "Look, Tony. Something is there."

"Yes," Tony said, letting the one word sizzle out of his mouth. "Yes. Attaboy, Stevie."

"They're on the other side of the lake, but they seem to be somewhere near the abbey," Brendan said. Tracking the screen with a finger, he said, "If memory serves me right, there is a series of underground rooms behind the main building. They might have Stephen and Dana there."

"Let's go," Tony replied, jumping up so fast his chair spun on its wheels.

"Do you ride?" Brendan called over his shoulder.

"Like—a horse?" Tony asked, his eyes crystal with fear. "Yes?"

"Yes, but I can handle a golf cart or a four-wheeler better."

"I've got both, but one is too slow and the other too noisy. You'll either have to take a horse, or stay here."

"I'm not staying here," Tony said. "I'm going out there with you. I promised Dana I'd have your back, no matter what."

Brendan didn't wait to decide. "Come on. But don't slow me down."

"Okay, then."

Tony tapped his way after Brendan's disappearing back, and realized he really, really wanted to find not only Dana, but Stephen and Leo, too, alive and well. Because somewhere in all of this espionage and chaos, he'd finally realized he did have a heart. At least heart enough to let Dana go to the man she loved.

If he could keep her alive.

## Chapter Twenty

Leo managed to crawl his way to the lone live oak that stood sentinel by the ivy-covered walls of the abbey. Now he watched and waited, sure that an FBI SWAT team was also out there somewhere, searching in the darkness for Caryn Roark and Dana Barlow. He didn't want them to mistake him for the enemy.

Leo only wanted to find Stephen.

Stephen had been left in his care, and he aimed to see to it that Stephen was found safe and sound—and alive. So Leo said a prayer to the God who had helped him overcome alcoholism and depression, to the God who had shown him that if he'd just hang on, someone would come along and need him again.

"I'm glad I waited, Lord," Leo whispered to the night wind. "But I could really use a drink right about now." Then he shook his head. "Strike that request. What I need right now is the courage only You can give me."

The pain in his shoulder throbbed a resounding beat through his temple. "Go in. Go in."

Leo had a gut feeling that Stephen was down inside the bowels of that old building somewhere. Gilda had told him her sister might be holed up in this creepy old place. It just made sense that they'd hide Stephen somewhere dark and scary, somewhere where others couldn't find him so quickly.

And since he'd found another set of footprints leading to the abbey, Leo had a feeling Dana was inside that building, too, maybe with her brother, maybe in another room. She'd come to get her brother, even if Caryn Roark had set the whole thing up, *because* Caryn Roark had set the whole thing up.

Leo leaned back, took a calming breath, and waited, sweat trickling down his back to his spine while blood ran out of the wound on his shoulder.

He'd learned a long time ago that waiting and watching could bring a man the ultimate prize—everyone got to live. That was why he hadn't called out yet. He didn't want to spook anyone, the good guys or the bad. And he didn't want to wait like a coward this time, hidden in a protective ball of pain. No, he wanted to be alert and calm, unafraid of what might come.

He had Gilda to thank for that. Gilda and God. Gilda had seen the good in Leo. Gilda had been kind to him from the first. Knowing that someone so pure and so loving had seen into his soul gave Leo the peace he'd been seeking all his life. And the courage to act.

Now he was ready to make his next move.

Trying to get a clear picture in his head, Leo knew from moving around that the building had been built on many levels. There was the main sanctuary, sitting on the broken and damaged rock terrace, that rose up like a dark gray skeleton into the trees, and then there was the one-storied dormitory-type wing that must have held sleeping quarters and other rooms at one time.

Squinting in the star-shrouded moonlight, Leo saw a set of stairs leading down at the very end of the dorm building.

"A cellar, maybe?"

The wind seemed to hear his question. It picked up with a mournful pitch. And Leo heard that throbbing instruction inside his head again. "Go in. Go in."

He knew what he had to do. And this time he wouldn't cower or panic. This time, Leo Ryan was going to display the courage of a real hero.

"Leo is still missing in action," Tony said as he held on for dear life on the back of one of Brendan's mean Arabian stallions. It had been a long time since he'd ridden a horse, but it was like riding a bicycle. It came back to him, but only because he didn't want to hit the ground and get trampled to death.

The horse Brendan was riding was even meaner, even blacker, and twice the size of the one he'd put Tony on. Tony was having a hard time keeping up with him. "Did you hear me?"

"I heard you," Brendan said over his shoulder. "And do I have to remind you that these woods are probably teeming with a SWAT team and all sorts of operatives who've come along with my sister. Don't shout out at me again, or I'll have to knock you off that horse."

"Yes, sir," Tony whispered, wishing with all his heart he'd stayed back in Kansas City. "I just want to find Dana and Stephen."

"So do I," Brendan said as he came along side Tony. "And we will. At least I convinced the FBI not to rush in with guns blazing. If Caryn doesn't have them in the abbey, then we're in big trouble. That means she's taken them somewhere else, maybe even out of the country."

"Not to Ireland?" Tony asked, trying to keep the squeal out of his voice.

"That would be the most obvious place, but I'm praying it hasn't come to that yet."

"Leo is out here somewhere," Tony reminded Brendan. "He won't let anyone catch him and he'll be the one to find them first, I guarantee."

"You could be right," Brendan said as they eased their horses along the lake. "We'll tie up here and walk the rest of the way to the abbey. If I know my sister, she's there, expecting us."

Tony followed Brendan's lead, and thankful to be off the big horse, secured his snorting animal to a nearby shrub. "This is one party I'd just as soon not attend," he replied on a thin whisper.

Brendan stopped him with a hand on his arm. "I can't imagine how we all wound up together, Tony, but I love Dana. And I love Stephen—"

"Hey, man, if you're about to tell—tell *me* you love *me*, it's cool, really," Tony interrupted, his stutter echoing out over the woods. "Let's just keep it light, okay, man? It's no big deal."

Brendan swatted his arm. "Shut up and listen. I care about all of you. I feel responsible for everyone who's helped me with this."

"This," Tony reminded him, "is all about getting your sister off the streets and behind bars."

"That's what I'm trying to say," Brendan continued. "She was my family and now—"

"And now you have us," Tony finished, his voice going soft with understanding. "And Gilda. She'll never desert you."

"I might have lost Dana, though."

"No, man, we're going in there to get her, remember?"

"I didn't tell her what I was doing."

Tony stopped in his tracks so fast, his sneakers threw dirt up. "What do you mean?"

"Before I brought you all here, I did my research. And I found out about Stephen."

Tony raked a hand over his jutting chin. "So are you telling me you don't want that boy around? 'Cause Dana won't go anywhere without him, trust me on that, buddy."

"No," Brendan said, the word tearing out of his throat. "I can't waste time explaining now, but I knew that Stephen was special. And smart. And I put two and two together."

"And figured he was the key to all of this," Tony said as Brendan pushed him along the bank. "You were analyzing that kid this whole time? That's just about as low as Caryn wanting to use him to control the world."

Brendan nodded, and Tony could see the self-disgust on his face, even in the waning moonlight. "I only did it so I could better protect him, but Dana didn't see it that way when Serena told her this afternoon."

Tony whistled low. "Oh, man, is that why Dana took off on her own?"

"It could be. I just don't know," Brendan said. Then he stilled Tony. "Look, we're almost there. Whatever we find in there, whatever happens, I need you to make me a promise."

Tony held up a hand. "Hey, I've already signed over my life to you. What now?"

"I want you to take care of them, Tony. In case something goes wrong."

"What could go wrong? We're only dealing with a loon and her whole loose-cannon cult."

Brendan backed him up against a sycamore tree. "I'm very serious, Tony. Don't make me regret asking for your help."

Tony held up both hands. "Sorry. Okay, okay. You know I love Dana. I'll do whatever I have to do. And…I love Stephen, too. This little forced vacation together has made me see the light, so to speak, about him. So, I promise." Then he went nose to nose with Brendan. "But I need that same promise from you."

"Deal," Brendan said, his dark eyes full of both dread and hope.

"Deal," Tony replied, then reached out a hand to Brendan. They shook on it.

Seeming satisfied, Brendan gently yanked Tony by the collar. "Thank you."

Tony straightened and stood tall. "No problem. Now, can we please just get on with this and get it over with?"

"He's coming," Caryn told Dana as she paced back and forth in the muted darkness. "I can feel it."

"Of course he'll come," Dana replied, her mouth so dry she had to force the words through her lips. "You knew he would. You don't care about me or my brother. You only want to see Brendan beaten."

"That's very true," Caryn admitted. "It's about time I beat him, don't you think? I mean, he took my father away, then he took everything that should have been mine."

"Brendan is not to blame for his father's misdeeds," Dana reminded her, her own feelings for Brendan too raw and exposed to explore right now. "You need to learn to forgive and get on with things, Caryn."

"Oh, I'm getting on with things," Caryn replied in a snapping voice. "I'm going to kill you, right in front of him, the same way I killed his dear little wife."

Dana stilled as the realization of that boast caught her in the gut. "You killed Shannon?"

"Yes," Caryn said, whirling to smile at her. "I pushed her right out that broken arched window over there. She hit the terrace and died instantly. Of course, Brendan wasn't here to see it that time, so he assumed it was a suicide, a desperate attempt to gain his attention. It got his attention all right."

Dana couldn't comprehend someone being so truly evil and uncaring. "How could you—"

Caryn came so close, Dana saw the icy blue of her lifeless eyes. "I could and I will. I can do anything I want. I have the power and the means, and once I have you and Brendan out of the way, I'll take your brother and build empires. I'll have what I need of Brendan's technology, enough hidden money to start over and the brilliant mind that's trapped inside your brother's head. He'll be like the son I never had. It's going to be glorious. My prayers have at last been answered."

"And what about Gilda?" Dana asked, the sick feeling in her stomach causing the words to sound shrill in her ears. "What about your twin sister? Haven't you hurt her enough?"

"Gilda is dead to me," Caryn replied, her robe flying out as she pivoted to stare out into the darkness. "Gilda is weak and submissive, so very pious and devout. She always loved Brendan, didn't care about his questionable parentage or what he took from us. She doesn't have any vision, you see?"

"I see that she is a good Christian woman," Dana countered, her hands still holding the ropes she'd managed to twist out of, her wrists burning with cuts from searing, raw strips of pain. "I see that Gilda has lived a good life, helping others, while you've lived a charade. Gilda has more vision than you can ever dream of finding."

Caryn whirled so fast, Dana didn't see the hand coming across her face until it was too late. The pain that followed left her reeling and dizzy, but she managed to keep her freed hands hidden.

"Shut up," Caryn said in a grating whisper. "Or I won't wait for my brother to get here."

"I see a light up there," Tony whispered to Brendan as they hunkered down on their bellies to work their way up the slope to the abbey.

"Aye, me, too," Brendan said through a struggling breath. "That would be my sister, waiting on my arrival."

"So what's the plan?" Tony wheezed, "Rush in with guns blazing, or sneak in on a surprise attack?"

"The element of surprise is always a good option," Brendan replied. "You will rush up the stairs, screaming for dear life, while I try to overcome my sister from behind."

"Could we switch places?" Tony whined. "I mean, I'm better at sneaking then rushing, I think."

Brendan patted him on the shoulder. "You'll be fine. You don't have to show yourself. Just distract her so I can get to Dana."

"Yeah, right, distracting. I'm not so sure I'm good at that, either."

"Just do it, Tony," Brendan retorted, all patience gone now. "Once we get Dana away, we'll find Stephen."

"Right, a piece of cake. I got it."

"Good," Brendan replied. "So here's the plan—"

Leo looked through the dirty window, down into the dark pit of the basement. Someone was definitely down there. He could just make out a shape huddled in the corner. A shape that sat rocking back and forth. Then he heard the distinctive chant of Stephen's high-pitched voice. "Dana will come. Dana will come. Dana will come."

That chant broke Leo's bitter old heart. And made him twice as brave as he felt.

"Now to get in and get you out," he said, his breath ragged, his right hand covered with blood from his wound. "Then everything will be all right, little Stephen."

Leo glanced around, making sure he was alone on the old stone and wood steps. Then he moved silently down the curving stairs, taking one step at a time until he was at the door.

"Locked," he breathed. "But then it would be, wouldn't it?"

It was a flimsy door. Leo looked around for something to pry the lock. Seeing nothing, he pulled out the pearl-handled revolver Gilda had given him just before he took off. Gilda was a very resourceful woman. He'd have to tell her that when this was over.

"Stephen, are you in there?" Leo asked in a high whisper. "Stephen?"

Leo heard rustling and then what sounded like jumping. "Leo. Leo. Stephen's here. Stephen's here. Let me out. Let me out now. Don't like her. Don't like her."

"Okay, sport. Stand back. Stand way back in the corner, Stephen. I have to pry the door."

"Okay," came the wail of a response. "Okay, Leo. Ready. Stephen's ready."

Standing back, Leo lifted the gun, turning the handle toward the door, planning to crack open the old hinged lock without taking a shot. With all his might, Leo hit the handle on the old lock, the effort causing him to see stars in his head to match the ones in the sky. The lock fell open just as Leo kicked at the heavy wooden door. The door splintered like the wound piercing Leo's shoulder.

He rushed into the room, waiting for his old eyes to adjust to the darkness. "Stephen?"

"I'm here. Stephen is here, Leo. Stephen wants out."

Leo wanted to hug the boy close, but he refrained. "Come on out, buddy. You're safe now. It's over."

"I knocked her down," Stephen said, pointing a shaking finger to the corner behind Leo. "Yeah, Stephen knocked her down. She's bad, bad, Leo. She held me too tight. I had to knock her away. Too tight. Don't like too tight."

Leo turned to find Serena crumpled and moaning in the corner. "Good job, sport." He bent to grab Serena, intent on either tying her up, or knocking her out. But Serena was already up. And she had a gun aimed for Leo's chest.

"Run, Stephen," Leo shouted, holding his arms out to

shield Stephen. "Run as fast as you can and find Dana. Run, Stephen."

Stephen screamed, then took off, his arms flailing as he hurried out of the dark room. "You come, too, Leo. Leo, please come!"

Then he heard shots and, because he didn't like loud noises, Stephen covered his ears and kept running, his own scream lifting out over the warm night like the cry of a wounded animal.

"Did you hear that?" Tony shouted to Brendan. "Gunshots!"

He got up to run toward the sound, but Brendan held him back. "Wait, Tony. Don't do anything stupid."

"That isn't good," Tony pointed out. Before he could get out any more protests, they heard several more shots, then a piercing scream. "Oh man, I think that's Stephen's high-trauma scream, you know, the one he saves for when he's really afraid or mad!"

"Okay, let's go," Brendan said, his heart hammering in a rapid beat that caught at his breath. "It came from behind the main building."

They rushed around the corner toward the screams, but another scream penetrated the suddenly still night.

"Brendan!"

Brendan looked up to the tall opening of what used to be an arched window in the turret room on the second floor of the abbey. The sight he saw there caused him to sink to his knees.

Tony sank down right next to him. "She's got Dana. She's going to push Dana."

Brendan didn't even hear him. He sat there, the last few days passing before him like a great river. Days of worry and anger, days of quiet times of brief laughter with the four peo-

ple who'd somehow stumbled into his life, days of wishing
he could be the kind of man Dana needed, days of hope, days
of fear, days watching Stephen with fascination and days of
falling in love with a woman and a child that could fulfill him
at last.

He saw it all there in the glow of a single candle, saw the
years stretching by, living with Dana and Stephen, having
their first child, doing the work that satisfied him, building
Dana a new farmhouse with a field of sunflowers in their front
yard.

But it wasn't to be. His sister had Dana perched like a delicate bird just over the lip of the jagged, scarred window. The
same window Shannon had jumped from.

"Dana," he called, her name like a flower floating out on
the night. "Dana."

He heard her sharp intake of breath, saw her struggle
against Caryn's restraining arm. But she didn't speak.

"I knew I'd bring you to your knees," Caryn said, her voice
shrill with anticipation and glee. "You're sitting in the spot
where our dear Shannon fell."

Brendan stood up on that, his heart beating with a new determination. "I've come for Dana," he said, the words controlled and calm. "I'm not leaving without her."

"Oh, that's not a problem, sweet brother," Caryn called
down. "I don't intend to let either of you leave. I only want
the boy now. The boy will be my family, my salvation."

Brendan watched, not daring to move, as she pushed Dana
farther out on the narrow ledge. He looked up at Dana and
saw that her hands were tied behind her back. He prayed
there wasn't a trigger-happy sharpshooter somewhere in a tree
about to open fire—both women would go over the ledge.
Tony lurched forward, but Brendan stopped him with a hand
on his stomach. "What do you want, Caryn?"

"What do I want? What do I want?" She threw back her head and laughed. "Oh, that's rich, coming from you. What I want is very simple. I want back what you took from me. I want back the happiness I felt as a little girl, before you came into the picture."

Brendan took one step forward, and with a subtle twist of his head, indicated to Tony the curving steps leading up to the turret room where Caryn was holding Dana. Tony took the hint and moved an inch in that direction.

"Caryn, I know you think you've been wronged. But I will try to make things up to you somehow. I need you to forgive me. Forgive me for whatever wrongs I did to you."

"You can't fix this," Caryn screamed, her white robes lifting out behind her. "You can't bring my parents back, or make Gilda and me close again. You ruined all of that for us. You ruined everything."

Brendan stood looking up at her. She was a beautiful woman, haughty and tall, porcelain and fragile. In the moonlight she looked like a white angel about to fly away.

"Caryn," he said, "I would do anything to change this. I would do anything to make you love me and forgive me."

"I will never love you," she replied, her hand tightening visibly on Dana's arm. "And I'm not going to give up everything I've worked so hard for, just to ease your guilty conscience. Forgiveness is not an option, brother."

Then Brendan saw it, just a brief view in the moonlight. Dana wasn't tied. She lifted her hands out just enough to show them that she was clinging to the ropes wrapped behind her back. Her eyes locked with his. Brendan saw her meaning in the bright glow of the stout candle Caryn held up. She'd somehow managed to free herself, but she didn't want Caryn to know that.

Brendan inched forward another hair, and held his breath

while Tony did the same. If he could just get Tony close enough to the steps, maybe Tony would be able to hurry up and do something, anything, to help Dana.

"Forgiveness is always an option, Caryn. It's a choice. It's a choice God gives us through His grace."

Caryn tugged Dana closer. "Don't talk to me about grace, Brendan. And don't preach to me about choices. Our father made a choice. He chose you. I can't forgive that, and I will never forget it."

From the corner of his eyes, Brendan saw a shape just underneath the trunk of the ancient oak tree. A dark, huddling shape. Then he heard it, a soft, gentle keening.

Stephen. Stephen was curled up against the tree, rocking back and forth, crying the silent, scared tears of a frightened little boy.

From that keening, a new hope emerged in Brendan's heart. He glanced over at Tony, flicked his hand toward the tree. Tony looked confused, then let out a little gasp of surprise.

Brendan stepped an inch forward. "Caryn, you want the Ruby Runners, right? You want all the formulas and designs for the SuperSensors, right? You need the information to take all the people I've trained, all the followers who will go with you to create your new world. I can give you everything you need, if you just let Dana go."

"I want the boy," Caryn shouted, her anger spewing forth like an electrical jolt into the dark sky. "I'm waiting for Serena to bring him to me."

"Serena isn't here," Brendan said. "I know she's not here, because I know Stephen is safe. Stephen is all right."

He said this, looking up at Dana's face, and was rewarded when he saw her body sink down in a visible shudder of relief.

"I don't believe anything you say," Caryn said, hissing the

words as she glanced around the eerie gray-washed ruins. "I don't believe you."

Brendan took a glance toward the tree. "Stephen can run very fast in his Ruby Runners. He's won three medals in Special Olympics. For running. He can run up steps really fast. I wish I could see Stephen do that right now."

"What are you talking about?" Caryn screamed, stomping and pushing at Dana. "You're just trying to distract me, Brendan. I'm telling you right now, if you don't show me that boy, I'm going to kill her."

Brendan's heart lurched right along with his sister's shove. Dana gasped and pulled back as she stared down the steep drop to the terrace rocks below.

"I'll show you the boy, but first let her go."

"No."

"I know Stephen is here. I believe Stephen is very brave. He can run right up those steps to see his sister. *Right now.*"

*Please, Lord, help this boy to understand.*

"Dana!"

Everything after that happened in slow motion in Brendan's mind. He saw Stephen stand up, heard Stephen call out Dana's name. He saw Dana turn to push at Caryn, saw Caryn grasp at air, watched as Stephen rushed past him and up the stairs, all the while calling out Dana's name.

Tony took off after Stephen, calling to the boy, "Run fast, run fast, Stephen."

Brendan stood frozen, his mind taking in the struggle between his sister and the woman he loved. Then he heard Dana's scream and snapped into action, rushing up the steps right behind Stephen and Tony.

Brendan made it up to the turret room just in time to see Stephen pushing at Caryn's robes, while Tony headed to grab Dana away.

"Get away. Get away, crazy woman," Stephen said in that high-pitched, singsong voice. "Don't hurt my Dana."

Caryn turned, a smile on her face, a smile followed by shock as Tony pulled Dana away from her and turned Dana toward her brother.

Brendan saw that as his chance to get to Caryn. He waited until Tony had Dana away from the ledge, felt the brush of her hand on his as he rushed forward.

And watched as Caryn tried to reach out to Stephen and lost her footing. She slipped, clutched at air, grasping until she felt Brendan's hand in hers, even as she was falling over the ledge.

"No!" Brendan shouted as Caryn fell. He felt the pull of her weight taking him with her, and dropped to the rotten floor in an effort to keep both of them from falling over.

Lying there, his head over the ledge, his body straining and bracing against the creaking, splintered floor, Brendan held his sister's hand with a death grip. "Caryn, don't give up. Hold on. I'll pull you back. I'll pull you back." Tears pricking his eyes, he said, "You can come back, Caryn. You can always come back to Christ."

She looked up at him, surprise glistening in her eyes as the moonlight swept over her with a delicate hand of pearl and gray. "Brendan," she said, her words rushing out as she held tightly to his hand. "'A brother offended is harder to be won than a strong city…and their contentions…like the bars of a castle'. I've always loved Proverbs."

"No, Caryn, no," Brendan said, tears streaming down his face. "I'll give it all up. I don't care. I'll let go of all contentions. I have no castles. Don't let go, Caryn."

She laughed, a soft tinkling sound that spoke of a carefree happiness. "Brendan, there is no contention now. You win."

And then she let go.

* * *

They found Leo near dawn. FBI agents and reporters, every form of law enforcement, and every form of curiosity seeker, swarmed the place by morning. But no one had thought to look down in the basement.

Except Stephen.

"That's the place, Dana. That's the scary room. Leo found me there. Leo had a gun. Yeah, Leo said 'Run, Stephen.' Stephen ran."

Dana was sitting in the back of an ambulance with a blanket around her. She pulled Stephen close, trying to hug him. He pushed at her. "Leo? Where's Leo?" Stephen pointed toward the moss-stained stairs. "Find Leo."

Brendan was sitting next to them, and Dana watched as he rushed into action. "Tony, we have to check the cellar."

Dana realized what Stephen was saying and pushed her blanket off to run toward the stairs.

"No," Brendan said, turning to hold her back. "Don't go in there."

"But—"

She looked down to where Tony stood just inside the door. And saw the tears falling down Tony's face.

"No," she said, trying to push past Brendan. "No!"

"He's dead, Dana," Brendan said, holding her close, his hands pulling through her hair. "He's gone."

"No." She whispered the word against Brendan's chest, the nightmarish hues of the sun's first rusty rays seeming to go on and on inside her fog of shock. "Not Leo. Not Leo."

"He saved Stephen," Brendan told her, the words harsh with pain. "Serena is down there, too, and she's dead. They must have both fought to the finish."

Stephen came up to tug on Dana's blanket. "Where's Leo, Dana?"

Dana turned to her brother, tears pouring down her face. "Leo was a very brave man, sport. Leo saved your life."

Stephen stomped his feet and stared up at her. "Where's Leo? I want Leo. Leo watches Stephen. Leo takes care of Stephen."

Dana couldn't speak. Instead, she pulled Stephen close and gave him a quick hug. Then she felt Brendan's hand on her arm. Tony stood beside him.

"They just took Serena out. Gilda is down there with Leo. She insisted on coming."

Dana put a fist to her mouth to keep from screaming. Brendan tried to comfort her, but she pushed him away. Looking over to Tony, she said, "Talk to Stephen. He doesn't understand."

Brendan gave her a look that caused her heart to break, but she couldn't face him right now. She sank down on the ground, looking up at the now-brilliant blues and golds of the morning sky.

Tony wiped his face and bent on one knee in front of Stephen. "Hey, sport, remember that tattoo on Leo's arm?"

"Star over tree. Lone star over a tree."

"That's right," Tony said, his voice cracking. "Leo is our star now, sport. Leo is up there with God, watching over us. Always."

Stephen hopped from foot to foot, his face squeezing in confusion. "I want Leo here, watching me. Here now, Tony."

"He can't be here, buddy. He has to be a star now. He's in heaven."

Stephen smiled then. "Heaven is nice. Mama and Daddy are in heaven. God lives in heaven. Yeah, heaven is nice."

Tony wiped his eyes and sniffed. "Yeah, heaven is a cool place, especially with Leo up there, that's for sure."

"For sure," Stephen said, flailing his arms, his smile widening. "Leo is my star." Then he looked down at his shoes.

"Leo said God put my feet in these shoes. He said I could run as fast as the wind. Yeah, my shoes helped save Dana. That's right. I ran fast. Fast as the wind. Leo said I could do it. Right, Dana?"

Dana smiled, shook her head yes. And watched as Brendan's head came up and his gaze locked with hers.

Stephen looked from his sister to Brendan. "Leo told me God brought all of us here. Yeah, together. God brought us all together. Ain't you glad, Dana? Huh? Huh, Brendan? I like together."

Brendan gave Stephen a weak smile. "I'm very glad, Stephen. I like together, too." Then he looked back at Dana, the smile gone.

Tony turned to Dana, shrugged, sniffed and walked away, his head down.

Dana sat in the bluestems, watching as they brought Leo out, Gilda behind the stretcher, her eyes red-rimmed and wide, her head bandaged. Then Dana watched as Gilda left Leo and went to the other ambulance where her sister lay.

Brendan stood off to the side, his dark gaze as deep and brooding as a windswept prairie. Dana knew she should go to him, tell him she loved him, but her heart hurt too much to even risk such a hope. He'd used her, tricked her, tried to manipulate her brother, but in her deepest of hearts, Dana knew he'd done it for all the right reasons.

He had protected them, fought for them, saved them.

He loved them. She knew that; could see it in the intensity of his misty eyes. And yet, she didn't know if that love was an echo full of danger, or a ringing of a new hope. She didn't dare try to figure it out in her current state of shock and mourning. So she turned away, into herself and stared out at the flowing blanket of crushed bluestems and rich, red clover.

And wondered if she'd ever find her way back home again.

\* \* \*

"It's over," Brendan told Dana the next day as they sat at the long butcher-block table in the kitchen. "It's all over."

Dana nodded, glanced over at Gilda. The room was quiet. Tony was outside with Stephen, playing football. Those two had somehow become best buddies.

It broke Dana's heart. It all broke her heart.

"The Universal Unity Church is no more. What's left of the building will be razed by the end of the week, and most of the culprits in the illegal schemes have been apprehended. Sharon Harper is safe at home with her family again—Serena hid her in a warehouse near the factory, but she's okay. A bit shaken, but all right. Ricardo Amodeo is dead. He died in the shoot-out at the church compound."

No one spoke. The sun streamed in the high, paned windows. The red geraniums on the windowsill contrasted sharply with the lone white-and-pink striped amaryllis that blossomed heavily in the center of the big table.

"Where will we bury her?" Gilda asked, her voice raspy from crying.

"In Ireland," Brendan replied, his eyes downcast, his food untouched. "At the old castle."

"She will be at peace there," Gilda said. Then she turned to Dana. "I want to bury Leo here, if you don't object."

Dana nodded. "Tony says he didn't have any family to speak of. But we should let his children know where he's buried, at least."

"He had us," Gilda replied, tears forming in her eyes again. "He will always have us."

Brendan patted his sister's hand. "Leo will be here, close by, sister, if that's what you want."

Gilda smiled then got up to take her dishes to the big aluminum sink. "I have arrangements to take care of."

Brendan didn't speak. He just sat there, his fingers drumming on the table in that way Dana had come to know. After a few minutes of a taut silence, Dana rose to go, too.

But Brendan's hand on hers stopped her. "Don't."

She looked down at him, loving him, knowing his pain was a biting, hurting wound that might destroy him. And her. "What do you want from me, Bren?"

He laughed, a bitter sound of anguish. "I want so much. But mostly I want you to understand—I never meant Stephen any harm. I only wanted—"

"You wanted to control the situation. Isn't that what rich, powerful men like you do? You have to be on top of any situation, you have to figure out all the angles. You have to win, at all costs."

He let her hand go, the sting of her words evident in the way he flinched and looked away. Dana started for the door, intent on going outside in the warm, clean air.

Then she heard him, and turned to find him with his head in his hands on the table. His shoulders shook.

Dana felt the last shreds of anger and bitterness slipping away like a great cloak. Ashamed that she'd been part of the source of his agony, she rushed to him, wrapped her body over his and held him tightly to her. He lifted up, his hands going around her waist as he put his head against her body.

Then she heard his simple plea. "I want forgiveness."

Dana fell down on her knees, and held his face in her hands. "Stephen was right, Brendan. God did bring us together. And God gave you the ability to create amazing things—like computer technology and shoes and beautiful flowers."

He hushed her with a finger on her lips. "But look at what I've destroyed. My own sister is dead. Samantha… Leo—they're dead."

She stopped his words with a touch of her lips to his. "We did our best to stop all of this. We had to do it, Bren. We had to."

"I don't know if I can—"

"*We can,*" she told him. "We can make a new life together. We can start over, with our faith, and a new promise to God."

Tears wet his face as he lowered his head. "I can't face God."

Dana pulled his head up. "Yes, you can. You have faced the worst a man can face. Don't turn away from Him now, Bren." Then she kissed his tears. "I'm sorry I ever doubted you. I was just so scared, so confused."

"Do you love me?" he asked, the sound of his words showing his fragile need.

"I do," she told him. "I think I loved you from the moment you held me."

"In the storm."

"Yes, in the storm. You are an amazing man. How could I not love you?"

"I will try to be the kind of man you can be proud of, Dana."

"You already are."

It was the fall of that year when they got married at the tiny church in Prairie Heart. They honeymooned in Ireland, with Gilda and Stephen nearby in the old castle there, while Tony Martin looked after business in Wichita.

And then Brendan Donovan took his new wife home to Kansas, to the rambling white farmhouse he'd had built for her while they traveled, and there, as the sun set over the prairie, he showed her the field of sunflowers he'd planted for her out their back door. The flowers stood tall and elegant, and they blocked out the memories of what used to stand across that field.

Brendan wrapped his arms around his wife's waist and leaned his head into the sweet autumn scent of her hair. They watched as Gilda and Stephen walked toward the smiling sunflowers, laughing and talking.

"I'm home," Dana said as she leaned back against the solid security of her husband's chest.

Brendan closed his eyes and felt the echoes of peace washing over him. "Aye, we're all home now, love."

\* \* \* \* \*

*Be sure to pick up Lenora Worth's next*
*inspirational romance from*
*Steeple Hill Love Inspired,*
*A PERFECT LOVE,*
*available December 2005.*

*Love Inspired®*

ENJOY ANOTHER

## Tiny Blessings

STORY WITH

# HER CHRISTMAS WISH

BY

# KATHRYN SPRINGER

Little Olivia Cavanaugh wanted a mommy for Christmas—and thought her new nanny Leah Paxson was the perfect choice! Leah took Olivia to church, baked cookies with her and made her daddy, Eli, smile a lot. All Olivia had to do was convince her daddy to marry Leah so that she would stay with them always....

**TINY BLESSINGS: Giving thanks for the neediest of God's children, and the families who take them in!**

**Don't miss HER CHRISTMAS WISH**
**On sale November 2005**

*Available at your favorite retail outlet.*

**www.SteepleHill.com**

LIHCW

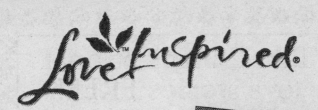

# IN THE SPIRIT OF... CHRISTMAS

### BY

## LINDA GOODNIGHT

Jesse Slater was raising his traumatized little girl, trying to reclaim his family's farm…and dealing with bitter memories of past holiday seasons. He didn't count on falling for his temporary boss Lindsey Mitchell. Lindsey sensed there were reasons behind Jesse's lack of faith, and wondered if she was meant to teach him and his daughter the true meaning of Christmas.…

**Don't miss IN THE SPIRIT OF…CHRISTMAS**
**On sale November 2005**

*Available at your favorite retail outlet.*

# Take 2 inspirational love stories FREE!

## PLUS get a FREE surprise gift!

### Mail to Steeple Hill Reader Service™

**In U.S.**
3010 Walden Ave.
P.O. Box 1867
Buffalo, NY 14240-1867

**In Canada**
P.O. Box 609
Fort Erie, Ontario
L2A 5X3

**YES!** Please send me 2 free Love Inspired® novels and my free surprise gift. After receiving them, if I don't wish to receive anymore, I can return the shipping statement marked cancel. If I don't cancel, I will receive 4 brand-new novels every month, before they're available in stores! Bill me at the low price of $4.24 each in the U.S. and $4.74 each in Canada, plus 25¢ shipping and handling and applicable sales tax, if any*. That's the complete price and a savings of over 10% off the cover prices—quite a bargain! I understand that accepting the books and gift places me under no obligation ever to buy any books. I can always return a shipment and cancel at any time. Even if I never buy another book from Steeple Hill, the 2 free books and the surprise gift are mine to keep forever.

113 IDN DZ9M
313 IDN DZ9N

| Name | (PLEASE PRINT) | |
|------|------|------|
| Address | Apt. No. | |
| City | State/Prov. | Zip/Postal Code |

**Not valid to current Love Inspired® subscribers.**

*Want to try two free books from another series?*
**Call 1-800-873-8635 or visit www.morefreebooks.com.**

\* Terms and prices are subject to change without notice. Sales tax applicable in New York. Canadian residents will be charged applicable provincial taxes and GST. All orders subject to approval. Offer limited to one per household.

® are registered trademarks owned and used by the trademark owner and or its licensee.

INTLI04R                                                    ©2004 Steeple Hill

# eHARLEQUIN.com

## The Ultimate Destination for Women's Fiction

### For **FREE online reading**, visit
www.eHarlequin.com now and enjoy:

**Online Reads**
Read **Daily** and **Weekly** chapters from
our Internet-exclusive stories by your
favorite authors.

**Interactive Novels**
Cast your vote to help decide how these
stories unfold...then stay tuned!

**Quick Reads**
For shorter romantic reads, try our
collection of Poems, Toasts, & More!

**Online Read Library**
Miss one of our online reads?
Come here to catch up!

**Reading Groups**
Discuss, share and rave with other
community members!

## For great reading online,
## visit www.eHarlequin.com today!

INTONL04R

*Love Inspired*
# SUSPENSE
### RIVETING INSPIRATIONAL ROMANCE

## Coming in November...

# Her Brother's Keeper

## by Valerie Hansen

An ordained minister turned undercover investigator is on a mission to uncover the truth about a young woman's past. But can he do that without hurting the woman he's come to love?

*Available at your favorite retail outlet.*
*Only from Steeple Hill Books!*

Steeple
Hill®

**www.SteepleHill.com**

LISHBK

*Love Inspired*
# SUSPENSE
RIVETING INSPIRATIONAL ROMANCE

## Coming in November...

# SHADOW
# BONES

by RITA® Award finalist Colleen Coble writing as

## Colleen Rhoads

**GREAT LAKES LEGENDS**

Skye Blackbird was convinced there were diamonds in her family's mine. Paleontologist Jake Baxter had the same feeling about fossils. But someone didn't want the earth disturbed and as the body count mounted, it appeared that that someone might not want Jake or Skye left alive....

> "Colleen Coble lays an intricate trail and draws
> the reader on like a hound with a scent."
> –*Romantic Times*

**Available at your favorite retail outlet.
Only from Steeple Hill Books!**

Steeple
Hill®

# New from RITA® Award-winning author Deborah Raney...

## On sale October 2005

When Valerie Austin is left at the altar, she leaves on a
mission to Haiti, where she falls in love with both the
Haitian people and the orphanage's doctor, Max Jordan.
Will Valerie return to life in the U.S. with Max, or will
she listen to her inner calling to stay in Haiti?

Steeple
Hill®

**Visit your local bookseller.**

www.SteepleHill.com

SHDR543